# Once Upon A Storm

# KIMBERLY CATES

OLIVERHEBERBOOKS

# CHAPTER 1

ENGLAND, 1843

The horse seemed formed of liquid gold, its coat shimmering in the sunlight, as exotic and hot-blooded as the spices that came from war-torn lands a continent away. Captain Simon Harcourt reined in the stallion, the horse's restlessness like his own, a wildness and sinew-deep knowledge that he didn't belong here.

He raked back his windblown hair back as he focused on the sweeping red brick towers and creamy stone columns of Everdene Hall, the manor house that had been a gift from the Tudors to the Harcourts for loyal service, a conglomeration of additions fitted together and torn apart through four centuries of upheaval, civil war, and intrigue. It stood perched on the crest of the hill, gardens spilling downward in rich greens and rainbow-hued blossoms.

Though it had been but five months since he had returned to England, it was nearly two decades more since he'd ridden from Everdene Hall, swearing never to return.

Nor would he have, but one dared not ignore a summons from the Earl of Ravenscroft. Not when that formidable nobleman was your father.

Simon grimaced at the thought that the old man loathed Everdene even more than he did. To his knowledge, his father hadn't set foot on the estate for years, leaving it in the capable hands of a land agent.

But a carriage accident en route to some political meeting had forced the Earl's hand, leaving Simon's father so badly injured there was no choice but to take him to his nearest estate. Something spooked the team, Simon's brother had written.

A ghost?

There had been a time Simon would have laughed at the notion, but war and regrets had proven that sometimes hauntings were real.

The estate of his boyhood seemed run-down and neglected, much changed from what he'd glimpsed in dreams that still mocked him, interspersed with those of battlefields littered with corpses, and villages burned to the ground.

He would meet with the Earl as commanded, then make his excuses and ride away faster than he'd come.

His horse had a race to run… such a simple excuse, but a good one. Caspian had only begun to make a name for himself. The first payment in a debt Simon owed.

He steeled himself and continued up the tree-lined drive. In the manor's courtyard, he dismounted, handing the reins to a freckle-faced groom. The servant's eyes nearly popped out of his head as he gaped at the horse. Simon had seen that starstruck expression before, had doubtless worn it himself the first time he'd encountered the breed.

"Gor, sir," the groom marveled, touching the stallion's neck as if to prove to himself it was real. "Never seen anything like this beauty."

"You will soon see more of them if I have my way," Simon said. "Cool him down. I will check on him ere long."

Simon watched the lad walk Caspian toward the stables. Then, he mounted the steps with a long-legged stride. Memory cut him, sharp and clear, the echo of laughter as his sisters hopped up and down the flagstone risers, singing a nursery rhyme, their golden curls bouncing. How was it that he'd charged into battle heedless, yet here, he paused at the door, uncertain whether to ring the bell.

He wanted to turn back. Before he could, the door burst open, his brother meeting him there. Lucien Harcourt, Viscount Everdene's lean countenance mirrored the planes of Simon's own, his blue eyes bright with a mixture of relief and delight.

"Simon!" The Viscount clapped him on the shoulder, the awkwardness of seven years apart making him seem almost a stranger. "By God, it's good to see you. It's been too long. I wasn't sure you'd come even if you did receive my letter."

Simon shrugged one broad shoulder. "Duty calls, and all that." He pasted on a wry smile.

"You've changed so much I might not have recognized you on the street!" His brother seemed much the same as they entered the hall—his breeches and coat impeccable, his face closely shaven, his cravat tied with painful precision, as if one mistake might tip his whole world off its axis.

Simon glanced in one of the gilt mirrors that flanked the entryway and rubbed a hand across the day's growth of stubble that shadowed his square jaw, ever more aware of his own travel-disheveled state. Grit from the road dusted his coat, his dark hair badly in need of a trim. Years under blazing suns and enduring harsh conditions had left his skin weathered and dark, making his ice-blue eyes so vivid they seemed to sizzle with a life of their own.

Lucien eyed him. "What happened to your face?"

Simon touched fingertips to the healing gash near his temple. "A mere scratch from an altercation over a hand of cards."

"Not another duel!"

"You needn't worry. I didn't kill the other fellow, though

putting an end to the incompetent fool is something his future officers would have thanked me for."

Despite his flippant attitude, he couldn't help wincing at his elder brother's expression.

Poor bastard had the weight of the family name on his shoulders, the honor of the Harcourts. Their old nurse, Betsy Rowley, had loved to describe the moment Lucien had looked into the Harcourt cradle and seen Simon squalling, claiming Lucien had added keeping his scapegrace brother out of mischief to his list of responsibilities. A duty that had grown in scope when only the two brothers remained together.

Lucien's brow furrowed as if the list of Simon's escapades was suddenly writ large across his face. "Simon, I'm begging you, don't make a muck of this. I think Father is ready to make peace with you at last."

Which translated to what? Simon wondered. Forgiving his rebellious son? Their last parting had been an ugly one.

"Father is not as hale as he once was," Lucien continued. "It's testimony to how badly off he's been that he was forced to stop his journey here. Spending six weeks in a house he loathes tells you just how serious the accident was."

"I can't imagine that my appearance is going to be good for his constitution. The mere sight of me often sent him into apoplexies." Simon kneaded the stiff muscles at the back of his neck. *Is he dying?* He wanted to ask, but couldn't quite say the words.

It was impossible to contemplate, the Earl as indestructible as the Tower of London. Powerful, grim, and arrogant. The granite-like planes and angles of his face harsh enough to frighten small children. Simon grimaced, recalling that he had been one of them.

Unwelcome warmth flooded his chest as he remembered Lucien attempting to get between them. But Simon had always been cursed with the need to confront whatever frightened him most. And much of the time, that had been his father.

Lucien's voice broke through Simon's musings. "He's been asking for you. There is some vital task he is determined only you should undertake."

The mere possibility that his father would entrust him with anything of importance was sobering.

"Then we shouldn't keep him waiting." Simon headed deeper into the entryway with its towering ivory arches and sweeping main staircase.

"He is upstairs in the Sky Chamber."

Simon's step faltered, and he paused to stare at his brother.

The Sky Chamber, with its banks of windows looking out over the gardens. Walls painted crystal blue, spangled with gilt stars that had sparkled like their mother's eyes. His mother... the beating heart of Simon's world, torn away when he was just nine years old.

Lucien couldn't meet his gaze. "Father was unconscious when he was brought in, and his servants were too new to realize the significance. I offered to have him moved the instant I got here, but he was too stubborn."

Simon could imagine the old man glaring at Lucien, the smallest sign of weakness unforgivable in anyone with a drop of Harcourt blood. Especially the Earl himself.

No, Barnabas Harcourt would act as if he didn't care. Truth was, Simon would rather face a horde of raging Turks than step into his mother's favorite room...

"I'll have the servants prepare your bath," Lucien offered. "I know you'll want to wash off the travel dust before—"

"Thank you, but no," Simon interrupted. "The sooner Father and I get this over with, the better."

Simon started up the marble stairs. It was almost eerie, as if he'd stepped through time. Even the peach-and-cream uphol-stered furniture had not faded, no doubt because it had spent the years covered with Holland cloth between his brother's rare visits, just often enough to keep things in order.

He could see the rails where he and his siblings had once peered down at the guests arriving for Everdene's balls and musicales, Jane and Cassandra cooing over the women in their elegant gowns. Their mother the most beautiful of all, slipping away from her guests long enough to give them each one of the exquisitely iced cakes and a kiss goodnight.

His shoulders stiffened and his gut tightened as he approached the heavily carved door. A footman was stationed outside to fulfill the Earl's bellowed commands. Simon had seen soldiers in battle shock who were more composed. The man's fingernails were chewed to nubs, his lips chapped from biting them. The servant sprang to his feet as if he expected someone to hurl a vase at him. Simon was relatively sure the footman's tenure with the Earl had made him quick to duck flying missiles.

It was a skill that had served Simon well in the army.

"M-m'lord…"

"I'm simply Captain Harcourt," he reassured the man in a tone he used to calm new recruits. "And you are?"

"Randall, sir."

Simon faced the portal, steeling himself for the encounter that he'd been dreading. "I'll announce myself, Randall," he said, then opened the door.

# CHAPTER 2

The view struck Simon like a blow to the chest. A bed was set up before a wide bank of mullioned windows, chairs with slender, gilt legs beside it. It seemed his father must crush them with the weight of his disapproval, as he had crushed the woman who once sought haven here.

"Who the devil—" the Earl began to roar.

"I'm the devil, indeed, or so you've told me once or twice," Simon kept his voice light. "But you've only yourself to blame for my appearance at Everdene, since you are the one who summoned me."

"Simon?" Did the old Earl's voice catch, or had Simon just imagined it?

"At your service, sir." Simon strode into his father's line of vision and sketched a bow. The Earl's iron-gray hair was thick as ever, as if it did not dare retreat without permission. Yet even he could not command the march of time. Deep lines carved a face that had once been hale and hearty, the pallor from his accident leaving him much altered, his powerful body enough changed that he seemed shrunken, somehow. Difficult as

Simon's relationship with his father had always been, he found himself both startled and saddened.

What was it his friend Jamie had said when they faced the desert tribes? *Even Colossus crumbled with time...*

Barnabas Harcourt regarded his son with that expression that was all too familiar to Simon. As if every flaw had become glaringly bright. "I heard about the ambush in the Khyber Pass."

Every muscle in Simon's body tensed.

"Dreadful business, that," the Earl continued. "Good thing you were in Jalalabad when the ambush came."

Simon swallowed hard. As ever, the old man went for the killing blow. He looked away, the room suddenly haunted by faces of the men he'd lost—Richards, with his slight stutter and sharpshooter aim; Carruthers, who had spent nights around the campfire sharing letters from his wife at home; and Jamie, the Scotsman, whose fiery hair was as fierce as his temper and loyalty, whose friendship had crashed past Simon's reckless façade. Jamie, whose dream of breeding the magnificent Turkoman horse in England had become Simon's own. Jamie hadn't given a damn when Simon tried to keep their friendship light, without going deeper. Jamie should have stayed far away.

Simon forced words from a throat suddenly raw. "We lost a lot of good men."

"Always said we must break those savages down to ash. More animal than human."

Simon wasn't surprised by his father's hatred of something he knew nothing about. The people he had encountered told a different story. He had found much that was enchanting in India and Afghanistan—civilizations and buildings and art, and the people themselves. An exotic world that enticed yet could turn lethal in a heartbeat.

He and Jamie had been captivated by their time spent there, discovering beauty they dreamed of carrying home... Not the gold and jewels, spices and assets other men coveted, but perfection in equine flesh and bone.

"Do you intend to return to what is left of your regiment?" His father's demand startled him from his memories.

Simon stifled a bitter laugh. *There is nothing left of my regiment to rejoin*, he wanted to say. Instead, he told his father, "I don't know if I will return to the cavalry. General Auckland gave me leave until I decide."

"Humph," his father puffed out is cheeks in a disgruntled snort. "It seems we have both found ourselves in places we did not expect to be." The Earl reached for a crystal goblet of port. It glowed blood red. "My unpleasant stay here has given me time to think. This estate has been a thorn in my side for nearly twenty years. It is entailed to your brother, so I cannot sell it, or I would have done that years ago. You and I are not in harmony regarding much, Simon, but our loathing of this estate is one. I've come up with a solution, and you are just the man to carry it out."

"I regret that I am occupied—"

"With those horses you are obsessed with. Lucien has informed me. Though what you know about good breeding I can't imagine. Other than attempting to break your own neck jumping impossible fences. Yet, your brother, for some reason, is much attached to you. He is determined you shall have the management of the Harcourt stables."

Simon waited for his father to dash his dream, much as he always had.

"I am doubtful that this preoccupation of yours will amount to anything, but find myself willing to indulge this little freak of yours until you lose interest in it and are off on some other wild enterprise."

Simon felt his hackles rise. "This is no passing fancy. These horses are extraordinary—"

"Spare me your flights of enthusiasm. I have agreed to

Lucien's plan. You shall have the property and the funds on one condition. Look down on that prospect," the Earl commanded. "What do you see?"

Simon paced to the windows. A green sweep of gardens spilled down the hill. Knots of a boxwood labyrinth, and banks of roses laid out with unnatural precision.

"Gardens."

The Earl waved his hand, impatient. "Beyond that."

The village of Everdene lay in the distance, edging the bottom of the green hill. Once, it had been the playground of Simon's childhood. Thatched roofs gleaming gold, whitewashed walls freshly painted each spring, cottages that had spilled out lads shouting and wrestling, sword fighting with sticks as they chased each other in mock adventures. Ribbons of lane winding through the village, and the near-forgotten woman in billowing skirts that somehow he'd never quite stopped looking for. My God, how he'd come to hate that.

"Well, boy, what do you see?"

Simon fetched himself a glass of port from the decanter on a table, hoping it might ease the hollow cavern that formed in his chest at the memory of his mother. It was as if the walls themselves held the echoes of Lenora Harcourt's essence, the gold of her hair, the blue of her eyes, her scent, like the potted rose trees she'd had brought into her special bower. But he said,

"I see cottages."

"I want you to tear them down."

Alcohol burned Simon's throat as he tossed it down in one gulp.

"What?"

"Erase it as if it had never existed. Prove yourself man enough to follow through with a job and I'll do as your brother wishes. I will leave the stables to you. You've made good sport of wrecking things in the past. Let us see if you can put that talent to good use."

"And if I don't?"

"Then someone else will tear down the village and I will do what I've long thought best. Disinherit you before I die."

For a moment, Simon considered the pleasure he'd take in telling the old man to go to hell. But at that moment he saw the young groom he'd left walking his horse. The Turkoman stallion pranced at the end of the reins, flanks gleaming, his form so exquisite it might have been poured of molten gold. He could hear Jamie's voice. *We'll pool every penny we have, Simon. Bring the stallion and three mares home. Start our stable with this bloodline. Imagine a whole fleet of these horses, and the two of us far away from cannon fire and the smell of death.*

The Earl cleared his throat, bringing Simon back to the present. "Perhaps I've grown soft in my old age. Perhaps I struck my head harder than the surgeon thought when I fell. Perhaps… I hope your years in the army have made a man of you at last, one who understands the honor due his name."

Honor. Simon's mouth hardened in bitterness. Yes, he'd learned what true honor was from the Scotsman who had the ill fortune to become his best friend. And it had cost the man his life.

"Let us put an end to this war between us here where it began," the Earl said.

Did some part of Simon hope they might be able to do so as well? He looked out over the green expanse. "Where will the people go?"

"I've spoken to the land agent. Inchwick says there is a valley some distance from here. If we build there, we'll see nothing unsightly from Everdene Hall. Look out the window, and it will be as if the village never existed."

Trust his father to decide to raze a village to clear the view of an estate he had no intention of ever visiting again, Simon thought. Or maybe the Earl was trying to erase the past. Simon peered down at the cluster of buildings at the bottom of the slope, remembering the boy he'd been, searching the lanes and cottages for any sign of the mother he'd loved.

But he was a man now, well used to that gaping absence in his life.

"Sell my soul for the stables or be disinherited?" he asked dryly.

"Not how I would put it, but yes. So, what say you?"

The old man's brow arched.

Considering Simon no longer had a soul, the choice was easy. "I say yes."

# CHAPTER 3

ONE WEEK LATER...

*A* cry of dismay startled Penelope Waverly, and she looked up from the list she was writing, to see the maid clutching one hand against her apron, the girl's face blanched white.

"Whatever happened?" she asked, as she bustled over to the girl.

"The kettle, miss. The handle broke."

One more item to add to the list of things to be repaired, Pen thought with an inward sigh. She noted the rag wrapped around Clara's hand.

"Did you burn yourself? Let me see."

"I tried to catch it before it fell into the fire. It's not so bad."

Pen leveled the servant a stern look, and the girl extended her hand. It was a nasty burn, but didn't need a doctor's care. Pen fetched the leather bag in which they kept medical supplies. She withdrew a tin of salve and spread it over Clara's blistering hand, then wrapped it in a clean bandage.

"Well, you'll not be carrying baskets to market with this hand," she said as she knotted the ends of the linen strip to hold it in place. "Go up to your room and rest."

Clara blinked back tears. "But who will do the shopping?"

"I'm perfectly capable of managing household chores."

The girl bit her lip. "Mrs. Waverly will be most put out."

No doubt it would be a dramatic performance worthy of Drury Lane, Penelope thought.

"I'll deal with Mama," Pen reassured.

Heaven knew, she was well used to the task. She had been managing her mother's changeable moods for as long as she could remember.

Fetching her shawl and bonnet, Penelope entered the parlor where her mother sat with her embroidery, a ruffled cap framing a face that might have been pretty once, but tended to look as if she'd bitten into a lemon whenever she gazed upon her eldest daughter. "Where are you going now? It's too early to pay calls!"

"There has been a mishap in the kitchen," Penelope explained, as she crossed to a mirror and settled her bonnet atop her dark curls. She tied a ribbon that matched her green eyes under a chin far too determined. "Clara burned her hand rather badly, and I need to do the marketing."

"I can't think why you employed that wretched girl in the first place!"

*Because I found her mother crying, terrified that Clara would go to London and be snatched up by the procurers who meet every stagecoach, looking for pretty, naïve country girls to fill the city's brothels...* Pen swallowed the explanation, knowing it would only add fuel to her mother's irritation.

"It's hardly Clara's fault that the handle on the kettle broke," Pen said instead. "These things happen."

*Especially to us,* she thought wryly.

"A Waverly shopping for vegetables like the most common sort! What will people think?"

"That I am determined to have carrots in my stew. And that our kettle is in need of repair."

"Send Hughes!"

Pen's heart warmed at the thought of their man-of-all-work, the loyal servant who had stayed with the Waverlys through their wildly shifting fortunes, too often without pay. "I'll not send Hughes to do an errand when I'm quite capable of handling things myself. Old Boney is vexing him again."

"Of all the ridiculous notions!" her mother huffed. "Napoleon Bonaparte has been dead for twenty years!"

"Unfortunately, a French soldier managed to fire a musket ball into Hughes's hip before Napoleon had the good sense to die. Considering that Hughes and men like him kept the wolf from our shores, we owe him some small accommodation. At any rate, I'm quite looking forward to a walk," Penelope asserted. "Alone."

"You are a gentleman's daughter! Yet you wander about like a common dairymaid with no care for what it does to our reputation. I cannot believe that we've come to this pass!"

Penelope fought not to roll her eyes. The 'pass' the Waverlys had come to had barreled down on them like a runaway coach, while the family stood in the middle of the road, practicing their dance steps.

"You have no one to blame but yourself for bringing our family so low, Penelope!" Her mother sniffed. "Throwing away a perfectly respectable marriage proposal…"

Penelope winced at the memory of the acutely embarrassing incident. "As I told Vicar Kemble, I have no wish to marry. Ever."

Her mother jabbed the needle so hard through the cheek of the cherub she was stitching, Penelope could almost hear the babe squawk in protest. "You are sorely mistaken if you think a woman's wishes matter. You must submit and do your duty."

"That did not serve us well with Father in the end." Pen regretted the sharp reply the instant it slipped out of her mouth. By mutual agreement they never spoke of those last troubled years. Once a respected architect, Ned Waverly had sunk deeper and deeper into drunkenness and gambling until he had stepped off of a scaffold and left his wife and daughters in dire straits. Even this house, deeded to Anastasia Waverly by a kind aunt, now belonged to someone else. It was a mere courtesy that they were allowed to remain.

Pen crossed to her mother, and patted her small hand. "We've done well enough thus far," Penelope added more gently. And though she found the idea of marriage alarming, that did not mean her sisters were of the same mind. "Besides, you have two other daughters who are of a far more suitable age to find husbands for."

"*Why* must you do everything the hard way?" her mother moaned. "I swear, from the time you were born you would not be reasonable."

"The general complaint is that I rely on reason too much, instead of being ruled by sentiment, as a woman should."

"Thank heavens your sisters are far more amiable."

Indeed, they were, Pen thought. So amiable that Pen was filled with disquiet whenever Fanny or Kitty crossed paths with a man in regimentals, or a handsome, feckless flirt. "They will make exemplary wives should they choose to wed," Penelope said. "But I am determined they'll be able to choose another path if they wish." Which was why they were currently off attending the lessons Penelope paid for, not only with the salary she'd earned as a governess, but a small bequest from her great aunt—pianoforte for Kitty, painting for Fanny, and French for both, so the sisters could open up a school together if they chose not to marry. If Fanny and Kitty *did* marry, Pen would do her best to wish them well, and then take what she'd managed to save and travel… perhaps to Italy or India to see the exquisite buildings there. Buildings her father had promised to show her before everything went wrong.

"As for me," Pen told her mother, "I shall make my own way in the world, thank you. Now I'm off to the village."

She looped the basket's handle over her arm and a gray kitten leapt out, scrabbling down her bell-like skirt and setting it swaying. "Mittens, you are quite incorrigible," she scolded, untangling the mewling feline's claws. She set the rogue down and smoothed her ruffle.

"Well, if you *must* go, stop and ask Dr. Finley for some of my physic," her mother said. "I vow I have a spell coming on."

"I will," Pen agreed.

Taking up her basket and reticule, Penelope hastened out into the yard. She smiled as she saw Rupert Hughes mending the gate, his felt hat pulled low over his eyes. The capable hands that had showed her how to wield hammer and saw when she was a child were repairing a hinge.

The grizzled veteran straightened up stiffly when he saw Penelope, the wrinkles that pleated his face smoothing out as he grinned. "Where are you off to, Miss?"

"I've errands in town and it's a lovely day for a walk."

"It's market day, so it'll be that busy. Are you sure you don't want me to drive you?" he asked, as he limped over. "I can hitch up the gig."

"There is no need, thank you. I am quite on the shelf, now that I've rejected the vicar's proposal, and everyone in the county knows it. Going about without the encumbrance of a chaperone is one of the benefits."

"Glad you sent that vicar packing, Miss. He's a joyless lot, crushing any pleasure simple folk get out of life. No holidays, no dancing, no drink or playing games. He'd douse the light right out of you, and you, well, you be able to find the humor in most anything."

A necessary attribute if she was to survive the Waverly household without dumping the contents of the washbowl over someone's head, Penelope thought.

"Should be an entertaining time at market day," Hughes said, waggling thick eyebrows. "There is quite a stir…"

Penelope laughed. "There is always a stir in the village." That was why she had loved her visits to the hamlet from the time she was a girl. She'd never had patience for needlework or girls' games. To sit like a lady, mind her dress and manners, and speak softly when she wanted to shout was pure torment. But in the village, she'd been loved, laughed with. Free.

During the years of her father's decline, she'd escaped the Waverly home whenever she could, watching the blacksmith at his hot forge or the Garveys mending things in their carpentry shop. But of all the people who fascinated her, the one she'd been most enthralled by was the fine lady from the big house on the hill who had shown her such kindness. The woman who had disappeared so suddenly.

She shoved the sobering thought away.

Hughes took off his hat and ran his fingers through gray hair. "Ruby up at Everdene Hall says something is afoot."

"There has been ever since the old Earl's accident," Pen said.

Everdene had never seen such a hurly-burly as that fateful day when the wagon rattled up to the Harcourts' great manor house with his lordship inside it. Anyone who could pass for a servant had been hustled up from town to put the rooms in order before he regained consciousness.

Hughes spat over his shoulder. "They say Mr. Inchwick is racing about like his coattail's on fire, but he won't tell anyone a thing. I don't trust him."

Penelope didn't either. There had been a time before her father's death that Walter Inchwick had been a frequent visitor to Laurel Cottage, playing cards, encouraging her father's impractical schemes. Like so many others, he'd disappeared from the Waverly family's sphere after her father's death.

"Maybe the Harcourt family finally realized how many repairs need to be made around here," Penelope said, without much hope. "Last time I was in the village, the baker's lad said four chimneys were smoking over on Tansy Lane."

But even the thought of smoking chimneys and Mr. Inchwick couldn't spoil Pen's pleasure in her solitude as she set out on the mile walk to the hamlet of Everdene.

Time alone to think without a jumble of problems to solve and bills to pay was a luxury she'd had far too seldom since she'd returned home from her latest foray as a governess. As she neared the village, she heard the noise from its eastern edge where a bustling market area had been set up, complete with stalls where farmers displayed their produce. Pen loved the colors and scents, the cries as sellers hawked their wares and buyers haggled over prices. She'd dropped off the kettle to be repaired and took a short cut to the market, slipping through a cluster of barrels that had been unloaded to block the end of the street. The narrow alley was solidly walled on either side, the back doors of shops shut and barred, the space between filled with shadow. As she made her way toward the bustling crowd at the main street, she heard an angry shout, running footsteps, and the barking of a dog.

She paused, wide eyed, as a tiny lad pelted around the corner, his face soot-smudged and eyes white-ringed with fear, an apple clutched to his chest. He slammed into her, her skirts swinging wildly and she could tell he expected her to scream and bring his pursuers down on him.

He stared at her for a heartbeat, something in his pinched face striking a chord in her heart. A shout sounded from the street and his gaze darted back like a trapped animal.

"Please," he whispered, then fell to his knees.

Pen scooped up the hem of her gown, dropping the bell of her skirt over the boy, just as a trio of ugly-looking strangers rounded the corner.

"Where'd 'e go, little brat!" a man with a pock-scarred face snarled. "Your pardon, Miss. You see a lad about so tall?"

She could feel the boy's heart racing where his chest pressed against her calf, his breath shuddering, his terror reverberating through her.

"Set the dog on 'im!" a man with bad teeth shouted. "Rags'll find him, sure. Tear 'im apart, 'e will."

Before Pen had a chance to move, a scruffy terrier charged straight toward her, snarling.

# CHAPTER 4

"Get back!" Pen cried, swinging her basket at the dog, knowing she couldn't fend it off for long. But as it lunged a second time, a deep baritone boomed out.

"Collar your dog!" The commanding tone froze even the terrier in its tracks, the alleyway suddenly filled with the most unnerving man Penelope had ever seen.

He towered over them all, his broad shoulders encased in a midnight-blue superfine coat, his long, powerful legs those of an expert horseman. His face was lean and sculpted and arrestingly handsome, the skin bronzed by foreign suns. In one strong hand he held a paper cone filled with something that smelled of cinnamon.

"We was chasin' a boy stole an apple!" Rotten Teeth explained. "He ran right in here."

"He's mine, he is," the ugliest of the men snarled. "Paid good coin for him and the ungrateful little beast ran away!"

Penelope tried to find her voice. "Well, you'd best seek him elsewhere!" she insisted, hoping the daunting gentleman wouldn't see her hands shaking. "There is no child here."

"But 'e ran right in here, gov'ner!" A lad of about twelve

addressed the stranger. "I earned that shilling, I did, chasing him down!"

"Are you questioning the word of a lady?" the gentleman asked sternly.

The boy looked from Penelope to the gentleman. "N-no. But Tripp's like a wee rat, darting about. Maybe she didn't see." He thrust his chin out at a pugnacious angle. "Perhaps the lady needs spectacles."

"I most certainly do not." Penelope dug into her reticule and pressed shillings into the boy's hand. "But here is for your trouble."

"Well, then," the gentleman said, choosing a sugary pastry from his paper cone. "I think this interview is over. I suggest you men leave Everdene before this situation becomes more unpleasant."

One man looked as if he were about to protest, but his accomplice nudged him with a grimy elbow.

"Never mind," he said. "That lad was nothing but trouble anyway. We'll find another one skinny enough to squeeze up a chimney when we get to the next town. Plenty o' families are anxious for one less mouth feed."

They turned and shuffled away, the terrier whining and looking back at his lost prey.

"I doubt we'll be seeing that lot again," the imposing gentleman said as they disappeared around the corner.

Pen tried to draw the scraps of her dignity around her. "There was no need for you to interfere," she told him. "I had matters well in hand."

"Or in *foot* as the case may be." He glanced at her skirts.

She fluffed the flounce to its fullness.

The man took a bite of his pastry, chewed and swallowed. "It's a good thing I got peckish on my way to the land agent's or I'd not have heard the disturbance," he said. "After years in the military I'm still getting used to the fact I can stop whenever I wish and indulge my love of sweets."

Pen tried not to be distracted by the bit of sugar clinging to lips that curled with a wicked sense of humor.

The ragged boy beneath her skirt tightened thin arms around her leg, and she hoped he didn't overset her entirely before she could be rid of this sugar-loving interloper. She set her gloved hand on the wall with what she hoped was a casual air.

The corners of the stranger's eyes crinkled, his ice-blue irises almost too vivid to be real.

"Forgive me if I'm mistaken," he said, in that rich voice that made a shiver of awareness skitter up her spine, "but I have the strangest feeling we've met before. Captain Simon Harcourt, at your service." He sketched her a bow.

Simon Harcourt. Of course. Pen swallowed hard. "I believe we had some *small* acquaintance when we were children," she said, trying to keep her voice level. "I'm Penelope Waverly."

He seemed puzzled for a moment, then those keen eyes lit up. "Of course! The architect's daughter."

"Yes," she said. The last thing she wanted was for him to inquire about her father. "Now, I am certain you have more important business to attend to than renewing our acquaintance. Especially when you and the other lads spent most of my childhood acting as if I carried the seven plagues of Egypt."

"I doubt any of them would think so now." He laughed, looking her over from head to toe, but he did not budge, merely stood there, regarding her with a stubbornly amiable expression. Why didn't the man leave when he was clearly not welcome?

She could hardly walk away herself with the boy clinging to her leg. Was it possible Simon... no, *Captain Harcourt* knew? His eyes sparkled as if he were in on some joke, then his gaze locked where a slight lump shifted beneath the bell of her skirt.

"I remember you were quite fearless as a girl," he said. "Which makes me somewhat surprised that your skirts are shivering."

Pen's temper snapped. "You would be shaking, too, if those hideous men had been accosting you."

"I have a feeling you knew exactly where the young thief they were chasing had taken refuge."

She started to sputter a protest, but his voice turned suddenly stern. "The game is over," he said, eyes on her skirt. "Out you come, my lad."

Her hem trembled, then lifted, the face that emerged sharp with hunger. Before the urchin could dart away, Captain Harcourt's empty hand flashed out, catching an arm so thin it seemed the slightest pressure would snap the bone.

"Easy there, lad," he said quietly, balancing his cone of sweets as the boy struggled to pull free. "I'm not going to hurt you."

"Let him go!" Penelope cried. "You're frightening him!"

"I must satisfy my curiosity first. While it's obvious this fellow was fleeing the rather ugly-tempered men pursuing him, I'm at a loss as to why a lady such as yourself would give him refuge beneath her petticoats. I remember you were quite the one for mischief when we were young, Miss Waverly. Are you in league with the wee rogue? Perhaps I should check your basket for stolen apples."

"Are you mad?" she choked out in affront.

"You'd not be the first to think so. But *you* are the one allowing this lad close contact with your clothing. You'd best take care. I'm relatively certain he has fleas."

"And so would you if you were sleepin' in filth," the boy fired back. "I tries to keep clean like me Mam showed me, but…"

Simon arched one brow. "And why isn't this mother of yours discouraging larceny? You know you could be hanged for thievery."

The boy's eyes filled with tears. "She had to sell me. Farley said he'd 'prentice me to a carpenter, but he lied. Gave me t' the chimney sweep. I'm scared o' the dark ol' chimneys, and can't breathe for the soot. Got stuck the first time up an' they burned me feet."

Simon's gaze swept the areas where skin showed through tears in his rags. There were scars and half-healed burns. He'd seen enough wounds in his time in the army to numb his response to them, but something about this plucky lad made him feel the horror sharply. Instinctively, Simon's fingers tightened on the child's arm.

"Ow! Ye're hurting me!"

"I'm sorry, boy. I'll let you go if you give me your word of honor you won't run."

The lad nodded and Simon released him. Simon turned to meet Miss Waverly's gaze, saw the tenderness there and the righteous anger. She'd hidden this ragged urchin, faced down men two times her size. If Simon hadn't come along, and the terrier had gone after the boy under her skirts she'd doubtless have been bitten or worse. Somehow, even then, he couldn't see her backing down. Unlike the mother who'd traded her own flesh and blood for a handful of coins.

"What kind of mother sells her own child?" Simon whispered to her.

The woman looked at him with a clear, unflinching gaze. "One who is more desperate than we will ever know." She turned to the boy. "What is your name?"

"Tripp. Me da called me that 'cause I was always gettin' underfoot."

"Or 'under skirt,' as the case may be," Simon quipped. He handed the lad the cone of pastries, and Tripp fell on it like a wild animal, his eyes darting from the man to the woman.

"Ye going to give me back to Farley?"

"No!" Miss Waverly exclaimed with such certainty the boy

calmed. "You said you were to be apprenticed to a carpenter. Do you still wish to be?"

"Don't matter what I want, do it?"

Simon saw something flash in Penelope's eyes. "We'll make it matter," she promised with a resolute tilt to her chin. "Come along with me."

# CHAPTER 5

*ou're doing it wrong...*

The long-ago memory from Simon's boyhood came back unbidden—Penelope's voice, chiding him—so clear that he had to look over at her just to reassure himself it was only in his head. But no, she walked through the lane in front of him, her hand firmly clasped around Tripp's, leaving him no choice but to follow. Even now, years later, he could picture Penelope as a child, standing beneath the oak where he and his friends were building a treehouse, her chin thrust out, hands planted on her hips as she glared up at them. She'd been infuriatingly sure of herself as she lectured about building techniques to lads whose pride had been far greater than their wisdom.

Who would ever have believed that stubborn girl would grow into the intriguing woman now marching down the street a step ahead of him? She wasn't beautiful in the fashionable sense. The notion of her as a delicate flower with pale skin and hands too dainty to do more than ply a needle or pluck a rose was absurd. And she certainly wasn't breathless with admiration because a gentleman had taken a difficult situation in hand.

As a child, she had been impossible to ignore. But now she fixed his attention in a way that both bewildered and amused him.

The barely discernable golden cast to her skin made him suspect she'd gone about without her bonnet. A few rich, mahogany curls had pulled loose from their pins, and teased flushed cheeks. Her green eyes still sparked with righteous indignation.

The dress she wore skimmed over curves that drew his eye, but most distracting of all were the glimpses he caught of full, red lips and a resolute chin softened by just a hint of a dimple in its center. Simon felt an unaccountable urge to touch the tiny dip with the pad of his thumb, to see if the skin was as velvety as it appeared.

"I assume you have some destination in mind," he called out to her.

Penelope glanced down at the urchin who seemed quite willing to go wherever his unlikely savior led, then back toward him. "Tripp hoped to be apprenticed to a carpenter, so it might as well be the finest carpenter I've ever known. Daw Garvey."

Simon started at the name. If he had been inclined to visit any of his old haunts upon arriving at Everdene—which he *hadn't*—the Garvey cottage would have been his first stop.

He remembered Daw as a gangly lad with a ready laugh and a thirst for mischief. They'd become fast friends, Simon entranced by the way Daw readily turned the entire village and surrounding countryside into one massive playground, opening a world of imagination and freedom that the son of an overly strict nobleman had been otherwise denied.

He'd met the carpenter's son when his mother was delivering calves' foot jelly to Daw's eighty-year-old grandfather, who always sat in the rocking chair. Simon had been fascinated by the things Daw's grandfather had whittled, watching the sharp snick of his knife, the long golden curls of wood shavings as they drifted to the floor. Curls as golden as Simon's mother's hair...

How was it that he only now realized that his mother's perceived annoyance in his and Daw's presence, shooing them out the door to go play while she visited, had been her way of protecting him? Covering for his red cheeks, scraped knees, and torn clothes with her gentle admonishments to take better care when walking, thereby allowing him to revel in that world without his father finding out?

It was expected for a nobleman's wife to visit the elderly and infirm. It was not expected for her to encourage her youngest child to fraternize with the villagers' children.

Simon put the memory from his mind. When they reached the familiar cottage with its attached workshop, he felt an edginess, as if his cravat pulled too tight. A sudden urge to make his excuses and leave. But before he could, Penelope rapped on the door, the boy hiding behind her. A moment later, a man flung the portal open.

Daw Garvey filled the doorway, his shoulders wide as an axe handle, his hands looking as if they could snap a brick in two.

"Miss Waverly," Daw began, then faltered, staring at Simon.

Guilt swept through Simon as he thought of the deal he'd made with his father and what was to follow, a feeling magnified as his childhood friend's kind eyes lit up in recognition. "Daw," he said, the name catching in his throat. "It's good to see you."

He was thankful Daw didn't seem to notice his discomfort. A wide smile spread over his weathered face. "Master Simon...? Almost didn't recognize you." He gave a hearty laugh. "You're a good deal taller than when last we met. Heard from your brother you'd come back from India." He turned to call over his shoulder, "Margery! Come quick! Master Simon is here! Or, er, Captain Harcourt now, is it?"

"To you? Just Simon," he said. *At least for a while longer...* He didn't want to think what Daw might call him once he learned of the Earl's plans.

Daw ushered them into the cottage, and the scent of the something delicious simmering over the fire teased Simon's nose.

A plump woman with pink cheeks and russet hair bustled over, wiping work-reddened hands on a buff-colored apron.

"This is my wife, Mrs. Garvey. Margery, this is Captain Harcourt, back home at last!"

Simon felt that odd hollowed-out sensation in his stomach at Daw's words. "Not home, exactly. But back. This is Miss Waverly and Tripp."

Daw's wife dipped a curtsey, wiping a bit of flour from her cheek. "Welcome. Come in, come in and sit a spell, sir, if you've a mind to, all of you."

Daw led Miss Waverly, Simon, and Tripp deeper into his home. Simon hadn't been in one of the Everdene cottages since the summer he was nine years old, but Daw's was exactly as he remembered it.

The main room was filled with special touches added by the skilled generations of craftsmen who had worked their magic with wood. A high-backed settle stood near the fire, rag rugs on the plank floor. A Welsh dresser held crockery and a few pieces of pewter. Shawls and a greatcoat hung on pegs. A flintlock musket hung over the door, while a rocking chair, carved with leaves and vines, nestled close to a basket full of mending.

Simon had vague memories of ginger cookies warm from the oven, and a whittled wooden puppet with jointed legs that would turn somersaults when you squeezed two sticks together. A gift from the grandfather who had once sat by the fire.

The wall above the fireplace was soot-blackened, but over the mantel was carved Able + Anna Garvey 1626.

"And who is this lad?" Margery asked and Simon noticed

that Miss Waverly had gently drawn Tripp forward. The boy's shoulders curled inward as if trying to make himself smaller.

God knew, he was already stunted enough after that bastard Farley starved him so he could squeeze up chimneys, Simon thought bitterly.

"Name's Tripp, ma'am." The lad licked his lips, his gaze flicking to the pot that hung over the fire on a chain.

Margery followed the direction of his gaze. "Well, I know a hungry lad when I see one, Tripp. I've got stew in the kettle if you'd like a bit."

"Yes, ma'am."

Mrs. Garvey flashed a smile at Simon as she settled Tripp and the bowl at the scarred oak table. "Daw used to tell our boys stories about the mischief you got up to, Captain Harcourt. You were quite the hero to our little rogues."

"You've sons?" Simon asked.

Sadness filled her eyes. "Twin boys. Hied off to Canada the day they turned fifteen. And you? Have you a wife and children?"

"No." Something in his tone made Daw clear his throat.

The carpenter laid a hand on his wife's back, deftly changing the subject. "I hope the Earl is gaining strength, Captain."

It was all Simon could do not to give a dismissive snort. *He's well enough to drive the maids to weep, and for my brother and me to exhaust his store of French brandy...* "His doctors say he's recovered to the point he can travel. He'll be going to his estate at Bitterne Tower on Thursday."

Daw nodded. "Best for all the family to leave Everdene for a while, to avoid the noise and mess of construction on the way. I vow, with so much lumber and so many supplies being delivered, Mr. Inchwick must be readying to build a castle."

Miss Waverly turned a curious gaze toward Simon. "What, exactly, are they building?"

Unprepared for such a question, Simon's throat went dry. He

coughed, trying to cover his reaction. "Something my father has planned. I'll be staying to see the project through, after which I will build the Harcourt stables into the finest England has ever seen."

A worried pucker showed between Daw's brows. "Have you been out to the site? Got to tell you, the place Mr. Inchwick is having things delivered is not where I'd want to raise horses."

"Or anything else for that matter," Miss Waverly said, her shrewd gaze locking on Simon's.

"Perhaps we should attend to the reason we've sought Daw out today," he said, hoping to direct their attention away from anything to do with the impending construction.

Thankfully, she turned back to the Garveys. "I'm afraid that Tripp, here, got into a bit of trouble."

Daw eyed the boy who was shoveling stew into his mouth. "Trouble?" he echoed, and the boy curved one arm around the bowl, clutching it to his chest as if he feared someone might take it away.

"We caught him stealing an apple," she explained.

"Is that so?" Daw asked.

Grateful for the change of topic, Simon gestured to Penelope. "Miss Waverly helped him evade his pursuers and paid for his contraband. Between the two of them, they were quite the resourceful pair," he added, trying not to smile at the memory of how she'd hidden the boy beneath her skirts.

Tripp glared at Simon. "Aye, I took the apple, but I'm a hard worker, I am! And the miss, here, is a right game one!"

"You were the clever one, Tripp," Miss Waverly said, bestowing a tender smile on him. She turned to Daw. "Poor boy. They'd abused him terribly."

Daw raked mouse-brown hair back from his brow and looked at the lad. "You're Zeke Raffy's eldest." The boy nodded. "Had the farm west of the brook," Daw informed them. "His father died in a farm accident last fall, and the family got a notice to quit. Tripp, here, and three other littler ones. Heard his mother sold him to the chimney sweep."

"Ye needn't talk as if I'm not here." The boy glared over his spoon. "'T weren't me mam's fault. Da got crushed under a cart and next thing, we was thrown out on our bums. Mam had to get to her people in Scotland or the wee 'uns would starve, but she got no money to get there."

"What about the parish?" Simon asked. "Isn't there a work-house?" He was certain he saw the grim building when riding to Everdene. True, it was a dismal-looking place, and they separated the mothers from their children, but surely that was better than selling one's own child?

Tripp shook his head. "Mam couldn't bear it for the little ones. Told her I'd get along on me own, I did. But that bastard Farley tol' Mam he'd teach me to be a carpenter. Instead, he stuffed me up a chimney and barely gave me a crumb to eat when I climbed down."

Raffy... Simon finally placed the name. He looked at Daw, a knot turning his stomach. "The Raffy cottage. It's on Harcourt land?"

"Aye. Mr. Inchwick leased it out to someone else a week after the wake was over."

If anything, Miss Waverly's expression turned even more determined as she looked from Simon to Daw. "We were hoping it might be possible to find some work for Tripp on the estate," she said, though Simon had not mentioned any such thing. "That you might be able to teach him some carpentry. I know he would work hard, wouldn't you, Tripp? And do whatever Mr. Garvey asked of you?"

The lad swallowed the lump of mutton he was chewing, his eyes on the big man. He nodded with a spark of hope as he locked gazes with the carpenter's.

"Well..." Daw drew out the word, tapping his knuckle against his chin as he studied the boy. "What do you think, lad?

Might be Mrs. Garvey and I could find chores for you to do around here, until we figure out what's to become of you. I suppose I could teach you a bit about how to use a hammer and saw if you're willing. But there'll be no more stealing. You want an apple, you ask for it."

Tripp nodded, then stilled. "But what if... what if Farley comes back an' wants to stuff me up another chimney?" Tears shone in his eyes, but he blinked them back fiercely, glaring at the four adults. "I won't go! I won't!"

Simon clenched his fist, feeling that old thirst for a fight. But it was Penelope who answered. "If Farley shows his face around here, you send him to the big house. Tell him to ask for Captain Harcourt. He'll no doubt settle his accounts."

Simon, surprised—and downright amused—by her audacity, uncurled his fist and placed it on the boy's shoulder, feeling the wing-like bones beneath far too little flesh. "Well, what do you say, Tripp?"

"I say yes, m'lord, your honor... I mean, your Captain, sir."

Simon looked up and saw that Penelope Waverly's eyes were shining at Tripp and Daw Garvey. He wanted her to look at him that way.

"Thank you, Daw," she said in that melodious voice. "And thank you, Margery. If there is anything you need for him—"

"I've got me own boys' clothes tucked away. I'm sure we can fit Tripp out."

Miss Waverly brushed the grimy hair from Tripp's forehead, then gave it a ruffle. "You listen to the Garveys, while you're here."

"He won't be no trouble, miss," Daw said. "We can use him to help stack wood and such for whatever business Mr. Inchwick is about. From the look of it, there will be plenty to do."

Simon felt a tightening in his gut. But he shoved the uncomfortable sensation away, reasoning that Everdene wasn't his estate, and decisions regarding it weren't his to make. If he'd refused, his father would just find someone else to carry out his orders.

He was grateful when they finally said their goodbyes, not relaxing until he and Miss Waverly ducked under the lintel and headed out into the village. The street was full of tenants going about their business, some laughing, a mother scolding a child for a tear in his breeches, a little girl shooing geese away from pies on a windowsill. None of them had any idea that before the year was out, there would be no sign this village had ever existed.

Simon would have traded it all, and for what?

He quickly shoved the thought to the back of his mind, erecting a wall he would later reinforce with a generous libation of brandy.

He turned toward Penelope, hoping for one of those irresistible smiles the woman had lavished on Tripp and the Garveys. "Well, I think that got settled nicely," he said.

Instead, she frowned. "I'm glad Tripp is safe, but helping him was the least you could do. It was your steward who turned his family from their home."

Simon looked back at the Garveys' cottage, remembering the mantel with its names and dates carved into the wood, dreading the moment he would have to tell Daw Garvey that he had to tear it down.

When he turned back, very much aware of Miss Waverly's presence, it occurred to him there was something that terrified him even more. That she would find out.

Apparently, his soul wasn't quite as dead as he'd thought.

# CHAPTER 6

The day after Simon had visited the Garvey cottage—a mistake if there ever was one—he was summoned by his father to meet in the mahogany-paneled study where the Earl held court. Unfortunately, Simon's memory of the event was somewhat muddled since he'd consumed a quantity of brandy beforehand, his customary way of dealing with his father's barbs.

"Good, you're here," his father had said, then nodded to his land agent, who stood as Simon entered the room. Mr. Inchwick wore a green silk waistcoat. His beard, trimmed to a precise point, gave his countenance a sharp appearance, while hair that might once have been brown, was dust-colored and curled.

Simon nodded in greeting.

"My younger son," the Earl continued, "Captain Harcourt will remain at the estate while construction is underway. I will leave matters in his hands once the Viscount and I depart, though I doubt he will pay more than a cursory interest to anything but these horses he's having brought to the stables, and the ladies hereabouts."

There was something about Inchwick's smile that rasped Simon's nerves. Then again, maybe it was the alcohol Simon had liberally consumed not only in anticipation of this meeting, but to dull his thoughts of the events at Daw's cottage, a mere day before.

"I shall, of course, be at your son's service." The land agent's words seemed cordial enough, making Simon think he had misjudged the man.

"Good to hear," the Earl said. "I'll leave it to the two of you." He waved his hand, dismissing them both.

Outside the room, Inchwick smiled again. "You needn't trouble yourself if you have other, more important matters."

Definitely not the alcohol, Simon decided. He simply didn't like the man. "I do, at least for the next few days." He figured it would take that long to dull his senses, allowing him to proceed with his father's plans. "Should I decide otherwise, you'll be the first to hear."

The man almost looked relieved. "You need only summon me." He started to turn away, then smiled solicitously. "I will, of course, be glad to meet you here, if it is more convenient."

"It is not," Simon replied, very much aware of his father's presence in the adjacent room. "Good day."

The land agent left, and Simon returned to the study below stairs, refilling his glass from the crystal decanter.

---

LESS THAN A WEEK LATER, AND NEARLY AS MANY BOTTLES OF brandy consumed, he finally forced himself to meet with Inchwick.

It was an easy walk from the manor to the land agent's red brick home, so that Inchwick could quickly cross from his private lodgings when he was summoned. Apparently, the stand of trees surrounding Inchwick's house concealed enough that it didn't 'pollute the prospect' of the Earl's view from the rear windows, because his father hadn't been disturbed enough to demand it be torn down.

*Not yet,* Simon thought ironically. *The old man was still alive...*

He grimaced as he mounted the stairs to the land agent's house and rang the bell. Obviously, he hadn't drunk enough brandy. His memory of Inchwick was hazy, but his father's words still echoed in his mind with astonishing clarity.

After a moment, a maid of about thirty years in mobcap and apron answered, then showed Simon down the hall to the land agent's office.

"Good afternoon," Simon said, striding in before the maid could announce him.

Startled, Inchwick looked up from the ledger spread across the large desk at the center of the room, a quill in his hand.

The man was stripped down to a cream-and-black striped waistcoat, his shoulders hunched, the points of his collar excessively high. Simon glimpsed pages filled with precise rows of figures before the land agent closed the calfskin-bound book he'd been writing in, then stood.

"Captain Harcourt! This is an *unexpected* pleasure," Inchwick said, with a smile that didn't quite reach his eyes. "I would have been happy to wait upon you at the manor house."

"It's no trouble to conduct our interview here. I have some questions you can answer."

"Of course, sir. Shall I have Mrs. Cullen order tea?" He leveled a rather quelling glance at the woman.

"Not necessary, though I'd be glad of a glass of Madeira." Simon gestured to the piecrust table where a decanter and an array of goblets stood.

The housekeeper curtseyed to him, then hurried out, closing the door behind her.

Inchwick laid his quill pen across the sharp-tined antlers on an inkwell shaped like a stag's head, then crossed to the table. As he filled two glasses, Simon noticed that the land agent had done well for himself. Rosewood surfaces gleamed, chinoiserie was displayed in a glass-covered cupboard. The drapes at the windows were crimson velvet. A portrait of a man in clerical garb hung over the fireplace.

Inchwick followed the direction of Simon's gaze. "My father. He was a curate in Northumberland."

"Ah."

"I assume your questions have to do with the new construction ahead." Inchwick handed Simon the glass of wine. "I can show you the plans I've drawn up, but I fear you would find it rather tedious."

"I am certain that you have those well in hand. But I suppose we must arrange a time to go over them and to visit the site as well."

"It will be my great honor at some later date. At the moment, our first order of business must be seeing that the stables are well fitted out for your magnificent horses."

"Excellent. However, I do have one question regarding our project that cannot wait. Do the cottagers know yet?"

"Know what?"

"About the plan to relocate the village? Has anyone told them?"

"No." Deep-set brown eyes narrowed, Inchwick's brow furrowing as if weighing his odds in a wager. "Your father and brother gave me leave to handle it as I deem appropriate. I decided it best to have everything in order first. The site laid out, the materials gathered, even some of the buildings finished before they are apprised of the situation. No sense giving them too much time to… ahem… work themselves into a lather."

Conscience was a prickly thing for a soldier. Especially in war. Do what your superiors order you to do, then get the hell away, try to outrun it on the swiftest horse a man could find. Simon had always been able to take the horrors he'd seen and done, and box them up like his campaign trunk. Surely he could do so now. Or so he thought, until the words slipped out. "Ah, so it is to be an ambush, is it?"

"You've been away from England for a long time, sir. Perhaps you've not heard of certain uprisings among the common folk. Between the Chartists demanding the vote for men who don't own land, to those protesting the Corn Laws, there has been a great deal of unrest. As for properties such as Everdene… the kind of changes we are about to make have incited violence in the past. Men riled up by nonsense written by the likes of Thomas Paine, and tales of revolution in France and America."

Simon thought of the sons Daw would likely never see again.

"Liberty," Inchwick nearly spat the word. "As if these people would understand what to do with it if it were given them. People getting above the station God placed them in. They should be grateful to have new homes, but I doubt they will be. I've recommended we not build too many cottages, since they'll not be filled. Plenty of folk will go storming off in high dudgeon as so many did during the last round of enclosures. Trust me, it will be far less vexing for Harcourts to raise sheep."

Simon drank deep. Yes, sheep were obedient and went where they were herded. Even into a narrow pass where they were perfect targets.

"Why your questions, Captain? Is something troubling you?"

"No." He tried not to think of Daw Garvey's wife in the kitchen where his grandmother had baked gingerbread. Nor Miss Waverly, who seemed to believe in the goodness of those around her. Simon tapped his fingers on Inchwick's desk. "I did have an interesting encounter last week. I met a boy who is going to help with construction. His name is Raffy. His father was a tenant here, I understand."

"Raffy…" The land agent tucked his chin back and frowned. "The boy must have belonged to Zeke Raffy, poor bastard.

Killed as his cart turned over when the edge of the road crumbled. I thought the family had moved on."

"The mother apparently was so desperate she sold the boy."

"It happens. Unfortunate that the family had to be turned out, but we cannot run a profitable estate without tenants who can work." Inchwick straightened the knot of his cravat. "There is no choice in such a circumstance. Not unlike soldiers who are sent home without an arm or a leg. They can hardly continue in the army, and you must march on."

The fact that it was true didn't mean Simon hated that reality any less.

Anger shoved hard against Simon's composure at the thought of men he'd seen wounded, and soldiers maimed in service of the Crown, left to beg on the streets. Inchwick's cavalier attitude made him want to plant the man a facer. He forced his mind away from the subject before he gave in to the impulse. "I encountered some familiar faces while in town," he said.

"Did you?

"I was wondering. What can you tell me about a Miss Penelope Waverly?"

"Miss Waverly?" Inchwick wrinkled his brow with faint distaste. "Why do you ask?"

Simon swirled the wine in his goblet. "She seems like a singular type of woman."

"Singular. Yes. She is quite the bluestocking. A meddling, unwomanly sort."

Simon's brows arched at the man's curt answer.

"Forgive me for being blunt, sir," Inchwick said, "but you did ask."

"I did."

"It will be better for Everdene when she takes herself off again to plague the offspring of whichever man is foolhardy enough to hire her as governess."

"She is a governess?" The thought came unbidden. How he

had longed for Nurse Betsy when his father had dismissed her after Simon's mother had disappeared. God knew, he had been a little devil to the woman who had ruled over the Harcourt nursery when he was a lad. He tried to picture the proud, stubborn Miss Waverly in such a position, minding her young charges. The thought made him smile. Heaven help the children in her care, because he doubted very much that they'd get away with anything.

"Miss Waverly," Inchwick continued, "is preparing for the inevitable, I suppose."

"The inevitable?"

"Her mother inherited property on the west edge of the Everdene estate from an aunt whose branch of the family had owned it for generations. However, Mr. Waverly—the architect, if you remember—got into some financial difficulty. A fondness for drink and reckless speculation. I advised the Earl to purchase the acreage to increase your family's estate. The house is to be surrendered after the mother's death."

She was to lose her home? Is that why Penelope Waverly had leapt to defend young Tripp?

Inchwick ran his fingers over the antlers on the stag's head inkstand. "I confess I'd imagined that we would take possession of the Waverly home sooner, rather than later. Anastasia Waverly has not been robust in health since the birth of her youngest daughter." The land agent cleared his throat. "If you are looking for a bit of diversion while you languish here, sir, anyone besides Penelope Waverly would be the wiser choice."

"Diversion?" he said, feeling an unexpectedly hot spark of outrage that anyone would paint Miss Waverly in such a light.

"Now that the Earl is out of danger," Inchwick replied, unaware of Simon's reaction, "I am sure that Squire Rendell or Sir Lewis Chapman will be eager to hold some ball or musicale with you and the Viscount on the guest list. Both families have marriageable daughters."

Of course, neighboring families of note would want his brother on their guest list, Simon thought. Lucian was the Earl's heir, and the most eligible bachelor around. A restlessness gripped Simon. After the visit to the Garvey cottage and now this meeting with the unctuous Inchwick, Simon was desperately in need of some way to rid himself of these damned uncomfortable feelings. But attending a ball was not what he had in mind.

"If I'm to remain here for a year at least, I will require a cavalry course set up in the west field, with straw dummies, etcetera," Simon said. "It won't do to let my skill with a saber grow rusty."

"I think that is a capital idea, sir," Inchwick said. He clasped ink-stained hands. "As I said to the Earl, I can see no reason you should waste your energy in the prosaic decisions about this project after the unfortunate episode in Afghanistan. You've naught to do here but amuse yourself. Hunting. Fishing. Renew acquaintance with the society to be found here."

The two acquaintances he'd renewed thus far had made Simon dashed edgy. Luckily, he'd already written to have his horses brought to Everdene—the mares he planned to build his stable with, and Brutus, the gelding he was training in cavalry maneuvers.

"Get on with this business as quickly as possible," Simon ordered, then stalked out of the land agent's house, trying not to think too hard about the inevitable.

His gut twisted, knowing the blow would come, imagining Daw Garvey and Penelope Waverly's faces when it did. One more item to be locked away in his campaign trunk.

One more reason to strike camp and move on.

# CHAPTER 7

$\mathcal{A}$fternoon sun streamed through the window of Laurel Cottage, falling across the pink sarcenet bonnet Penelope was determined to refurbish for her sister, Kitty.

Much as Pen loathed needlework, Kitty's efforts were usually better spent on her piano practice. But at present, Kitty was banging out Bach as if his *Well-Tempered Clavier* was in a most disagreeable mood. Little wonder, after a breeze had swept Kitty's favorite bonnet off her head and into a puddle as she walked down the lane.

But banging the piano was better than tears, Pen thought as she carefully stitched a cluster of silk pansies over a stain. She'd just pricked her finger and glanced out the window when she glimpsed a blur in sunny yellow skirts whisk through the gate.

Fanny. Pen's middle sister flung open the front door, then shut it, rushing into the parlor as if wolves were one paw behind her. Yet instead of dismay, her cheeks glowed cherry-red with excitement.

"Pen! Kitty!" She gasped, tucking a wayward ash-blond curl behind her ear. "You'll never guess who I met on my way to Rebecca Caine's! Squire Rendell's footman coming to Laurel

Cottage with *this*!" She brandished an engraved invitation before her and read aloud.

"*Squire Jacob Rendell cordially invites Miss Waverly, Miss Katherine, and Miss Frances Waverly to a ball to be given at Malvern Way…*"

"A ball!" Kitty leapt up from the seat of her pianoforte, her hands thumping out a discordant sound that set Penelope's teeth on edge.

"Oh, Fanny! Do let me see it!" Kitty raced to snatch the invitation from her sister. "I've been *perishing* from boredom!"

"It's to be the most exciting event we've had all summer," Fanny enthused. "I ran into Lavinia Chapman while paying calls, and she said that Maria Rendell said…" She paused for effect.

"Well, if Lavinia Chapman said it, it *must* be something extraordinary," Pen muttered wryly. The girl had a tongue that could wag on about nothing until Pen longed to be able to tie it in a knot.

"The Viscount Everdene and his brother, Captain Harcourt, are both going to attend!"

Fanny had Pen's attention now. "I thought the Earl was still recovering," Pen said.

"He's so much improved that Maria convinced her papa to host the affair before the Harcourt brothers desert us again. She's hoping she might snare the Viscount. Since the Earl's accident, it's no doubt more imperative than ever for the Viscount to come up to scratch and sire an heir. Though all of the girls in my French class claim that Captain Harcourt is the one to turn a girl's head. He's devilish handsome."

That much was true. If Fanny and Kitty were this infatuated by the mere idea of Simon Harcourt, one of those wicked smiles would send them into ecstasies…

Fanny twirled around, nearly upsetting Penelope's sewing

basket. "Rebecca Caine saw Captain Harcourt on a horse of pure gold and said he looked like the Sun God Dedalus."

Pen raised her eyebrows, amused. "You might want to loan Rebecca my book of myths. It's Apollo, if you are speaking of the Roman sun god. Helios in Greece. Dedalus was the father of Icarus. You know, the boy who flew too close to the sun."

"Don't tease, Pen!" Fanny pouted and shot her an accusing glare. "Rebecca claims that the whole village was abuzz because *you* were seen walking down the street with him on Market Day, cool as you please!"

That was hardly how Penelope remembered it. The encounter had seemed rather heated, actually.

"Well, aren't you the sly one!" Kitty gasped. "You didn't even mention it!"

"Because you two would turn our meeting into something romantic when it was not so at all."

Kitty fluffed out her charming plaid day dress, her pique giving way to laughter. "The encounter was totally wasted on you! You are completely hopeless."

"Is that why you've been aimlessly wandering about this past week, Pen?" Fanny asked. "Were you hoping to see him again?"

Pen rolled her eyes. She'd been more restless than ever since her encounter with Simon Harcourt, but her 'wandering about' had been far from aimless.

She'd visited the village several times to see how Tripp fared, and to post letters to contacts she'd made through school and lectures, hoping someone might know of a family seeking a governess.

True, there were times she'd caught glimpses of the golden horse and its rider in the distance, but she'd quickly turned the opposite way.

If *he* was going to the ball, it was the last place Penelope should go, but she quite loved dancing. The thought of whirling around the floor in the arms of Simon Harcourt was quite appealing. *Too* appealing, like a goblet of fine spirits—a temptation in which a less controlled woman might lose her head. Fortunately, Pen knew better than to take that first sip...

Still, it wouldn't be the worst thing to indulge in a bit of fun before returning to the twilight world of some wealthy employer's nursery to teach recalcitrant children.

There would be no dancing then.

"I shall wear my green satin," Fanny exclaimed, "and Pen, you must loan me Aunt Phaedra's necklace." Penelope couldn't help but smile as her sisters chattered in excitement about gowns and jewelry and dancing slippers. After a moment, the pair turned to her.

"What will you wear?" Kitty asked.

Pen shrugged and stitched another silk pansy into place. "I don't know. It's been three years since I've been to a ball. I suppose I'll wear my blue gown."

"Oh, that color is lovely on you!" Fanny enthused. "What if we remake it a bit so it doesn't look so out of fashion?"

"You know I don't pay heed to such things."

"Please, Pen! Let us add some pretty touches!" Fanny's smile lit her whole face. "You might as well get some benefit from my artistic flare! A little gauze draped here and there to give it an airy look, and I could make some pink silk roses."

Kitty clapped her hands. "I just finished a wide swath of lace we could baste about the neckline. It would be fun to dress you up. Please. You'll be back to drudging as a governess soon enough."

They both looked so eager, like the little sisters she'd often bought lemon drops for in an effort to distract them from their father's drinking. Pen gazed at them fondly. Her sisters could be flighty and try her patience, but there were times their kindness warmed her through.

"I surrender," she said. "You two can arrange me however you please. But no feathers! They make me sneeze!"

"When we're done with you, every gentleman in the room will be clamoring to dance with you," Kitty predicted. Penelope couldn't suppress a spark of excitement.

"I very much doubt the gentlemen will lose their heads over me when you are about," Pen said, "but I confess, it will feel good to dance." To set down her responsibilities for one night, and just be one more young woman in a glittering chamber full of music and laughter.

*It's very likely some of the guests will be laughing at* you... caution whispered. *The governess playing lady...*

But her Waverly forebears were as estimable as any in the county, Penelope thought.

For one night, she'd remember the life she'd been born to, before she returned to the life that *was*.

# CHAPTER 8

$\mathcal{S}$imon leaned close to the horse's neck, feeling the power of the of the stallion between his thighs as it ran down a lane near Laurel Cottage. He loved the times he exercised the animal. Strands of cream mane whipped back to sting Simon's cheeks, the hammering of hooves echoing the racing of his heart, bringing him a sense of freedom almost as if he were in flight. He wasn't exactly looking for Penelope Waverly. Or maybe he was. For a woman who was supposed to be a diversion, Miss Waverly had proved damned elusive.

Inchwick might have intended to quell Simon's interest in the lady, but cautioning Simon *not* to pursue something was a sure way to get him latch onto the forbidden.

Every other young miss of marriageable age in the vicinity of Everdene had crossed Simon's path whenever possible, praising his horsemanship, raving about Caspian, and inquiring if Simon and his brother were attending the Rendells' ball.

Only Penelope Waverly had been like a will-o'-the-wisp—almost as if she'd been avoiding him.

But today, it seemed he might be in luck. As he turned a corner, he spied a lone figure walking at a no-nonsense pace, a familiar chipped straw bonnet on her head. He grinned, a frisson of excitement buzzing under his skin. It seemed his bluestocking had finally come out of hiding.

As he cantered toward her, he saw her observe him, shading her eyes with the flat of her hand as if the sun was too bright. Simon knew what it was like to see Caspian the first time, a splash of living gold.

He drew rein beside her, pleased with the picture she made. A soft-green walking dress showed the womanly curves of her body to advantage, the thin batiste skirts rippling in the gentle breeze. Some kind of flower was printed on the fabric. Tucks marched down the front of her bodice in military precision, so that Simon wanted to reach out his finger and trace them from the frill at her neckline, over the swell of her bosom to where the point of her bodice arrowed down past her waist. He tried not to think about the womanly charms it pointed *to*.

"Lovely morning, Miss Waverly," he said. "Out searching for waifs to rescue?"

"I only do that on Thursdays," she said, straightening the green streamer on her bonnet. "Tuesdays I check the post."

"I'll have to make a note and be certain to ride in the opposite direction from you on Thursday." He winked.

A becoming shade of pink tinted Miss Waverly's cheeks. Simon felt an absurd amount of pleasure that he'd caused her to blush. The prospect was so entertaining that he swung down from the saddle, so he could see her face more clearly beneath the brim of her bonnet.

His boots struck the ground, kicking up a cloud of dust, and Caspian danced to the side, lifting his hooves with an elegance almost like ballet.

"I must say you have made quite the spectacle of yourself hereabouts," Miss Waverly chided Simon. "My sisters have been raving about your horse. I thought they were exaggerating, but there is a sheen to his coat, as if the sun were striking a gold ring. He's quite remarkable."

"He is, isn't he?" Simon noted Caspian stretching his neck toward Miss Waverly. "Have a care," Simon warned. "The breed tends to be wary of strangers."

"In other words, he is a very intelligent horse." Undaunted, Penelope offered the animal the flat of her hand.

Simon stared in disbelief as the horse sniffed her fingers, then leaned forward and lipped the streamer on her bonnet.

She shoved the brim back until the chipped straw tumbled off her curls to dangle between her shoulder blades, her ribbons out of reach. The sunlight set her ringlets aglow. "You're a fine fellow," she told the horse, "But you mustn't eat my bonnet! What is your name?"

She spoke as if expecting the stallion to answer.

"Allow me to make a proper introduction," Simon said. "Caspian, this is Miss Waverly. Miss Waverly, Caspian."

"Named for the Caspian Sea, are you?" She continued to address the horse.

Simon raised one eyebrow in surprise. "You know of the Caspian Sea?"

Penelope ran her gloved hand down the horse's elegant nose. "I used to study the atlas when I was a little girl, imagining all of the places I hoped to visit one day. The Taj Mahal. The Parthenon." Wistfulness softened her voice, but something else as well. A hint of vulnerability he'd not recognized before.

He'd realized from their first encounter that she was a singular woman, but these new discoveries piqued his curiosity.

She sighed. "How I'd love to see all the things I've read about, wonders the world holds. Wonders like this horse. Who would ever have believed such a creature lived and breathed?"

He'd felt the same way when he'd seen horses like Caspian traverse the rugged mountains of Afghanistan. Slim-bodied, with long, slender legs, their small, round hooves shaped for racing across desert sand.

"He's a Turkoman horse," Simon explained. "One of the oldest breeds known to man. Bred to travel the desert, sure-footed in mountain passes. It's said that Alexander the Great loved his so much he even named a city after it."

"Alexandria Bucephalus," she exclaimed, her eyes shining.

Simon smiled, astonished. "Yes."

The stallion pricked his ears forward as if hearing the name of his illustrious forebear, his liquid brown eyes large in a long, delicately shaped face.

"I hope to breed these horses here and take the racing circuit by storm," Simon confided. He'd told no one outside his family what he'd planned, some part of him superstitious, as if voicing his dream might cause fate to snatch it away. What was it his friend Yadav had called it in India? Karma? That your mistakes, your own misdeeds would ricochet back on you, and exact the kind of consequence you deserved?

*God help me if I get what I deserve.* Simon thought of the village he was to destroy.

"Caspian is fast, then?" Penelope's voice brought him back to the English countryside and the woman who stood beside him.

"He's like wind across the desert. On my last mission, he outran a dozen Afghan warriors in the Hindu-Kush mountains."

Her gaze shifted from the horse, to Simon, then back again, and Simon could almost see her imagination trying to conjure the scene. But how could a sheltered English gentlewoman ever know the gut-churning sensation of seeing Ghilzai tribesmen sweep down a mountain? How could she picture their long flintlock jezails firing, their loose trousers and flowing shirts making them a blur of color and rage. Warriors, one with their horses and the unforgiving landscape. He pulled his thoughts away from the memory, looking at Penelope once more.

"Caspian saved my life," Simon said softly.

"Then England owes Caspian a debt."

Simon's mouth went dry as Penelope looked up at him from beneath thick, dark lashes. "You were in Afghanistan then? What was the country like?"

"Harsh. Beautiful. More a cluster of separate tribes, really, with the misfortune to lie between Russia and India."

India, yielding riches beyond measure to the conqueror who possessed it, silk and cotton, tea and spices… opium.

"The Jewel in the British Crown," Penelope murmured the name the British colony had been given. "I remember hearing Russia was determined to gain territory and claim India's wealth for their own."

"All that stood between India and Russia was a band of countries in Eastern Asia. Lord Auckland, who was in charge in Bombay, decided to send troops into Afghanistan to keep that border secure."

"So, you wound up fighting the Afghans instead."

"Yes. He felt the Afghan ruler, Dost Mohammad, was too friendly with the Russians. So, we removed him, and put Shah Shuja in power, a corrupt, weak, arrogant man, known for hacking off noses or ears of his servants when they displeased him. I suppose you can hardly blame them for objecting."

"I should think not." Penelope hugged herself, and he could see her shudder. "I saw a caricature once—the English lion and the Russian bear snarling with Asia between them. They called it *The Great Game*."

Simon felt a sharp burn of anger at the term, as if men were pawns on a chessboard… But Penelope couldn't know how the words would affect him.

"Whatever we call it—*The Great Game* or, as the Russians say, *The Tournament of Shadows*—the conflict between us is only the beginning," Simon said. "Russia wants India's riches. We want to keep those riches for ourselves. Russian and British conquests will collide at some border in earnest one day, and when they do…" He looked off into the distance. "I fear how much blood will be shed."

She was silent for long moments, then turned her attention back to the horse. "I'm glad that you managed to carry something beautiful out of Afghanistan in spite of the war. Caspian is such a magnificent creature." A dimple appeared in her cheek, impish and endearing.

"What are you smiling about all of a sudden? Remember, I met you when you were a hoyden girl. That sly smile of yours was one the lads and I learned to be wary of."

"I've no desire to add to your high opinion of yourself—*or* your horse—Captain Harcourt. But I can't help being amused by things I've heard young ladies chattering about since you've been riding around the countryside. Apparently, you and Caspian are being compared to figures out of mythology. Helios, or Apollo… or…." She looked up at him with a mischievous grin. "Dedalus."

"That is a rather low blow, Miss Waverly. Isn't Dedalus a doddering old papa? Icarus's father?" Simon rubbed his jawline. "Please tell me I've not begun to show silver in my hair."

"Not a single thread, but I'd wager you've caused more than your share of gray hairs to sprout on other heads."

"*Touché*, madam. Though I'll match your wager and double down on the fact that you are equally guilty of turning people's hair white. I doubt that chimney sweep and his cohorts have recovered from your encounter."

Penelope tipped her chin up. "I certainly hope not."

"As for Caspian leaping out of Olympus, my friend Jamie and I thought the same thing when we first saw this breed in the desert. We couldn't take our eyes off of them. But they are far more than beautiful. It was their stamina that stunned us. Our guides claimed the wind itself couldn't outrace them. The breed could go three days without water, cross the most treacherous desert or snowy mountain pass." He expected her to be impressed by such a feat of endurance and courage. Instead, that soft, pensive look crossed her face again.

"So, his life was full of challenges he was meant to triumph over," Penelope said. "I wonder if he misses those wild lands." She looked around at the piled stone fences, the neatly laid-out fields. "I fear England must feel very tame. Does it to you?"

"It did." *Until I encountered a certain crusader fending off a chimney sweep and his cohorts.* Simon shifted the reins to his left hand, remembering how restless he'd been in the five months since his return from Asia. The nights he'd spent in London in a whisky-soaked haze, burning for a fight, grateful when someone challenged him. He just hadn't expected his most adept opponent to wear a bonnet and have the most delectable lips he'd ever seen. He tried to pull his gaze away from the temptation of her mouth and focus on something else.

"I can't wait to see the first foal out of Caspian," Simon said. "The mares Jamie and I chose should arrive here any day."

"Your friend must be very excited as well."

"Jamie is dead."

Green eyes widened, flooding with empathy. "I'm sorry."

For a moment, it seemed as if she might ask what had happened, but she did not, perhaps wise enough to know that if he wanted to add more, he would. Simon yanked his thoughts away from Jamie's death as if he'd thrust his hand in hot coals.

He feigned a carelessness he did not feel. "There is to be a ball at the Rendells'. Will you be attending?"

"Yes. I'll escort my younger sisters there. Someone must make certain they do not get caught up with some incorrigible."

"We incorrigibles can be quite exciting. Will you be at risk of stealing off to some secluded place with a shameless rogue, Miss Waverly?"

"I'm far too sensible," she said primly. "I'm in no danger."

Simon looked down at her lips and wondered. She was so certain she could handle a rogue. He'd like to test her theory.

Every feminine curve enticed the man in him… and he wondered what it would be like to press his lips against the graceful arch of her throat.

An errant breeze set her skirt swaying and for a moment he glimpsed the white frill of her petticoat and a flash of stocking and half-boot. What would it be like to curl his hand about her ankle? Inch his fingers up to bare skin…

Where the devil had that thought come from? Simon had a man's appetites, but deflowering virgins was hardly his style. As a cavalry officer, he'd found plenty of willing women, experienced widows, courtesans eager to satisfy his needs and their own. Dallying with young well-born ladies could get a man legshackled in a hurry.

He stepped back, eager to turn his thoughts away from shadowy corners and stolen kisses and the temptation of testing the resolve of this beautiful woman. Her cheeks washed a deeper shade of pink, as if she sensed his train of thought, and she turned her attentions to Caspian again. "You said that this breed is wary of strangers. I cannot imagine this lovely animal behaving badly. He's such a gentle horse."

"Yes, well, tell that to the groom at the last stable where I boarded him. Took a chunk out of his shoulder. Of course, I found out later that the man was a thief, so perhaps he deserved it. I look forward to having my own stables, and choosing the staff accordingly."

"Perhaps you should have Caspian present at the interviews."

"I can see it now… *Your credentials seem impeccable. You're hired, unless my stallion bites you.*"

Penelope laughed. The sight mesmerized him. With her bonnet hanging from its strings down her back, her face tipped up, the dimple dancing in her cheek, she reminded Simon of the brief moments in his youth, before clashes with his father had become so bitter. And before his own glorious dreams of what it meant to be a cavalry officer were drowned in blood.

He surprised himself by asking, "Do you ride?"

"When I get the chance. Riding is one of my greatest pleasures, but since I've spent most of my time away from Laurel Cottage the past few years, my mare got no exercise. That was hardly fair to her. A friend bought Epona and she seems happy enough when I visit her. He lets me ride her whenever I wish."

*He?* Simon felt a surprising sting of jealousy.

"It's just hard to find time," she continued, unaware of his reaction, "when there are so many practical matters to catch up on at home before I leave again."

"Perhaps you might find time to ride with me one day. I will make certain Caspian is a gentleman and minds his manners."

The stallion blew a puff of air out of his nostrils and stamped his hoof, as if insulted by the aspersions cast on his manners. Simon couldn't blame the horse. After all, Caspian wasn't the one imagining curving his hand around Miss Waverly's bare leg.

"I'd keep my horse to a sensible pace," Simon promised.

"Would you?"

He nodded. He could keep Caspian reined in, but there were no guarantees a certain part of his anatomy would be willing to 'keep a sensible pace' when it came to Miss Penelope Waverly.

"Perhaps we can ride, if there is time," she allowed. "As to the stables you plan to build, they must be very large if the materials down in the vale are any clue."

Simon's impure thoughts scattered at the reminder of his true purpose at Everdene and what Miss Waverly's reaction to it would no doubt be. "Er... I do hope for a large stable. Eventually."

What was it about this woman that intrigued him so?

He'd seen how fearless she was, how quick of wit in a crisis. How willing to step beyond a woman's accepted role and challenge men. She was a delicious, irresistible riddle, Miss Penelope Waverly.

Even more so when a wicked look crossed her face. "When I was eight, I used to love to watch the blacksmith work. He warned me never to touch the iron when it was hot, but finally, I couldn't resist. I had to know what it felt like."

"Burned your fingers, did you?"

"Yes. I'm feeling the same urge to touch something now."

Was it possible that she was experiencing the same fierce attraction to him? He peered down at her gloved hand and imagined it running down his neck, splayed over his chest, caressing lower…

"Caspian's coat is so beautiful it almost doesn't seem real. You'll think me a featherhead, but I need to touch it with nothing in between."

Simon almost groaned aloud. Her fingers went to the button on her glove.

His throat worked as she slipped the tiny loop over the pearl button. It was only a glove, but seeing her draw it off, revealing her bare hand one inch at a time made his groin tighten. All he could think of was clasping her hand, turning it over and pressing his lips to the tender inside of her wrist.

Once her hand was free, she pressed her palm to Caspian's shoulder. Her eyes slid shut. Simon's mouth went dry.

Who would have guessed Miss Penelope Waverly, champion of abandoned children and disdained by Walter Inchwick as a bluestocking spinster, was such a sensual being? Beneath that proper façade was a woman who had repressed urges to explore by touch… Penelope Waverly would keep a man on his toes.

"He's so soft," she breathed, so caught up in the moment, the glove tumbled from her fingers. They both bent to retrieve it at the same time, their fingers colliding. Simon felt a sizzle of sensation go through him. He straightened, and held the glove out to her.

She thanked him, drawing the glove on with an air of brisk efficiency. But she must have felt the charge of awareness between them, for she fumbled with the pearl button, the little loop evading her fingers.

Simon stripped off his own gloves, thrusting them into his pocket. "Allow me," he said, his voice gravelly as he took her fingers in his own. He turned her hand to expose the troublesome button. For an instant, he peered down at the inside of her wrist, the delicate tracery of blue veins beneath warm white skin. He took his time, reluctant to end the contact. After a moment, he slipped the loop over the pearl, fastening the glove, but it didn't ease the arousal pulsing through him. There, beneath the button, remained a teardrop-shaped opening that revealed bare skin. He stared down at it and wondered what would happen if he touched his mouth to that vulnerable place

"I'd best let you be on your way," Penelope said, withdrawing her hand from his grasp, then hiding it in the folds of her skirts. "It's hardly fair to keep poor Caspian here when he's longing to run."

"I'm astonished he was patient this long," he said. "You seem to have cast a spell on him, just as you did on Tripp Raffy. I look forward to seeing you at the ball," he said, and meant it. Crowds could bring out the worst in him. There was always some idiot raving about British conquests, their superiority over all others. More than once, he'd planted such arses a facer.

He closed his eyes, remembering bloody battlefields, too many lost comrades.

He bade Miss Waverly farewell, imagining the oblivion to be found in the bottom of a bottle of whisky.

Then he mounted his stallion, leaned over the horse's neck, and spurred him to a gallop, flying across the meadow as if he could outrun the howling madness in the passes of the Hindu Kush…

# CHAPTER 9

*I*n the days leading up to the Rendells' ball, Penelope tried to convince herself that it was the horse's fault she'd lost her wits enough to dally with Simon Harcourt. From the time she first opened *Classic Fables of the Greeks and Romans* as a child, she'd imagined soaring away from her everyday world on the winged horse Pegasus. Harcourt's Turkoman stallion was the closest to such mythical beauty she'd ever seen.

*And what of the stallion's rider?* A voice whispered in her head. She didn't even have to close her eyes to picture Simon Harcourt, his hair windblown, his body powerful. There had been a moment she hadn't been able to breathe as the ethereal pair had thundered toward her, the man as wild and beautiful as the horse itself, the flash of gold against the sky like lightning.

When he'd reined in beside her and dismounted, he'd made her laugh, his teasing lightening her mood in a way few people could.

And when she'd dropped her glove… A shiver of heat went through her at the memory of how he'd taken her hand to help her refasten the glove's pearl button. For a heartbeat, time had frozen, and she'd seen his eyes go smoky before he grasped her hand. She'd wondered if he was going to press those sinfully sensual lips to the pulsebeat in her wrist. Most alarming of all, there was part of her that had wanted him to.

She'd broken the spell, tugged her hand free and buried it in her skirt, but that didn't quell the feeling that she'd somehow been stripped bare in those intense moments. Reminded that she had a body as well as a mind. She wondered what it would feel like to have masculine hands on her skin, Simon Harcourt's rein-hardened hands, the fingers that had been so deft as he slid a delicate loop over a pearl button...

*Stop it, Penelope,* she castigated herself. *You're no better than Kitty and Fanny, dazzled by a handsome cavalry Captain.* She was far too old for such nonsense, even if Simon Harcourt looked like Perseus reborn. She'd almost convinced herself that her reaction to him was a moment's madness, was all. *You will take yourself in hand, now you realize just how dangerous he is.*

Yet she couldn't control her dreams.

The man haunted her nights, not only kissing her wrist, but other parts as well, until she'd awakened, restless and tingling and far too curious for her own good.

*If he does claim his dance at the ball,* Pen resolved, *I will make it clear to him that I have no intention of more than a harmless flirtation before I'm off to a nursery classroom again.*

Heaven knew, she was fretting over nothing. Simon Harcourt would be awash in the most eligible partners the county could offer. Young beauties with large dowries and parents anxious to make a match with the wealthy Harcourt family.

Noble connections able to help him realize his dream of the equine bloodline he'd hoped to start with Caspian.

THE DAY OF THE BALL DAWNED BRIGHT AND CLEAR, PENELOPE'S sisters fluttering about like drunken butterflies while they donned their finery, fussing over this flounce and that ribbon, and who should wear which piece of jewelry. Their mother was eager to attend as well, and take her place among the clutch of matrons who listened to her complaints about ill health and lavished her with sympathy. Let Mama prattle on about how kind the Honorable Mrs. Davies had been, offering to take the Waverly women to the ball in her carriage. Let Mama recount happy tales from her time at Miss Primrose's Finishing School for Young Ladies and the thrill of her first season. At least she was not languishing in bed, grieving over Pen's refusal to marry the curate.

Embracing the spirit of the day, Penelope surrendered herself to her sisters' ministrations, much to Kitty and Fanny's delight. They had not allowed her one peek in a mirror until they put the last touches on her ensemble. When they finally whisked her before the cheval glass, the woman who stared back at Pen seemed a stranger. The blue gown had always suited Pen, despite being out of fashion, but it had been transformed by her sisters' efforts. Just as they'd promised, festoons of gauze gave it a fairy-like aura. Clusters of silk roses caught up the blue hem, revealing a pink silk underskirt Fanny had insisted Pen borrow. They'd altered the bodice to reveal her décolletage, and while the effect was more daring than Penelope was accustomed to, she didn't have the heart to complain.

"It's beautiful," she said, hugging them both.

"No hugs!" Kitty exclaimed, horrified. "You'll crush your roses and put creases in the skirts!" But Pen only hugged tighter.

Fanny pursed her lips with great satisfaction. "I'd like to see Lavinia Chapman and her set call you an old maid *now!*"

Pen couldn't deny that the thought of silencing such nasty asides pleased her.

"You'll dance as much as you like tonight, Pen," Kitty promised.

For a moment, a dark, ironic visage flashed in Penelope's mind, and she imagined Simon Harcourt claiming his waltz, his blue eyes raking over her with the heat that had simmered in them as he'd buttoned her glove.

***

NO EXPENSE HAD BEEN SPARED BY THE RENDELLS IN PREPARING for this night's entertainment, Pen thought as she took a respite after her second country dance. The whole house was like a confection designed to show their world—and especially the Harcourt brothers—the family's wealth and position. Hundreds of beeswax candles set crystal prisms aglow, the chandeliers bathing the guests in flickering rainbows of light. The Rendells' conservatory must be denuded of flowers, every blossom from the tiniest rosebud to fragrant lilies arranged in lush displays along the walls. The refreshment table was laden with the most elegant fare imaginable to fortify breathless dancers.

Pen reveled in the spectacle, the rainbow of gowns swirling by, the music that rippled from the musicians in the loft above, and most of all, her sisters' delight as they joined their friends, cheeks flushing when gentlemen asked them to dance. Pen felt a poignant tug remembering how innocent she'd been when she'd attended her first ball. Worry pricked that her sisters had no understanding of the reality that awaited them beyond the bridal door.

Pen glimpsed her mother across the room, grateful to find that she and Mrs. Davies were still together on a divan arranged for chaperones' comfort. Glad as Pen was that the rest of her family had found their friends, she realized there was nowhere among the casual groups gathering that she really fit. Her friends had mostly married now, young wives and mothers chattering about children's antics and the challenges of careless maidservants or wayward husbands. She couldn't bear one more pitying glance or question about suitors.

Kitty and Fanny's set were too flighty, concerned with little but romance and gowns. Her mother's friends looked through quizzing glasses and dispensed criticisms, praise, or the straight pins needed to fix torn flounces, while boasting about their daughters' accomplishments.

The men gathered in groups as well. Viscount Everdene had yet to appear, but Simon Harcourt had been commandeered by Sir Jacob since his arrival and was presently engaged in conversation. Pen had caught Simon glancing her way once or twice, but he'd made no move to approach her.

Feeling out of place, Pen strolled about the room, inspecting the paintings the Rendell family had collected over the years. It was easy to discern the originals from copies of portraits and landscapes Rendell's daughter had made during the family's recent trip to the Continent.

Penelope was pretending to be engrossed in a badly executed copy of Botticelli's *The Birth of Venus* when she heard the sure tread of approaching footsteps behind her. She knew without turning that it was Simon, caught the subtle scent of some exotic spice, felt a frisson of awareness. He was standing too close, his long legs brushing the back of her skirt as he leaned over her to examine the painting.

"I'm afraid this particular Venus looks rather out of sorts, Miss Waverly," he observed, the warmth of his breath caressing her bare shoulder.

She wheeled around, and took a step backward, praying he couldn't see the telltale flush climbing above the neckline of her gown.

He was garbed in evening attire, his black coat and breeches perfectly tailored, his waistcoat a blue that deepened the hue of his eyes. It was embroidered with gold thread that caught the light of the candles, his wide, white smile flashing as though the blackguard knew the effect his presence had on her.

His gaze traced over her from head to toe, the curve of her bare shoulders, the short puffed sleeves, and the lace that fluttered softly as she waved her fan. Then he turned his attention to the painting she'd been viewing.

"It seems Venus is taking a chill," he said, examining the nude goddess in all her feminine glory. "Unfortunately, I am not." His eyes held for a moment on the small pink bow nestled between her breasts, her skin heating even more under that lazy ice-blue gaze. "It is quite warm in here, I fear."

"Perhaps it is because your chin is buried in your cravat. If you looked up, it would improve matters. Or you might like to take a turn outside where the air is cooler."

"With you?"

"Certainly not. You may be feverish for all I know."

"I find it has cooled significantly." His impish grin belied his words. "Perhaps you would do me the honor of claiming you for the next waltz?"

She wanted to refuse him, but her glance strayed across the ballroom, where Lavinia Chapman stood, staring daggers at her. While Pen had no intention of marrying, that didn't mean she was immune to the allure of being whisked out onto the floor by the most dashing man in the room—and pricking at the pride of the proud miss who'd scorned her.

*Be careful...* a voice whispered in her head. *You already know how dangerously charming Captain Harcourt can be...*

His eyes twinkled as if he could read her mind. "Perhaps," he whispered, "you find the room too... warm for your taste." The challenge that made her stiffen her spine.

"You're incorrigible."

"We established that a long time ago. Fortunately, so are you. Come, Pen. Rescue me. My brother was called to London unexpectedly, leaving me the sole Harcourt to be netted by some matchmaking mama. I fear the last Miss I took out onto the floor was planning her trousseau in her head."

She couldn't help but laugh as the orchestra struck up a waltz. "Fine," she said, tucking her gloved hand into the crook of his elbow. "I'll dance with you. If only to have an excuse to tread on your toes."

He led her onto the floor, exuding a confidence that seemed to command the entire room. The eyes of every woman followed the dashing Captain as surely as they did the golden Turkoman horse that he rode, both magnificent animals, potent and masculine, with a dangerous, irresistible fascination.

When he placed his hand on her waist, even the layers of bodice and corset and chemise were unable to keep that touch from feeling searingly intimate as the first notes of the waltz swirled out. He whisked her around the floor with athletic grace, and she felt every nerve in her body come alive in a way she couldn't explain. She could see a glint in his eye, the fan of pale white lines at the corners from squinting against foreign suns.

She tried to converse, but felt breathless, aware of people staring, doubtless speculating as to why the handsome captain was dancing with her. Kitty and Fanny were beaming from the sidelines, waving at her in a most improper manner, while the so-called eligible misses and their mothers glared in disapproval.

When the dance ended, Simon escorted her from the floor, but he did not simply bow and walk away to seek another partner. Instead, he walked with her down the corridor to where the company thinned and the garden doors stood open to the night breeze. Truth was, she was glad to get away from so many speculative glances herself. But now Simon was the one regarding her quizzically.

"You're staring at me as if I'm a bug beneath a magnifying glass," she said at last. "Have I got a spot on my nose?"

He leaned one broad shoulder against a pillar, his lips curling in a bone-melting smile. "No spot. It's just... I could never resist a mystery, and you puzzle me."

"Do I?"

"You look quite fetching tonight, you know. The blue of your gown does something wonderful for your eyes. And when you dance... you seem... younger."

"I'm six-and-twenty," she said crisply, determined not to let him charm her. "Well on the shelf."

"That is what I can't reconcile. I realize you're not the usual type of miss on the marriage mart, but surely you've had offers."

She snapped her fan open. "Offers to put myself completely in the power of someone else? No, thank you."

"You've no desire to be the angel of the house?"

"How I loathe that description! No woman is an angel, nor should she be expected to live up to such a ridiculous ideal." The melting sensation he'd evoked when he had whirled her around the floor vanished, and she felt wholly herself again. "Those who describe a wife's role thus have no idea of what they're speaking. When a woman marries, she doesn't own anything, not even her children. Men jest about being 'leg shackled' when they wed, but the true shackles are snapped on brides naive enough to plunge into such an arrangement."

"Indeed?"

"All men would be tyrants if they could." She was prepared to walk away, or have the Captain stalk off in affront. Instead, his brow wrinkled.

"You are more outspoken than any lady I've ever known."

She lifted her chin. "I take that as a high compliment."

"Dare one ask how you came to be so?"

Part of her wanted to fling off a comment and walk away, yet his question surprised her. There was admiration in his eyes, curiosity that drew her out. She was astonished to hear herself saying, "When I was defiant, my mother devised a punishment that was pure agony. I would be forced to sit perfectly still on a stool at her side for hours on end, without saying a word. If I spoke, the time would begin again with an hour added. She hoped that would put an end to the unflattering habit of my speaking my mind."

"It is obvious that had the opposite effect."

"I decided when I was twelve that no one would ever silence me again." She shot him an ironic grimace. "My mother was *so* pleased."

Penelope watched for his reaction and to her amazement saw the admiration in his eyes deepen.

"It is no small thing to be a defiant daughter."

"I'd gotten my hands on a copy of *A Vindication of the Rights of Woman*."

"You are a devotee of Miss Wollstonecraft?" Simon asked.

Her gaze sprang up to meet his, and she tilted her head in surprise. "You have heard of her?"

"My best friend was partial to Romantic philosophies and poets. Wollstonecraft's daughter, Mary, wrote—"

"Frankenstein," Pen tried to hide an inward shudder. She hadn't finished the book. Once the creature was brought to life by harnessing lightning.

"Miss Wollstonecraft's commitment to the rights of women did not mean that she eschewed curiosity about men," Simon said. "You do realize that Wollstonecraft did marry?"

"And died of childbed fever soon after."

"Ah, but before that, she shared a great love… and passed her brilliance on to the daughter born of it. Perhaps it was destiny."

"I don't believe in predestination," Pen asserted.

Simon's brows rose. "Don't you? I find that surprising… considering."

"Considering what?"

"I remember something of the tale attached to you. That you were one of those injured in the Great Storm."

There was no question what storm he meant.

People still spoke of that storm in awed tones. The tempest had swept through the county with a ferocity that left wreckage in its wake. Her shoulders stiffened and she looked away, remembering the rain pounding down on her as she dashed beneath a tree, the crackling white light surrounding her in the heartbeat before the tree fell. Wood splintering and fire blazing, the searing light and pain as she was crushed beneath the branches unable to breathe…

She still had the scars…

"It's a miracle you survived," Simon said. "People said you must have a special gift or be destined for some remarkable fate to be spared."

"Or that I'm a witch." The whispers echoed in Penelope's mind. *She's a queer one, she is. No wonder. Struck by lightning.*

"Do you remember much about that day?"

"I was disobeying, as usual. We'd come down from London to visit Mother's aunt while Papa was looking over investments with his friends. Ships and mines or something. I had promised Fanny that I would take her and Catherine to see the baby lambs in one of the neighbor's pastures."

"How old were the three of you?"

"I was seven, Fanny was three. Catherine might have been three hundred for all we knew. She certainly looked it."

Simon laughed. "Not a very flattering description of your sister."

"Oh, our Kitty wasn't born yet. Catherine was Fanny's doll."

"Ah."

"Mother insisted we stay inside. It was going to rain, and Fanny was too little to get wet. I argued that a little rain was nothing to fret over. After all, Mother was the one who made us take baths."

Simon's eyes sparked with amusement. "God help England if you ever stand before a judge."

"I was chafing at the injustice when Fanny stole up to Mama's room, curled up and fell asleep. I saw my chance. I grabbed up the doll and raced out."

"You took Fanny's doll?"

"Promises to dolls are very solemn things at that age."

Simon felt a twinge of tenderness in his chest as he imagined Pen as a naughty little girl, racing out with the doll under her arm.

"You know the rest," Pen said briskly. "The storm struck. I ran beneath the tree to try to keep Catherine dry. When they found me, I was unconscious. I woke up at Dr. Clay's surgery. Perhaps it was the pain from the burns, or the medicine they gave me, but everything was a blur for weeks after. By the time I finally asked about Fanny's doll, it was gone. Fanny might never have forgiven me if Kitty hadn't come along."

"Kitty... Catherine?" He drew out the names, considering.

"That's right. Kitty is named after a doll. We never tease about it, though. Mother is sensitive on the subject." A wave of melancholy wisped over Pen, and she turned away. Truth was, her mother had become sensitive about everything after the storm. Her parents never said a word, but underneath, it was as if they blamed each other. Mother blamed Papa for encouraging Pen to be so headstrong she'd disobeyed, and Papa had blamed Mother for not keeping better watch.

Simon obviously sensed the change in her mood. "I'm sorry," he said, with such gentleness it surprised her. "I didn't mean to bring up something painful. I'm just curious about what shaped you into this strong, independent woman."

"I wasn't the only one who was hurt in that storm." She forced herself to smile. "Besides, it was all a long time ago." And sometimes, when the rain came, it seemed like was about to happen all over again. She smoothed her dress.

"I was lucky. Dr. Clay and his daughter, Isabel, were lovely to me. I had other visitors as well."

Pen looked at Simon and remembered a blonde-tressed countess who smelled of lilies, pale, motherly hands stroking back Pen's tangled hair. "I remember your mother was very worried about those of us who got hurt in the storm." Penelope pressed her fingertips to her breast. "She was so kind. I still have the picture book that she gave me. When you see her, please tell her I've not forgotten."

She looked up, startled by Simon's stony expression.

"I'm afraid that would be impossible," he said.

She winced at the edge to his voice. "Your mother is well, I hope?"

"I wouldn't know. I've had no contact with her for the past twenty years."

"You… what?" There were times Penelope guiltily imagined escaping her mother's complaints for a few weeks, but to go years without seeing her mother, contacting her…? Penelope remembered watching wistfully from a distance as the beautiful countess laughed and frolicked with her children. Of all four young Harcourts, Pen had seen the special love she had for her younger son. The delight she'd taken in Simon's antics, how enthusiastically he'd run up to her, sure of being scooped into her arms. How Penelope had envied him.

"I don't understand…" Pen stammered, trying to imagine any power on earth that could have shattered that bond. "I knew that she'd left Everdene, but everyone assumed she'd merely gone to one of your family's other estates. She obviously loved you so much."

"So much that she slipped out of the house in the dead of night without saying goodbye. All I have to say is good riddance."

"You can't mean that."

"Oh, I assure you, Miss Waverly, I do." His hands curled into fists. "I will be glad when the village is gone, obliterating the last reminders of her."

Penelope's breath snagged in her throat. "What? What do you mean when the village is gone?"

Simon's face paled, the edge to his voice sharper. "It's to be leveled."

Her jaw dropped. "Leveled?" she choked out. "But why?"

"My father prefers to have a clear vista. I'm to oversee relocating the people to an area where they're not visible from the manor house windows."

She stared at him, her stomach roiling in horror. "You can't be serious. Those are people's homes!"

"They will have new ones. Those cottages were built during Tudor times. Surely we'll be able to make improvements."

"Improvements? Is that your intention?"

"Inchwick assures me that he has an appropriate site chosen. He's already having materials delivered—"

"I've seen where those piles of supplies have been placed!" Penelope fought to control her anger, keep her voice low. "If you tried, you couldn't have picked a worse site than Blagden Valley."

The dashing partner she'd waltzed with was gone, those blue eyes that had tantalized her cold and blank as stone. "Miss Waverly, I admire your concern over my family's tenants, but situating a village and its construction is the purview of land agents and architects. It's not something that women should concern themselves with."

"Oh, no. Women should not concern themselves with such matters. They should just go meekly where men direct them and bury their children when sewage runs into the water and the air is rife with God Knows What pestilence. Ask Daw. He told you the site wouldn't be healthy for horses. Yet, you'd put children there? What kind of a man are you?"

*A soldier who follows orders.* "The decision is not mine. The land is not mine. It is my father's and, thereafter, my brother's."

He swore, his fists knotting. "What they order *will* happen whether I oversee it or not."

"And you will help them lay waste to people's lives. People who depend upon your protection, who have served Harcourts for a hundred years. Find a way—"

"There *is* no way." Simon's face contorted with anguish. "Don't you understand? There is nothing I can do to stop it."

Penelope felt as if someone kicked her in the stomach. Tears sprang to her eyes. "Of all people, I never would have expected this of you… You're Daw Garvey's friend! You looked him in the eyes and… How can you do this to him? To everyone?"

Simon shuttered his gaze, then sketched her a stiff bow. "No doubt there will soon be plenty of other people asking the same question."

She pressed her hand to her mouth as he wheeled and stalked away, disappearing into the crowd.

# CHAPTER 10

(W)hat the hell had he done? Simon sank into the coach seat, cursing as the equipage jolted into motion.

One moment he'd been thinking of kissing Penelope Waverly senseless, the next he was lashing out, telling her the village was to be razed. By morning, the whole county would know their homes were to be destroyed to provide the Harcourts with a more picturesque view. Penelope Waverly, champion of runaway chimney sweeps, would probably show up at Everdene Hall leading an army of villagers set to burn the manor house to the ground. She'd probably throw the first torch through the window herself.

He drove his fist into the side of the coach, wishing he was at Gentleman Jackson's where he could pummel an opponent and be pummeled in return. But he was far from London with its boxing salons and fencing academies, gaming hells and brothels, and scores of other rakes happy to help him go to the devil.

He'd made a muck of things. No doubt Inchwick would be furious. Let him be. Part of Simon was glad the truth was out. He'd loathed the sensation of riding across Harcourt land, greeting tenants with a false smile, knowing what was in store for them. Let the poor bastards in the village know what they were facing instead of being lied to, made fools of, believing that the building project in the valley had nothing to do with them. That they were safe.

The way he had once felt as a boy, before—

Simon's jaw clenched. Hadn't memories of how his mother abandoned him been the flashpoint that had led to his outburst? Penelope Waverly dragging memories of the woman into the light.

The interior of the coach couldn't black out the scenes her words resurrected from his childhood. Those rare visits when his father came to Everdene in the last year before his mother vanished. His mother's forced brightness, how she had had Nurse Betsy keep the children in the far wing of the house, out of the way.

*Your father is a very important man. He cannot be vexed by children racing around…*

Everyone, from the scullery maid to the butler, had held their breath until the Earl's carriage rolled away.

But in spite of Nurse's efforts, Simon and his brother and sisters had all known something was wrong. Their laughing, beautiful mother seemed a different person, her eyes swollen and red. Simon had hated it, and cut up in antics that usually delighted her, won him hugs, his hair ruffled with her hand, that bell-like laughter… Instead, she had been a ghost of herself.

*Your mother loved you… you were her favorite…* Penelope had said. It must be true. Penelope Waverly was the last woman to coddle one with platitudes. And yet, how could he believe it? His mother had abandoned him, hadn't she? And abandoned his brother and sisters. He closed his eyes, haunted by the other words Penelope had spoken…

*When a woman marries, she doesn't own anything, not even her children…*

He'd never heard a woman speak so plainly. What struck him more was the fury in Penelope's eyes, her heartbreak, and impotence to change the constraints women faced—and the stunning realization that everything she'd said was true.

He closed his eyes, remembering the interlude in the ballroom before his temper had gotten the best of him. Miss Waverly's cerulean gown, her joy in the music lighting up her face. Her ability to laugh at herself and others, tempered with the empathy he'd witnessed. Yet, she was no prim do-gooder looking down her nose at human frailty or squeezing all joy out of people's lives with strictures to be obeyed.

No. She'd been warm and vital and… and *real* in a way that made his heart race. He'd held her in his arms, waltzing, and the world had spun away. He'd been mesmerized by the way one long curl lay along her proud throat, silk against the velvet of her skin. The tempting way the tops of her breasts swelled above the neckline of her gown, the pink bow at that deep vee where he had imagined pressing his lips.

For God's sake, she wasn't the first young beauty he'd ever danced with. He'd had liaisons aplenty, but his couplings since returning to England had been like the drinking he'd done, drowning himself in brandy and sensation to dull the knife-edge of regret. But both had left him even emptier than before, that failure making him so angry, that he'd tried to outrun the pain with a recklessness Jamie would have checked…

And yet, he'd never felt the way he did when he was with Penelope, almost as if his past was washed away and he was that young captain who'd just bought his colors, his dreams not haunted by war scenes and betrayals, mistakes he could never make right.

There had only been the pleasure in her face. A woman reaching for so much more than society would ever allow her. And in that moment, he'd wanted her with a fierceness he hadn't felt in what seemed a lifetime.

Penelope Waverly was different, awakening him after the nightmare that had held him in thrall far too long. She made him wonder what else lay in that most unconventional mind of hers, beneath her gown and in her heart.

The coach rumbled to a halt, and Simon shoved open the door and leapt out before the footman could let down the step.

He walked into Everdene, hating the place more than ever, a gilded trap snapping shut around him.

His valet, Martin Flynn, met him in the entry. "Sir, you are home early."

"Not early enough." Simon tore off his cravat. "Bring whisky to the study. A lot of it."

The valet cleared his throat. "Yes, sir. Whisky. And a bandage for your hand? You are bleeding."

Simon glared down at his glove and saw the blood seeping through it. With an oath, he stripped the fine kid off of his hand and regarded his split knuckle. "It's nothing."

"The glove would disagree since it is destined for the rag bag unless I can get the stain out. I assume that some gentleman was objectionable at the ball?"

"*I* was the objectionable party, according to a lady. I struck the coach wall and it may never be the same."

"Well, better to hit the coach than another fellow," Flynn observed cheerfully. "It's been rather a relief not to have to patch you up."

Was there any way to 'patch up' what Penelope Waverly had set loose in him?

"Whisky," Simon repeated, knowing there were some things no one could fix.

Flynn hurried off, and Simon stalked to the study, haunted by memories of that night when he'd wakened to the sounds of his parents fighting, then his brother being thrust back into the dark nursery. When morning came, finding the door locked from the outside. And afterwards…

Every morning, when he first woke, he'd believe she was still at Everdene, would come to have breakfast in the nursery. Every morning, he'd faced the realization that she was gone. The sharp, tearing away of her presence, like losing her again and again and again.

His sisters became strangers, packed up and sent away—to aunts in Italy, he found out later. After a brief stay at Bitterne Tower, he and Lucien had been sent to Eton, their only contact with their father rare. The harsh regimen had been hell at first, being bullied by older boys. But Simon had learned to fight there, embraced a man's world, one of order, testing athletic strength and skill. He'd fought his way to become a leader among the lads. The dreams of his mother had come less often until at last, he'd amputated that part of him, like a limb too shattered to save. He'd acted as if that life never was....

Yet now, Penelope's words about a woman's lot challenged him.

Yes, he'd been devastated as a boy. Abandoned. Bewildered. Heartbroken. He was a man now. He knew how ruthless his father could be. Simon and his sire clashed whenever they had the ill fortune to be in the same room—a prospect he avoided whenever possible.

But a wife would not have the power to escape. She was chattel, her husband's property, Simon's mother one more possession for the Earl to dispose of as he chose.

Like the tenants who would soon discover they were helpless against their landlord's whims.

He looked around him, bitterly. This was his father's study. His brother's. *This estate isn't mine,* Simon had told Penelope. *This will be done whether I take charge of it or not.*

But the reasoning that had proved so handy at easing his conscience when he was alone, only stuck in his throat when faced with her unflinching gaze.

*If you tried, you couldn't have picked a worse site,* Penelope's contemptuous words echoed in his memory. Hadn't Daw said something similar?

He should have ridden there weeks ago to see the site for himself, but when he'd pressed Inchwick, the man had found one excuse after another. Simon had let it go, assuming that his father and brother had chosen the site where he was to build. It had already been settled. Simon crossed to a red leather chair beside the hearth and lowered himself down in it. His jaw set, grim. He'd order the servants to have his horse ready first thing in the morning. It was time to judge the site for himself.

As for his major gaffe in revealing the truth about razing the village… It wasn't as if Inchwick could have concealed the truth forever. Simon would deal with the consequences tomorrow. But tonight should be quiet enough.

Surely even Miss Waverly would hardly ring the church bell and raise the alarm in the middle of the night. He had at least until tomorrow before results of this night's blunder would come home to roost. But they *would* come. His stomach knotted as he pictured Daw Garvey's face.

Flynn returned with a tray, a glass, and a cut-glass decanter of whisky. He filled the glass to the brim and served it to Simon.

Simon lifted his glass and drained it, the whisky burning down his throat.

"Is there anything more I can do for you?" Flynn asked with an impassive face.

Simon gave a pained laugh. "Wake me if you see a woman in a blue ball gown leading a mob with torches up the drive."

Flynn's brows raised. "Sir?"

"Just go to bed and leave me alone."

"Yes, sir," Flynn said, then he hastened away, leaving Simon to drain the decanter until there was nothing left.

# CHAPTER 11

"*P*en? What on earth are you doing?" Kitty's voice startled Penelope awake.

She jerked upright, lifting her head from the desktop where she'd laid it down sometime during the night—for just a moment, to rest. Something stuck to her cheek—a piece of paper?

She brushed it away, and blinked, trying to get her bearings. The candles in the study had guttered out. Pen's hair straggled down from its pins. Her fingers were stained with ink, the desk littered with broken quills she'd cast aside.

"Wh-what time is it?" she stammered.

"Seven in the morning. I came down to get some ointment for a blister on my heel and heard you muttering in your sleep. You didn't even change out of the gown you wore for the ball," Kitty chided. "Mama will have a fit of the vapors if you got ink on it!"

The ball! The night before came flooding back to Penelope. Waltzing with Simon Harcourt, the dizzy sensation she'd felt when she'd looked up and seen his gaze turn to blue flame.

He'd led her away from the crowd, and she'd wanted him to

kiss her… then the words that had stunned her, sickened her. The lives he would shatter, homes he would raze, the destruction of the village that was the bedrock of her childhood, now to be obliterated at his family's command. She had been angry with him, hurt and disappointed, yet in the hours after his confession, she couldn't forget the anguish in his face before that cold mask had concealed it.

*The land is not mine. It is my father's and, thereafter, my brother's. What they order will happen whether I oversee it or not.*

She'd fled into the Rendell's garden, pacing until her head whirled, wishing she could run to the village and warn the people about what was coming. She wanted to shriek at the carefree dancers in the ballroom, all with homes no Harcourt could destroy, rail at their heedlessness. Simon Harcourt's words had reverberated through her head as the other guests danced, had tormented her during the ride back to Laurel Cottage, where she'd hastened to this room with a desperate plan.

"Is something wrong?" Kitty asked. "You've been acting so strangely ever since you danced with Captain Harcourt last night."

For a moment, she wanted to confide in her sister, spill out the truth. But she couldn't be sure Kitty would keep it to herself. The thought of rumors spreading, people panicking was unbearable. Not when Pen still had a chance to change things.

She quickly rolled up the drawings she'd made. "Yes, something's wrong, but don't worry," she told her sister. "I'm going to fix it."

---

DEMONS FROM HELL WERE ATTACKING THE INSIDE OF SIMON'S skull with pickaxes when Flynn appeared at the study door the next morning, a tray in his maddeningly capable hands. The light from the corridor was uncomfortably bright, and Simon thanked the fates—or the maid—who'd left the heavy draperies shut.

"I've brought you the *remedy*, sir," Flynn said.

With a gimlet eye, Simon regarded the vile mixture of raw eggs and garlic that the valet swore could cure a hangover. "Next time I tell you to bring me whisky, perhaps you could show some restraint. I am obviously not to be trusted…"

Flynn handed him the glass. "Drink up, sir. I fear you'll need bolstering today."

Simon drained it. "The taste alone should make me forswear ever imbibing again."

"Yes, well, we will soon put that declaration to the test. Last night you asked me to warn you if a lady carrying a torch arrived at Everdene. One has. A Miss Waverly."

Every muscle in Simon's body clenched. Of course, it was she.

"No torch was immediately visible," Flynn added, "though, considering her militant expression, she might have concealed one in the bundle she's carrying. She insisted she must see you at once."

As if he wasn't miserable enough, Simon thought, as he ground his knuckles against his closed eyes. He was tempted to send her away, but he doubted that even a cavalry charge would dislodge her from his doorstep until she'd had her say.

The crisp click of her heels on the marble floor pounded in his head like a battalion marching. Apparently Miss Waverly had decided to mount an offensive herself. She strode into the room wearing a dove-gray walking dress with some red bits as trim, her arms filled with large rolls of paper, a small streak of ink on her cheek.

Unfortunately, Flynn's 'remedy' seemed to strike Simon's queasy stomach with a thud. He glanced at his valet, then at

Penelope. "Miss Waverly. I was about to send Flynn to fetch you."

"I decided to find my own way here. My burden is rather heavy."

"Heavy?" He squinted at the bundle she carried. "Have you got a dueling pistol wrapped up in that batch of scrolls, Miss Waverly? If so, I beg you to use it *before* our interview and put me out of my misery."

"*Your* misery?" she exclaimed, affronted.

"Miss Waverly, I got little sleep last night and I've the deuce of a headache. So, if you've come to ring a peal over my head—"

"*I* was up all night *without* the benefit of the whisky you've obviously indulged in." She dumped the scrolls on his desk. When Simon raised his brows, she wrinkled her nose. "Don't bother trying to deny it. I recognize the smell, after living with my father. Unfortunately, my errand won't wait until you are sober. It is imperative that I show you these right away."

"Show me what?"

She crossed to the window, flinging the drapes open wide. Simon winced and swore under his breath as shards of light pierced his eyes.

"Have mercy, Miss Waverly."

"You can hardly be expected to see what I've brought without light," she said briskly as she opened the other drapes. "As for mercy—I've none to offer. I was so angry when you left the ball, I could hardly contain it. I wanted to announce to the whole assemblage the wicked deed your family planned to carry out, but before I could do it, I realized most of the Rendells' guests wouldn't care. Those few who might would fling up their hands and declare there was nothing they could do to stop it."

Simon could picture the scene all too well. "I applaud your restraint."

"In fact, it would be far more expedient to go to the village and bang on doors."

"Raise a mob to tar and feather me? That was my prediction as to how you would proceed."

"But then I realized that someone *did* care!"

He kneaded his temple. "Perhaps you could go and discuss the issue with them."

"My thought exactly! Which is why I came to you."

"Me?" Simon tried to shake the cobwebs from his head.

"It was obvious you care for the Garveys," Miss Waverly said. "Last night there was one unguarded moment when I saw how pained you were at the idea of tearing them from their home."

Simon groaned inwardly. "I fear you are attributing to me a decency that I do not possess."

"If the situation had not pained you, you'd not be sitting in a darkened room with your head aching from drink! You do look like the very devil."

He choked out a laugh that made his head throb. "Miss Waverly, that is hardly an expression a lady should use."

"And you are hardly looking or behaving like a gentleman, Captain Harcourt. Regardless, it is the perfect description for what I see before me."

Simon rubbed his hand over his face, feeling the stubble Flynn had not yet shaved away. Having spent the night on the settee, sleeping in his clothes, he was suddenly aware of how disreputable he must look. "Miss Waverly, it's hardly proper that I receive you in such a state."

"I do not care if your cravat is perfectly knotted. Anyone can see that you are distressed, but I have come here this morning on far more important matters—your well-deserved chagrin over destroying people's homes."

He wanted to deny it again, but damnation, what was the point? Penelope Waverly seemed to have an unerring instinct for unearthing the truth, and she'd not let go of it. Too bad they hadn't had her in Afghanistan to wrench information out of captured enemies.

"Fine. You've found me out," Simon growled. "Will it please you to hear me say it? I loathe the idea of giving Daw and the rest of the village this news. But what I feel about the plan to raze the village hardly matters."

"I have to admit that you do make a valid point," she replied. "It pains me greatly, but there you are."

"My head must be worse than I thought. It sounded as if you just said that I was right. Which begs the question, why are you here?"

"Because once I accepted that you were telling the truth about not being able to stop the destruction of the cottages, I began thinking. They are your father's property, and your brother's after that."

"I should be relieved to hear you agree, but strangely, I am not. You look far too... frenzied."

"You would be, too, if you'd come up with a perfect solution to this coil."

"I tremble to hear it."

"You said that you could take this chance to make improvements in the new cottages. So... here they are!"

She smacked a scroll onto the table then unrolled it. Simon gaped, wondering if last night's excesses were still playing tricks with his eyes. Sunlight poured across a neatly drawn image of a cottage.

It was not the type of sketch ladies often displayed to show their accomplishments, but rather, precise lines, exact measurements.

"These look like... building plans." he said, bewildered. "Where did you get them?"

"I drew them myself."

"*You* drew them?" He angled them to get a clearer look.

"Yes. I had little patience for girlish pursuits when I was growing up, and preferred building things to needlework, and geography to drawing lessons. My father indulged me shamelessly before he died, teaching me to draw plans for fairy castles and pirate lairs. He took me with him to building sites, explained things like load-bearing walls, trusses, and foundations. We even built a doll's house for my sisters."

"No wonder you were able to out-build us lads when it came to the tree house."

"My last employer, Mr. Tremayne, was also an architect. I was lucky enough to study plans one of his colleagues had sent him for a model village. The drawings were filled with quite the most progressive ideas, with cottages built for the comfort and health of those who would live there." Penelope pointed to a second drawing showing the layout of the rooms as if on a map.

Simon dragged a hand over his face, trying to focus.

"This is a floor plan." Penelope told him. "You enter here..." She pointed to an open space where the door would be. "This is the main room. The chimney is designed to effectively draw smoke up and out of the cottage, and the built-in cupboard is heated by the fireplace," she said, tracing a path through that area, then through what looked to be another doorway. "Here is a kitchen and scullery, perfect for cooking meals. I've designed it for greater convenience. Later, after a hard day's work, the cottager and his family will be able to gather around the fire and keep warm, no matter how blustery it is beyond their door."

She'd not only drawn the dimensions of the room but made sketches of what it might look like furnished, pots of geraniums on the windowsill, a rocking chair near the fire. And a cradle...

"There are three bedrooms for modesty's sake, so brothers and sisters won't have to share and the parents will have their own private chamber," she continued. "This shelter over the door will allow the cottager to step out into the yard without rain and dust sweeping in. A covered staircase will lead to the loft area."

Was it the way Penelope had drawn the images that made him picture the cottage so clearly? As if he could walk inside and warm his hands at the fire? He might have loved to see Daw's reaction to such luxury, but Simon knew all too well what the Earl of Ravenscroft's reaction would be.

Penelope pulled out another drawing that plotted out the entire village. "Build a well here, so it's easy to get the water people need. And if we situate the privies carefully, they won't overflow into the houses or foul the water."

Simon could hardly fathom a gently bred lady mentioning privies by name, let alone determining where he should situate one to prevent overflow of waste. He stared as she launched into further explanations, her cheeks flushed with excitement, her breath quick and light. Tiny curls escaped from her hastily twisted chignon, baring the tender nape of her neck. His heart beat with some emotion he could not name. The thought that this woman had gone to all of this effort for the villagers of Everdene moved him beyond words.

*It's something my mother might have done...*

He shoved the thought away and tried to ignore the tightening in his throat at the comparison. Of course, it was absurd even to *consider* taking Miss Waverly's proposal seriously, he told himself. He couldn't just accept building plans from a woman who knew nothing about construction. The cottages would tumble down on people's heads.

Not that he was about to spoil the moment and mention so. When she turned to face him, it was all he could do not to gather her in his arms... And though he longed to ask her how she survived when the world was bound to disappoint her, he felt this effort of hers deserved a serious response.

"This is all quite remarkable," he said, wishing to give her some small triumph before he crushed her dreams. "I did listen to what you said last night. I plan to ride out to Blagden Valley to see for myself if it is an unhealthy place to live."

She beamed at him. "I'm sure you'll wish to move the location once you do!"

He held up a hand to stem her enthusiasm. "I can't promise anything, but I intend to examine the area. As to the structures to be built there—I meant to meet with Inchwick and see them, but there has always been some other estate business that caused him to delay. I didn't press the issue since I considered the matter already settled."

"But Mr. Inchwick's plans can't be written in stone if you are to oversee them. Surely you can make changes as you see fit."

He remembered his father's almost contemptuous words to his land agent. *I will leave matters in my younger son's hands... though I doubt he will show more than cursory attention to anything but his horses...*

Before he had a chance to comment, Miss Waverly laid a hand on his sleeve. The warmth of her touch penetrated the cloth to the skin beneath. "It will still be hard for people to leave the village, but you can give them so much more." Her eyes shone so bright with hope that he could scarcely bear looking into them. God, what would it mean to feel such passion? To care so damned much?

He said as gently as he could, "I deeply appreciate the work you've done on these drawings, but we must leave construction to the men who possess the skill."

Her chin bumped up. "It seems to me that you and your crowd of lads told me exactly the same thing when you were building your treehouse on the heath."

The memory of simpler days gave him a pang. "I suppose we did."

"Perhaps you'd care to revisit the site of our first quarrel," she said with a toss of her head. "Join me in a ride tomorrow. That is, if you can keep up."

Simon was surprised to find himself smiling, realizing just how much he wanted to see Miss Waverly on horseback. "Caspian and I never turn down a chance to take a good run," he said. "But I seem to remember you had to sell your horse."

"I'm sure I can borrow her for the day."

"Tomorrow then," he said. "Shall I call for you around ten?"

"Not unless you want my mother to insist I take one of my sisters along in hopes she might make a match with you."

"Heaven forbid." Simon feigned an eloquent shudder. "Shall we meet at the crossroads, then?"

"Yes. The crossroads."

He had Flynn fetch her shawl and bonnet, then Simon escorted her to the door. "It is a long trek to Laurel Cottage, and you had little sleep last night," he said. "Would you like me to summon the carriage to take you home?"

"No, thank you." She tied the bonnet's rose-colored ribbons beneath her chin. "I always get my best ideas when I am walking. Perhaps I'll think of something wonderful to add to our cottage plans."

He felt a wave of sadness as he stood on the steps, watching her stride off in search of something ephemeral—ideas, hope.

The outing tomorrow would not change his decision regarding Penelope Waverly's untutored building plans, but maybe he could gently show her how impractical her dream village would be.

# CHAPTER 12

$S$imon was astonished at how much he looked forward to spending time with Miss Waverly, even under strained circumstances. He found her waiting at the crossroads, mounted upon a dapple-gray mare. Her emerald riding habit was a bit faded, but it set off her figure to perfection, filigree buttons glittering on the bodice. A round hat tilted at a jaunty angle atop her curls.

Caspian pranced as Simon greeted her then patted his saddle bag. "I took the liberty of having Cook prepare a picnic."

"Lovely." Green eyes sparked with a smugness he couldn't quite decipher. "I will have luncheon in my tree house. You may have it in yours."

She touched her heel to her mare's flank, and the horse cantered off. Simon kept pace, enjoying the picture Miss Waverly made, her cheeks pink with pleasure, the mare responsive to her slightest command.

When they reined in atop a hill, Simon gave her an admiring nod. "You are an excellent horsewoman. My compliments to whoever taught you."

"My father." She angled her face away.

*Her father*, Simon thought. The man who gambled away her home, whose carelessness had left his daughters in such straits that this proud, capable woman had to seek work in service.

A hot coal lodged in Simon's belly, anger at this man he'd never met. Trying to put it from him, he focused on her horse. "It's obvious you and your mare have a special bond," he said.

"They claimed no girl could ever ride Epona, so of course, I couldn't resist." She ran her hand down the mare's graceful neck. "I bought her with part of a bequest my great-aunt left me when she died. The aunt we were visiting the year of the storm. I think she always felt a bit guilty because I was injured while under her roof."

So, Penelope hadn't been left completely without funds. Simon was glad. "I'm sorry for your loss."

"Don't be. Aunt would never have had the patience for a long illness such as her husband suffered. She always said she hoped she'd drop dead while in the midst of something interesting. She was doing what she loved most—arguing with the vicar, and simply slumped over and was gone."

Simon thought of the men he'd seen, dying slowly of battle wounds. "I suppose we could all wish for such a death," he said. "Do you miss her?"

"She told me I was not to waste time on grief. I was to live my life, and if I did not, she vowed she would haunt me."

"I believe I would have liked her very much."

"The bequest made it possible for me to take this time away to set my family to rights. Though I did miss discussing architecture with Mr. Tremayne and the antics of his children quite desperately at first."

Simon felt a prick of something uncomfortably like jealousy. "And Mrs. Tremayne? Was she an amiable mistress?"

A line appeared between Penelope's brows. "Our ideas

regarding education were not the same. Fortunately, Mr. Tremayne was less… *restrictive* in his views about women's minds. He opened the doors of his vast library to me, day or night."

Was that the only tension between the governess and the mistress of the house, Simon wondered. He could certainly understand why Mrs. Tremayne might be less than pleased with a woman such as Penelope Waverly in her husband's library at night. There was something about her that challenged a man. A quick wit and intelligence some would find hard to resist.

"I was able to teach the girls classics and Latin and the sciences," she continued.

"Mr. Tremayne seems like a forward-thinking fellow."

"Yes, well. There are far too few, in my experience. Now, shall we?"

At the light touch of her heel, her mare sprang forward leaving Simon vaguely disturbed and curious as to what had just transpired.

When they reached the copse of trees where he and Daw Garvey had once played, a wistfulness washed over him.

"We'll need to dismount here," Penelope said. "The underbrush is a tangle."

"Ah, so our pirate lairs have not been discovered by the village children," Simon said with some satisfaction.

He tied Caspian to a low hanging branch, then slung the saddle bag over his shoulder and crossed to the mare's side intending to hand Penelope down. Before he could do so, she'd landed lightly on her feet, shaking out the skirts of her riding habit.

After securing her own horse, she headed deeper into the grove with Simon a pace behind. It was like stepping through a window in time to summers past, he thought as he took in the scene around him. The scent of wildflowers and fresh loam drifted on the slight breeze. Underbrush tugged the legs of his breeches, the wonderful coolness of the shade wrapping around him. For a moment, he could almost see Daw Garvey and Freddy Trevor crashing through the brush with him, the handles of hammers and hatchets thrust through their belts, their pockets heavy with bent nails they'd straightened. He could hear the thud of cast-off boards they'd dragged behind them.

And he could picture a little girl with a daisy crown in her hair scowling up at him as he wedged a support beam between forked branches.

*You're doing it wrong.*

Who would ever believe he'd be returning here with the woman that girl had grown into? He held back a prickly spray of berry branches, so Penelope could pass by.

"Surely we must be getting close," he said.

"Right up there." She gestured to an oak tree, and he looked up. Three boards that had been part of a makeshift ladder were nailed to the nearest trunk. The tree had grown, but he could just see the remains of a platform among the leaves. What was left of the treehouse floor had caved in, a few boards dangling overhead. The slanted roof that Simon had hauled up the tree with a length of rope had slid off and smashed on the ground below.

"How unfortunate," he said with a grimace. "The ruin of a perfectly good pirate ship. Perhaps we should have our picnic on a blanket on the ground instead."

"Just because *your* ship is not seaworthy, does not mean *I* should be marooned as well."

She set off with a determined stride to a tree some distance away.

He looked up and saw glimpses of a second treehouse among the branches.

"Miss Waverly, I seem to remember you broke your arm in some escapade during our childhood. You needn't risk another just to spite me. It's obvious our treehouses leave something to be desired structurally."

She scooped up her skirts, looping them over one arm. A flash of shapely calves in white stockings drew his attention as she placed the toe of her half-boot on a ladder rung that appeared straight as the day she'd nailed it there.

Simon felt a twinge of concern. "It's not worth hurting yourself," he said. "Don't be stubborn."

Her eyes flashed and he realized he'd said exactly the thing that would impel her to scale the tree. He strode across the space between them, hoping to haul her down, or at least catch her when she fell, but she scaled the makeshift ladder, nimble as the girl she had been. His heart lurched when her boot slipped halfway up, but she merely steadied herself, then pushed onward, until her head emerged at a dizzying height.

He tensed, waiting to hear a crack of rotten wood beneath her weight.

"Oh, my," she exclaimed. "Such a wonderful view. Pity the boys' treehouse tumbled down. I did warn you back then that it would," she said, looking so damned pleased with herself he had to laugh.

"You did indeed." He peered up at her and shielded his eyes with his hand. She looked particularly fetching in her riding habit, with that ridiculous hat at a rakish angle. "Now, come down before the whole thing falls apart and you break your pretty neck."

"I seem to recall that we agreed to a picnic in our respective tree houses, rather than share anything as pedestrian as a sedate meal on the ground." She looked down at him, the glint in her eyes far too smug as she added, "Perhaps you should join me instead."

"No, thank you. I weigh far more than you do. You come down."

"Not until you come up here and I've proven my point." She

brushed a wayward leaf from her sleeve. "I could build a sturdier treehouse than Daw Garvey when we were children. Have him look at the plans, and I wager he'll declare them sound. If he does, you must at least consider implementing them."

Simon cast another worried glance at the branch bearing the treehouse's weight. "I'll consider it. As long as you come down."

"Really, I promise you the platform is sturdy. Trust me."

Did she have any idea what she was asking him to do? He'd trusted only two men in his life—his brother, and Jamie, who was lying somewhere in Afghanistan in an unmarked grave. But the longer she was up there, the greater the chance she'd trip over her skirt or one of those boards would give way. It made him damned uncomfortable to realize how scared he was that she might fall.

With a muttered oath, Simon scaled the ladder. He emerged through the tangle of leaves. Bracing a booted foot on the thickest branch, he touched one sole to the treehouse floor, careful not to put weight on it. He held out his hand. "There. You've proven your treehouse is sturdier. Now, let me help you down."

She drew even further away from him. "There is nothing to fear. It will hold our weight. There is a wonderful view."

"You're not going to be reasonable, are you?" he grumbled.

"I'm completely reasonable," she insisted. "I know how strong my work is." He tested the platform, and the boards didn't even creak. Slowly, he edged to where she stood, her grin so triumphant he wasn't sure whether to shake her or kiss her.

Instead, he examined her workmanship. Even he could see that the treehouse was not just well-built, but well-maintained. "You can't have done all this when you were ten."

"Of course not. I returned several times over the years to brace the framework. My sister, Fanny, liked to come here to get away from—" She cleared her throat, then added, "to sketch."

Simon narrowed his eyes, sensing that wasn't what she'd

started to say. But this was no time to open some long discussion. The whole point was to get Penelope Waverly back on solid ground. Still, his curiosity was piqued by the structure on which he stood.

"I'm amazed that you learned how to construct things this way," he said, running a hand along one of the solid joints.

"I have always been determined to learn how to make things hold together. Fix things."

Simon peered into the distance, seeing the church spire and the golden thatch of roofs. In the weeks since his father had told him of the plan to raze the village, Simon had held himself aloof from what he'd become a part of. At first, he had wanted to obliterate the last tangible reminder of the life he'd lost. But now, it wasn't so simple.

Penelope Waverly made him remember who he'd been before his world crashed down. The boy who had loved the way his mother had moved among the tenants, carrying gingernuts for the children and draping shawls over infirm shoulders in winter.

"Maybe I was trying to repair what was broken in my family." Penelope's admission broke through his thoughts.

Hadn't he done the same thing when he'd cut up in antics with his mother, trying to rekindle the laughter he so loved? "I fear there are more broken families than we know."

"Father had always promised me that we would go to Italy together when I was older. He would show me the Duomo de Milan and St. Peter's Basilica. But it was not to be."

"What happened?"

"To my father?" A pensiveness shadowed her face. "He began to drink, to come up with wild, reckless schemes. He gambled. Once, my sister Fanny did an ink drawing that blew into a stream. I splashed in to fetch it, but the lines had bled until only the slightest resemblance remained. That is what happened to the father I'd known. It wasn't long after we discovered he had lost the house Mother's aunt had left us, that we received the news he'd fallen from the rafters of a building he'd been working on."

Fallen? Simon wondered. Or jumped to his death to avoid facing his wife and daughters?

"I'm sorry."

"I am, too. But the father I'd known and loved had been lost long before. I try to remember him as he was then."

Did he have any memories of his father that were warm? Simon wondered. No. Only the harsh rasp of him upsetting everything, only relief when he was gone.

"I think your father would be proud, if he could see the drawings you made."

"Perhaps." She touched one of the support beams he could see she had replaced, the wood fresher, new. "I spent so much effort trying to fix things, but perhaps there are times you do need to tear something down completely and start over."

She looked vulnerable suddenly. Desolate.

"Penelope..."

Her gaze met his, held.

His voice sounded rough even to his own ears. "May I call you... Penelope?"

"Yes."

He plucked a leaf out of her hair. Why did he suddenly feel the stirring of...

Connection...

He'd wanted to kiss her at the Rendells' ball, but this urge was different, deeper. His knuckles grazed her cheek, lingered. "Sometimes," he murmured, "starting over is the only choice left."

Simon curved his hand under her chin, tipped her face up, and lowered his lips to hers.

Her lips parted as he traced his tongue along the seam, then slipped inside. She moaned softly, and opened to him, heat spearing down beneath the flap of his breeches. His arms slid around her waist, gathering her against him, her breasts firm against his chest as he explored her mouth with a hunger that all but unmanned him. What the hell was he doing? he thought the split second before all reason swirled away.

# CHAPTER 13

*P*enelope gasped as Simon's mouth explored hers, tasting of forbidden pleasures, more sensual than she had ever imagined.

Yet it was the tenderness layered beneath it that made her feel as if nothing was solid beneath her feet anymore.

She'd been kissed when she was seventeen by one of Rendell's sons. An uncomfortable exchange of inexperienced youth. But this... this was a man's kiss. Masterful, knowing secrets that made her core melt. He seemed to sense her knees threatening to give way, his strong arms pulling her closer, anchoring her in a world that suddenly seemed uncertain. She pressed herself against the hard wall of his chest, the heat of his body penetrating layers of fabric.

His hand slid to her nape, and she felt a soft tug on tendrils that had come loose from her chignon as he tilted her head back to give himself more freedom in his kiss.

Her nipples seemed to burn, and she looped her own arms around his neck, threading her fingers through his hair. Her tongue tangling with his, her body as eager.

He smelled masculine and mysterious, spice and leather,

recklessness and a hint of something she couldn't identify, but craved nonetheless.

His tongue delved deep into her mouth, and his other hand slid down to her bottom, drawing her hips tight against the hard ridge of his arousal. Sudden, sharp awareness cut through the haze of desire that had her in its thrall.

This kiss might ruin everything…

She pulled away, every nerve in her body still tingling as she stumbled against the hip-high wall. Simon caught her by the arms, to steady her.

His eyes burned with hunger, his breath shallow. And she couldn't forget the hardness of his arousal against her, and the truth it betrayed. He wanted her.

"I—I'm sorry," she stammered. "I didn't bring you here to…"

To what?

She'd come here to convince him her plans were to be taken seriously. Did he think she was trying to entice him to do so by allowing him liberties?

"I only wanted to show you… that I can build things."

He swallowed hard, watching her with a wariness as evident as her own. "Perhaps we had best continue further discussion on solid ground. Let me start down the ladder first," he said. "That way I can loosen your skirts if they get tangled."

She suddenly pictured him loosening her skirts with a far more intimate purpose. Just because she'd decided never to marry didn't mean she wasn't curious about what a man felt like, tasted like. She'd been impassioned about righting injustices her whole life through. It wasn't possible to feel emotions so intensely, and not wonder about what it would be like to experience physical passion. Especially with a magnificent male animal like Simon Harcourt.

With athletic grace, he descended a half-dozen rungs, then stopped. She glanced down at him, realizing he was waiting for her to follow.

Penelope scooped up her skirts again, but found it far more difficult to back down the ladder. Simon's arms bracketed her legs, and she was acutely aware that he must be awash in petticoats. Cool air nipped through her thin cotton stockings, but something warmer penetrated them as well. Simon's breath. She was aware of a small hole she'd torn on a sticker bush on the way into the grove, and imagined the patch of bare skin he must be able to see.

This predicament was her own fault, she thought as she groped with one foot, trying to find the next strip of board below. Between the lack of sleep, her over-excitement at the ball, and the tumultuous emotions of the physical intimacy she'd just shared with Simon, she'd let her guard down. And when the hard, heedless expression on his face had relaxed as they stood in the treehouse, she'd glimpsed something deeper beneath. Something she'd seen in his dealings with Tripp and when he recalled the friend he'd lost. Pain he'd tried to hide when he spoke of his mother.

It seemed to take forever to reach the ground, but at last, she heard Simon's boots thud against the dirt and felt his hands spanning her waist, swinging her down before him. She tried to get her balance, letting her skirts fall in a cascade of lacy petticoats to cover her legs.

Simon led her to a quiet spot, then drew a blanket out of the saddlebag and spread it out so she wouldn't soil her dress. She sank down gratefully, putting a respectable space between them as she busied herself laying out the feast his cook had packed: bread and butter, roast chicken, and strawberry cake. A flask of water with a touch of lemon slaked their thirst. But even that couldn't cool the fever that had sprung up between her and the man now lounging on his side some distance away from her. He was propped up on one elbow, the meal largely forgotten before him.

Worried about the strain of trying to have a normal conversation after what had transpired, she was grateful when he brought the topic back to business. "You've gone to a great deal of trouble, drawing those plans and bringing me here," he observed. "Why do you care so much?"

"Because it's not often that you get the chance to take something that is meant for ill, and change it to something good." She nibbled on a bit of cake, though she tasted very little of it, her mind still on their encounter in the treehouse. Forcing her thoughts back to the more important matters at hand, she said, "I have questions as well. You haven't been to Everdene since you were nine. It isn't your estate. Why would you agree to do this?"

"If I complete this task, my father will deed me the Harcourt stables. The breeding program with Caspian will become a reality. In the space of a year, the stables will be larger than I'd even dreamed of."

"As long as you destroy a place your mother loved."

His jaw hardened, and he looked away. "Yes."

"I'm sure the Earl won't give a moment's thought to what being part of the destruction of the village might do to you." She watched as Simon crumbled a bit of bread and tossed it to a bird hopping nearby. "Surely you must realize that even an earl can't rip the love of a place out of someone's heart? Memories are always there, buried perhaps, ignored, but they pop out at the strangest times. Today it happened to me. The last years with my father were painful ones. When he drank, he became… ugly. After I learned he had gambled away Mother's house, that was what I remembered most. But when you asked who taught me to ride, I remembered the day he first put me up on a horse and led me around. *Heels down, Penny! Back straight. Hold the reins gently now…*" she said in a gruff mime of his voice, then added, "Despite how broken he was during those last years, I will always remember how tender he was when he taught me to love architecture and horses."

Simon pushed himself upright. "Building this stable is about more than a horse. It's a debt I owe to Jamie."

"Then help me understand. I want to."

She regarded him, silent, waiting. He shoved himself to his feet, crossed to a nearby tree, looking, of a sudden, so alone. When he spoke, it was low, pain deep in every word.

"Jamie was my best friend. More than a brother to me. We served for eight years together, from West Indies to India, to Central Asia. We were green lads with our first commissions when we met. He was the only man in the regiment who could ride as well as I could, and it made me mad as blazes. Our men set up all sorts of contests, pitting us against each other, and it's a wonder we didn't break our necks. Then, during a skirmish, my horse was shot out from under me and I got separated from the rest. Seven *thugees* were trying to kill me, when Jamie came out of nowhere, and suddenly we were back-to-back, sabers swinging. Maybe it was because we'd competed against each other so fiercely. I knew every move he would make, and could predict every feint, every blow, and aim mine accordingly. It was the same for him. We didn't have to speak a word. We just knew. From that moment on, no one could best us."

"That must have been a sight to see."

"He was the only man I ever trusted as much my brother." Simon paused for a moment. "Every soldier has to trust the next man to watch his back in battle. But Jamie and I... our bond ran far deeper."

"So you protected each other as you made your way into Afghanistan."

"We fought like fury to reach Kabul, but once the garrison occupied the city, things went well enough. Jamie and I wandered the bazaars, frequented the tea houses. Our daring on horseback was legendary, and we befriended Afghans who were as fascinated by horses as we were. At first, they believed our garrison was just there temporarily, but when Englishwomen and children began to arrive to join their husbands and fathers there, the Afghans began to fear we'd come to stay."

"Had you?"

"We've never willingly ceded territory we've colonized. But there was another issue that lit the fuse that destroyed our relations with the Afghans. That involved the Afghan women." He went silent for a moment.

"The women?" Penelope echoed. "How so?"

"Women were never allowed to go out without a brother or husband or father accompanying them. They were not allowed to speak to anyone but family. To do otherwise was a great insult. But soldiers who are far from home, lonely... they're going to seek out feminine company. We were warned to stay away from them, but I suppose it was inevitable that lonely English soldiers would find ways around that." He glanced back at Penelope, her eyes green, her hair softly curling under her hat. "We underestimated the danger," he said.

"One day, we were breaking in some new colts, and some dolt of a young officer lost control of a horse. It charged through the bazaar and knocked over an Afghan woman. She was enveloped in a *chadari*, covered head to foot as if by a sheet, only a bit of netting over the eyes allowing her to see. She struck her head on a stone ledge when she fell. She lay there, unconscious, blood soaking through her veil. Later, I learned her uncle had just stepped inside a building to haggle with a merchant, but it seemed no one was with her. I raced over to her and pulled the head covering off, used my neckcloth to put pressure on the wound." He closed his eyes, remembering the chaos of the moment, the shrieks of those in the bazaar, the roars of fury from the men.

"Was she terribly hurt?"

"The injury wasn't as bad as it looked. Just... bled profusely as head wounds do. But her uncle came charging out, furious. I tried to explain, but... he couldn't understand. Only the swords of Jamie and the other soldiers kept onlookers from drawing their blades. Afterwards, I took an interpreter to the woman's house to see about her recovery and try to make amends. It was too late. Rumors flew that I had dishonored her."

Penelope looked down at her hands. "But you were only trying to help."

"Unfortunately, the people of Kabul were already outraged by women's encounters with other soldiers. The fact that I'd bared her face infuriated them. They put a price on my head. The garrison was already in trouble. Complicating matters, Afghanistan is really a collection of independent tribes, each with their own chief. Our commanders had been bribing them with British gold to keep from attacking our patrols or supply trains." He paced, remembering the tension in the garrison, the feeling of a noose tightening around their necks. Supply lines cut, the civilians growing angrier, the chiefs feeling cheated. It was like watching a lit fuse inch closer and closer to a powder magazine, and being unable to snuff it out.

"It didn't take long for the chiefs to realize they could get rich, each one demanding larger and larger payments. The cost became too great for our superiors in Bombay to bear. When they demanded that we cut those expenses, it didn't take a brilliant military mind to realize we were at the tipping point and would not be able to hold Kabul much longer."

"Is that why Jamie was killed?"

"He was supposed to carry a message to Jalalabad to ask the British commander to prepare for our retreat... warn that an entire garrison would be landing on his doorstep soon. I know Jamie hoped to convince them to send reinforcements to help our men make it through the passes. Jamie convinced General

Elphinstone to send me with him. He claimed it might settle things down in Kabul if I were gone."

"Or it could leave you totally exposed! Two men at their mercy."

"Two men meant nothing, compared to the entire garrison, our servants, the wives and children of our men. That night, Jamie drew me aside and told me he wasn't riding his cavalry mount. He was taking Caspian. I knew damned well Jamie would be in trouble with our commanders, but the Turkoman horse would have a better chance of outrunning the tribesmen who would pursue us. And there was no question they would when they realized what he had done. Their golden horses were treasured."

"I can certainly understand why."

"It's strange, what men speak of when they know they might die," Simon mused, memories carrying him far away. "Here, the garrison was in danger, and a perilous road lay ahead of us. But that night, we talked of the stable we'd build, our bloodline of golden horses. We vowed that if either of us made it through the mountains, we'd ship Caspian to England and make that dream a reality."

"You told me once that Caspian had saved your life. It was on that ride, wasn't it?"

"Yes. We were halfway there when we were ambushed. We were both hit, but Jamie was shot in the hip. I got him to cover, but there was no way he could make it the rest of the way. He gave me the message and told me to take Caspian. Jesus, I didn't want to leave him. He said I had no choice. Caspian and I were all that stood between the Afghans and the total destruction of our troops."

He could see the empathy in Penelope's eyes.

"Oh, Simon."

"Somehow, Jamie managed to prop his rifle on a rock and fired to give us cover. Without it, we never would have gotten away." Simon paused a long moment. "Even then, we barely made it through. I tore the message into pieces so they wouldn't be able to read it if they captured me. The tribesmen got so close I swallowed one of the bits of paper." He grimaced at the memories of his near-capture. "Yet, in the end, I rode into Jalalabad, wounded but alive."

"Thank God."

"I delivered the message, then... I don't remember much for several weeks. I was feverish, in pain... The surgeon said he removed three bullets, one from my side, two from my leg. He tried to give me laudanum, but I wouldn't take it. I wanted to know the moment the garrison arrived."

Penelope stood and crossed to Simon. "I read about the retreat from Kabul. It must have been torture not knowing what was happening to your men."

"We waited. And waited for the troops to ride in," he said, trying to breathe past his anguished memories. "At last, on January 13th, one man rode in, hideously wounded. They asked him where the army was. He said *I am the army*. And the story he told..." Bile burned the back of Simon's throat.

"The Afghans had promised General Elphinstone safe passage for the army and all of the camp followers and our Indian servants. They claimed they would provide supplies on the journey as long as the British left Kabul. So, four thousand five hundred British and Indian troops set out, accompanied by twelve thousand camp followers, many of them women and children. It was January. Freezing, the snow deep. Some officers begged the general to return to the cantonments. Elphinstone didn't listen. As they began winding through narrow mountain passes, snipers picked our soldiers off one by one."

"The same mountain passes you had just ridden through," Penelope said softly.

"Tribes would sweep down in lightning-fast attacks, kill as many as they could, and then melt into the landscape. By the time the column reached Gandamak there were only sixty-five soldiers left to make a last stand. The Afghans left a lone survivor to tell us of their victory. The commander of Jalalabad had a trumpet blown all night in case anyone else had escaped, the sound of it drifting off into the winter stillness. We counted the hours, hoping any other survivors could hear the sound of the trumpet, that it might guide them to the fortress, even in the darkness. My God, it seemed as if we waited forever. No one else ever came."

He looked into Penelope's face, saw tears dampening her cheeks, her lips quivering, no doubt trying to picture it. But how could anyone who wasn't there?

She sucked in a ragged breath. "I heard what happened to— to those they killed. There were newspaper accounts…"

Of course, she would have found a way to read newspapers, even when women were forbidden by society to do so. The thought brought him some small bit of comfort as he recalled the horrors of what had transpired next, something he didn't dare mention out loud. The tribesmen gelding the fallen men. Cutting off fingers. Severing their heads and putting them on pikes at the gates of their cities.

"And Jamie?" she asked, her voice a near whisper. "Did anyone ever go back to find him? Bury him?"

"Between the snow leopards, wolves, and tribesmen, there was nothing left. Some months later, a merchant came to Jalalabad, told the officers that the tribesmen who chased us hoped to collect the bounty on my head. If anyone else had been with Jamie, maybe he would have been the one safe in Jalalabad." His throat convulsed. He took a deep breath, focusing on Penelope, the sunlight in her hair, the breeze wafting loose strands about her face, her eyes the color of forest glades shimmering with sadness. The sight of her brought a calmness that he hadn't felt since leaving Afghanistan, and he clung to that as he finished his tale. "Jamie should be the one waiting for Caspian's first foal to be delivered. I keep thinking—why didn't I leave the injured woman alone? She wasn't my responsibility. Surely someone would have fetched her uncle to tend her. If I hadn't leapt in..."

"Simon," she said, reaching out, placing her hand on his. "You can't alter that decision you made. What good does it do to rake it over in your mind, when you'd help her again if you were faced with the same situation?"

"But would I?"

"If you thought it would save that woman's life? Yes." Her smile was tender. "Regardless, building that stable won't change the fact that Jamie died under those hideous circumstances. You were almost killed yourself in that wild race to Jalalabad."

"I left my friend behind."

"He knew he was dying. What good would it have done for you to die by his side? By forcing you to go on, alone, through hostile country, you at least had a chance. A testament to his belief in your own skill and courage and tenacity, believing that you would reach Jalalabad. Under these circumstances, I don't think he would fault you if you left his horses behind."

"Do you have any idea what you are asking of me?" his voice cracked, anguished. "To break a vow to my best friend. A brother-in-arms who gave his life in my place?"

"Would you have survived if you had taken him with you?"

He didn't answer. He knew he would not have.

She tightened her clasp on his hand, her eyes focusing on his. "I can imagine how difficult this choice must feel. But Jamie is dead."

"Because of my recklessness! He had his whole life before him."

Pen reached up, laying one hand against his cheek. "War is brutal. It robs people of life. Wounds them, body and spirit. I love that you intend to honor your friend by creating some-thing, making the dream you shared real, but—"

"Don't you see? The only way I can pay back some small measure of what I owe Jamie is to build this stable."

"I believe you will," she said softly. "But not this way, Simon. Not by flinging together flimsy houses and causing people like Daw and Tripp to suffer needlessly. Jamie is dead. Pray God, he is at peace. But the villagers are alive, and I truly believe your friend would not want his dream to be realized at their expense. You have a chance to make their future better. I know it isn't what your father or Inchwick intended. Perhaps even your brother will disapprove. But surely you can see that, in the end, defying them will be worth it?"

Simon's jaw tightened for just an instant. What did she know about what was best for his family? Of his father and the fragile peace Simon had struck between them? Of Lucien and his pleas that Simon mend that rift? Yet there was something in her face, a depth of character, courage to stay true to her ideals.

"You're so sure you know what is right," he said. "I envy you that."

Doubt shadowed her face for a moment. She looked away. "Take my drawings to Daw, or even to Mr. Tremayne. Ask if my plans are sound. Then *you* decide whether carrying out your father's orders to the letter is worth the cost."

He looked into those eyes that were so earnest, so forthright. He could see something downright terrifying in her expression.

She believed he would do the right thing.

Sadly, she didn't know him at all.

# CHAPTER 14

The last place Simon wanted to go was Daw Garvey's workshop, but there was no way to put off this reckoning any longer. He found his friend hard at work in the barnlike structure, long curls of wood drifting around his boots as he ran a plane over rough wood.

Tripp sat on a stool, sanding a spindle of some kind. Blond hair, freshly washed, wisped around sharp features, his face and neck free of grime. Simon wondered how many hours Margery Garvey had spent scrubbing away the soot ground into his fair skin. There were still red burn scars on his forearms and cheek, but they would heal in time.

Yet, would there be new scars, hidden scars, once Tripp lost another home, Simon thought as he approached Daw through the maze of tools, kegs of nails, and boards of various shapes and sizes.

"Why, isn't this a grand surprise, sir!" Daw said, flashing a grin so wide that Simon knew Penelope hadn't breathed a word about the destruction of the village. "Say hello to Captain Harcourt, lad," Daw told his small charge.

Tripp hopped up and straightened a jerkin that must have belonged to Garvey's sons. "H'llo, Captain, sir."

Despite everything, Simon felt a warmth in the center of his chest. "Are you liking carpentry as much as you anticipated?"

"Oh, yes, sir!" Tripp exclaimed. "Mr. Daw even let me turn this piece myself! I'm making a stool for Widow Bevans to rest her foot on. She's got gout, y'see, and Mr. Daw an' me are going to surprise her with it. A stool, not more gout. She's got plenty o' that on her own."

Both men chuckled.

"Tripp here is turning out to be a big help. Don't know how I got along without him." Daw's eyes twinkled as the boy thrust his thin chest out, bursting with pride. "Is there something I can do for you, Captain?"

Simon's fingers tightened around the plans he had tucked under his arm. "There is, as a matter of fact."

Daw set the wood-plane aside. "Let's head up to the house. Have some of those oat cakes the missus made this morning."

"Thank you for offering, but it's better we talk here. I've some news for your ears alone." Simon glanced at the boy, then back.

Daw dragged his forearm across his sweat-sheened face, wiping away the sawdust that clung to his skin. "Tripp, run over to the house and have your tea."

The boy set his spindle aside and raced off. Simon watched in silence until he disappeared around a corner.

"I scarcely recognized the boy when I came in," Simon said.

"He's right clever and even more willing than my own lads were. We had a few rough nights at first. Poor lad waked up screaming." Daw winced, his face grim. "First time, Margery thought a horde of thieves had come to murder us in our beds. But once our heads cleared… the three of us have done well enough since then. My grandfather made that rocking chair by the hearth plenty big enough for me an' the wee fellow."

Simon could picture the scene so clearly, Tripp on Daw's lap, the carpenter's powerful arms wrapped around the child's thin body.

"Wish I could get hold of whoever was chasing Tripp the day you found him." Daw's big hands clenched into fists. "I'd give that lout nightmares of his own t' keep him awake. Thinking of Tripp stuffed up that chimney, well, ties my own stomach in knots."

The two men stood quiet for a moment, then Daw continued. "Tripp told me what Miss Waverly did for him. How she hid him in her skirts..." The carpenter's cheeks went crimson. "All I can say is the lady is an angel."

She was anything *but* an angel, Simon thought. That was why she appealed to him so much.

Daw dusted off his hands. "Miss Waverly brought such life back into our home. Didn't know how much Margery missed having a little one to fuss over since our boys are all grown and moved away. Like a hen with a chick, she is, grumbling about the holes in his stockings and shooing him to wash up and urging the boy to eat and loving every moment." Daw smiled. "I'm taking the lad with me to building sites. He's curious about everything. Speaking of curious..." He nodded to the papers in Simon's arms. "Have you got something at the big house you want me to repair? Or plans for that stable you want to build?"

Simon stiffened. "Not exactly. I finally rode over to take a look at the site at Blagden Valley. You were right. It's not a wholesome place to build."

Daw crossed his arms over his chest and harrumphed. "It's not fit for horses, that's for sure."

"Nor for people, I'd wager." Simon said.

Daw's brow puckered. "People?"

Every muscle in Simon's body knotted. "There is no easy way to say this, Daw. My father has given me orders to move the village."

"What do you mean *move the village?*" Daw's eyes went round, then narrowed, a knot appearing alongside his jaw.

"Tear the buildings down and rebuild elsewhere. The site he and Inchwick decided on is Blagden Valley."

Color drained from Daw's weathered face.

Simon pressed on. "I've been given *carte blanche* to oversee this project."

"You are to oversee it?" Daw's gaze drilled into Simon's. "How long have you known about this plan?"

"Since the day I arrived at Everdene."

Stark betrayal seared across Daw's face. "I welcomed you as a friend. You came into my home, knowing full well your family was going to tear it down. You laughed with me about old times as if nothing was amiss…"

Simon's stomach churned, sick with guilt. And for an instant, he hated Penelope Waverly for her interference. If it weren't for her, he would have maintained a comfortable distance from people like Daw, avoiding reminders of a time when this village was his world. When he was happy here, *whole* in a way he never would be again.

But it was too late now, with Daw glaring at him as if he were the vilest of traitors. Maybe he was… but traitor to whom? The villagers? His father?

He drew a deep breath, searching for the words to explain. "Seeing you and your home is the reason I'm here right now. You know this land better than anyone. That's why I'm asking you—where would you build if you had the choice?"

"I *don't* have a choice," Daw raged. "No simple folk do! My sons were right. We're batted about like our lives are a child's game, then thrown away with no more thought than a broken cricket bat."

"Your sons aren't wrong. I wish to hell they were." Simon kneaded the back of his neck. "I'm asking you. As the man who knows this estate better than anyone. Where would you build?"

Daw hesitated, then raked a hand through his salt and pepper hair. "There is a pretty place up by Havelock Meadow with a clear stream where Margery and I used to take the boys. But what does that matter? That land is too handsome for the likes of us, isn't it? The Earl will never allow tenants to build there."

"I know it's a gamble. But it's one I'm willing to take."

"Easy for you," Daw scoffed. "You're not the one paying the price if you fail."

What if he did fail? Would he prove Inchwick's point, that tenants were more trouble than they were worth? That Everdene would do better to raise sheep? As for paying a price... Simon knew his father. Defiance would be punished. How brutal would that retribution be? Cutting Harcourt support for the stables themselves, or disinheriting Simon completely? Unless Simon could prove to his father and brother that this plan for Everdene would benefit the family coffers as well...

*All you have to do is walk out of here,* temptation whispered in Simon's head, *turn and walk away, the way you should have done in the streets of Kabul the day the woman fell...*

But the sight of Daw's clenched fists, huge, work-rough, but somehow helpless, stopped him.

"If we manage things the way I hope to, my father won't know about the change in plans until it is too late," Simon said. "I'm wagering I'll be able to convince him and my brother that these improvements to our village will be better for the estate as well. At least this way there's some hope."

"Don't." Daw's hand cut through the air, his expression steeled. "Don't promise things you can't deliver. To give people hope, then crush it, is cruel. You should know that better than anyone."

His gaze bored into Simon's. Suddenly Simon could see himself as a boy, searching for any sign of his mother. He and Daw had asked everyone in Everdene if they had seen her. He'd been so sure someone would give him a clue, and he would find her.

Daw was right. Hope came with a price that could cut to the bone.

Simon drew a steadying breath and shoved the memory back into a past buried deep. "The truth is, I don't know if I can carry this through," he confessed. "It could end in disaster, but I have to try. Will you take a look at these?"

He unrolled Penelope's plans on the work bench.

Daw's gaze locked on the drawings as he picked them up, and carried them near the window. The workroom grew so silent, Simon could hear the hammering of his own heart.

If Daw said the plans were flawed, could Simon abdicate responsibility for the pain the people of Everdene village would suffer? No. Sometime in the hours between Penelope's challenge and Daw's devastation, Simon had crossed a Rubicon of his own. He would build the village in the meadow, whether he used Penelope's plans or not.

At last, Daw confronted Simon, suspicion darkening his face. "Where did you get these?"

"Penelope Waverly drew them."

"Miss Waverly?" The carpenter didn't sound near as surprised as Simon expected him to be.

"She charged into my house with these the morning after I slipped and told her about the fate of the village. Gave me no peace until I promised to have you take a look at them."

Daw's Adam's apple bobbed in his throat, his voice a trifle thick with emotion. "I've seldom seen anything like this in a tenant's cottage. Three bedrooms instead of one? The separate room for the kitchen and a gathering place as well? It would be a lucky man who lived in such a place."

Tension buzzed inside Simon. "Tell me, Daw. Are the plans structurally sound? I need to know."

"I'm a carpenter, not an architect. But from what I can tell, this is as fine a plan for a cottage as I have ever seen."

Relief and dread poured through Simon in equal measure. "If I have my way, Havelock Meadow will have streets lined with them."

"I don't see how this dream village of yours can come to be," Daw insisted. "Mr. Inchwick will raise holy hell if you flummox his plan to put us in that benighted valley. He wants to use every decent hectare of land to run sheep and put more coin in the Earl's pocket. First thing he'll do is write to your father, and between them they have the power to do whatever they please with us."

"It's true. They have the power. And yet, how many times as boys did we pull off impossible capers?"

"This isn't a game. People's lives hang in the balance."

"I know. Just give me a chance to see if I can push this through. Don't tell anyone about this until I have matters settled."

Daw bristled. "I'm not as good at lying to a friend's face as you are."

Simon winced inwardly.

"People deserve to know what's in store," Daw insisted. "To make plans, find somewhere to live. Winter will be coming and Blagden Valley's not only foul, it can't possibly hold more than half of the cottages you see here."

Jesus, God—could Daw be right? Were Inchwick and the Earl planning to evict tenants as well? Simon hadn't even considered that. "We won't be turning anyone out in winter," he said.

Daw's eyes blazed. "Tell Tripp's mother that—if, by the grace of God, she and her babes made it all the way to Scotland without starving by the road." The carpenter started to turn away.

Simon grabbed him by the arm. "Give me five days. No

matter what happens with Inchwick, I'll call a meeting in the assembly hall and announce it myself."

Daw's glare pierced Simon, his voice gravelly. Rough. "Five days," he said, and stalked away to the home he was fated to lose.

# CHAPTER 15

*P*enelope hadn't been able to sit still since she'd gotten home from her ride with Simon. She'd exchanged her riding habit for a simple day dress, covered the blue print skirt with an apron, then taken up a feather duster and attacked the high shelves in the library with an energy that sent dust motes whirling before every window. Her father's books on architecture still filled the shelves, some of them strewn about the desk from the hours of research she'd done before drawing her building plans.

She'd felt jumpy as a cat in a pack of foxhounds ever since she'd returned from the outing to the tree house. Simon's kiss had flung doors open inside her that she couldn't quite close. Even her lips felt different, as if her sisters and mother must be able to see what she'd been up to.

At least Mama had finally tired of complaining that it was unseemly for a gentleman's daughter to go riding alone. Fortunately, Mama hadn't guessed just how 'unseemly' Pen had been, or Anastasia Waverly would be attempting to march Simon Harcourt to the altar.

That was the stuff of nightmares.

For the moment, Pen was busy concocting bleak visions of her own. Her nerves wrenched tight with anxiety as she pictured Simon showing her building plans to Daw Garvey and the carpenter passing judgement on her work.

What if she had made mistakes when she'd figured measurements and positioned load-bearing walls? Simon would be forced to dismiss her idea. Or would he be downright relieved at the slightest excuse to do so?

She had seen the war waging inside him when she'd proposed her plan—wanting to do what was right for the villagers, yet knowing that if he did, he'd have nowhere to build the stable he'd dreamed of creating with his best friend. The wish he owed a dying comrade who was more a brother to him even than the Viscount who shared his blood.

Even if Daw Garvey *did* approve Penelope's plans, Simon might refuse to take action. And there were still Inchwick and the Earl to deal with—powerful men who could crush any hope of moving the project forward. She fretted her bottom lip, as she dusted the atlas she had loved as a child. Should she have warned Simon not to let the land agent know the plans were her creation?

The idea that she should hide her abilities was anathema, yet she could swallow her pride in this case, endure that injustice, to keep a far worse one from crashing down on the cottagers' heads. *She* would know she'd had a part in making the progressive village a reality. That would be enough, she reasoned. How many women had society forced to conceal their true identities behind men's names? Authors of books, scientists, any woman who dared step outside her accepted sphere and use her intellect and talent?

A sharp rap on the door startled her from her thoughts, the feather duster knocking on the shelf, sending a cloud of grit into her nose and eyes. She went into a fit of sneezing, then scrubbed her eyes with her sleeve and glanced out the window.

An unfamiliar barouche with canary yellow wheels stood at the gate. The Waverlys' manservant, Rupert Hughes, held the reins of an exquisite pair of matched bays. A hubbub rose in the hallway, a feminine greeting drifting through the library door. "Captain Harcourt! What an unexpected honor!"

Penelope's heart leapt into her throat as she heard that deep, familiar voice answer. "I hope you will indulge me, ma'am. I know this isn't the appropriate hour for calls, but I am most eager to speak to Miss Waverly." Pen pressed her palm to her mouth, her pulse racing.

"Penelope? Of course, but I rather thought..."

Pen gasped in dismay. Hells bells! That was her mother's voice! The last person she wanted involved in this situation was her mother.

Pen leaped off of the stepladder, tugging on the ties of her apron. She muttered under her breath as the knot clung, her mother chattering on.

" ... you both seemed most vexed when you parted at the ball..."

Simon chuckled. "I've never been dealt quite so crushing a set-down, but it turns out that I'm in Miss Waverly's debt."

The stubborn knot gave way and Pen threw the apron on a chair and dashed into the entryway, breathless.

"Captain Harcourt!" Penelope tried to stifle another bout of sneezing. The sneezes won, but before she could grope for a handkerchief, he provided one. Fine Holland cloth, with his initials in the corner.

A pucker formed between his brows. "I was hoping I might take you for a drive, but perhaps you have taken a chill?"

"Penelope has always been in ridiculously good health!" Mama protested eagerly. "It's almost indecent!"

"I am relieved to hear it," he said with mock solemnity.

"She just took it into her head to dust—"

Pen could see dismay dawn on her mother's face as she realized she had just told an earl's son that her daughter was doing a servant's labor. She had to admire Mama's quick recovery. Mama pressed a thin, pale hand to her bosom. "I begged her not to exert herself, but she was devoted to her poor, dead papa, and cares for his books in his honor."

Simon made some inane comment about dutiful daughters, and Pen felt the urge to cuff him in the arm. He knew exactly what had driven her restlessness. He thrummed with tension as well, while she tried to guess whether the plans had been a success or failure.

She knew she was asking a great deal of him to even consider altering his father's vision at the possible cost of the vow he'd made to his friend. But, as she'd pointed out earlier, Jamie was dead. People like Daw and the other villagers were alive. They would have to deal with the consequences of Simon's decision the rest of their lives, for good or ill.

Her mind a whirl, she decided it would be best to take their looming conversation away from her mother's ears. "I would very much enjoy going for a drive with you, Captain," she said.

Her mother beamed. "I will summon Kitty to join you."

"I never take a chaperone with me when I'm governessing, Mama," Penelope insisted crisply. "I do not need one now. Captain Harcourt and I have been friends since childhood."

"I give you my word, I will be a perfect gentleman." Simon sketched her mother an earnest bow, but when his gaze met Pen's, a roguish gleam twinkled beneath his lashes.

Pen's cheeks warmed. There had been nothing gentlemanly in his kiss, his tongue breaching her lips, so shockingly intimate she'd been imagining the act it had imitated.

She fetched her bonnet and shawl, then Simon offered her his arm. Slipping her hand through the curve of his elbow, she felt the hard sinews beneath the superfine of his coat, remembered how his sleeves had brushed her legs, only the thin barrier of her stockings between them as they climbed down from the tree.

He helped her into the barouche, thanked Hughes for minding the horses, then climbed up beside her with athletic grace. With a gentle snap of the reins, the horses fell into a perfect trot, Laurel Cottage fading in the distance.

Pen clasped her hands in her lap. "What did you find out?" she asked, feeling as if her heart would beat its way out of her chest. "You must tell me and put me out of such misery."

"Daw says it would be a lucky man who lived in such a cottage."

Relief welled up in Penelope. Yet, she tempered it, knowing she'd only cleared the first jump in a course that would make the wildest steeplechase look tame. "So, what do *you* think?"

"Honestly?" He darted a glance at her, his lips curled in a wry smile. "I'm not sure if I'm glad or disappointed. Part of me was hoping that the plans would be insufficient, and that I'd not have to seriously consider your proposal."

A cold lump formed in her throat. "What do you mean to do?"

"I rode back to Everdene Hall to think about that. Visited Caspian… looked over the mares that have just arrived."

She nibbled her fingernail, grateful she'd forgotten her gloves. There were so many ways he could reject her proposal. Reasons most of their world would laude. Surely a vow to a dead comrade-in-arms who died in his place would hold more weight than the fate of simple cottagers. Pen could almost hear the arguments: So what if the cottages Inchwick would build in that ague-filled valley were cheaply constructed and cramped? The common folk should be grateful to have a roof over their heads at all! "Simon, please—"

He cut her off before she could finish. "I intend to show your drawings to Inchwick and tell him there has been a change in plans."

A thrill ran down her spine. "That will be wonderful!" she cried, grasping his forearm. "I can't wait to hear all about it."

"What do you mean, *hear about it*? You're coming with me."

"Wh-what?" Pen choked out.

"When I present these building plans to Inchwick, I need you to be there, to answer any questions. The plans are yours, Penelope. You're the only one who can fully address Inchwick's concerns."

She reeled inwardly at his assertion. "I thought you would present the plans to Inchwick, concealing the fact that they were drawn up by a woman. Not because you wanted to take undue credit, but because a land agent—and anyone else for that matter!—will take the plans far more seriously if they think they were done by a man."

"You went to a great deal of work to make clear, superior plans," Simon said, guiding his team expertly around a corner. "You convinced me."

She felt a fluttering in her chest as she looked at Simon Harcourt's handsome profile. "Just so that you know, Mr. Inchwick and I... well, we don't exactly have a history of being amiable," she confessed.

"Ah. Butted heads with him as well, did you?" Simon raised a satirical brow. "Somehow that does not surprise me."

She'd confronted the man when she'd learned that Laurel Cottage was lost.

Pen could still hear her mother's wailing, her father smashing things.

"Inchwick mentioned that Laurel Cottage was now Harcourt property," Simon said solemnly. "To be surrendered after your mother's death."

"Which is why I used much of the money from my bequest to pay for lessons to prepare Kitty and Fanny to support themselves. It is inevitable that they will lose their home."

"They know the situation?"

Pen laughed without mirth. "They believe some miracle will happen, a knight on a white charger will race in and save us."

"Ah, hence the curate."

"Yes."

"Thank heaven you had the intelligence to refuse him," Simon teased with an eloquent shudder. "You would have made the very devil of a curate's wife. You're more of a thieves' kitchen mastermind, kidnapping urchins and hiding them under your skirts."

"That urchin was hardly an unwilling victim. His arms were wrapped around my legs so tight, it's a miracle he didn't topple me right into that terrible chimneysweep's clutches."

"Well, I did catch a glimpse of your legs as we were climbing down from the treehouse and they are very lovely. Though a gentleman shouldn't mention it."

Her cheeks burned as she remembered the warm, moist feel of Simon's breath penetrating the thin fabric of her stocking. She imagined all too clearly him pressing his lips against the inside of her knee. Feeling her face heat up even more, she pressed her thighs together and slapped his arm, feigning her best governess frown.

"*You* are no gentleman."

"No. No, I'm not. And *you* are no angel, though the Garveys and young Tripp are convinced otherwise." He grinned. "That's why I like you so much."

They rode in silence for a few moments, the horse's harness jingling.

"Frankly," he continued, "I'm looking forward to seeing Inchwick's face when you spread these plans out on his desk. I tell you in confidence that it's been rather thin of excitement since I arrived at Everdene, excepting my encounters with you."

Couldn't she have said the same thing? Crossing swords with him sparked her temper and challenged her wit. Something she might even miss once she returned to governessing and he returned to his command. But the idea of facing off with the land agent filled her with both excitement and unease.

"Your confrontation with Inchwick is a bit of excitement I had best forgo," Pen said. "My mere presence might end any chance you have of convincing him to move the village."

"Actually, you are just the partner I need for this venture. If he is distracted and angry at your presence, he's more likely to make a misstep." The corner of his mouth ticked up in a wry smile. "And you *do* have a gift for testing people's nerves."

"I don't understand."

"I've spent enough time in gaming hells to read people's faces when they're hiding something. When I glanced at Inchwick's ledgers the other day there was a shifty glint in his eyes. I'd wager a thousand pounds there was something in them he didn't want me to see."

"Inchwick has been cheating his lordship?"

"I don't know. Not yet. But if we can uncover what he's hiding, we might have the leverage we need to coerce him into cooperating with us. My father cares little about people, but he does not like being cheated."

Pen felt the first real hope that they might realize her vision for the cottagers.

"Will you come with me?" he asked.

She looked into his ice-blue eyes, felt the tug of something warm and new inside her, and nodded. "I wouldn't miss it for the world."

# CHAPTER 16

*I*nchwick's housekeeper answered the door, her hair raked back in a knot at the nape of her neck, her face sour as an unripe cherry. "Captain Harcourt!" Mrs. Cullen exclaimed in surprise, glancing from Simon to Penelope. "I fear that Mr. Inchwick is not at home. There has been some problem with the water wheel at Jonesy's mill."

"It seems there is always some coil to untangle on the estate, is there not?" Simon said with a smile. "And I fear I'm about to deliver another one. I've brought Miss Waverly to discuss some matters regarding the building project I am in charge of." He nodded to the roll of papers in his arms.

"I will give him the message as soon as he returns."

"I'm sure he will be back in no time. We will wait for him in his office."

"H-his office?" Mrs. Cullen's brow furrowed in confusion. "I am sure you'd be much more comfortable in the parlor."

"The desk in his office is much better for laying out these plans," Simon said brusquely. "Perhaps you could bring us tea. Miss Waverly mentioned that she is a bit peckish. I believe we saw some fresh berries as we walked up the lane. You might gather some for her. I would take it as a personal favor."

Penelope's lips puckered and he knew she was suppressing a smile.

"I suppose I could." Mrs. Cullen pressed her fingers to her breast, all aflutter.

He nodded amiably, then ushered Penelope toward the office where he'd met Inchwick before.

The moment he shut the door behind them, Penelope gave a soft chuckle. "I see it's not only *young* misses who are impressed by cavalry officers. I had no idea I was so particular about my tea."

"You are a most discerning woman. I'm counting on it. You search the room, and I'll search Inchwick's desk. We should have a quarter hour while Mrs. Cullen is occupied, but we'd best be quick, in case she has sent someone off to fetch her employer."

Simon strode to Inchwick's desk chair and sat down, the better to open the drawers. He was struck again by the quality of his surroundings, the rosewood and porcelain, the gleaming silver candlestick, and the stag penholder with its exquisite antlers. Inchwick's grim-faced clergyman of a father scowled his disapproval at the havey-cavey goings-on from the frame on the wall. The drawers were in an order so precise Simon sensed Inchwick would notice the slightest deviation. Carefully moving and replacing things was taxing, but nothing he found seemed untoward. Penelope was making an efficient search of bookshelves with the thoroughness that could earn her the respect of any rogue from thieves' kitchen. They'd made a decent job of it when Simon heard a commotion in the hall, then footsteps approaching.

Before the door could open, Simon closed the drawer and swung his booted feet up on the desk, leafing through one of the ledgers as if it were a sale sheet from Tattersall's. Penelope slid the book she was examining back into place, then stood stiffly beside the shelf she'd been searching.

Moments later, Inchwick rushed in, his face red with exertion. His gaze swept the room, from Simon to Penelope and back again.

"Captain Harcourt. Miss Waverly. Mrs. Cullen said you had a matter of some urgency to discuss."

So, she *had* sent someone running to fetch him, Simon thought.

The land agent's eyes narrowed on the ledger in Simon's hands. "What is this about?"

Simon shut the volume with a snap and set it aside. "Some vital concerns regarding the reconstruction of Everdene Village. I looked over the site you've set out at Blagden Valley. I found it lacking."

"The new location has already been determined."

"I've decided to make adjustments to the plan. I asked Miss Waverly to show me around the estate."

Inchwick looked as if he'd swallowed something bitter. "I would have been happy to do so."

"You always seemed far too busy with other matters. Besides which, you're not half so pleasing in a bonnet. Miss Waverly and I were friends as children, and struck up our acquaintance once again. She took me to revisit treehouses we built in our youth, and before we knew it, we were discussing the plans for the village."

Inchwick's nostrils flared. "I cannot see what business a woman would have discussing anything but frills and furbelows."

Simon gave a hearty laugh. "Have you seen the intricate construction of their bonnets? Most ladies might not be informed regarding architecture, I will allow. However, I find Miss Waverly is *exceptionally* talented."

"Talented?" Inchwick lips pursed, as if to ask *in what?*

The man grated Simon's nerves, and it took work to keep an amiable expression on his face. "I've chosen a far more salubrious site for the village up near Havelock Meadow."

The land agent blinked. "That is good grazing land. I cannot think that the Earl would approve."

"I have already sent for surveyors to lay out the streets."

"Sir, you cannot expect to make such a vast change without consulting the Earl or Viscount."

"I will deliver the information to them myself, and if there are questions, have their man of business examine the expenditures in your ledgers to determine whether or not my plans are sound. After I have examined them myself."

"Examine… That is certainly unnecessary! It would be my pleasure to provide any information you require."

"I am counting on your expertise! I'm sure I will have questions once I familiarize myself with the costs of materials, etcetera. I've been made aware that I have not taken my responsibilities here at Everdene seriously." Simon shot a purposefully teasing look at Penelope. "Truth is, mathematics and finance have never been my forte, but I intend to do my best."

Some of the color came back into Inchwick's cheeks. Simon's self-deprecating words seemed to have eased the land agent's nerves. Either that, or he'd regained his composure. Simon gathered the scrolls he had set on the table. He unrolled them. "Let us begin by examining these plans."

Inchwick bent over the drawings. After a moment, he made a guttural sound. "I see what you mean about overspending your accounts, if these are any sample, Captain. Whoever drew these must have a fortune to burn and no conception of the type of people we must house."

"Miss Waverly drew them." Simon might have said a cat had made the drawings, considering Inchwick's reaction. Contempt curled the land agent's lips.

"That explains it. Leave it to a female to be impractical,

wasteful, and foolish. What do cottagers need with three bedchambers? They'll just fill them up with more mouths to feed. Make more of a burden on the estate!"

"I thought they supply the labor to run Everdene," Penelope said.

"These people are no different than the livestock they raise! Put a pig in a palace, and they'll turn it into a pigsty."

Simon saw Penelope's anger flash in time with his own. She started to respond, but stopped, her gaze fixed on a shelf across from her with a sudden intensity that sent a hum of excitement rippling through him. Simon rose to draw Inchwick's gaze away from her, angling his body to block her from the land agent's sight.

"That comparison speaks more about your short-sighted-ness than the people I've conversed with," Simon protested.

"I know you are untutored in such matters, Captain," Inch-wick said. "But these changes are costly."

"Not such a great amount as to be prohibitive. I am convinced the benefits will outweigh the inconvenience. However, I'm concerned that there are fewer cottages being built than will accommodate our current tenants. Perhaps you could explain why."

Inchwick straightened his collar. "One must be willing to cut away dead wood, so to speak, to keep an estate productive. Some evictions are necessary, just as casualties are to be expected on a battlefield."

"You cast out the word 'casualties' as if they were no matter. I assure you, numbers in newspapers are far different from men you've sat at campfires with, and shared bits from letters home. *I know the villagers in Everdene.*"

"Sir, I am certain your intentions regarding this matter are worthy, but I urge you to trust those trained to command this enterprise."

Simon's jaw knotted. "My comrades were massacred in the

retreat from Kabul because they trusted generals who were sure they knew best. Generals who had no idea how to lead. I'll not make the same mistake here."

"Your father seemed quite certain you would not concern yourself with the intricacies of construction when you accepted the project here."

Simon saw the land agent's baleful glare fix on Penelope. Simon flattened his palms on the desk, his face close to Inchwick. "It seems even my father can be wrong."

The man drew himself up, doubtless trying to form another plan of attack. "Captain Harcourt, you are a soldier. A hero of the empire. You are a man who has faced hard decisions without the sentimental weakness of women. You may not have your brother's cleverness at mathematics, but you understand that there are sometimes necessary losses for the betterment of the realm."

"Yes," he said, keeping his voice calm, though he wanted to rail at the man. "I have seen exactly what those losses are. As to whether they are necessary, I would have to argue. The location I have chosen will give us room to build the correct number of cottages. And there will be plenty of grazing land with the present area of the village cleared for that purpose."

"Captain—"

Simon struck the plans Penelope had drawn so carefully, silencing the man. "I have engaged surveyors for the Havelock Meadows site. These are the buildings we will construct there."

Veins pulsed in Inchwick's temples. "Captain, you cannot—"

"Oh, I assure you I can, and I will." He paced back to the desk and waved a careless hand over the ledgers spread across the desk. "As for these, I've decided to become more informed as to the financial aspects of this project, so I will be taking these ledgers to examine for the next few days."

"That—that is not possible."

"The ledgers are the property of the Harcourt family, are they not?"

"Well, yes, but—"

"They belong to the Earl and Viscount who put me in charge of the estate in their absence. I seem to recall my father directing you to give me *carte blanche* when the three of us met."

"Captain Harcourt, I cannot..." The land agent's face blanched. "How will I record the details of the day?"

Simon tapped his fingertips on the volumes. "I have every faith you will manage. Perhaps write notes on foolscap, then make the entries once I return your ledgers."

Penelope's voice startled him. "I believe you might wish to examine this volume as well."

Both men turned. She stood beside the shelf she'd been looking at earlier, her hands grasping the calf-skin bound ledger Simon had seen that first day. Inchwick's eyes bulged, and Simon wondered if he would have an apoplexy.

"Those are my personal records," Inchwick blustered. "There is no need for you to bother with them." The land agent started toward her, but Simon was quicker, taking the ledger out of Penelope's hands.

"I'm sure this will be helpful as well. Something tells me that your ledgers will make fine examples of how I should set up mine. They should provide plenty of inspiration, if I'm to make a success of my stables." Simon thumbed through the pages. "I'll not find you betting exorbitant sums on races or keeping an establishment for a ladybird, will I? Not that I'd blame you for either."

Inchwick huffed, flustered. "Of course not! Miss Waverly—"

"Beg pardon for speaking of subjects that should never insult a lady's ears, Miss Waverly," Simon said, with a mischievous wink. Penelope stood, erect, calm, beautiful in her strength and power. The sight sent a prickling sensation at his nape, suddenly aware of the potential danger he'd put her in—danger that might increase once he rode away from Everdene for good.

He put that thought from his mind. "I can only hope I'll be able to decipher enough to feel somewhat informed of the basics," he said, as he collected the other ledgers. "I'm rubbish at keeping accounts in order. He nodded at the plans. "I should be back in three days, once I confer with my family. Use the time to examine these plans. Should you have any questions regarding the drawings, Miss Waverly will answer them in my presence only. I do not wish to miss any of the details. Do we understand each other?"

"Yes, Captain," Inchwick said grimly. "I understand perfectly."

Simon bowed, then escorted Penelope to the carriage. He helped her up and handed her the ledgers, aware of her quick intelligence and dauntless determination, wrapped up in an all-too-compelling feminine form.

Only someone who knew her well would guess that she was worried. He wanted to drive back that stiffness, warm her into the woman who'd kissed him in the treehouse, who'd defended Tripp from his tormentors, who'd challenged him and dared him to remember something beyond the pain he'd suffered here at Everdene. Yet, the strange feelings in his chest were too new and unnerving for anything save humor.

He bumped his thigh against her leg and flashed her a grin, hoping to smooth the crease from her brow. "Just for honesty's sake, I'm not really rubbish at sums," he teased.

"I would imagine you could master whatever you set your mind to."

"Miss Waverly, did you converse with my tutor all those years ago?" He glanced at her, wanting to tease out a smile. "Hopefully Inchwick will be fooled. I'm counting on the fact that he'll think me too dull to uncover whatever mischief he's about. And he'll dismiss your intellect because you are a female."

He waited for her temper to flare, wanted a glimpse of the fiery woman who'd championed the village, but she only looked out over the landscape as it whisked past them.

"Penelope, what is it?"

"I know this seems like a prank to you, outwitting Inchwick and your family. But a man like Inchwick does not take well to being challenged."

Simon drew rein beneath a willow tree, then angled himself the better to look at her.

"I thought you'd be pleased once we pulled off our caper."

"I am… glad we got the ledgers, but we are far from achieving our goal as yet. How will you move forward now?"

"I thought we could go over Inchwick's records together, if you are willing. I could use your discerning eye." And he wanted to spend more time with her, honesty forced him to admit to himself. "But first, I need to ride posthaste to see my father and brother, on the off chance that Inchwick musters the courage to write them himself. I am more certain than ever that there is something in these ledgers Inchwick does not wish us to find. We can bend him to our will."

"I am not so sure. Mr. Inchwick is a small man. Small in ethics and consequence. He will strike out where he can."

Against her? Did she fear Inchwick might take vengeance on her family? Simon tensed at the possibility. Surely Lucien could be trusted to make sure she suffered no repercussions. He was the one who would own Laurel Cottage, after all. Simon would call in a favor.

Penelope's voice broke into his thoughts. "Do not underestimate Mr. Inchwick."

"Do not underestimate me. I will be gone three days, then we will set about building your village." He looked down into her face. That determined chin, the soft cleft in it, those direct green eyes. His chest tightened. She was far from naïve, no missish innocent. She knew exactly the cost her defiance of convention would exact, but she marched forward anyway. The front line of a Forlorn Hope? Or a harbinger of generations to come?

All he knew was that she touched something inside him buried deep. Made him want... not to conquer her, not even to shield her, but to fight this battle at her side.

# CHAPTER 17

"For God's sake," Lucien pleaded as Simon strode into the entryway of that bastion of Harcourt power, Bitterne Tower, "tell me there isn't some problem with the project at Everdene?"

Simon felt a stab of irritation as he shed his riding cloak and hat, handing them to the footman. Must Lucien always expect the worst? "On the contrary. I'm finding I'm quite wrapped up in the doings there."

It was strange to consider the changes a few weeks had wrought. He'd been sizzling with tension when he'd first ridden to Everdene to answer his father's summons, every hoofbeat that took him closer, tightening the vise around his chest.

Yet now, the miles stretching between him and the home of his childhood—and a certain woman with uncompromising eyes—made him edgy, as if he were pulling away from the center of some force he couldn't name.

Simon assessed his brother, noting the wariness in his eyes. "I've come to discuss some matters regarding construction with you."

"Construction?" Lucien echoed with a bewildered frown. "Is not Mr. Inchwick handling that angle of things?"

"That was the expectation; however, I have decided to take a more active role. We can discuss it over a glass of port once I wash away the dust from the road." Simon gestured to the valise on the marble floor beside him.

"Shall I call Father?" Lucien asked. "I believe he is in the west wing. This is his usual time for napping."

The idea of the Earl napping startled Simon. His father had rarely appeared to need those human luxuries such as sleep or regular meals. He'd seemed almost like an automaton whose gears never wound down. "I can wait upon him later. How is the old man doing?"

"Better here."

Yes. He would do better at Bitterne Tower. Built in the reign of Richard III, the dark, forbidding house had always been one of his favorites. The exact opposite of his mother's lovely touches around Everdene. "I'm glad to hear it."

"There is no telling what internal damage was done when he was injured, or how it is healing." Lucien twisted the signet ring with its family crest. "He will be pleased to hear things are going well at Everdene."

Simon stifled a wry smile, thinking just how 'pleased' the old man would be if—*when*—he learned the purpose of this sudden visit.

Simon bathed and donned a kerseymere jacket and cream waistcoat, then joined Lucien in the study. His brother was waiting for him, a newspaper in his hands, a tray bearing sandwiches, cheeses, and a decanter of port atop a black bogwood table.

Simon poured himself a glass as Lucien folded the crisply ironed paper and set it aside.

"You look… different," Lucien said, his gaze sweeping Simon from head to toe. "Better."

"Yes, well, it's amazing what a bath and a change of clothes can do."

"It's not that. When you returned to England you seemed… brittle. As if you were looking for a way to kill yourself. Everdene and being industrious agree with you. Like the brother I knew."

Simon stopped to consider. He *did* feel different since the day he'd ridden up to Everdene. Or was it since the day he'd run across a bonnet-clad warrior righting injustice?

He took a sip of the port, grateful for the superior quality of the Earl's wine cellars. "I find that a sense of purpose agrees with me. It really is a handsome estate."

"You didn't think so before."

"I did, once. It seemed perfection when I was a boy. After Mother disappeared, it felt as if the estate itself had betrayed us. But it turns out, matters were quite reversed. *We* are the ones preparing to betray *it*."

"Betray… what do you mean?"

"You know that demolishing the village is wrong—to merely wipe away everything familiar to these tenants without a thought to the harm it will do to the people who've served our family for generations."

Lucien shot to his feet. "*You*, lecturing *me* on matters of responsibility regarding the estate? That's rich. You haven't bothered to give a moment's thought to Harcourt holdings —ever!"

Simon met his brother's stormy gaze. "You're right. I'm the first to admit that I haven't noticed anything going on around me unless it had a mane and a tail—but I actually met my conscience on the streets of the village." A warmth filled his chest. "She was hiding a runaway boy under her skirts." He couldn't suppress a smile whenever he pictured that scene, and he pictured it far more often than he should.

"She?" Lucien snagged his own glass of port and drained it.

"That explains things. It's about a woman. Please don't dally with one of the villagers' daughters or wives. The last thing we need is to give them one more reason to be up in arms."

Simon's hand knotted. "Miss Waverly is a gentleman's daughter."

"Waverly? Why does that name sound familiar?"

"Remember that girl who tormented us when we were building our treehouse?"

"The one who was struck by lightning during the Great Storm?"

"Yes. She showed me the site where Inchwick was planning to build the village. It's not a fit place for anyone to live."

"What would you know about it?"

"Lucien, I wouldn't put my horses there, let alone people. I've given orders to move the village to Havelock Meadow."

"You what?" Lucien choked out.

"There's a much more suitable site that doesn't flood and allows for all the cottages to be replaced. I expect to return to Everdene with a signed document from you confirming that decision."

Lucien kneaded his brow as if he'd been struck with a blinding headache. "Simon, for the love of God, *think* for once in your life. Don't make a mess of this chance just because a pretty filly caught your eye. A year from now you won't even remember her name, but you'll be disinherited for the rest of your life."

Was that true? Would he forget Penelope when he rode away? Would *she* forget him? Why did that thought suddenly sting? As for being disinherited... he'd known from the first when Pen had proposed her plan it would put him at risk

"I can't say where I will be a year from now," Simon confessed, "but *you* will be landlord to these people the rest of your life, which is why I don't understand why you would approve this debacle. The valley you've chosen to build in is known to be full of ague and sickness. It has terrible drainage. The water is unclean. When our father dies, you will be left as the lord that caused the death and disruption of the people working your land."

"I didn't choose the site. Father didn't either. Mr. Inchwick—"

Simon cut him off with a wave of his hand. "Then neither of you will object when I move it."

"Jesus, Simon—" Lucien stalked away, his face contorted with frustration. Then he stopped, wheeled to glare as if Simon's words suddenly struck home. "Is Blagden Valley really so vile?"

"Yes. I spoke to those familiar with the land. Then I rode out there to see for myself. Lucien, you and I both know that what Father is doing to the villagers is wrong. It may be legal, within his rights, but it's wrong. I'm here to appeal to you one last time. Is there any way to convince Father to leave the village as it stands?"

"Do you think I didn't try? You know how manipulative he is. The only way he got me to agree was—" Lucien's voice broke, and he turned away.

"Was what?"

"I managed to extract his promise to fund the stable you wish to build. He will raze the village no matter what, Simon. Don't fling your entire future away on a Forlorn Hope. This stable you're bent on building is a perfect use of your gifts. No one is better with horses than you, and that Turkoman stallion is the finest animal I've ever seen. You've been searching for something to pour all of your passion into for as long as I can remember. You're a fine soldier, I have no doubt. But I don't want to lose my brother in some hideous massacre like the one you barely escaped."

"Lucien—"

"Father has agreed to set aside a sizeable inheritance in your name if you accomplish this. You will never have to fight some hellish battle again."

Simon stared, noting the pain in Lucien's face. "I had no idea my circumstances troubled you."

"Why the hell wouldn't it? From the time Mother and the girls left, you've been the only family I have."

"A state you could easily remedy. Half the county was at Rendells' ball, hoping to match their daughters with a peer of the realm. Marry some pretty miss, then set your mind to filling up the nursery like a viscount should."

"And end up like Mother and Father?" Lucien gave a harsh laugh. "I may have to sire an heir eventually, but the longer I can put it off, the fewer years I'll spend in misery."

Simon could see the deep scars his brother bore, things he had seen, heard… still carried with him. "Lucien, Father won't live forever. The damage he's doing will."

Lucien swore under his breath and stalked out of the room.

***

THE DINNER HOUR LOOMED GRIM, AS SIMON STRODE INTO THE vast dining room, haunted by memories of how silent those first months had been without his sisters, without his mother's laughter. So cold his teeth had ached, and he'd not been able to swallow, food congealing in his throat. Even the fires in the vast fireplaces that bracketed each end of the huge dining room had failed to drive back the chill, because it didn't come from the air. It came from his father.

Simon pictured the picnic he'd had with Penelope, lounging on the blanket. And the meals shared with his fellow soldiers, filled with noise and teasing, laughter and comradery. The food had been rough, simple fare, yet it had tasted far better than the fine cuisine served at the Earl's table.

This world his father ruled chafed like an ill-fitting saddle, making Simon strain to stay upright. Every moment making him more certain that it was wrong.

As he entered the room, he saw that a footman had wheeled his father to the head of the table in an invalid chair. During the weeks since Simon had seen him, the Earl had lost flesh, his jowls sagging, his belly shrinking beneath his scarlet-and-gold embroidered waistcoat. Even his skin seemed tissue-thin, ropes of blue veins visible.

The Earl leaned toward Lucien, oblivious to anyone else in the room, the pair of them discussing something important. A closed circle that had grown tighter after Simon's mother had disappeared.

Steeling himself, Simon pasted on an amiable expression and strode to where a place setting had been arranged for him partway down the vast table. "Good evening, sir."

The Earl leveled Simon such a grim look from beneath bushy iron-gray eyebrows that, for an instant, Simon feared Inchwick might have written about the village after all.

"To what do we owe this unexpected pleasure?" Barnabas Harcourt demanded.

"I wished to clarify some matters regarding Everdene with Lucien," Simon said. "Nothing you need trouble yourself about."

"If I wished to be involved in such nit-picking, I would have overseen the project myself," the Earl grumbled. "Though, I must say, you've lost a bit of that reckless, wild look since you first waited upon me. Proof that attention to duty and sense of purpose make the man."

"Trying to stay alive in battle is not purpose enough?" Simon attempted to jest as the footmen began to serve from silver platters.

"Are you mocking me, boy?"

"Not at all. I would agree that purpose is bracing." Simon selected something drowned in cream sauce. "It does make me curious, though, Father. What has your purpose been all of these years?"

"My seat in the House of Lords!" the Earl blustered. "Expanding the empire and crushing any chance England could be poisoned by the revolution that shattered France. Destroying anyone who would overturn the God-ordained order of society or sully the Harcourt titles."

Simon looked at his father as if seeing him for the first time —a man who destroyed without thinking of the cost. What was it Penelope had once said? "All men would be tyrants if they could." He wasn't aware he'd said it aloud until he heard Lucien's quick intake of breath. His father banged down his silverware with a force that rattled the china.

"Tyrants? Keeping order, that is what my purpose is! I've devoted my life to it. Do you have any idea how many insurrections we have been forced to crush? Chartists, mobs. Two years ago, someone attempted to assassinate the queen! Rabble, jealous of our wealth and land and power."

"From what I can see, most are men and women simply wanting enough to keep body and soul together, a roof over the children's heads, full bellies—"

"Their children's bellies are their concern, not mine. Let them make their own way! My duty is to the Crown, to the empire, to myself!" Selfishness and contempt hardened the lines in his features, reflecting generations of greed.

Simon pictured the windswept, exotic lands he'd ridden across as a cavalry officer, taking whatever resources the native people had to give, scooping more and more into the treasuries of men like the Earl of Ravenscroft. To fund elaborate entertainments, mountains of delicacies, rich fabrics, diamonds and precious stones to adorn throats and ears and fingers. No wonder they had hated him.

The great Earl of Ravenscroft would not even have seen Tripp Raffy during market day, nor cared that the boy's mother and sisters might be dying by the side of the road somewhere between here and Scotland. But then, the Earl had sent his own daughters away without the slightest qualm, hadn't he? Flesh and blood children were far more troublesome than gold a man could lock in a vault.

How had his mother ever come to marry such a man, Simon wondered. Had she ever loved him? He remembered the bits of stories Pen had told him, the memories Daw had awakened. He could see his mother easing a shawl around Daw's grandfather's shoulders. See her racing about after the horrible storm that had torn through the county, aiding those who were injured, comforting those grieving the villagers who had died. How much cold had she suffered—in her body and heart—bound to this man who had held complete power over her?

Simon had joined the army, ridden away. What could a wife do?

His father took a drink, then pointed a finger at Simon. "It's time to apply yourself now you are home."

***

DAMNED IF SIMON COULD SLEEP. HE KICKED OFF THE COVERLET and thrust himself upright, crossing to the chair over which he'd draped his banyan, bitterly surveying this room that had been designated as 'his.' *Now you are home...* His father's words reverberated through him. *No,* Simon thought bitterly. *This is not home. Nowhere has felt like home since the night Mother left Everdene.* He'd felt like an inconvenient guest any time he'd visited his father or brother, their rigidness bringing out the worst in him, leaving him rash and raw and reckless.

Oh, for the days of buttering the banister to slide down more swiftly, of putting ink into people's tea and slipping mice into his father's desk drawer. Their tutor had tried to beat the mischief out of him, but there hadn't been a switch sturdy enough. When their tutor had loaded them into a coach bound for Eton, the man had been drunk with relief.

Perhaps he should get drunk himself, Simon mused, remembering the decanter of port in the library.

He took a candlestick and walked through the night-silent house intending to numb his memories. Yet before he could lift the cut-glass stopper and pour himself some blessed relief, Penelope Waverly's face rose in his mind, a reminder that he needed all his wits about him if he was to manage his father and brother.

He closed his eyes, trying to bring forth the scent of her hair, the tenderness in the curve of her mouth, the earnestness in her green eyes as she cupped his face in her hand.

Tenderness. Understanding. A heart that ached for a little urchin. Thunder rumbled in the distance, and he remembered another time he'd witnessed empathy much the same. Wisps from his own past winding through his fingers like silk.

His mother, the night of the storm, creeping into the nursery long after midnight, her hair clinging damply to her chalky face, the window flickering as lightning streaked the sky. A single candle wavered in her hand as she bent over her own children, one by one. First Cassandra and Jane, then Lucien and Simon. Simon had seen her through sleep-dazed eyes, heard her voice —whisper-soft, thick with tears.

*So many were hurt. It could have been any one of them...*

Nurse Betsy had stolen up to her, slipping an arm around his mother's waist. *They're all safe and sound, my lady. Would God that you were...*

Why had he only now remembered that? What had his mother feared?

Drawn by that slender thread from the past, he made his way to the far wing of the hall and mounted the stairs he was certain no one had trodden on for years. Halfway up, he paused to spill candlelight over the mahogany rail, seeing the place where he'd carved names with a penknife. He ran his fingertips over the awkward letters. Lucien. Simon. Cassandra. Jane. Then the last name... Mother...

It was as if he'd been trying to carve them into his memory. Into his heart.

He walked into the deserted schoolroom where he'd faced the fact that his mother and sisters were never coming back. The table where he'd sat with Lucien was still there. The ink wells were dry, the slates clean, the books stacked neatly. The map of the world still hung on the wall, its edges brittle now, and curled.

He remembered the day he and Lucien first entered this room, a month after his mother disappeared and his sisters were sent away. Nurse Betsy had been replaced by a harsh tutor, ordered to mold the Earl's sons into men unpolluted by women's weakness. The whole manor had seethed with upheaval, his father ordering that every sign of his countess be wiped from the house. Simon crept down to see the pile servants were making of anything that had to do with his mother. The oil portrait of the whole family had been cut from the frame. Mountains of clothes his mother had worn. Her embroidery hoop with its half-finished spray of roses. Even the porcelain horse Simon had given her on that last Christmas lay on the marble floor, it's tail broken.

*We're to put it in the fire,* Simon heard a maid say. *Sinful, it is to burn such as people could wear!*

He'd waited until the servants' backs were turned, then darted out, snatching two objects from the pile. Heart hammering, he'd dashed to the nursery where he'd found loose bricks in the fireplace. He pulled the rough blocks away, thrusting his treasure behind them, determined to retrieve them one day. But then, the bitterness had begun to settle in...

Simon went to the place where the mortar had loosened, wedged his fingers between the brick's rough edges. Gently, he wiggled the block free, the nook it revealed lost in shadow. Setting the brick aside, he held the candle closer to the opening, frail tendrils of light penetrating the darkness.

Carefully, he drew out a chipped porcelain horse. He ran his thumb over the slick, cool nose, then reached into the nook again to pull out a gilt frame the size of his palm.

He peered down at it, so lost in the image of his mother that he didn't hear footsteps until the door creaked open. Yet, he wasn't surprised. Lucien had always had the devil's own knack for knowing when Simon was wandering, restless, especially after their mother and sisters had vanished. A candle illuminated the harsh planes of his brother's face, the banyan he'd drawn over his nightshirt. The candle he held…

"Don't you ever just sleep?" Simon asked with a frown. "You look like the very devil."

"I thought I heard a noise."

"Perhaps you should get a job as the night watch. I came to retrieve something I hid away long ago." He could almost hear Penelope's voice, stitching those tattered memories of his mother back together.

His brother crossed to him, looked down at the miniature. Simon could sense the tension in Lucien wrenching tighter. He said nothing.

"Do you ever think of her?" Simon asked softly.

He saw Lucien wince. "No. It's hard enough to deal with the present. We both agreed on that."

They had, after too many nights of grief that tore at Simon, too many battles with their father as heartsick boys demanding to know where Mama had gone. Simon, running away, determined to find her. Lucien had been the one who found him.

*She left us, Simon! You can't run away, too!*

He'd never seen his brother so shattered before, or since…

"When I was in the village, with Penelope… Miss Waverly… I was stunned that she still remembers Mother after all of these years When she spoke... I remembered Mother, too. Not how she left and that emptiness after, but the way things were before."

"That was all a lie, though, wasn't it?" Lucien's lips thinned. "She left us. That's all you need to know."

Ignoring him, Simon said, "Penelope made me think. Wonder. Our mother cared so much about the villagers when they were sick. The people hurt in the storm..." Simon's voice trailed off. "I still don't know what happened that night. I was half asleep when someone shoved you in the nursery door and locked it. Tell me what you saw."

Lucien's jaw knotted. "I don't remember."

"Do you ever think of finding her? Asking why she left?"

"Bloody hell, no! I wouldn't even know where to start. She's dead for all we know. Better for us if she were."

The words cut deep. Had Simon felt the same way long ago? No. No matter how hurt he'd been, no matter how lost, he couldn't bear the thought of a world without his mother in it.

"Leave this alone, Simon," Lucien rasped. "For God's sake... leave it alone."

"I need to know what happened that night. You saw something. And you do remember. I can see it in your face."

"They were arguing. Mother and Father. He caught her sneaking out with a valise in her hand. After that, she disappeared because she wanted to, and never looked back. Why would you want to rake it up after so many years? She's not worth it. What's done is done." Lucien's face contorted. "Your hurt was so raw for so long. You've barely started healing from what happened in Afghanistan. Just... leave it the hell alone and I'll let you build the village wherever the hell you want. I'll sign your damned letter."

For a long moment their gazes locked. Simon wanted to push for more information. His hand tightened on the miniature until the frame cut into his palm.

Lucien looked as if he were about to say more, finally tell what truly had transpired that awful night. Suddenly, Simon heard Penelope's plea echo through him. *Jamie is dead... Daw and his family are alive...*

What mattered was building the village where people could live a decent life. Not have to bury their children. It's what his mother would have wanted as well.

"Tell Inchwick you approve relocating the village. That I have your blessing to do whatever I choose."

"I will. If you give me your word you'll quit poking around in the past. Live in the here and now." Lucien thrust out his hand, part challenge, part gentleman's agreement. "Your word," he repeated grimly.

Simon pictured Tripp Raffy. Daw. And Penelope, believing in him... helping him to remember the mother who'd laughed and embraced him and loved him.

He nodded, then shook Lucien's hand.

---

LUCIEN SAT AT THE WELL-ORDERED DESK IN HIS BEDCHAMBER, HIS head throbbing as he dipped his quill in ink and signed his name to the letter Simon required. There it was, license to give Simon the power he requested—to relocate the village, and very possibly destroy any chance Lucien's reckless brother had of inheriting the funds to build his stable.

Simon had always been stubbornly independent, defying their father and refusing to take the easier path. But this refusal to obey the Earl's edict could affect the rest of Simon's life.

Was agreeing to his brother's request even now making a horrible mistake? Lucien wondered as he glanced at his signet ring, the lion rampant, the Latin words in a curled banner. *Dum vigilo tutus.* While I am vigilant, I am safe...

He had been vigilant for so long, feeding Simon's anger

toward their mother, like adding tinder to a fire. And now he wondered if he had made a mistake in bringing Simon to Everdene. Lucien should have guessed that returning to the home they'd abandoned decades ago might stir up questions about their mother. But was his purpose to shield Simon from the pain? Or himself from what he'd done...

Sweat prickled Lucien's brow, and he wiped it away with the back of his hand.

*You do remember... I can see it in your face...*

By God, yes. Every moment was seared into his mind.

But it would be all right now, Lucien reassured himself. Simon had given his word that he wouldn't dig around in the past any longer—a past filled with razor-sharp edges and consequences that would never let Lucien go. He melted a stick of sealing wax over a flame, cursing that Waverly woman for opening doors from their pasts that should have remained nailed shut.

What spell had she cast over his brother, breaking down the barriers Lucien and Simon had built around such unspeakable loss? She had no idea the devastation that lay on the other side, he thought as he spilled the blood-red liquid beside his signature, then pressed his seal into the wax.

# CHAPTER 18

*P*enelope had rarely passed days so long. From the moment Simon had ridden away, she'd found herself on edge. Simon had left the ledgers in her hands for safekeeping, and she'd spent hour after hour squinting at the columns of numbers, trying to unlock the secrets therein. When eye strain brought on a pulsing headache, she had closed the books and hidden them away, taking a walk with Fanny to buy thread to match a gown she was remaking for herself. Once her current dresses had been turned and mended, Pen knew she would need something to replace the two beyond saving. One had a stain where young Roger Tremayne had upset his inkwell all down her front. The second, she had ruined herself. She'd been so engrossed in an architectural tract that she'd stood too close to the fire and scorched the back of her skirt.

It was a relief to get out into the fresh air, driving the gig to the linen drapers. But once they went into the shop, Pen's temples ached again. She cast a wistful glance at a length of forget-me-not blue and one in that elusive green that misted tree limbs when leaves budded out in spring. Then she marched resolutely to examine a serviceable brown that wouldn't show grimy hand prints or smudges of charcoal dust from drawing lessons. A gown she would have made up in such severe lines that it would not attract undue attention from the gentlemen of the house.

"Don't you ever wish for something pretty?" Fanny asked, regarding the brown fabric unhappily. "This green would quite match your eyes."

There had been a time Penelope had been able to choose colors that pleased her and took pretty gowns for granted. But never again. A spinster governess dared not draw the attention of powerful men who could cause her harm.

She'd made peace with that fact, and yet, the idea of Simon seeing her in this beautiful gown made her sigh. She smiled at her artistic sister. Fanny's longing caused a pang in Pen's heart as she imagined the graceful lines and delicate colors Fanny captured with her paintbrush.

When Maria Rendell fluttered in amidst a cluster of friends, Fanny begged to run off with them. Pen was grateful for the respite. She purchased the thread, then stopped at the post office. After retrieving a parcel and packet of letters, she tucked them in her shopping basket and went to sit on a bench an obliging merchant had set up under the shade of an elm.

She opened the parcel, delighted to find three books her beloved schoolteacher, Miss Firth, had sent her, but no news of potential employment. Next, she turned to her letters, recognizing Hannah Tremayne's childlike penmanship. Smiling, she opened it and read.

*Dear Miss Waverly,*

*We had to come home from Italy because Mama did not care for all of the foreigners about. She is very vexatious. YOU would never be vexatious when there were so many interesting things to see.*

Penelope chuckled at her former charge's innocent complaint until she read the next sentence.

*Papa says so, too...*

Pen did hope her former employer had not made this comment within his wife's hearing.

*He says we must be patient until Mama feels quite well again.*

Suddenly, Pen's gaze caught on a familiar, masculine script at the bottom of the page.

*Miss Waverly. I stumbled across Hannah in the midst of her letter, and could not resist adding this postscript. The exquisite Italianate buildings we saw on our recent trip to the Continent made me think of you. I know you would have been as thrilled as I to see St. Peter's Basilica and the Biblioteca Maricanna. Truly breathtaking works of art. Hannah chattered on and on wondering 'what Miss Waverly would think,' and I confess that I could not help wondering as well. I quite miss our talks in the library once the children were abed...*

*Your friend,*

*Richard Tremayne*

A flutter of discomfort rose in her chest as she remembered those talks now. Of course, Mr. Tremayne had done nothing ungentlemanly, yet there had been more admiration in his eyes than was prudent.

She was still staring down at the letter when she heard hoof-beats nearing. She glanced up to see an exquisite golden horse, and Simon grinning down at her.

"You're back!" she cried, her heart leaping as she folded up her letter and thrust it into a book.

He swung down, looping Caspian's reins around a low hanging branch. "I was checking on a lumber order, then planned to come looking for you." He reached into his coat pocket and drew out a piece of foolscap. He handed it to her.

Penelope read swiftly, her hand smoothing over the wax seal with the crest imprinted on it. "You did it!" she exclaimed. "I admit to spending most of the time you've been gone trying to convince myself it was even possible. How did you ever get your brother and father to agree?"

"Agree may be an overstatement," Simon said with a

mischievous glint in his eyes. "I didn't consult my father, and my brother doesn't know about the improved cottages we're building. My hope is that by the time they discover the truth, it will be too late to change course."

"Your brother just... just gave you the letter?" Pen asked, incredulous.

"My brother and I struck a gentleman's agreement. I can build at Havelock Meadow as long as I let the past lie."

Penelope frowned. "What does the past have to do with this?"

He looked a little sheepish. "My brother caught me in our old school room in the middle of the night. I couldn't sleep, you see. I got to thinking about a place I'd found there when I was a boy. A little nook where I'd hide treasures. I hadn't thought of it for years. I might never have, were it not for you."

"I still don't understand."

He pulled off his riding gloves and set them aside, then drew something from his waistcoat pocket. He laid the oval object in Penelope's hand. His fingers lingered on hers for a long moment, his hand rein-callused and warm. When he drew away, she saw a gilt-framed miniature.

Her heart twisted as she stared down at the face that had seemed like that of a guardian angel after the horror of the lightning strike. Instantly, she could see herself lying crushed beneath branches, feeling as if she were going to die.

Golden hair curled around a face, fine-drawn as cameos in a jeweler's window, Lady Ravenscroft's mouth too tender, painted a rosebud pink. Her eyes peered shyly out at the world beyond the schoolroom with an innocence that wrenched at Penelope's heart.

"She can't be much older than my sister Kitty in this," Penelope breathed. Kitty, who still believed the maiden was always rescued and the dragon always slain, and glittering happiness would be hers for the taking. One day, she would learn the hard truth.

"She looks very much like my sister Cassandra did the last time I saw her," Simon said.

"I remember your sisters. They used to deck their ponies' manes with ribbons. When they drove that lovely wicker cart, they looked like princesses to Kitty and Fanny."

"And to you?"

"I was only wanting to take the ponies for a run, and wondering how the poor things could bear all of those streamers flapping around their heads."

Simon chuckled. "I felt the same. I used to sneak them out, just to stretch their legs. Once, just before my sisters were about to drive them to a friend's birthday party, I took the ponies for a run, and got them so full of mud my mother made me scrub them down until they shone. And then she forced me to give all of those giggling girls rides in the cart the whole afternoon."

"Undoubtedly, a dreadful blow to your boyish dignity."

"It was. But when the day was over, Mother called me up to the Sky Chamber… her favorite room, and shared a whole plate of pink cakes she'd saved for me." He stopped, giving Penelope a rueful smile. "There you go again. Making me remember things. You'll have to stop that now. I made a gentleman's agreement with my brother that I would stop delving into what happened to her. In exchange, he would write the letter I requested, giving me full power to do what I wish here at Everdene."

Penelope frowned, troubled. Building the village at Havelock Meadow was far more important than an event that had happened long ago, and yet, why would quelling Simon's curiosity about their mother be so important to the Viscount? She studied the painted image, the vulnerability of Lenora Harcourt's eyes tugging at Pen's conscience.

Simon nodded out to the countryside. "I intend to turn all of my energies to building this village as quickly as possible.

Beginning with the vastly unpleasant task of breaking the news to the people of Everdene that they will be losing their homes."

"I don't envy you." Penelope returned the miniature to him. "Though their situation will be improved in the long run, I expect they'll be angry at first."

"Considering Daw Garvey's reaction, I'm sure you're right," Simon said, slipping the miniature into his pocket. "I thought I would summon them all to a meeting at the assembly hall."

"Yes. Best the news comes from you, and the sooner the better. If they believe you've been hiding things from them, they'll wonder what else you might be concealing."

"I'll have notices posted that there will be a village meeting tomorrow, and that someone from each household must attend." Simon rubbed the back of his neck. "Now I just have to figure out what I'm going to say."

"I'd like to be at the meeting once you do."

His gaze warmed. "Would you?"

She fretted with the string that had tied up her parcel. "I – I know this course isn't without personal cost to you. You're risking a great deal."

Something flickered in his eyes, a wry expression that made her wonder. The corner of his mouth ticked up. "When you look at me like that, I count the risk worth it."

She wanted to dismiss it as teasing, mere flirtation, but he sobered, their gazes holding. He cupped his palm over her cheek. And then he dragged the pad of his thumb over her lower lip, pulling gently at the plump curve. Warmth pooled between her thighs.

"The project is far from out of danger," he said, unaware of the effect his touch had on her. He lowered his hand, his gaze distant. "If my father discovers what we're doing before we are past the point of no return, he would put an end to it once and for all. I'm going to fling myself into the work like a fury. I'm not sure how I'll be able to manage the site, and comb through the ledgers as I need to, once the building is underway." He grimaced. "I'll manage. I'll have to."

"It's definitely most important to break ground on the cottages," Pen agreed. "I've been going through the ledgers while you were gone. I could continue to do so, if you like. I could list whatever I find suspicious, and you could examine those sections."

"Would you?" He looked almost boyish in his enthusiasm. "Once the sun goes down on the building site, I could stop by to see what progress you've made. I've asked Daw for a list of supply costs, and we can check with those contractors to see if the amounts match. Unless they are in on whatever scheme Inchwick is about. It will be intensive work. Tedious."

"More tedious than teaching fidgety children their times-tables when it's been raining for a week and they're trapped inside?"

That won a grin from him. "As a former fidgety child, my sympathies lie with the enemy on that one, Pen."

"I've some experience with snarls in bookkeeping," she said. "My father's business affairs were a nightmare when he died. I was so angry when I opened the books and saw the insane schemes he'd been investing in, but I hoped I might still be able to turn things around." Her voice trailed off, bitterness curling her lips. "I'm only telling you this so you know I am capable…"

"I never doubted it. Nor can I think of anyone I'd rather cast my lot in with than you."

"I feel as if… as if there is more. Something to do with your brother that you're not telling me."

"Ah. Doubtless that instinct you gained as a governess, from uncovering secrets. It's nothing that should concern you. I will pay you for your time laboring over the ledgers."

"No! I couldn't possibly take—"

"I insist. Your family is obviously facing some financial hardship. You hardly became a governess for the pleasure of it. The estate can easily afford the expense."

"Simon—"

He laid a finger upon her lips.

She grasped his wrist, the sinewy surface lightly dusted with coarse dark hair. She meant to pull his hand away, reminded of years of her parents silencing her. But when he spoke so earnestly, the timbre of the exchange altered. "Please let me, Pen. We are already in your debt."

Was it the earnestness in his eyes that made her hand feel so heavy, pulling his arm down. His fingertips skimmed her chin, trailed down her throat, ghosted featherlight across the swell of her breast before she released him.

"Pen?" Fanny's sudden cry made the pair draw apart. "I was looking all over for—oh, Captain Harcourt!"

Penelope saw her sister's face light up with curiosity.

"Good afternoon, Miss Fanny. I was just saying goodbye to your sister," he said gallantly, tipping his hat, then turned back to Pen. "Until tomorrow," he said softly. His eyes held Pen's for a long, heated moment, then he swung astride Caspian and cantered away.

# CHAPTER 19

The assembly hall was stifling, packed with villagers murmuring nervously among themselves, casting wary glances up toward the front of the room where Simon now stood. Like horses just before a storm, they were restive, as if they could sense danger carried on the wind, sensing imminent destruction.

In that sea of faces, there was one his gaze sought out, a slim woman who sat with quiet dignity, her posture perfect, her bonnet tied beneath her chin. He longed to ask her to remove the headgear so that he could see the whole of her face, and none of the quicksilver expressions were lost to him.

God, he didn't want to fail these people. He didn't want to fail *her*.

He checked his pocket watch, braced himself, and stepped onto the dais. A hush fell over the room.

"Thank you for taking time out of your day. As many of you are aware, building supplies have been delivered to the area near Blagden Valley for some mysterious construction. One I have been given charge of. As you know, my father, the Earl, was lately injured and brought to begin his recovery here at Everdene. Before he moved to a more favored estate at Bitterne Tower, he decided to make sweeping changes on Everdene."

Faces paled. The crowd went very still. Simon could feel the sudden pulse of fear.

"What kind o' changes?" the blacksmith shouted, bolder than the rest.

"He wishes to move the location of Everdene Village."

A roar went up from those gathered, and Simon could see the gamut of emotions, confusion, grief, downright anger. The cacophony of responses deafened him, people leaping to their feet, shaking fists.

"Move? That's impossible! He can't--"

"He can and he will!" Simon boomed. "He has that right, under law."

"Law!" a cooper named Okum Landry yelled in outrage. "You nobs have been choking the life out of us for years!" he said, pulling the strip of leather he wore around his neck up to mimic a noose, a bit of metal flashing at the thong's end. "Time to take things into our own hands! I'm not the only one thinks honest workers have been taken advantage of long enough!"

"I agree with you, Okum," Simon said. "That is why I'm here today. How many of you have been to Havelock Meadows?" From the grudging shouts and nodding heads, Simon knew Daw's wasn't the only family who had picnicked there. "Have some of you seen the surveyors there?"

"Been surveyors at Blagden as well."

"At Havelock Meadows they're laying out new streets, sites for buildings, cottages with more room for your families. You'll have better drainage, more modern conveniences."

"Why would the Harcourts do that?" the innkeeper demanded. "Haven't hardly spit in the direction of Everdene in years. Now you want to tear everything down? Why should we trust you?"

Jesus, why should they? Simon thought. There were times he didn't trust himself.

The roar grew louder, and he thought of what Inchwick had warned against, manor houses burned to the ground by infuriated tenants.

Okum grabbed Tripp by the arm. "See this boy? Look what happened to the Raffys! Threw 'em right out into the streets, didn't they, boy? You tell 'em."

"Captain Harcourt knows what happened to me ma and da," Tripp shouted, as far as his high-pitched voice could carry. Tripp yanked free. In a shot, the boy squeezed through impossibly small spaces, his straw-colored hair visible in flashes as he darted through the crowd. Suddenly he popped up and pressed himself against Simon's leg. "The Cap'n knows," Tripp repeated, glaring fiercely at the villagers. "He was right there with Miss Waverly when they took me in to the Garveys. Got me a full belly. Kindness. An' he didn't just walk away since. Been to check up on how I fared. Even got me a new toolbox an' told me each time I master using a tool, he'd have the blacksmith make me one for my own."

Penelope's mouth opened on a gasp.

"No need to tell about that," Simon said. "It's nothing to do with these people."

The boy looked up at him with a hero worship that made Simon's chest knot. "But it is, sir!" Tripp insisted. "Shows just how different you are from that ol' miser, the Earl."

"Tripp!" Daw Garvey's voice cut through the hubbub as he shouldered his way toward the boy. "You mustn't speak that way about the Earl."

"Well, 'e is a miser, isn't he, an' everyone here knows it. But Captain Harcourt isn't."

Daw reached the dais, climbed up as Tripp continued. "Captain Harcourt's a man o' his word. Cares about the folk here. Ye say so yerself t' Mrs. Garvey."

The murmur grew, here and there someone in the crowd looked bemused.

Daw's strong, work-rough fingers curled around Tripp's narrow shoulder. The big man looked out at his neighbors. "I was as angry as any of you are feeling when I first heard of this plan."

"You knew about this and stayed silent?" Okum roared. "Why should we listen to you? You're as bad as the Harcourts!"

Simon stepped forward, angling his body in front of Daw, hating the danger he'd put his friend in. "You have valid complaints against my family, fine," Simon challenged. "Leave Daw out of it."

"Put himself in it, he did—" Okum accused, but others in the crowd seemed torn. For years, Daw had been the one they turned to when they needed to shore up whatever was falling down. Barns. Roofs. Tables and chairs. They depended on the big, gentle wood smith, trusted him in a way that humbled Simon.

Daw's voice carried through the hall, deep and sure and calming. "Captain Harcourt came to me with architectural schemes. Showed me what he hopes to build. He asked me where we should build—"

"In hell! How about we send all the Harcourts to build in hell —and you with them, Garvey!" Okum spat. "Siding with the bloodsucking landlords."

Suddenly there was a ripple through the crowd, and a clear, strong feminine voice cut through. "Okum Landry, how can you offer any informed opinion at all?"

Simon stared, aghast. Penelope had climbed up on a chair and towered above the crowd, her bonnet shoved back until it dangled down her back by its ribbons.

"You haven't even seen the plans for the cottage, nor where it is to be built," she challenged. "You have no notion how hard Captain Harcourt has worked for all of you." She looked like one of the furies from Greek myths, her green eyes snapping fire. "Who among you wouldn't like to have a bedchamber of your own, where you and your husband or wife can go to rest without climbing over a half-dozen children? Can you imagine what a respite that would be after your work is done?"

"And where would the children sleep? Out in the barn?"

Pen turned toward the woman who had asked. "Your sons would be in one room, your daughters in the other. You'd have a kitchen separate from the keeping room. Far better drainage. Clean water…"

Simon couldn't see the village woman's reaction, but from the glow on Penelope's face, he guessed she'd made an impression. "Yes," Penelope said. "The Earl gave an order that hurt every one of you. But I promise you, Captain Harcourt means to make this the best thing that ever happened to you."

"How many families are you going to turn out?" a man with a farmer's deep tan and weathered face demanded.

"None, if I have my way," Simon vowed. "But I can't do this alone. If I'm going to carry this project off, I will need your help." People canted their heads, suspicious. Simon could almost hear their thoughts—what does a nob like you need our help for, when you're already bleeding us for rent? "I know you have lives of your own, livings to make, children to raise, crops to tend. Most of you are working more hours than there seem to be in a day. I'm asking anyone who can squeeze out time to come to New Everdene and help us build a village we can all be proud of."

Some of the men started to shove toward the door, led by Okum Landry, every line in their bodies hostile, bitter. Okum held up the metal disk dangling from the strip of leather and shook it. "I'll bet my China coin that he'll make a fool of the lot of you!" Okum snarled.

Simon glimpsed a stooped figure making her way toward the dais, Widow Bevans limping painfully, leaning on her cane.

Garbed in black, she looked like a plump crow, her face that of a dried apple doll, wrinkled and misshapen by age, her bright button eyes gleaming. Tripp rushed over to take the old woman's arm. Daw extended his hand as well, steadying the widow as she joined him on the dais. She sent her neighbors the kind of stern, yet loving glance that came from knowing most of them since they were still in leading strings.

"We can trust him," Widow Bevans insisted. "Take him at his word. He's our dear lady's boy to the marrow o' his bones."

She raised a gnarled hand and laid it on Simon's cheek. "Like your sainted mother you are, Captain Harcourt," she said softly, her eyes misty. "I know you'll see this through."

Simon was taken aback at the tenderness toward his mother. One more echo reminding him of the woman who had disappeared, the woman whose kindnesses had not been forgotten.

"I'd sooner trust Daw and the widow than Okum any day!" someone shouted.

"And Raffy's boy," the farmer called. "No one has more cause to hate the Harcourts than the lad does. If Tripp can trust him, we can give the Captain a chance."

"Miss Waverly, are there truly three bedchambers?" a rather harried-looking mother asked, shifting the fussy infant on her shoulder.

"Yes," Penelope said. "And the prettiest prospect looking out over the meadow…"

A girl of about fifteen gazed up at Pen with admiration. "It almost sounds like you drew the cottage plans up yourself."

"She did," Daw affirmed. "I looked them over, and the plans are sound as one o' Captain Harcourt's fancy horses. I'll stand under the roof myself and dare it to fall!"

Simon's chest squeezed with gratitude, as he looked from Penelope to Daw and Tripp to Widow Bevans. He remembered this feeling… the feeling he had when he'd ridden along the line of raw recruits before leading them into their first battle. Felt their loyalty, their resolve, his own need to protect them. He hadn't felt such a bond since Jalalabad, a sense of purpose even realizing the dream of his stables could not give him. This was a cause to fight for. But he wouldn't be tearing things apart this time. This time he would be building something that mattered. No matter what it cost him, he would see it through.

"This afternoon, we'll be out at the building site. Anyone who cares to take a look at what we're going to do, come join us. I'll lay out the plans drawn on paper for you so you can see them for yourselves. I'll pay good wages to those willing to work."

But he couldn't help but wonder what Okum and his cohorts would do. It wasn't just Inchwick and the Earl Simon would have to concern himself with now.

The villagers began to shift toward the door, their conversation a buzz of half-understood words. He couldn't tell for certain if he'd moved them, convinced them, but they'd soon find out. A hand thumped his shoulder. "You did well," Daw said, the carpenter's honest face solemn with approval.

But had he done well enough?

The villagers were gone, except for Daw and Tripp, Penelope lingering as well. Sometime during the furor of people leaving, she had climbed down off of the chair. He could almost see her heart pounding with excitement beneath the prim, burgundy-hued gown she wore. Her eyes gleamed, sunlight streaming through the window onto the soft curves of her face. Simon longed to gather her in his arms, share things he could never put into words.

Instead, he cleared his throat. "Miss Waverly, may I see you a moment? I have some questions about the plans."

"Of course," she said, her business-like tone belied by a sudden spark of eagerness she hid behind lowered lashes.

Daw glanced between them, then looped his arm around Tripp's narrow shoulder. "We'd best head out to the construction site and get things organized, lad. I have a feeling we'll have several crews of workers to keep busy when morning comes."

"Time will tell," Simon said, unwilling to hope too much.

"Oh, they'll come, Captain," Daw called back as he urged Tripp toward the door. "They'll come."

The room seemed incredibly large and empty now that Simon and Pen were alone. Their footsteps echoed in the silence as he drew her behind a small screen, hiding them from any curious eyes that might glance through the windows. The minute they were alone, Pen spun to face him.

"Did you see the expressions on their faces?" she said, beaming up at him. "You were wonderful!" The pride in her gaze sent sparks of awareness through him, feeding something inside him that had seemed lost for too long.

He clasped her hands, his throat suddenly tight. "Having you there made all of the difference. Thank you for speaking on my behalf. I swear that you and Tripp and Daw and Widow Bevans turned the tide."

"We all know the kind of man you are. We believe in you."

His heart thudded in his chest. Oh, God. What if he failed them?

"I'm so grateful you came back to Everdene," she began, then suddenly seemed to notice the change in his expression. "What is it?" she asked, pressing her hand against his chest.

"I don't know what would have happened if you and the others hadn't supported me."

"You would have found a way to make them listen," she said with such certainty it startled him. "They will follow you, Simon. We would have followed you anywhere, you know. And now, looking out across that crowd, I can tell you that most of them would, too."

"Do you have any idea how beautiful you were? Standing up on that chair, speaking out."

Two sweeps of color pinkened her cheeks.

She leaned toward him, lips parting.

"Ah, Pen…" he whispered, "you take my breath away."

He curved his hand around her nape, his mouth seeking hers. He wanted her, more than he'd ever wanted any woman. Wanted her naked in his bed, challenging him, demanding everything he could give. Their tongues touched, and he gave a low growl in his throat.

Someone shouted outside, and he drew away, his gaze searching to be sure she was shielded from view. He smiled inwardly, thinking of her reaction if he'd told her he was protecting her… "You could have been Boudicca, leading a Celtic army against the Romans. Or Athena on horseback. I wish I'd had a dozen like you in my regiment."

The mischief in that curve of her kiss-reddened lips struck straight to his heart. "I probably would have been court-martialed for telling you that you were doing something wrong."

He could feel some barrier cracking inside him. He caressed her cheek, speaking softly. "Ah, but this time, I would have listened."

# CHAPTER 20

The meadow was a hive of activity as Pen guided the gig along the dirt path. A half-dozen sweating men were busy grading the surface, a mountain of gravel that had been delivered waiting to be spread upon the newly leveled road. The main street of New Everdene.

She marveled at how many villagers had joined the effort to raise the new buildings. Despite Mr. Inchwick's constant litany of warnings and complaints, the process was moving forward with a haste that stunned her. Simon and Daw had gone to a hiring fair as well, bringing in workmen from all around. It was as if the two men had made a bargain with the fairy folk, for work continued late by torch and lantern light, and it was always a surprise, come morning, how much they'd gotten done. The sight of their wives bringing hampers with food warmed Penelope's heart. The women bustled about, spreading blankets out on the grass to observe their menfolk's progress on houses they would one day inhabit. Their children frolicked around the meadow, exploring their new surroundings.

Penelope loved listening to them chatter about what they'd

do once the cottages were finished, some of them stitching curtains for windows that weren't yet framed in.

Simon was part of it all. He'd worked beside them with a vigor and good humor that made him far more attractive than any cavalry uniform could, his laughter ringing out, bringing with it the memories of that shared kiss, leaving her wanting...

Perhaps it was fortunate that Pen's mother and sisters were hovering nearby when they were at Laurel Cottage. Their presence also had the effect of counteracting Inchwick's sour attitude toward Simon's success. In fact, she and Simon had little time to focus on anything but the plans, the construction site, and the ledgers during the past two weeks. And still, she couldn't dispel the lingering effects of that kiss, nor forget his husky voice whispering through her memory.

*You take my breath away...*

She put it from her mind, focusing on Simon perched atop the skeleton of a half-finished roof, securing one of the rafters in place. He balanced precariously as he wielded a hammer, like the boy who'd once climbed trees. Flushed with exertion and the unseasonable warmth, Simon and some of the other men had stripped off their coats. Simon's sleeves were rolled up to bare forearms sprinkled with dark hair, his shirt collar open, the skin gleaming. He saw Pen watching him, a grin spreading across his handsome face before he turned back to the task at hand. Once the rafter was nailed in position, he swung down to greet her, a puff of dust rising from around his scuffed boots as they struck the ground.

"You look very pleased with yourself, Captain Harcourt," Pen said as she alighted from the gig. A new energy pulsed through him, an irresistible force that reminded her of the powerful stallion he loved.

"I never could bear idleness," Simon replied with a smile that made her stomach flutter. "It feels good to be working again.

Come with me to the stream so I can wash up." They walked down to the water's edge, and he knelt, splashing his face and rubbing the moisture over his neck where the dark curls clung, in need of a trim. Without thinking, she slipped her fingers beneath the damp white linen collar and pulled it away so it wouldn't get wetter. Her knuckles grazed hot skin, his nape deceptively tender, sensual. For a moment, she thought of the others who might see, but she didn't care.

He stepped back, then shook his head like a wet dog, silvery droplets flying from the tips of his hair, the mussed, dark curls so enticing she couldn't resist reaching up to brush them back into some sort of order.

His eyes heated. "You're aware we're surrounded by prying eyes?"

She glanced around, momentarily worried, until she noticed that—thankfully—no one seemed to be paying them the least bit of attention. Even so, she stepped back, deciding it more prudent to change the subject. "I'd imagine you were always busy in the cavalry. Do you miss it?" she asked, then stopped, suddenly thinking of the friends he'd lost. "I'm sorry. That was insensitive of me."

His brow furrowed, and he stroked her knuckle, his back to the workers, shielding her from view. After a moment, he said, "I witnessed men at their most brutal. Did things myself that I will never forget. Or forgive. But I saw heroism that awed me as well." He took a deep breath, finally looking into her eyes. "The military gave me lessons I desperately needed. Discipline. Purpose. I'd always been wild, despite my mother's steadying hand. After she—" He looked away, his eyes turning cloudy. "After my father took my brother and me from Everdene, I became reckless. Once I donned my colors, I had something to fight for again. My men and I... we fought for each other."

"I'm sure you were a wonderful officer."

"That's debatable. I didn't care about promotion for ambition's sake. Only because it gave me more power to shield the men who served under me. And, God knew, battle was hell. I was raised on tales of Agincourt and Waterloo. The reality was far different."

"How so?"

His expression darkened, and she suspected that he was holding back much of what he witnessed. "Officers bought their commissions instead of earning promotions through merit, while men far more fit to lead were passed over and ignored. I saw the results in India—and became aware just how unjustly we treated the people who lived there. After we occupied Kabul, I knew in my gut that invading Afghanistan was a mistake."

She could only imagine the horrors he'd seen. "What changed your mind?"

"Jamie. He was the one who formed a bond with some of the Afghans. He understood them." Simon glanced toward the north. "Jamie was a Scotsman. He spoke about what it was like to have someone rip away your identity as a nation... your language, your heritage..."

Though she was no longer sure if they were talking about the Afghans or the Scots, she nodded. "I can understand why they would hate that."

"The bitterness still runs deep." Simon frowned as they strolled through a cluster of elm trees that grew near the bank. "I remember Jamie telling me that it's like someone had stripped the very blood from your veins. Those nights spent talking to him about what happened in Scotland helped me see England's thirst for conquest in a different light."

"Yet he was fighting for the English Army?"

"He was." Grief darkened Simon's eyes. "He died for it."

They walked in silence for a few moments as she mused on the changes in him, so impressed by the man she was coming to know. The rakehell soldier who'd first ridden up to Everdene and drowned his anger in spirits and carousing was nowhere to be seen.

"What do you think of our progress on the cottages?" he asked at last, then gave her a rather sardonic grin. "I do hope our efforts are up to your standards?"

"I'll admit to being *somewhat* satisfied," she teased back. She glanced toward the group of men and rubbed at a spot of ink on her sleeve. "I spoke to Daw about a few adjustments on Widow Bevans' place, and there were a handful of measurements we needed to correct. I'd like to have an architect inspect it in a month or so, just to be sure I've made no mistakes. I thought I might write to ask my former employer if he'd be willing."

"I've no objection if you think it best."

She smiled at his words. He was trusting her to make that choice. To know what should be done. She basked in his trust. "I'm astonished how quickly the village is taking shape," she said. "You really are a miracle worker."

"Hardly. Commanding workmen isn't so different from commanding soldiers."

"Inspiring them, more like. You work as hard as any man here. Then you come to Laurel Cottage and attack the estate finances."

"How is your project coming?" he asked.

That first week, she'd written until her fingers ached, making exact copies of the ledgers as he'd asked. They'd had to return the actual volumes to Inchwick, but once they did, Penelope had begun sifting through the figures.

"It's frustrating, but I'm making progress," she said. "On the surface, it seems it's just a question of comparing prices charged with those paid. It's tedious work for me. I can only imagine what it's like after a long day at the construction site. You probably want nothing more than to sit before the fire and sip brandy."

"I don't mind it." He laughed. "As for brandy, I'm quite clear-headed most nights. Either the quality of my father's cellars has deteriorated, or manual labor is spoiling my palate when it comes to spirits. About the ledgers… what are your thoughts?"

"I've been studying ways stewards might be dishonest," Pen said. "They might charge the estate more for materials than they actually pay. They might order more of a product than needed, then sell what is left over. Sometimes they might coerce suppliers."

Simon's brow raised in interest. "How would they do that?"

"By giving merchants the estate's business only if the supplier gives the steward goods that he can sell to line his own pockets. That particular method is more difficult to detect or to prosecute, since they never actually take money out of the Earl's pockets."

Simon nodded, and Pen watched a droplet trickle from his temple down to his square jaw. He absently swiped at it, his focus seeming far away. "Men did the same kind of profiteering in the army. The catch was that they had to store the excess somewhere until they could sell it. If Inchwick is doing something similar, he'd have to store his ill-gotten gains somewhere as well." He stopped, suddenly, looking over at her. "I wonder if any of the servants at the house would know. One of them might have noticed something. The cook, minding her larder or the butler or housekeeper aware of some irregularity."

Her brow furrowed.

"What is it?" Simon prodded.

"Is that necessary now? You've the letter saying you have *carte blanche*."

"Yes, but you can see as clearly as I do that Inchwick resents every minute of it. I won't be at ease until we have leverage over him. A cornered rat will bite."

"Would he really do something?"

"Without a doubt. Which means I'll need to be cautious with

anyone I question. Inchwick could threaten them into silence if he got wind that we were nosing about. And once I'm gone from the estate, anyone who cooperated with us would be at his mercy. The question is, whom do I approach first?"

"I'm quite certain that Ruby Smith is still working at the big house. I saw her younger sister the other day and she mentioned it. I would definitely ask Ruby. She's a clever girl, and loyal to a fault. Nothing untoward gets past her."

"Perfect. I'm confident that we'll have Inchwick boxed in soon."

THAT NIGHT, SIMON HAD RUBY SENT TO HIM. THE GIRL, WITH flame hair and freckles and wide-set, lashless eyes, looked confused and a trifle wary as she bobbed him a curtsey.

"Captain, sir. I heard ye called for me."

"As I understand it, you just came up from the village when the Earl was recovering."

"Aye, sir. 'Twas a great opportunity, working in a fine house. I was happy to have it." She clasped her trembling hands together, her gaze at her feet.

Trying to put her at ease, he said, "Miss Waverly tells me you're a very clever young woman and an honest one."

The young girl blushed, but still wouldn't look at him. "Miss Waverly's the clever one, sir. Taught me to read, said that way people couldn't fool me. I could judge matters for myself."

"Very wise. Which is why I've asked you here. Have you noticed anything strange going on?"

"About what, sir?" she asked, daring a glance, then quickly staring at the ground once more.

"Anything at all," he said, figuring it best to leave the question open.

Seconds ticked, before she started to finally raise her head. "Do you mean the label?"

"What label?"

Her gaze shot to the ground, and if anything, the knuckles of her clasped hands turned white. "I-I came upon Randall rushing up from the wine cellar. He was fiddling with the labels afore he served it to you. Dropped one and I picked it up to show me brother. I didn't mean anything by it," she said, tears springing to her eyes. "I just wanted to show him what sort of fancy drink a nob has with his dinner."

"Do you still have it?"

She shook her head. "But there's more. I didn't think anyone would miss the one. I found a whole pile o' them when I was dusting. Struck me as strange, it did. He was real furtive-like. Said the other labels were dirty, and not fit to serve to the Earl or his sons."

Simon's interest sharpened.

"They was in some foreign language, I think. But not the label I found. It was crumpled up and kinked. Don't recall the words, but they was in English."

That explained why the liquor from the Everdene cellar had been so utterly disappointing. Simon realized something must show in his face. The girl looked even more nervous.

"I don't mean to make any trouble, sir. I just notice things sometimes. Me pa says I need to keep my eyes lowered, modest like a girl should."

"You're in no trouble. You've been very helpful."

He drew a coin from his pocket and pressed it into the girl's chapped hand. "Say nothing to anyone about our conversation, do you understand? And if you happen to see another such label, bring it to me." The girl bobbed a curtsey, then darted from the room.

Simon thought of Randall, the footman he'd first encountered outside the door to the Sky Chamber the day he'd arrived at Everdene. He'd assumed the lad was chewing his fingernails to nubs because of the convalescing Earl's tyranny. Maybe the footman had more to be nervous about than the Earl's rages. He couldn't wait to tell Penelope what he'd discovered.

# CHAPTER 21

As Penelope drove the gig up to Laurel Cottage's stables, she found it hard to forget the picture Simon Harcourt had made at Havelock Meadow: the vee of his chest exposed by his open collar, the sinewy strength of his bared forearms, and the enthusiasm that lit his eyes when he walked through the building site. The left rear wheel wobbled, drawing her mind back to the present, even as her stomach fluttered with the memory. It was far easier to blame the jolting ride than attribute it to the cavalry captain with his disarming smile, never mind the way his sensual lips parted when his gaze found her mouth.

She drew rein and set the brake as Rupert Hughes came to greet her. The devoted old servant walked out of a stable that had once been filled with fine hunters and matched carriage horses, as well as Epona, the mare Penelope had tamed so long ago.

It was a strange, echoing place now, all the stalls empty except for the one that their patient old horse Dobby shared with barn cats and the occasional inquisitive mouse.

It felt strange, thinking how different Laurel Cottage once

was, the stables bustling, the house and garden neat, her father and his friends riding out to view the races.

She patted the horse's flank. "He was favoring his right hoof a bit," she said to Hughes. "He may have picked up a stone."

"Ah, well, he'll be able to rest a bit. Maria Rendell took your sisters to town. Miss Kitty just got back with the mail."

Penelope felt the muscles in her shoulders tense as they did whenever the mail arrived now. She knew full well she needed to accept a post if one was offered, but she didn't want to leave Everdene until the village was further along. Or was it that she didn't want to leave the man who was supervising the project, the man who asked her insights, sought out her opinions, and seemed to be watching for her whenever her gig rattled up to the hitching post in the shade of an elm.

She flushed, needing time to think, then glanced at the gig, grateful for such a mundane task to keep her thoughts from the Captain's roguish grin. "I fear the wheel needs looking after again. Perhaps a bit more grease. And Dobby might need a bit of liniment on his left fetlock."

The horse had practically fallen asleep by the time they got the traces unhitched.

"Good old girl," Hughes said, stroking the mare. "Made for work, not for pleasure."

Pen felt a jab of discomfort. Wasn't that what she had felt about herself for as long as she could remember? She was the plumbline destined to hold the walls of her family straight, her determination keeping the whole thing from tumbling down.

Only since Simon Harcourt had charged into her life had she felt... how to describe it? Free... to laugh, to let her true self show, that intelligence and insatiable curiosity that made most people pull away as if she carried the plague.

Traits that drew scorn, then alarm from men who strayed into her path.

She'd been able to argue with Simon, he'd not expected her

to water herself down, like wine, until only the faintest pink was visible instead of the rich color of her thoughts, her ambitions, her logic. As long as she could remember, she'd felt out of place. But with Simon… she could scarce wait to share ideas.

Suddenly, she wanted that spring green fabric to make a pretty dress. To wreath herself in something that pleased her, that would bring that feverish light to Simon Harcourt's eyes.

*You take my breath away…*

His words seem to ripple through her veins.

He'd left her aching, wanting… imagining what it would be like… to what? To see that magnificent body bared, the skin that had glistened in the vee of his damp shirt hers to touch.

What would he think if she ever unbuttoned the front of the placket? Explored the ridges of muscle. Explored *him*… with the curiosity that was all but driving her mad?

"Miss Penelope, are you well?" Hughes' gravelly voice shook her from her musings. "You're that flushed. Haven't got a fever?"

"N-No. I just got a bit too much… sun at the building site."

"Humph," Hughes said. "Perhaps you should take a parasol next time. It's a fine thing you're doing, helping with the building there. Why, I was talking to the folks at the store when I was in town last, and they're buzzing like bees in an apple orchard, they're so excited about the prospect of moving. Made me laugh to hear 'em complaining about the drainage last time it rained. Been enduring it for generations, but now it's unbearable. And Captain Harcourt working as hard as any of 'em. They're that stunned and glad of it. He's as fine a gentleman as ever walked these lands, is Captain Harcourt. Nice to have him coming around to Laurel Cottage."

"I must say, he seems to have a positive effect on anyone around him."

"He'd make a fine match for you, he would, the way you both have with horses…"

Penelope's cheeks grew even hotter. "It's not—not like that."

But was it? In a way that had nothing to do with forever after and wedding rings? She'd vowed never to marry. That remained unchanged. Yet, considering that, would it be so wicked to take one sip of what others took for granted? To explore the mysteries of his body and release the secret longings in her own?

Made for work, not for pleasure...

She stifled a sigh. "He's only coming here for business purposes," she told Hughes firmly.

The beloved retainer made a harrumphing sound. "If you say so, my lass."

She moved restlessly to the house, where a pile of letters was waiting on the tray in the entry way.

The bill from the green grocers, one for repair of the leak in the roof. Drawing pencils and paints, French and piano lessons. New sheet music and the bill finally due for the few pretty luxuries Kitty and Fanny had bought for the Rendells' ball. Trinkets Pen hadn't been able to deny them.

*You should be attending your own accounts, rather than raking over Everdene's ledgers,* she scolded herself with a sigh. But the money Simon was quietly paying her would help. She wondered what would it be like to be able to use these skills openly and collect a fee, to draw up plans, to supervise the construction of buildings she'd designed, and be able to go to university, to truly study anything she wished.

In some ways, this interlude had only given her a glimpse into a world that was still beyond her reach, like someone dangling a candy before another child's eyes then snatching it away.

How difficult would it be now to go back to teaching in the schoolroom? To make herself small enough to close herself into that confined space again, physically, mentally, when Simon Harcourt had given her abilities free rein? Not just that—encouraged her, delighted in her, made her a full partner in building something that would last years after she was dead.

Was that the danger? She had been free of society's confines for a brief time. Would that make the years ahead only worse?

What was this new feeling? This feeling that made her body alive in a way she'd never felt before. Her skin hungry for Simon's touch, her imagination straying to what it might be like to see all of him, touch all of him.

She sifted through the letters, one from Miss Firth, her beloved teacher from her days at Miss Allen's Academy for Young Ladies. She was just reading about Miss Firth's humorous adventures with a sprained ankle when she glimpsed a letter written in a bold masculine hand, sealed in the same way Simon's directive from the Viscount had been.

*Miss Penelope Waverly,* the direction read.

Pen set aside the letter from Miss Firth, and picked up the second missive. She frowned in bemusement. What could Viscount Everdene have to say to her?

Unnerved, she carried the letter into the library and closed the door, then sank into her favorite chair and broke the letter's seal.

*Dear Miss Waverly,*

*During my brother's recent visit to Bitterne Tower, he spoke of your involvement in his recent project. As I am certain you know, I have agreed to his plan to relocate the village against my better judgment. While he seems most enthusiastic about your contributions to this ill-advised venture, I am most concerned by other subjects he discussed with me regarding family matters from the past, specifically our mother.*

*Do not interfere in matters you cannot understand. My brother has only lately returned to England and his family. Perhaps he has not seen fit to tell you what a precarious state he was in when he returned. Captain Harcourt suffered a great deal during his time in Afghanistan. The effects were so grim that there were times I feared for his life. During his stay at Everdene, it appears he has been improving. Inquiries about our mother can only cause my brother pain. Though I cannot fathom why a virtual stranger would pry into private family affairs long past, I am compelled to order you to desist if you have the slightest regard for my brother's healing or happiness. Please be advised that I will take whatever steps I deem necessary to insure that he is not troubled by such inquiries in the future. They can only do my brother harm.*

*Lucien, Viscount Everdene*

A hot flood of irritation and embarrassment rushed through her veins. It was hard to identify why. It was as if Viscount Everdene was scolding her like... like a child. As if she couldn't possibly reason things out for herself, as if she were poking her nose in other people's business far too important for a mere woman to understand. And what about the veiled threat at the end of the letter. *I will take whatever steps I deem necessary...*

She could never bow to even subtle bullying.

Yes, she'd known that Simon had suffered a great deal because of what he'd endured in Afghanistan. The memories he'd shared with her had horrified her, sickened her, made her wish for the power to wipe away the gruesome scenes imprinted on his brain as she would the spoiled slates of her students.

Perhaps he had been balanced on a knife's edge when he'd first returned to England, but who would not have been? Losing his men in a massacre, down to his very best friend? Yet Viscount Everdene wrote as if Simon were brittle enough to break. That was not the man Penelope had come to know.

She had seen the tender light in his eyes when he spoke of his mother, the way he'd cradled the miniature in his broad palm.

Perhaps Penelope *had* reminded him of his mother's love for him, but wasn't it possible that was responsible in part for the positive change in him? That those memories had called to a part of him shrouded in shadow. That part of the spirit that longed to love and be loved.

*And what if you are wrong?*

Pen nibbled at her fingernail. What had happened at Everdene Hall so many years ago? If the Viscount would write so openly to a casual acquaintance, revealing his brother's vulnerability, things must have been bad. How much danger was Simon truly in? What if her prying made things worse? Was she prepared to risk doing real damage?

She pictured Simon as he was working on the Havelock site, adding his own touches. Since the moment they'd hatched their plan, some of the edginess, the recklessness that haunted his expression had left his eyes. When she'd met him, it had been as if he couldn't bear being in his own skin.

Now, she glimpsed hints of the boy she had known.

He no longer fell prey to dissipation, drowning himself in drink, as if still trying to escape through the Hindu Kush mountains. Years destroyed by war, or his father's expectations. Since he'd returned from the meeting with his father and brother, there was something new about him.

From the first moment she'd encountered him in the alley where they'd saved Tripp Raffy, there had been an energy emanating from him. A physical tug that was always sensual, fascinating. He was the kind of man women's eyes followed with desire and he exuded a strength men envied. But this sudden burst of industry, purpose, enthusiasm had stripped away the dissipation, and she could see who he had been... an officer. The leader of men he was meant to be.

*Do not interfere in matters you cannot understand. Inquiries about our mother can only cause my brother pain.*

The Viscount's warning echoed in her mind.

He'd promised to take whatever steps necessary to prevent her interference. She wished it were an empty threat, and yet...

he owned Laurel Cottage, did he not? Could he turn them all out into the street, as he had Tripp's mother?

If he wished to levee a more personal attack, it would be easy to destroy Pen's reputation among the local gentry. There were already whispers about how improper her behavior was. Going to the building site without a chaperone was scandalous enough. A hint from the county's most eligible bachelor that she was of easy virtue would make her a pariah. She might risk such gossip herself, but that would mean Kitty and Fanny would be outcasts as well. Not to mention that a soiled reputation would mean no one would hire Pen as a governess.

She paced the room, her head a whirl of dread and defiance.

What was she going to do?

# CHAPTER 22

By the time evening came, Penelope felt as if her nerves were ready to snap, the letter's contents leaving her in a maelstrom of confusion and indecision. She'd begged off attending a musical evening at Mrs. Davies' house, claiming a headache, and had nearly shoved Kitty out the door when her caring sister had offered to stay behind to keep her company. That was the last thing she needed. Simon was meant to be busy tonight as well. When last she'd seen him, she'd given him a sheaf of papers to go over at Everdene Hall, carefully marked pages that would require hours of concentration.

That was why the sound of someone rapping lightly on the window made her jump, and she set her plate of spice cake aside and pulled back the curtain to find Simon standing outside. He pointed to the rear of the house, and she hastened to the back door. She saw that he'd brought Brutus, the cavalry horse he was training. A patient fellow Simon had tied in the rear of the house, out of sight.

"What are you doing here? Is something wrong?"

"I know I shouldn't have come, with your family away, but I

couldn't resist stopping by on the chance you might be home. I have news that couldn't wait."

Pen looked over her shoulder, grateful to hear Clara whistling in the kitchen. She nibbled at her lower lip, aware of the risk they were taking.

"They should be gone for another hour," she whispered. She held her finger to her lips to urge silence, and gestured for him to follow. When they reached the library, she quietly shut the door, feeling daring and a little bit wicked as she turned to look at him.

His shirt was rumpled, the first two buttons on his collar open. He'd donned his jacket again, though, his tousled dark hair tempting her to run her fingers through it to straighten it. He smelled of fresh air, sawdust, and horses.

He glanced at the spice cake as he sank down into a chair and his stomach growled.

"Go ahead and take this." Pen passed him the plate of cake, then sat beside him. "You sound like you're starving."

"I should say that you needn't go to the trouble of feeding me, but I'm too hungry to dissemble." He took a bite, and closed his eyes savoring the cinnamon-laden treat.

The sweep of his inky lashes on his cheekbones gave a hint of what he'd look like in slumber, and she pictured far too clearly his head on a pillow. Her whole body felt too tender, her nerves raw after the letter from the Viscount.

"I've had two illuminating conversations since we last spoke," Simon said, opening his eyes to look at her.

"Did you?" Her mouth went dry as she watched his tongue sweep a crumb from his full lower lip.

"The first was with Ruby Smith, who is every bit as clever and observant as you implied. You remember my complaint about the quality of my father's wine cellar?" Simon didn't wait for a response. "It turns out that Inchwick has been ordering bottles of inferior wine, and is relabeling the bottles with forged, superior vintages. By charging the estate the premium price, he has the potential to rake in a considerable sum."

"We have him, then!" Penelope clasped her hands in relief.

"Not quite. After all, I doubt he's made much in the short time we've been here. The wine aside, it occurred to me that Mr. Inchwick always makes certain *he* is at the building site when lumber is being delivered."

"And?" she said, as he took another bite of cake.

He finished chewing. "This is really good."

"The lumber!" she said, impatient.

"Right. This morning, I gave him an errand he could not evade and got him out of the way. When the deliveryman came, I noticed we'd not only been shorted on the amount, but there were cracks in some of the wood. The bill was for a price far too high for anything but top quality. When I asked about it, the deliveryman claimed his employer was the one who oversaw all the dealings with Inchwick."

Simon frowned, considering. "I'm more convinced than ever that Inchwick has been skimming coin off of the accounts, purchasing supplies that were not the highest quality and charging the estate the premium price. I doubt this is his first foray into stealing from the estate. He has it down to a fine art."

"You'd think he wouldn't dare with you actually being here."

Simon shook his head. "On the contrary, my father led him to believe that I would not care enough to notice. For him, it's business as usual."

"That would explain why he was disgruntled when you took more than a passing interest in the village."

Simon's lips flattened in a white line. "I've even puzzled out what his motive was for choosing Blagden Valley as a site. If there were accidents, or the buildings weren't sturdy due to subpar lumber, he could blame the flooding and the valley itself. And when that happened, it would be easy to convince my father and brother that estate farming is no longer profitable.

That turning the fields to grazing sheep or building some sort of factory would be better for the Harcourts."

"How much do you think he's swindled over the years?" Penelope asked.

He folded his arms over his chest, and gave her a look of shared triumph. "Enough that he will no doubt remain quiet in regards to the improvements we've made to the village. In fact, I intend to confront him tonight, to ensure such."

*We...* The way he said that word, his eyes warming when he looked at her, as if they shared a connection beyond measure... She scarce dared to breathe.

"I wanted to rush over here right away and tell you," he said, unaware of how his words affected her. "It about killed me to finish the work day. I nearly dropped a hammer on Daw's head, because I kept looking in the direction of Laurel Cottage, hoping to see you driving up the lane."

Rising, she paced to the window, readjusting the curtain. "My mother and sisters needed the gig," she said. And she'd been trying to decipher the meaning of the Viscount's letter. Pen glanced at the desk where the broken seal gleamed red. She wondered if she should show it to him. And yet...

She looked into Simon's face, so filled with excitement, eager and warm as he grinned at her. Something new shivered to life inside her.

Oh, God. When had it happened? This fierce need to touch him? A pull she felt in her chest.

He rose as if drawn by the same irresistible force. His eyes narrowed with concern. "I thought you would be pleased that we've caught Inchwick at last."

"I am."

Her pulse tripped as he cradled her cheek with one work-hardened hand. "Something is troubling you," he said in a low voice. "What is it that you're not saying?"

He'd noticed—not only her strengths, but the slight shifts in her expression, the vulnerabilities she kept so carefully hidden. It made her feel exposed, trembling with excitement and gratitude and dread, and a yearning for something that left her shaken.

He drew her into his arms, and held her gently, resting his lips against her hair. She curled against the warm wall of his chest, allowing herself to lean on him just for a moment. "What is it, sweet?" he breathed.

The murmured endearment made her want to melt into his embrace. To lift her lips to his, seeking out that kiss that had so altered her world.

She wanted to spill out her worry over the Viscount's letter, and yet wariness stopped her. What if the truth about his mother could only wound Simon more deeply? She owed it to him to be certain she would not do more damage.

When she drew away, she saw a flicker of something unexpected in his gaze. Hurt? She wondered if he felt the same thing she did... a loss of that warmth, that connection. Of not being alone. Worried, Penelope walked to the desk and shuffled papers, hiding the tell-tale red seal beneath Miss Firth's cheerful letter. What was happening to her? Her whole life, she'd known what she must do. She'd never been torn with indecision. But now, suddenly, she felt as if she were teetering on bare rafters. No matter which way she turned, she would fall...

"Penelope," he said. "What is wrong?"

"Nothing," she said, fairly certain her smile was overbright as she held up Miss Firth's missive. "I wanted to tell you that I received a letter from my favorite teacher. A woman who is now a dear friend. She's asked me to visit several times, but now she's had a mishap and I really must go." Go to seek out the wisdom of a woman whose counsel she trusted. Sort out the conflicting feelings that gave her no peace.

There was a long pause as he stepped toward her. "Must you?"

She nodded, entirely too close to him to think straight. "I - I should be gone three weeks, perhaps four."

He removed the letter from her hand, placing it on the desk. "I suppose we'll have to contrive to get along without you. I only hope you will not return to Everdene to find the roofs all cockeyed."

"I'm sure you'll manage just fine without me," she said.

"Will I?" The searching timbre of his voice made her knees go weak. She glanced up at the clock. "Oh, dear. It's later than I thought. You'd best go. My mother and sisters will be home soon." She strained on tiptoe to brush his lips with hers.

In an instant, that peck flared into something far hotter. Steely arms surrounded her, pulling her tight against his chest, his mouth searching hers as if to burn the taste of him into her, make sure she could still taste him when she was gone. His hands roved up and down her body, as she wrapped her arms around his neck. His hand slid around between them and cupped her breast. He made just enough room between them to unhook enough fastenings of her bodice to slide his fingers inside it, burrowing beneath chemise and corset to pull the soft globe free. Penelope arched against him as he feathered his thumb over the nipple, his lips trailing from her mouth, across her cheek, to her earlobe, his teeth gently teasing her in time with his thumb.

She felt as if she were melting, as he rolled the tender bud between his fingers. And she stifled the moans lest anyone hear.

Anyone hear...

The sound of harness jingling outside penetrated the thick haze of desire she was lost in, and she pushed at his chest.

"My mother... the girls..."

They sprang apart, Simon swearing as voices drifted in, Fanny laughing with Hughes as he took charge of horse and gig. Simon tried to do up Pen's fastenings, but she looked around in a panic. "If they catch you here..."

She didn't have to finish. She'd be ruined. A forced march to the altar. "The window… go out the window," she said pushing him toward it. He opened it, as she fumbled with her bodice. Pen could hear Kitty coming closer. "Hurry! Go!"

He paused one last moment, kissing her fiercely on the mouth, then leapt through the opening into the darkness. Pen fastened the last of her hooks as the library door swung open.

"Oh, here you are," her mother said. "You look rather flushed, dear. Have you taken a fever?" Her mother raised a hand to Pen's brow. Her heart hammered, her breast still tingling from Simon's touch as she glanced at the window. Her hands shook as she thought of how close they'd come to disaster.

A fever? Yes, she'd caught a fever indeed, momentary madness brought on by Simon Harcourt's kisses.

# CHAPTER 23

That was too damned close. Simon crouched in the bushes beneath the window, not daring to move. The last thing they needed was for a rustle to give him away. He could hear her mother fussing. Could imagine what Pen looked like. Her clothing askew, her hair mussed, her lips swollen red with kisses. He'd barely heard her family arriving home in time. Three minutes sooner, and they'd have caught him with his hand cupping that velvety soft breast, his cock straining against his falls, moments away from tumbling Penelope onto the settee and settling between her legs...

A fever... her mother was fretting. He'd never felt so on fire. With a need that coursed through him, made his falls pinch at his still erect cock. It seemed as if he'd crouched there an hour before the library went silent, someone blowing out the candles, and hopefully making their way up to bed. But the thought of Pen in her bed did nothing to calm the hunger coursing through his veins.

For an instant, he wondered which room was her bedroom, whether she might cross over to the window, and he might see her in her nightgown... or even less.

Simon swore, and unfolded himself and crept back to the rear of the house, retrieving Brutus, grateful for the cavalry mount who would draw far less attention, the gelding's brown coat blending in with the darkness. He walked the horse away from the house, until it was safe to mount. Swinging up on the horse, he cantered off toward Everdene Hall, each thud of Brutus's hooves seeming to drive the harsh truth into Simon's mind. He wanted to kiss Penelope again, caress her breasts and explore all of the parts of her denied to him. And now she was leaving to visit a friend? For a month, no less!

He didn't want her to go.

The realization landed like a blow. *This* is what it would be like when she left to be a governess once more. Or when he rode away from Everdene to whatever his life would hold. A future hazed in vast uncertainty, now that his hopes of financing a stud farm might be in jeopardy because he risked his father's wrath. He winced, recalling ideas she'd offered him, ways to construct that remarkable stable that might never be.

Maybe it was better to get a taste of what days without Penelope Waverly would be like, a voice whispered. Face the inevitable.

He spurred Brutus to a run, as if he could escape the sudden ache in his chest, grateful when he finally reached Everdene. He needed a damned distraction, a way to put Penelope Waverly out of his mind, her eager lips and the hardening of her nipple against his palm.

What better way to quell those thoughts than to summon Inchwick? He scrawled a note to the land agent, sent it off with Randall, then went to wait in the room he liked least in all of Everdene.

This study, with its dark, heavy draperies, grim dark furnishings and dour paintings, seemed permeated with his father's essence, the arrogance, hateful words, and contempt hanging in the air like the cigar smoke that had once swirled about the room.

Yet tonight, Simon needed the gravitas of the Earl's unseen presence, the threat that would put the fear of God into Inchwick and bend him to Simon's will.

The land agent had been surly since their initial encounter over the ledgers, seething about the slight to his dignity. But it would be hard to maintain that sort of high-handedness now that Simon's suspicions had proved true.

The clock on the mantel was striking nine when there was a scratch at the door—Randall announcing Inchwick's arrival. The footman's cheeks were pale, his eyes avoiding Simon's, after the discussion that had followed his delivery of the wine bottle on the desk.

"Forgive me for rousing you from your house so late, Mr. Inchwick." Simon regarded the land agent with a lazy eye. "But I wanted to hear the report regarding the errand I sent you on this morning. Did you leave the grist mill in good order?"

"It was an issue anyone could have resolved," Inchwick complained. "I still cannot see why I should have been sent to deal with such a minor problem."

"An affront to your dignity, was it? But not so great an insult as the fact that I insisted upon reviewing the estate's finances."

"Any man of business would be insulted by the implication he did not have his employer's confidence, not to mention having my personal finances rifled through."

"Yes, well, I could not help but be curious as to how you managed your money. When I visited your home, I noticed that your surroundings are most... refined. You have a taste for the finer things in life, don't you?" Simon ran a finger down the bottle. "Wine, for example."

"I have always believed that quality matters."

"Indeed, it does." Simon poured two glasses and gestured for Inchwick to take one. "This vintage from Bordeaux has always been a favorite among us Harcourts." He took a sip, then eyed the man. "Though I must say, it is not as exemplary as I remember it."

"Perhaps your palate has changed after so long in foreign lands," Inchwick observed blandly. "The drinks there are quite exotic, I would imagine."

"Hmm." Simon swirled the ruby-red liquid in his goblet. The crystal glass sparkled like the edge of a blade. "The quality of building materials is even more important," Simon continued. "Any failure there could have far more serious consequences than drinking a glass of inferior wine."

Inchwick's eyelid twitched. "Perhaps you should consult Daw Garvey on the subject, since you place such value in the carpenter's guidance."

"Garvey, yes. Or Mr. Crawford. I had a most illuminating discussion with him when he delivered a load of lumber from the woodworker's yard today."

"Is that so?" Inchwick's fingers began to tighten on his glass, but Simon could see him forcing his hand to relax. "I hope you found the delivery satisfactory."

"What there was of it was not up to the standards one might expect for the price charged."

"I will speak to Crawford directly. If I had been on site—"

"Mr. Inchwick, you have been a very busy man." Simon interjected, drumming his fingertips on a crisp new ledger. "Running the estate is difficult business, but it seems you've been enhancing your own financial affairs on the side—at the Harcourt family's expense."

Inchwick cleared his throat. "I'm sure I don't know what you mean."

"Oh, I think you do," Simon retorted, in the tone that made subalterns sweat. "I have checked and double-checked your calculations—so thoroughly, in fact, that I had the pertinent ones copied in a new volume of my own." He opened the book, and shoved it across the desk. Inchwick stared down at lists written in Penelope's delicate, precise hand.

The man blanched. "Who is responsible for this—this outrage? Have you shared my personal finances with someone else?" Inchwick's eyes narrowed to slits. "It has to be that Waverly chit! Ever since she began interfering, it's been a disaster. I should have thrown them out of the house when that wastrel of a father died."

"You're good at throwing people into the street, aren't you? Like you did with Tripp Raffy's family?"

Inchwick's neck swelled with outrage, a stippling of sweat on his upper lip. "Tell me you didn't allow some fool of a woman to pry through my personal records—"

"Miss Waverly is no fool, as well you know," Simon enunciated with deadly calm. "And you are not in a position to complain about my methods. You will accord her the respect she has earned, especially over these past weeks as she assisted me with matters regarding New Everdene. I could not have accomplished what I've done without her."

"What you've accomplished?" Inchwick scoffed. "That remains to be seen, does it not? We've yet to see if the houses tumble down on people's heads. As to her conclusions regarding my records, she is hardly qualified to make judgments." Suddenly, Inchwick tried to sound conciliatory. "Captain, you are not the first man to have your head turned by a skirt, and a pretty face. You cannot trust her. I swear—"

Simon leaned forward, keeping his voice low, even, and ensuring there was no mistaking his meaning. "You will leave Miss Waverly out of this."

"But—"

"Choose your next words with care."

The man nodded. "I meant no disrespect."

"We both know you are a thief," Simon continued. "The question is why? You make a handsome salary, live in a fine house, and for the past decade have had the run of this estate as if it were your own. I understand a starving boy snatching an apple, but my patience fails me when I encounter a man filling pockets that are already bulging with coin."

"Perhaps you need look in the mirror, sir," Inchwick said bitterly. "Your father and brother do not care what I do here as long as the tenants' rent is paid. Where did you get this false information regarding accounts? From some servant or merchant plotting against me?"

"You're the one doing the plotting. I have the record right here." He tapped the ledger again. "Lumber. Kitchen supplies. Wine… Did you truly think that I could not tell the difference between French vintage and this cheap swill?"

Inchwick darted a glance at the bottle, his tic worsening.

Simon steepled his hands together and tapped his lips. "It is one thing to pad these orders for personal gain, but you had to find a place to store your ill-gotten goods until you could find buyers. Fortunately, with the right pressure, Mr. Crawford was happy to show me where he delivered the first part of Everdene's lumber order. Imagine my surprise when I discovered a barn on the old Raffy place filled with things my family bought and you intend to re-sell. A location out of the way, where the new tenants were assiduously ignoring the comings and goings of your cohorts."

A trickle of sweat ran down Inchwick's cheek.

"No wonder you wanted the Raffys out of the house after Zeke had his accident. You needed someone on site to help with the unloading. And with children about, one of them might have let something slip to a friend or a neighbor."

"Captain Harcourt, I assure you—"

"Spare me your protestations. It seems you and I face a conundrum," Simon mused. "The question is what to do? I would love nothing more than to dismiss you right now, but I've given some thought to the matter and believe we should strike a bargain."

"A bargain?"

"My silence for yours. You halt all embezzling of Harcourt funds. I will stay silent regarding your crime. You will stay silent as well."

"Silent?"

"Once the village is finished, you will inform my brother and father that you have found another position. You will leave Everdene voluntarily or I will expose what you have done."

Inchwick paused, a malevolent gleam in his eye. "What if I expose all you've been up to with moving the village?" It was exactly the threat that Simon had anticipated, and so he let the man continue. "What if I tell your father and brother that an interfering chit has drawn the plans that *you've* approved? They'll storm down to Everdene in a rage which could halt construction in a flash!"

Simon steeled his voice. "Do not attempt to bait me, Inchwick. You do *not* want to make me your enemy." He gave a grim smile. "What is the penalty for embezzlement? Transport to a penal colony, last I heard. Hard labor... walking on a treadmill or breaking rocks. No doubt, my father would use all of his considerable power to see that you paid the highest price the law allows. There would be a certain justice to that, after what happened to the Raffys. However, I realize that sending you off in shackles would be less satisfying than seeing families like Daw Garvey's settled in their new cottages before the snow flies. Better to avoid anyone's interference, don't you agree?"

"Except for Penelope Waverly's!" Inchwick blustered. "Her father had his flaws. Perhaps the worst was allowing his daughter to spit in the face of God's natural order."

"You wish to speak of flaws?" Fury jolted through Simon. "A father is meant to protect his daughter. Instead, he gambled away her home, her future."

Inchwick flattened his palms on the desk and Simon could smell the fear on him. "You don't even know this woman!" Inchwick roared.

"I do know her," he said, more certain than he'd ever been in his life. It was madness to think so, but Simon remembered his time in India, listening to servants speaking of past lives, reconnecting with those they'd known and loved before. Perhaps he did not believe in such things, but he could finally understand why others might. "And I am coming to know you, to my disgust, Inchwick. With the help of Miss Waverly, I will be monitoring the estate's accounts for the duration of your tenure here. If one scrap of lumber is misplaced, one bottle of spirits is mislabeled, or one delivery for the kitchen is over-priced, you will learn what it feels like to be flung out in the street. And straight into the hands of the law. Do we understand each other?"

"Completely."

Simon could see the avid gleam in Inchwick's eyes—the look of a man offered a reprieve from gallows, yet eager to pick the pockets of those who had come to see him hang. No doubt, Simon would have to tread carefully, stay alert.

"If you trouble Miss Waverly in any way, I'll do far more than simply burn your reputation to the ground." He leveled Inchwick a deadly glare. "And should you have any doubt, you need merely ask the foes I've fought and men I've dueled as to what happens to those reckless enough to cross me."

His gaze locked with Inchwick's. As much as he wished he could believe the land agent was cowed into submission, he knew it would be risky to make such an assumption. Something told Simon that Inchwick was only biding his time until he could strike.

# CHAPTER 24

It was a relief to get away from Everdene for a little while, Pen admitted to herself. Not only to escape the demands of her family, but also the threats hanging over her head from Simon's brother, never mind Inchwick's displeasure in everything she said or did. More importantly, it would give her time to clear her head after the kiss and the feel of Simon's hand exploring her breast, a touch so intimate it still made her knees go weak. She needed to think without distraction. About Simon. About her. Them.

It had been pure luck that they hadn't been caught when her mother and sisters had returned from the musicale. Mere minutes between ruination, and barely squeaking by with mussed hair, a hastily fastened bodice, and a flush that might have betrayed them. Should they be caught, there was no doubt Simon would do the right thing and marry her. But she hadn't fought for her independence her whole life just to have it whisked away because of some indiscretion. And marry they must, should the worst happen. Her ruin would mean the ruin of her sisters as well.

A dangerous game she was playing. She needed to fight this

attraction, and fight it she must, she thought, as the cart she'd hired at the coaching inn arrived in front of Miss Firth's small cottage. The driver pulled Pen's trunk from the back of the equipage, setting it at her feet, then rumbled off.

Pen looked up at the neat cottage, a welcome refuge after so much confusion. She felt blessed to have time with the mentor she had so admired during the three years she'd spent at Miss Allen's Select School for Young Ladies. Miss Firth had taken Penelope under her wing at once, when other teachers, ground down by poverty and exhaustion, grew impatient with her ceaseless questioning and refusal to be fobbed off with rote answers. It wasn't just Penelope who had benefited from the woman's generosity. Miss Firth had taken it upon herself to gather all the 'troublesome chits' in her tiny chamber. The cozy winter evenings they'd spent, sitting at her feet as if she were a female Socrates, were some of the happiest hours Pen had ever known.

Now, in the small cottage where Miss Firth and her fellow teacher, Miss Collins, made their home, Penelope experienced an echo of that same sense of peace. She had seldom felt as if she belonged anywhere, or was much more than a nuisance to be tolerated. Her sisters loved her and she loved them, but the weight of responsibility for Kitty and Fanny always weighed on her shoulders. Only with her great aunt and her beloved teacher had Pen been able to be fully herself.

Until Simon…

She put him from her mind as Miss Collins led her to the parlor where Miss Firth waited. The small home the two teachers had made was filled with books and paintings. A pianoforte stood in the corner, laden with an eclectic collection of sheet music. Two chairs were drawn up beside the hearth, where tables held an assortment of sewing baskets, half-read volumes, and newspapers women were widely forbidden to read. Her former mentor sat in one of the chairs, her lame foot propped up on a stool.

"This is such a lovely home," Penelope said, imagining what it might be like to have such freedom away from the strictures of society.

"A bit small at times," Miss Firth said with a smile. "Especially when Rachel is playing her music, and I am trying to read. But we do like it."

Penelope had always noticed a unique tenderness in the teachers' relationship, a gentle touch, a love that many of the girls at the finishing school had whispered about. Penelope hoped the women had found happiness together.

"Dear, dear Penelope," Miss Firth said. "To think you're here, at last. A pleasant trip, I hope?"

"Indeed," she said, attempting to shove all her uncertainties and fears to the back of her mind. "I couldn't have asked for a better day for travel."

Miss Firth's brow furrowed as she examined her former student. "And yet, I can't help but think something is troubling you."

Even had she wanted to, Pen wasn't sure how to voice her concerns as she regarded this woman who had always seemed so wise. She gave what she hoped was a bright smile. "I am quite sure that once I have a chance to settle in, I'll be right as rain."

"Of course. I was so eager to see you, I asked Miss Collins to bring you in here straight away. We'll talk when you come down for tea."

It was an hour later when Penelope returned to the parlor, finding Miss Firth busying herself with a skein of yarn, unfurling the thread bit by bit to wind into a neat ball.

Perhaps, sensing Penelope's earlier reluctance to talk about anything too personal, she handed Penelope a skein to wind, and kept their conversation light, something Pen was grateful for. It was wonderful to just sit quiet for a little while and attempt to untangle her thoughts along with the yarn.

"So," Miss Firth said, once tea was served and they set the neatly wound balls of yarn into a basket. "Tell me about this village you have written about."

Pen poured the steaming tea into two delicate cups rimmed with blue flowers. She hadn't realized how much pressure she'd felt these past weeks, as she pushed to make the village at Havelock Meadow a reality—and to unravel the unfamiliar feelings that swirled inside her whenever she was near Simon Harcourt. Leaving out the latter, she regaled Miss Firth about the village, her architectural ventures, and her need to find a new position as governess before winter came. "Part of me still expects to wake up and find the village is all a dream," she confided. "Yet, then I go to the building site, and see that it is truly happening. The buildings I drew taking shape."

"It must be quite exciting."

"Beyond anything I imagined possible."

Miss Firth smiled tenderly. "From the time you first walked into the classroom, I sensed something remarkable in you. So much promise. Yet I know you well enough to see that crease between your brows that always appeared when you were troubled, or trying to solve a truly difficult problem. What is it?"

Penelope stared down at her teacup, wrestling with what she should say. Finally, she looked up at her friend. "The man who is my partner in this enterprise. Simon... Captain Harcourt. The younger son of the Earl of Ravenscroft."

Miss Firth tipped her head to one side, her gaze unflinching. "Is he making things difficult? Attempting to take command?"

"Quite the opposite. He regularly seeks out my opinion, relies on my calculations and trusts my insights. There is some question that the man who manages the Harcourt estate is dishonest, and Captain Harcourt trusted me with the estate ledgers, hoping I might unearth whatever mischief is going on."

Miss Firth's brows arched in surprise. "It sounds as if Captain Harcourt knows your worth."

Penelope felt a rush of pleasure. "Occasionally he has come to Laurel Cottage after working all day at the building site, so that we can share our thoughts and plans."

And though she left out how some of those visits were made when her mother and sisters were gone, Miss Firth saw right past that. "Do you... enjoy his company?" she inquired delicately.

Penelope's cheeks burned. "Perhaps too much."

"Ah," Miss Firth said, placing her teacup on the table, then shifting her injured ankle upon its pillow. "From what you say, the two of you have struck up an equal partnership."

They had, Penelope realized. And therein lay the crux of the problem. She wanted that sort of partnership, craved it, but without risking her independence. "I've never had anyone listen to me more intently. He actually hears what I am saying. Shares triumphs as well as failures."

Miss Firth glanced through the window where they could see Miss Collins in the garden. "Is that not what we all wish for?" she asked.

"Is it?" Penelope sighed. "I've always been so sure about what I wanted in my life—to keep my independence, not conform to society's expectations. And now, when it is all within my reach, the thought of surrendering that independence to a man?" Perhaps it was because she'd bottled this up inside of her for so long. Or that she was finally able to tell someone who didn't censure her for harboring secret hopes that society frowned upon. Whichever the cause, she was surprised by the sudden show of emotion that welled up inside her. Tears sprang to her eyes, and she quickly looked away, trying to blink them back. "I'm sorry. I—"

"You have nothing to apologize for, my dear." Miss Firth smiled kindly. "You are a remarkable woman. Designing a village certainly defies any normal feminine pursuit that I have ever heard of. It's nothing to be ashamed of, society be damned." Miss Firth turned her attention out the window, watching Miss Collins working her trowel in the vegetable garden. "Do you believe in soulmates?"

"Soulmates?" she echoed, following her gaze. It was a term she'd heard somewhere, but had given little thought to.

"The chance to share life with a partner who is your equal could be a gift, could it not? To work together to make the world a more just place?" She turned back, brushing a few crumbs from her skirt, before looking at Penelope. "Your Captain Harcourt sounds like an exceptional man."

"He is. When I'm with him, I feel…" She hesitated, trying to put it into words. When that failed, she stood, then paced the room while Miss Firth watched her patiently. "I feel… *different.* There's so much excitement, anticipating seeing him, sharing ideas and hopes and aspirations, but it's mixed with uncertainty. Fear. Freedom lost. Putting myself in a position in which another person is in control of my life. How can I possibly entertain such an idea?"

"A wise sense of caution, and yet… Do you not risk losing control any time you step out your front door? Think of the horses you love. Riding is a question of trust, weighing your own skill and the horse's loyalty, an understanding that you will balance your strength and faults for the good of both."

"I allow that is true. But one can sell a horse if it becomes too difficult to deal with."

Miss Firth laughed. "Tell me, Penelope, what is it that makes a truly gifted scholar?"

Pen canted her head, considering. "Accumulating knowledge. Demanding more of one's self than simple answers. The ability to evaluate new evidence and change your mind."

"Precisely." Miss Firth nodded in approval. "Keeping that in mind, have you ever considered that ridiculous attitudes toward women persist because people refuse to examine new information and change their minds?" She waited a beat, then added, "Yes, to love another makes you vulnerable. You will never be quite certain how it will sort out. But think about it. If I recall, when you first got on that horse you love, people claimed no girl would be able to ride her. There was no way to guarantee the outcome, but if you hadn't tried, imagine how different things would be. Nothing would change."

Wasn't that what Simon had done during these past weeks? Realigned life-long expectations of a woman's capabilities and proper sphere? He'd taken a great risk, regarding her plans seriously, putting them into action. He'd consulted her, acceded to her greater knowledge of architecture, delighting in her success.

Yes, Simon Harcourt had a face and physique formed to tempt the most reasonable woman to sin. He was as dazzling and dangerous as the stallion he rode, exuding potent masculine beauty. But he'd rewritten every rule to give her the chance that she'd craved. He had laid siege to those barriers so that she could charge inside.

Miss Firth broke into her thoughts, her tone gentle. "I have no doubt about what amazing things you could accomplish alone if the world would open its doors to you. But it won't."

"I know… But I'm afraid I'm falling in love with him," she confided. "And now I know why they call it falling. The sensation is terrifying, out of control, and yet, exhilarating."

"Like flying?"

She nodded. "If only I wasn't afraid of what will happen when I hit the ground."

"Maybe you never will."

"But marriage…? That was not part of my plan."

"But you could not conceive of a man the likes of Simon Harcourt, when you set your path. Frankly, neither of us could. As I see it, you have two choices. Hold tight to the world you knew before Simon Harcourt, or reevaluate, and open yourself to the possibility of something beyond it."

Penelope stared into the fire, thinking of Simon's embrace, the feel of his mouth on hers, the temptation and danger. To her. To her sisters, should she and Simon continue down this path without benefit of marriage. "It's all so much to take in…"

"You know, you do not have to leap into this as if jumping off a cliff, though that is your nature. You could merely test the waters, step by step. See what comes of it." Miss Firth's cheeks turned a soft shade of pink. "I spent most of my life alone, thinking that I could never find… happiness. Now I have. Perhaps it was not in the common way, but it is *my* way."

"Would that a man and woman could live together, free of the legal restraints a woman suffers in marriage, without bringing censure upon the whole of their families…" Penelope fretted her lower lip.

"Something else to consider," Miss Firth said, as an orange cat leapt into her lap, nudging its head under her hand, "I have learned there is a family in Ireland who might wish for a governess for the daughters. I meant to send out inquiries on your behalf. But now I'm wondering, would you prefer I cease my inquiries about positions for you for the time being?"

"Yes. No." She looked at Miss Firth in desperation. "I'm not certain. I need to care for my family."

"You *need* to care for yourself, as well. My family is not pleased with my choices, but I am happier than I have ever been. The day I chose to stop molding myself to fit their expectations was the day I was finally free."

Pen closed her eyes, picturing Simon beside the stream at Havelock Meadow, his skin glistening as he'd scooped up handfuls of water to splash on his ruggedly handsome face. But along with that thought came the recollection of the Viscount's letter, his warning, and the soft yearning she'd seen in Simon's eyes as he gazed down at the miniature of his mother.

The one thing she knew for certain was that time was fleeting. As quickly as her time with Miss Firth sped by, it reinforced the fact that her days with Simon were slipping through her fingers, and any chance they had could soon be gone.

She had to *do* something. She was not a woman to sit and passively accept whatever proper society—or a man—dealt her. She must take some sort of action.

The only thing left to do was to face Simon and… and what? Ask what his intentions were in this partnership they'd forged? The very thought of doing so made her palms sweat.

There were only two possible outcomes, unless she was willing to cause a scandal and dash any chance her sisters had of making a match. He would reject her outright, which meant an end to this yearning, or offer her marriage, which meant an end to her freedom.

Neither was a choice she could bear. There was only one thing to do. She would have to end things with Simon, as soon as she arrived home.

# CHAPTER 25

The trip back to Laurel Cottage had been pure misery, the jouncing of the coach making her queasy as she tried to frame what she was going to say to Simon. Her frustrations were only magnified after she was dropped at her doorstep. She'd been determined to go to the building site and get the interview over with as soon as possible, but that was not to be. Their maid, Clara, had gone to help her cousin deliver a new baby, and Pen's mother had taken Kitty and Fanny off to spend the day with the Rendells.

Aside from the wind gusting outside, she should have been grateful for the quiet house, but in spite of her need to end things with Simon, she'd been chafing to drive out to New Everdene to see what the workers had accomplished in her absence.

She ignored the lingering thought about wanting to see Simon after spending nearly a month away. Little good would come from such thinking. Not when she needed to end things with him, secure a position, and ensure she didn't risk her sisters' places in society.

It all seemed so easy, ending things with Simon. Quite

another when actually faced with the idea that it meant the end of… everything else that might happen when they were alone. In spite of Miss Firth's gentle counsel, to test where this unexpected sense of connection with Simon might lead—reevaluate, now that she had new information—she knew she had to do more. Unlike Miss Firth, Pen couldn't simply abandon her sisters. She could never be happy knowing she had caused them any sort of pain.

A sharp rap caught her attention, making her wonder who was so impatient at this hour in the morning. She glanced in the hall mirror, whisked a tendril of hair up, and refastened a hairpin, the chignon she'd hastily twisted that morning half tumbling down. Satisfied she didn't look as though she'd just tumbled from bed, she opened the front door.

A rush of pleasure washed through her.

Simon stood in the doorway. A lock of hair had fallen across his brow, his eyes sparkling. His grin made her feel as if bubbles were filling her chest.

"Simon!" she exclaimed. "What are you doing here?"

He looked beyond her into the hallway. "Is anyone home?"

Her throat went dry as she shook her head.

He pushed the door behind him mostly closed, then drew her into his arms, holding her for a long moment. "I couldn't wait to see you," he whispered against her ear.

"Nor I, you." She reveled in the warmth of his embrace as she breathed in his familiar scent.

He stepped back, slightly, then used his finger to tilt her chin upward. "It feels as if you've been gone months instead of a matter of weeks." He stared at her mouth, his eyes smoldering.

Pen took a steadying breath, trying to calm her racing heart. She couldn't get the words out, too worried that anything she might say would end this tenuous relationship. A gust of wind blew open the door, startling them both. They quickly pushed away from each other, Penelope relieved that no one was about to see them. And though their moment of intimacy was lost, she was grateful for the timely interruption.

"I hope the wind isn't getting in the way of the work," she said, glancing out the open door at the treetops swaying in the distance.

Simon, apparently sensing her need for space, moved back several feet onto the threshold. "Only those working on the rooftops. There's much to be done elsewhere in the meantime."

"I'd hoped to drive over this morning, but my mother and sisters needed the gig for the day..." Realizing he didn't need a reminder that it was hardly proper for him to wait upon her alone, she quickly changed the subject. "Did you speak to Inchwick?"

"We've come to an understanding." He explained the conversation. "I'll be keeping a close watch on him. If he bothers you at all—"

"I can deal with Mr. Inchwick."

"I have no doubt you can." The wind gusted again, bringing with it a handful of dead leaves that rattled across the threshold. Simon glanced outside, then once more, partially shut the door, this time, using his foot to hold it in place.

"I've missed you, Pen."

The world be damned. She wanted to race into his arms, not caring if the door blew open or everyone in their family walked in at that very moment. Even so, she stood resolute. "I've missed you as well," she said, painfully aware of exactly how much.

His eyes danced. "I have something for you."

"What is it?" she said.

"You'll have to come see." He opened the door, then stood aside. "After you..."

Curious, she stepped outside, then stumbled to a halt, her gaze locked on the dappled gray horse tied to the hitching post.

Her breath caught. "Epona..."

"How do you like my new horse?" Simon asked with almost boyish excitement as he secured the door shut against the wind.

"Your...?" She crossed the space to her beloved mare. Liquid dark eyes fixed on her, the horse whickering, then daintily lipping at one of Penelope's loose curls. "Wh-what in the world? I don't understand."

"Your absence made me realize just how much I need you at the site, and so I purchased her from the farmer you sold her to. The perfect solution to having to share the gig with your family."

"Simon—"

"What would make me most happy would be to give you Epona as a gift.

"A gift? I couldn't possibly accept."

A solemn expression stole over his features, softened with a tenderness that made her heart skip a beat.

"It would be little enough to pay you back for all you've done for the village," Simon told her. "Were it not for you, I might never have realized the great wrong my father was doing by building at Blagden Valley until it was too late."

She swallowed hard, touched by his earnest praise. "Much as I'd love to keep her, I can't." Her voice quivered. "I can't afford it."

"Then let's make a deal. We can use a good horse once my stables are built. They can't all be brood mares. But until then, I will pay for her upkeep to board her here at Laurel Cottage so that you can visit the building site without imposing too much hardship on your family or your time."

Penelope shook her head, her mind reeling. "This is all so..."

"New Everdene is as much your creation as it is mine. At least think about it. I hope you'll ride with me this morning so that you can answer any questions the men have regarding the design."

He strode to her side, cupped her cheek and ran his thumb

over her lower lip. "I do understand the reasons you surrendered Epona still remain. My groom will deliver oats and hay to feed her. When you are gone, I'll keep her in my stables. She'll be cared for and exercised. Ready and waiting for you whenever you visit home."

Tears pushed at the backs of her eyes. "Simon, that's too much to ask of you."

He caught hold of her hands, pressing them firmly. "You didn't ask it of me. I want to do it." His gaze found hers, his eyes sparkling once more. "Wouldn't you like to be able to go for a race across the meadows whenever you wish?"

"Of course, I'd like that very much. It would be pure heaven, until I secure a new post..." Her words trailed off, and she felt an ache at the undeniable fact that she would be gone long before New Everdene was finished. She would miss the joy of moving day, the celebration. And Simon... the triumph in his handsome face.

"Right, then." Simon angled his shoulders away, his face hidden from her as he smoothed a hand down Epona's back. "Let me help you settle her in her new stall."

He untied the reins. They led Epona into the deserted mews. Pen was intensely aware of how dingy it looked. The dim interior showed the wear of the past years, only the dray horse Dobby's stall was filled with straw. Names were painted on each stall door, all that remained of horses who had been sold one by one to pay off her father's debts. She felt a pang as she passed the stall where Jupiter, her father's thoroughbred, had been kept. Simon stopped when he saw the faded letters she'd painted before her world had fallen apart.

*Epona.*

He smiled softly. "It looks as if you're home at last, little lady," he told the mare, then handed the reins to Pen. "I'll put down some bedding for her," he said.

She watched him pitch in forkfuls of straw, the muscles of

his back and shoulders rippling as he made a soft bed for the horse she loved.

Had anyone ever given her such a thoughtful gift? Could he possibly guess how often in her troubled youth, during the shattering of her family, that she had stolen out to this stable long after dark to lean her cheek against the soft, arched neck of Epona? How the scents and soft sounds had soothed her! There had even been times she'd allowed herself to cry with her face buried in Epona's mane.

It had torn her heart out when the farmer had led Epona away. She'd clenched her teeth so hard it seemed her jaw should crack. Yes, her heart told her. Simon would understand it all. Her grief, her anger, her determination not to let anyone see the wound she'd suffered. He turned and flashed that beautiful smile, and it struck like an arrow to her heart.

In that moment, she knew what she had to do.

She released Epona into the stall, caressing the mare's velvet nose one more time.

Then she took hold of Simon's hand. He followed her as she led him out and bolted the stall door closed. She turned and faced him.

"What is it…?"

The way he spoke, his soft inquiry more like an endearment.

She pushed past what she wanted, determined to say what needed to be said. "I-I have been doing a great deal of thinking while I was away."

"Something about the design of the cottages?"

"No. About you. Me. This—" She didn't even have the words to describe what they were.

His brows drew together and he waited, quiet, for her to continue.

"I've given our situation consideration," she plunged on, "and it seems that I can't stop… stop imagining what it would be like to—to…"

His Adam's apple bobbed convulsively, his eyes blue fire. "Penelope, you needn't feel that this gift, Epona... I have no expectations..."

"But you *do* think of me that way as well." She was tempted to run her fingertips down his chest, feel if his heart hammered as hers did. "I can't have mistaken..."

"If you're asking whether I imagine what it would be like to kiss you the way I want to, to touch you and take you to..."

"Your bed?" Her throat tightened around the word, her voice more a rasp.

He caught her hand with his and pressed it harder to the wall of his chest. "I've thought of it. There are times I can think of little else."

"While I was away, I researched... possibilities," Pen plunged on. "There are ways that one can lessen the chance of... complications."

"You mean conceiving a babe?"

"That would be a complication, since neither of us has any intention of marrying. But considering that you are a soldier, something of a rake... I'm certain you are far more informed on the subject of... *prevention*... than I."

Simon choked back a tender laugh. "I have some knowledge of the subject."

"I'm glad to hear it. You see, I find that... that you have tempted me in a way I never expected. I'm... not willing to return to my old life without exploring subjects I previously had very little interest in. What is between a man and a woman."

Simon swore under his breath. "Oh, Pen. Do you have any idea how much I want you? But it's not... not something you can test, like a theorem or hypothesis, then go merrily on with your life. If I take you to bed, it changes everything."

"You've changed me already." She rose on tiptoe, and pressed her mouth to his, kissing him on the lips.

He seemed to hold back. And just when she thought he

meant to reject her, his mouth opened over hers, his tongue parting her lips, dipping inside. His arms tightened around her like iron bands, molding her against the steely strength of his body. His hands roamed up and down her back as if he couldn't get enough of her, one palm cupping her bottom and pulling her hard against his hips. She could feel the ridge of his sex, and was startled by the length of it straining beneath his breeches. Her head fell back, her knees melting until they could scarce support her. Simon's mouth trailed down her throat, exploring the vulnerable place behind her ear, the curve where her collarbone arched. His calloused fingers stole between them and he took her breast in his hand, her nipple hardening at his touch, hot sensations spearing to the secret place between her thighs.

He hesitated, moving his mouth to her ear, whispering. "Ah, sweet. I'm a mistake you don't want to make."

"But I do," she said. "Just for now."

WHAT THE DEVIL WAS WRONG WITH HIM? SIMON THOUGHT, drunk on the taste of her. He'd bedded women in the past, never thinking beyond their mutual pleasure. Yet what he felt for Penelope was different. Fiercer. More dangerous.

If he'd been a bad bet before, scarred by the horrors of war, he was a worse one now. He would be disinherited soon, the price to be paid for building New Everdene. His only choice: rejoining his regiment. The last thing he'd want for Penelope was the harsh existence of a woman who followed the drum, like the British officers; wives who had made their homes in foreign lands and suffered in the Hindu Kush. Every fiber of his being sickened at the thought of Penelope at an enemy's mercy in that blood-soaked snow.

He put it from his mind. She'd made it clear she did not want forever. Only this moment. Were there not ways that he could show her pleasure without ruining her?

*Selfish bastard... you're making excuses because you want her... like breath in your lungs, like blood in your veins... like life.*

She grasped his hand, tugging him toward the deserted house, and he followed her. Would have followed her to hell, if that was where she led him... maybe it was.

Her skirts brushed against his legs as she led him up the stairs and down the hall. Somewhere in his sex-hazed mind, he had the vague awareness that the deeper into the family quarters they went, the more faded and threadbare things became.

Lighter patches showed on walls where pictures had hung. Here and there, he could see where the leg of a demilune table had been broken and clumsily repaired, the lower panel of a door cracked where someone had kicked it. The rugs were threadbare. Pen led him to the room farthest from the stairs.

He stepped inside it, closing the door behind them.

Light spilled through simple white curtains, an escritoire scattered with drawings of buildings, a ruler, and books on architecture and history and science. A chair with worn patches on the arm was drawn up by the hearth, a mending basket on the floor. A dressing table displayed a tortoiseshell brush and comb, a bowl of hairpins, and few of the toiletries he'd seen his various mistresses display. The bed stood in the middle of the room, its slender spindles draped with moss-green bed curtains. He'd caught her in the midst of unpacking. Her traveling trunk stood open, lacy things spilling out of one of the built-in drawers. A nightgown draped over a chair.

Simon imagined the filmy garment on her body, candlelight filtering through the delicate cloth.

She turned to him, her eyes huge and filled with curiosity and passion—and a sudden hint of shyness he'd not seen in her before.

Tenderness speared through Simon, and he forced himself to

draw a deep breath. His hands went to the fastenings of her bodice, unhooking them one by one until he bared her corset. The tops of her breasts welled over the undergarment's edge, tempting curves that he burned to taste. A blue silk bow was tucked in the shadowy cleft. Simon's cock ached as he dipped his finger into the sweet, secret mysteries between her velvety breasts. He pulled the end of the ribbon, untying the bow, then set his fingers to unhooking the top of her corset. The garment had wrinkled her chemise and pressed tiny patterns into her skin. A touch of narrow lace along the scooped neckline tempted him as he reached beneath the edge of the thin fabric and filled his hand with her bare breast, lifting the globe free.

Her breath hissed softly, and he felt her nipple, diamond hard against his palm. It half-maddened him to feel how much she wanted him. He slid the callused pad of his thumb over the bud, and looked down at the coral-hued aureole.

"Lie back, love," he breathed, easing her onto the bed, then lowering himself half over her, taking her nipple into his mouth. She tasted like lemon ice on a summer day, tart and sweet and so delicious he would never get enough of her.

She moaned as he suckled her, teasing and tormenting. Her hands tugged at the back of his shirt, until she found the skin at the base of his spine. The feel of her nails, softly abrading that sensitive skin made his cock throb where it pressed against her thigh, aching with a need the like of which he'd never experienced before.

He reached down to the hem of her skirt, tugging layers of petticoat and skirt up, his hand skimming along the strong, slender length of calf, then thigh.

His mouth went dry as his fingertips found the slit in her drawers. He drew lazy patterns on the fragile skin of her inner thigh, then touched the downy, secret curls. She started, gasping as his fingers found the tender petals and folds of her sex.

Penelope's senses tilted and spun as if she were no longer on solid ground. The hot, wet pull of Simon's mouth on her breast and the feel of his fingers edging up the inside of her thigh was dizzying, dazzling.

Every nerve quavered like a harp string, her inner muscles clenching with an aching emptiness, a longing to be filled.

Simon murmured praise against her breast, her throat, his teeth nipping exquisite trails he soothed with the sweep of his tongue, the faint rasp of his close-shaven jaw sending shivers cascading through her.

"Open your legs for me, sweet," he said, as the tip of his finger found a place so sensitive that pleasure jolted through her, electrifying every cell in her body. Her thighs clenched around his hand.

A hot flush burned her cheeks. "I'm… I'm… damp…"

"It's just your body readying itself for pleasure." He skimmed his fingers through the silky dew, parting the delicate folds, teasing, circling. She writhed, soft moans escaping her. Something built inside her, a pressure, a throbbing, a need so fierce she couldn't breathe.

Simon edged downward. She raised herself on her elbows and saw his face darken with lust as his gaze locked on the fragile place beneath the mound of ruffles and petticoat. "You are so beautiful." His head dipped down and he pressed his lips to the inside of her knee, working upward, kiss by kiss. Hot breath ghosted over her inner thigh. "So brave…" The tip of his finger dipped inside her.

She stiffened at the intrusion, the sensation strange, yet igniting a thrill deep in her belly. She arched her hips toward him, wanting something… needing more. It panicked her to feel control slipping from her grasp, even her own body, and responses in Simon's hands.

"Easy, love, easy," he urged, as if he could feel her resistance. "Let me take care of you… just this once… let go."

He blew softly on the swollen bud, his tongue seeking her

there, hot, silken. She arched, cried out, a half sob. She bit her lip in an effort to silence it, tried to twist away before the last thread that anchored her slipped out of her grasp. But Simon caught her hips, held her fast as pleasure, wild as any storm, broke over her, and her world flew apart.

When all was done, she drew a steadying breath, her body feeling warm and relaxed as she'd never been before.

Simon kissed the tuft of down, and gently smoothed her petticoats and skirt over her legs. He glided his fingertips over her breasts, the tight pink buds painfully sensitive after all that had occurred.

She dared a look at him, shaken, embarrassed at the way she'd cried out, the things they'd done. "I-I didn't know… people did such things." She breathed as he drew her into his arms. "That I could feel so…" Her voice trailed off. "I don't… don't have words for what I felt."

"Your sweet body doesn't need words. I know… without them." Simon held her close, breathing in the scent of her hair, his hand sliding down her body in long, firm strokes.

She felt his erection, a steely ridge against her. "But what about… you? I want to—"

"Not this time, sweet."

She felt a sudden wash of uncertainty. "Was I not…?"

"You all but drove me mad. There's nothing I would have loved more than to bury myself inside you. But you surprised me. I wasn't expecting you to offer me what I've been craving since the day I met you. You trusted me to prevent filling you with a babe. I wasn't prepared."

Penelope felt him pulling away from her. She should have been grateful he was being so careful. She'd asked him to, after all. Yet she couldn't help feeling vulnerable, a trifle hurt.

"There must be some way—"

"I'll not risk it. We have the village to finish. And then I'll be gone from here. And you... you'll be off working as a governess."

She'd forgotten that they both had lives to live outside this moment. "Miss Firth said she might find me a position in Ireland."

"Ireland?" he echoed, and she felt his body stiffen. "When do you expect to leave?"

"Nothing is certain yet. I'm not even sure I want to go. But I've always longed to see the world beyond my doorstep. It's not the Caspian Sea or the Alps or the Silk Road, but it's not England."

"I've traveled the world. One thing I've found. Wherever you go... you carry 'home' with you. The burdens. The pain and the love."

His gaze sought out hers. He touched her cheek. "Now, I'll carry today with me as well."

All she could do was nod.

# CHAPTER 26

What had he been thinking, all but making love to Penelope? Simon berated himself. What the hell had happened to him in that virginal bedroom, sharing the most shattering sensual experience of his life without even finding his own release? He'd been consumed by an almost primal need, understood why a stallion might kick its way out of a stall to reach the mare of his choosing. He'd never know how he kept himself from sinking into Penelope's wet, welcoming body. Had he been protecting her? Or himself?

It was pure torture not to. And yet, giving her pleasure, awakening her to the power of her own body, was the most erotic thing he'd ever experienced in his life.

In that moment, he had wanted to beg her not to go to Ireland. To stay with him… and what? He would be leaving Everdene when he was finished building the cottages, wouldn't he? Likely disinherited, with only an officer's pay and the exquisite stallion he was determined to build a future on. Or was another outcome possible? He'd fought his way out of seemingly impossible corners before by changing strategies.

He'd seen building the village as the end of his involvement here. An act of defiance—improving the village despite his father's greed and hardness of heart, then riding away. What if he convinced Lucien and his father of the benefits of the structures he and Pen had built, and drew up plans to improve the rest of the estate in ways that wouldn't hurt the villagers and yet increase profitability? He could outline them so clearly even the Earl couldn't dismiss it. During long work days, he'd listened to the tenants as they spoke of challenges they faced, asking them what solutions might be.

Inchwick had been jealous of his position, seeing any suggestions as an insult, threatening anyone who questioned his decisions with eviction. As for Simon's interference—it was a threat to Inchwick's skimming profits off the estate undisturbed.

Was it possible Simon might at least get Lucien to see reason —and together they could convince their father?

*Not bloody likely…* Simon scowled. Yes, it would be a hellish road ahead, and he was certain his father would throw as many barriers as possible in his way. But he'd charged into battle and beaten bad odds before.

For the moment, he had nothing of value to offer Penelope except the chance to realize her vision for the cottages at New Everdene—that, and the pleasure she'd found in his arms. But what if he could change that? He had to try.

Simon closed his eyes, a shiver of sensation, of need wracking his body. He'd told her that if he took her to bed everything would change, and he'd been right. *He* had been changed.

Either he would win this war with his father, or he would carry Penelope Waverly with him into every battle and relive the moments he held her in every midnight dream.

For days now, Pen had felt as if her nerves were too close to her skin, one smoldering look from Simon across the building site, or the library, and she was sliding down into that sense of total surrender, of reaching for that sensation that had burst upon her when he'd sent her body over the edge. That bone-deep craving for more, a mere taste of sensual pleasure not enough. The need to explore his powerful masculine body with the same abandon.

The breakfast table was hardly the place to be thinking such things, but neither was the building site or the library, when she was doing preliminary sketches of the stable Simon hoped to build. She thought about it in bed, when she touched the tender petals he'd kissed, finding them slick just from the memory of his fingers and mouth and low growls of desire.

She startled as the rattle of delicate porcelain pulled her out of her improper musings. Kitty's teacup clattered on the saucer, the steaming liquid wavering dangerously near the rim.

"Penelope?" she called out, waving her hand. "Did you not hear a word that I said?"

"No. I'm sorry. I'm afraid I was woolgathering."

"Again." Fanny complained, taking a bite of toast. "Are you feeling quite well? You've been acting fidgety ever since we got back from visiting Maria. It's not like you to forget things and stare into space."

Kitty narrowed her gaze as she studied Penelope's face. "Do you think Mama might be right, and all of this work at the new village is a strain not meant for a woman's mind?"

Pen started to snap a retort, but Fanny broke in.

"I think she's distracted by that lovely Captain Harcourt who brought Epona home. He must be very fond of you."

"It's far more convenient for me to be able to visit New Everdene. I'd think you'd be too grateful to tease me, considering that he brought her so that you'd have use of our gig."

"Of course he was thinking of Kitty, Mama, and me," Fanny

said with a laugh. "The fact that he can't take his eyes off of you has nothing to do with it. Not to mention that you get pink as a peony anytime we mention him."

"I do no such thing!"

"Of course, no woman in the county could blame you. He's certainly set hearts a-flutter. Cordelia Bing and her maid take the long way on their walks every day, just for the chance to see him in his shirtsleeves."

Pen made a show of rolling her eyes, but it was a half-hearted effort. She'd always scorned Miss Bing and her maid as hopeless flirts, the pair of them ogling any fair-looking young buck in the neighborhood. But Pen could scarcely blame them for their fascination with Simon. A less-than-decent glimpse of that iron-honed physique was well worth going an extra mile or so out of one's way. And Pen was doing far worse, picturing Simon as he had been that scandalous day in her bedroom, the black silk of his hair brushing her skin as he traced his lips up her inner thigh in a kiss more intimate than she'd ever imagined.

She'd heard whispers from married friends, how fierce a man's appetite for the marital act could be, a force men could not control. Yet Simon had given her pleasure while refusing to risk taking his own, even when she'd offered, been willing to give it to him.

She suddenly understood what she'd once thought of as foolhardy. That instinct, older than time, to fold herself into Simon's arms. Be his safe harbor as he was her own, allowing herself to sink in and trust his strength, share all of the pieces of herself, the strength, and also those flawed, vulnerable places she'd hidden for so long.

"Pen, do confide in us," Kitty pleaded gently. "Fanny and I have known for a long time that these meetings with Captain Harcourt were about far more than house plans, and the fact that he gave you Epona proves it."

"He's merely loaning—"

"The way he looks at you when you're not paying attention… If only you could see his face. I swear, Mama is ready to order your trousseau."

"Of all the absurd notions!"

"You *do* care for him!"

Pen tore a bit of crust from her own toast, and her hand trembled. "I do. As any friend would. But you must not make more of it than it is. Captain Harcourt and I have… have a mutual respect for each other and…"

"Has he kissed you?" Kitty asked, eager.

"Of *course* he has!" Fanny exclaimed. "Look at that blush! Is he a wonderful kisser? Forrest Bing kissed me behind a potted palm at the Rendells', and he tasted of fish."

There was a sudden bustle at the breakfast room door, and Clara hastened in. "Miss Penelope, there is a gentleman come to see you."

"Captain Harcourt?" Kitty piped up in a teasing tone.

"No. He's not from around here. Never seen 'im before. But he's quite handsome in his own way."

Pen, grateful for the interruption, pushed her chair back from the table, the pleasant morning with her sisters gone. "Show him to the parlor," Pen said with a sigh.

"I hope it's not another debt collector," Kitty gave her a sympathetic look. "Mama keeps forgetting to give you the bills."

*Forgetting* was one way to describe it, Pen thought with irritation, remembering the drift of receipts she'd discovered stuffed in a hatbox three days ago.

Whatever it was, a visit from a strange man at this improper hour of the morning was unlikely to be good news.

Peering in the mirror, she straightened the collar of her dove-colored morning gown, then went to face whatever new challenge fate had dealt her.

The moment she let herself into the parlor, she started,

taking in the familiar rangy body, clean-cut features and pale red-gold hair of her former employer, Richard Tremayne.

"Hello, Penelope."

The fact that he used her Christian name startled her. He looked weary, his smile a trifle sad.

"Mr. Tremayne... This is a surprise."

"I beg you forgive me for giving you no warning that I would visit, especially at this hour. And for not responding to your request that I come see this village of yours sooner. I fear things have been somewhat... complicated at home. When I had to travel to London to deliver plans for a new townhouse, I determined to stop here as well."

Pen noticed a thin black mourning band fastened around his upper arm. "I see you have suffered a loss."

"Yes. My wife succumbed to her illness a month ago."

"I'm so sorry. How are the children?"

"As one would suspect. Grieving. Confused. Angry. My sister is staying with them for the time being."

Penelope didn't know what to say. Any words that came to her mind would be poor comfort to a man who had recently lost his wife, and more useless still to motherless children. "I so appreciate your willingness to inspect the buildings, considering all you've been through. I was just about to go to the site."

"Perfect. It will give me a way to take my mind off of a home without my wife."

Penelope had Hughes hitch Dobby to the gig. As they set out for New Everdene, she tried to make conversation, asking Tremayne about his London project. She was eager for him to see her work, yet there was an undercurrent of nervousness that she couldn't quite define.

When she pulled the gig to a halt and set the brake, she saw Tremayne look over the building site with astonishment. "I cannot believe how much progress you have made. Your letter led me to believe that the work had barely begun."

"Captain Harcourt is resolved to have everyone housed before the snow flies," Pen said. "I wouldn't have imagined it possible, but as you see, he is well on the way to achieving his goal."

As Tremayne helped her down and fastened the lead rope to the hitching post, Pen glimpsed Simon helping Daw and other men raising the cumbersome skeleton of an exterior wall, while Tripp hopped around them, like a sparrow stealing crumb cake. She couldn't hear their banter, but it was easy, full of laughter, and made her heart feel too big for her chest. Once the wall was in place, Tripp tugged on Simon's sleeve and gestured to Penelope.

There was no doubt the moment Simon saw Mr. Tremayne. His eyes narrowed as Tremayne offered her his arm, saying that construction sites were notoriously uneven, known for twisting ankles. She had been traipsing around New Everdene for nearly two months now, with no mishaps, but what could she do but lay her hand lightly in the crook of his elbow?

By the time they reached Simon, he had smoothed the displeasure from his face, though the introductions between the men felt strained. They spent the morning inspecting cottages in different stages of construction. While Tremayne's approval pleased her to no end, she sensed that Simon was a trifle jealous. Not that she had time to dwell on it. They'd just stepped out of Widow Bevans' cottage when Mavis Bailey, the wheelwright's wife, came to get Pen's opinion on a rash her young son had sported on his chin. She excused herself and left the two men together with one backward glance.

<hr>

SIMON DIDN'T WANT TO LIKE RICHARD TREMAYNE, BUT HE couldn't find anything specific to object to. The man had pointed out remarkably few flaws, offering advice on how to correct them with clarity. As to the workmanship, he had praised it in a way that had left the laborers grinning.

The architect might be well-spoken, gentlemanly, knowledgeable, but there was no doubt in Simon's mind—especially on noticing the band of mourning on the man's sleeve—that inspecting this village damn well wasn't the only reason he'd gone out of his way to call on Penelope.

Simon leaned against the wall of what would be Widow Bevan's cottage and regarded the architect with an appraising glance.

"It's a wonder, what you've accomplished here," Tremayne said, oblivious to Simon's growing suspicions. "I'd never have believed you could achieve so much so quickly."

*It's amazing what you can accomplish when the devil is nipping at your heels*, Simon thought, picturing his father's stone-hard face. "It's not so different than setting up encampments in the army," Simon offered. "Giving the men their orders and reminding them how comfortable they'll be once the tents are pitched and campfires burning. But I can't take credit for the buildings themselves. Pen—Miss Waverly—it is her vision taking shape."

"It's a remarkable achievement for a woman."

The muscles of Simon's face tightened, and he felt stung. "Could you have done better, just by virtue of being a man?"

"You needn't bristle on her behalf. I just mean this isn't a woman's usual province. I know what a treasure Miss Waverly is. That is why I am here."

Simon bristled against the appreciative look in the other man's eye. Tremayne's gaze followed Penelope as she bent down to examine the wheelwright's child, speaking to the mother, no doubt about some salve or other.

"I've just buried my wife, you see, and my children were quite attached to Miss Waverly when she was their governess."

Simon scowled. "You terminated her employment, did you not?"

"My wife became rather... fractious as her illness progressed. She was somewhat intimidated by Miss Waverly's intellect."

*Or those hours you spent with the pretty governess in the library, teaching her architecture, leaning over books together...* Simon thought bitterly. *No wonder she objected if you were looking at Pen like this...*

"Rest your worries, Captain Harcourt. Nothing improper happened. I did not want to cause my wife any discomfort when she was already suffering so much."

So he had discharged a young woman who'd desperately needed the salary she'd been promised. Simon wanted to scorn him, but he could understand Tremayne's dilemma.

And his dismissal of Pen had been one of the luckiest events of Simon's life.

*It's too late for you to snatch her back,* Simon wanted to warn. *She is mine now.*

There was no doubt what Tremayne's intentions were. Luring Pen back. And had he done so the day before Simon had lain with Pen in her bed, he might have been able to let her go. Tell himself that she would be better off with this architect with his fancy house, his expertise in the profession Pen was fascinated by, with children she already cared for.

But it was too late, now, Simon thought. He loved her.

---

The sun was starting to set when Richard Tremayne handed Penelope up into the gig and they returned to Laurel Cottage. The trip back quieter, with long pauses Pen hadn't expected. When they arrived home, he surprised her by asking, "May I step inside for a moment? I wanted to check something in one of the books I have loaned you."

"Of course." She ushered him into the library where her

drawings and calculations were arranged in neat piles. He ran his fingers over *The Builder's Guide or Complete System of Architecture*, but he didn't open it.

"Where are you staying?" she asked.

"Nelson's Public House. I'll be catching the stage out tomorrow."

"Please tell the children how very sorry I am for their loss. I will write letters to them tomorrow."

"Thank you. It's a difficult time for them." He ran his finger over the embossed title of the book. "They are very fond of you."

"I'm fond of them as well. And glad your sister is there to comfort them."

"Yes. She'll remain until November, but then must leave. She has a family of her own." He hesitated a moment, then looked up at Penelope. "I was hoping that, when she leaves, you might consider returning as governess. It would do the children a world of good to have your steadying hand on the tiller. You are so very capable. So familiar."

Before she had a chance to respond, he closed the space between them and took her hand, his fingers smooth and soft compared to the callus-roughened strength of Simon's. "It would do me good as well. I have never forgotten those evenings we spent together, discussing architecture and science and books we'd read. They were the most fascinating conversations I ever shared with a woman. I know they troubled my wife, and I'm sorry for it. But they were so invigorating, I couldn't resist."

Penelope gently drew her hand from his, regret stinging her as she thought of Tremayne's wife growing weaker and weaker, fearing her husband might stray. How Pen wished she could have reassured her, and yet, truth to tell, she had been tempted by those evenings in the library, the companionship, her first taste of a man truly listening to her. It had been a heady experience, if an uncomfortable one with Mrs. Tremayne upstairs. It had also been the merest sip of what partnership could be when compared to the wholehearted belief Simon had in her abilities. His understanding of her need for independence. His passion as he taught her the secrets of her own body.

Pen gave him an apologetic smile. "I regret that my time with your family caused Mrs. Tremayne any concern. But it is all in the past."

"Is it? These last weeks, I've been unable to push the thought from my mind that, after mourning a decent interval, perhaps you might consent to be more to me than my children's governess."

Pen pulled back in dismay, suddenly uncomfortable in the realization that some of Mrs. Waverly's fears had not been wholly wrong. "I... I don't think..."

"Please, don't misunderstand. Mrs. Tremayne and I were happy once, but as she grew weaker and more withdrawn... you provided a warmth that I've missed. Perhaps my thoughts were not the most honorable, although my actions were beyond reproach. Even so, I know that she would want what is best for the children. I can imagine no better stepmother than you. There is even a small house at the rear of my property that we could convert into a residence for your mother and sisters, in time."

"Mr. Tremayne, I–I don't know what to say. I'm aware of the honor you do me, but it is far too soon to even contemplate..."

"I wish you to know that I admire you above any woman I've ever met. When we were in Italy, the children and I were constantly wondering what you would think. I'd look at the architecture and wish I could share it with you, discuss the fine points. Think what it would be like to explore it together. Italy and France, Prussian castles and Austrian cathedrals."

There was a time it would have been as if he'd offered her the most exquisite sweets to gorge on, but now it left her stomach unsettled. "It is far too soon..."

"I understand. I hope you will accept when the time is right. We already know we are well-suited. We are both past our hot-blooded youth, and appreciate contentment."

Before she realized his intent, Tremayne drew her into his arms. He kissed her softly on the cheek, her lips. It was pleasant, but she felt anchored to the ground, none of that heart racing out of control feeling. There was none of that dizzy reaction she'd felt when Simon molded his mouth to hers, igniting inner fires as his sensual mouth kissed her bare skin, his tongue trailing over her as if she were spun sugar and rich cream.

Pen flattened her palms on his chest and gently pushed away, gaining space between them. "Mr. Tremayne, we mustn't."

"I didn't mean to ask so much of you today," he said. "I only meant to ask you to return as governess. I'm not ignorant of how—how this might sound. But from the moment I saw you, I knew that I needed to make my intentions clear."

"You have. I appreciate that you've been honest."

"You will consider my offer?"

"Mr. Tremayne..."

"Richard."

"Richard. Let us revisit this at a later time. I have to focus on New Everdene. And you must concentrate on your children and on healing your heart."

"Of course, you're right. Perhaps, while you are corresponding with the children, you might write to me. As a friend," he added quietly. "Surely we are that, Penelope. You know I would do anything for you."

"I do."

He offered her his arm, and she walked him outside. As they waited for Hughes to drive Tremayne to the village, Pen caught sight of Epona in the small, fenced paddock. She felt a pang, remembering the day Simon had pulled the miniature of his mother from his pocket. He'd seemed so vulnerable, and for an instant, she had seen the wistfulness of another child who had lost his mother.

An idea took hold of her, and she turned to Tremayne with a flutter of hope. "I was wondering if you might be able to help me with something."

"Of course. Anything within my power," he said tenderly.

"I know you travel widely for your work. You have contact with many people. There is someone I am searching for who tended me after an accident when I was a child."

"Not a serious accident, I hope."

"It was. I was struck by lightning."

Tremayne gasped. "How terrible. You're fortunate to be alive."

By instinct, she touched the scar beneath the bodice of her dress. The twisting reminder of the force that had jolted through her, changing her forever. "I would have died without the care of Dr. Clay and, Lady Ravenscroft, Captain Harcourt's mother. Being back in Everdene, those memories have returned. I'd like to thank Dr. Clay in person after all this time."

Richard's brow furrowed and his rubbed his jaw. "Clay... Clay... why does that sound familiar to me? Ah! Now I remember! I did some work on a church in Galen's Well a year or so ago, and sliced open my finger. I had to have it stitched up at a surgery there. That doctor's name was Clay. William Clay, I think. Nice fellow."

"In Galen's Well?" Excitement bubbled up in Pen.

"Yes. Is he the man you're looking for?"

"I think so." On impulse, she flung her arms around him. "Thank you, Richard. Thank you for sharing your books and your wise counsel regarding New Everdene. And for this news about Dr. Clay. I'll never forget your kindnesses."

He closed his arms around her, and kissed the crown of her head. "I hope to make you happy for the rest of our lives."

Suddenly aware he'd misinterpreted her embrace, she drew away. Her face flushed as Hughes ambled out of the stable.

Richard smiled at her, so warmly it made her regret her impulsiveness. "Goodbye, my dear. For now," he said.

"Goodbye."

Hughes climbed in to the gig, waited for Tremayne, then set the wheels in motion.

Penelope watched them as they drove off, her mind whirling, until they disappeared.

She'd found him. Dr. Clay. Found him at last. Maybe, just maybe, he was the thread that could help her unravel the mystery of what had happened to Simon's mother so long ago.

And yet… Was she right to pursue this further? Caution whispered. What if the truth was something even more painful than what Simon already believed? Was better to know it rather than imagine a hundred ugly possibilities?

She'd only known Lady Ravenscroft a brief time. Those weeks as she'd recovered from the lightning strike, when her body had been in pain. She had few memories of her own parents visiting, the world a strange, blurry haze lit only by the beautiful lady and the young doctor who had spread salves on her burns and cared for her with such tenderness.

Lady Ravenscroft had seemed the soul of kindness, but after Pen watched her father's descent into drunkenness, she knew better than anyone that the face a person showed the world and the face shown to family in the privacy of their own home could be completely different. Concealed behind a mask…

She bit her lip, thoughts of her father bringing the Viscount's letter to mind. Simon's brother had warned there would be repercussions if she defied his wishes, let alone angering the ruthless Earl who had such power over her family.

*You have no idea what you are meddling in...*

Yet, she had seen the wound in Simon's spirit when he'd shown her the miniature of his mother's face. She had seen the longing, the wistfulness in his eyes when Widow Bevans had called him 'our lady's boy'... She remembered the love she'd seen in Lady Ravenscroft's countenance as her wild-spirited son flung himself into her arms, sure of being welcomed.

She would seek out Dr. Clay herself. As much as she wanted to solve this mystery, she couldn't involve Simon until she knew she would not hurt this man she'd come to love.

# CHAPTER 27

*P*en had often contemplated seeking out the doctor who had fought for her life that horrifying day of the lightning strike, but somehow there had always been other demands on her time. The town of Galen's Well was about a two-hour ride from Everdene, and boasted a quarry and a silk factory, as well as a foundling home and a hospital complex surrounded by a high wall.

Dr. William Clay's surgery was a tidy building nestled between a bakery and a milliner's shop. The sign outside it sported an accurate rendering of the human skeletal system, Pen guessed had been painted by Clay's daughter, Isabel.

The waiting room was empty as she stepped into the surgery. It was sparkling clean, with a familiar scent of soap, medicines, and herbs that Penelope found strangely soothing. The door to what must be Dr. Clay's office was cracked open, and Pen crossed to it and knocked softly.

Dr. Clay called out. "I've just returned from the operating theater and will be ready for patients in a quarter hour."

"I'm not a patient. At least, not anymore." Pen peeked in the door.

Dr. Clay peered over the rim of his spectacles, eyes that had seen far too much suffering widening in surprise. "Well, if it isn't my lucky Penny," he exclaimed.

Pen grinned at the tender nickname he'd called her because she'd survived the terrifying storm with no life-altering injuries. Others had not been so fortunate.

"I'm amazed you recognized me, Dr. Clay."

"Some patients you don't forget!"

She'd heard once that beauty was something you were born with, a mere lucky toss of the dice. But in age, you got the face you deserved. He'd been rather non-descript before, reminding Pen of a hound who'd lost its master, even though his smile had been quick and tender. Now, there was a depth of empathy that made him beautiful in her eyes.

He stood and crossed to her, clasping her hands. "What brings you to Galen's Well? You are in good health, I hope."

"My mother recently informed someone that I'm in such good health it's almost indecent."

Dr. Clay laughed. "That is what I like to hear. You never were a lukewarm miss."

"I always meant to visit you, after you moved away. I wanted to thank you for the care you gave me after the lightning strike." It was true that she owed him thanks, but her cheeks flushed, knowing she was using it as an excuse, a way to open up a line of inquiry regarding Simon's mother.

Dr. Clay made a faint, *tsking* sound. "Terrible business, that. So many injured in that storm. As for you, I'd never seen a braver little girl. I'm only glad that your parents allowed you to stay at the surgery so I could see to your recovery."

As long as she lived, Penelope would never forget the burns, or bruises from the tree splintering. She gave him a somber smile. "Between you and Lady Ravenscroft, you made my recovery as easy as possible."

The elderly physician patted her hand, and she noticed his

fingers, once elegantly shaped and deft, were large-knuckled with arthritis. "It was a joy to have you at the house. You were a grand companion for my Isabel."

Dr. Clay's daughter was an only child, whose mother had died giving birth. Pen had faint memories of Isabel distracting her through her weary convalescence, but any hope of continuing the friendship had been lost when Isabel and Dr. Clay moved away soon after Simon's mother had disappeared.

"How is your daughter?"

"She is in Edinburgh. Studying." His eyes twinkled with a mischievous glint Pen couldn't decipher.

"Studying what?"

"I'm not at liberty to say, but she is enjoying herself immensely." His half-smile faded, and he said gently, "We both wished I could have kept you at the house even longer than I did."

"I don't remember much from that time, only snippets, but there was something about a fairy named Lily."

"Lily was Lady Ravenscroft's creation. She cut out paper dolls for you and Isabel and told you stories. It was the first thing that made you smile."

A lump formed in Pen's throat. "You worked with her ladyship often while you were lived in Everdene. It was obvious you cared for each other."

"Yes. We were… friends." The timbre of his voice changed.

Was there more to it than that? Pen wondered.

He cleared his throat. "Lady Ravenscroft worried about you, even after we sent you home. But then, she worried about any wounded creature she stumbled across."

Then how could she callously walk away from her own child? No. Pen couldn't believe that. "I recall her as being very kind."

"Too kind for some." He looked away. His eyes grew misty. "She could never bear to see children or animals in pain. The first time I met her, she brought a horse to me at the surgery. Someone had abused it. I bandaged it. Cared for it. She came to check on it every day with her youngest boy."

"Simon," Pen supplied.

"Yes. He was a wild lad, that one. I patched him up more than once."

"I'd like to thank her for caring for me as well. I thought, if anyone would know where I could write to her, it would be you."

He looked perplexed for long moments, as if he were considering some weighty decision. At last, he crossed to his desk, opened his inkwell and took up a quill. But before he wrote anything, he set it down again and walked to stare out the window. Penelope followed the direction of his gaze, could see the hospital in the distance, a tangle of ivy scaling the high brick fence. He seemed to be wrestling with something that weighed on him.

"Dr. Clay," she probed, "are you quite well?"

"Come with me," he said softly, and started out the office door.

# CHAPTER 28

Simon frowned as his gaze once again locked on Penelope where she stood beside the stream, making him uneasy. Oh, she still came to the building site, still gave instructions, but for the past few days it'd been as if the vibrant woman he'd come to love was lost in shadows. She'd been making excuses to avoid him whenever possible—her gaze distant, as though something weighed heavily on her mind. An invisible gulf had opened between them that marred his deep satisfaction at the row of structures marching along the main road like the houses he and Lucien had built out of blocks as boys.

The site swarmed with workers, some framing in their sixteenth cottage, while Daw and others finished the completed structures inside, worked on roofs or hung front doors. It would be a while before people could begin moving in, but with every day, the time grew closer.

All of this seemed lost on Penelope, he thought, eyeing her from the peak of the roof he and Daw were currently working on. She'd been this way ever since that last odd trip she'd taken shortly after Tremayne had arrived. At first, Simon thought it had been the presence of the architect, his private meeting with her before he'd examined the construction of the cottages, declaring it sound. But the man's presence seemed to bother Simon more than it did Penelope. She'd seemed oblivious whenever Tremayne's gaze had followed her, or he leaned a trifle closer to hear her words.

The way his hand had covered hers when she had taken his arm.

Simon had wanted to shove Tremayne aside like some green lad staking his claim. But he'd resisted the impulse, whether for Penelope's sake or the knowledge that the fellow was in mourning, he couldn't be sure. Of course, he'd asked Pen about the visit later, and she'd admitted that Tremayne had asked her to return to care for his grieving children.

Simon had guessed there was more to it than returning as a simple governess from the flags of color high on Penelope's cheeks, even as she insisted that she'd remain at Everdene for the present.

So, if not Tremayne, then perhaps it was Inchwick. Simon searched the grounds, finding the fastidious man astride a drab brown horse, glaring as Tripp helped Widow Bevans plant seedlings for a flower garden that would bloom alongside her newly built cottage.

The land agent had been careful to keep his distance from Penelope, finding plenty of fault with everything that Simon had done. It seemed that Penelope was doing the same—keeping her distance from Simon. He'd scarce seen her since he'd begun working on the plans for the stables. He was near to finishing— eager to show her his newly revised plans—making him wonder if she would guess why his vision had changed. There was now a house, big enough for a family. A library that could be Pen's own, with a large table she could use to draw building plans. A bedchamber with windows looking out over the pasture he hoped to fill with long-legged foals. And maybe, in time, babes of his own.

Did he dare share his hopes with her? Hopes that now stretched beyond these newly constructed buildings? They'd spent some evenings together—unfortunately, highly chaperoned by her sisters and mother after the day he'd all but made love to her, pleasuring her and tipping his own world off of its axis. But ever since her day trip to who-knew-where, she'd been fidgety, easily distracted. And in the week since Richard Tremayne had called upon her, Simon had begun to fear she might regret those kisses and intimate caresses she and Simon had shared, while he'd wanted nothing more than to steal her away and continue where they'd left off.

Her secretive manner was so unlike forthright Penelope that it set his wits off-balance. Which was why he about fell off the ladder when he noticed her at the bottom, looking up at him.

"Do you have a minute?" she asked.

"Of course."

"I was wondering..." She stared down at his hands, before finally meeting his gaze. If anything, she looked as flighty as a sparrow in front of a hungry cat. "Might you have time to take a drive with me?"

Much to his dismay, her expression told him this was not for some hidden rendezvous. "Is it something that can wait?"

She shook her head.

She knew damned well it was hard for him to be away from the site. He was about to decline when Daw, apparently having overheard as he climbed down the ladder behind them, said, "Go. She's moved heaven and earth for ye. I'll pick up any slack here."

"We should take your team and carriage," Pen suggested. "They'd be swifter than poor Dobby and our gig."

Which is how he found himself sitting next to her in an open carriage driving down the lane toward destinations unknown.

He looked over at her, curious. "You're silent as a sphinx," he teased, as he drove the carriage along the road. "Where exactly are we going?"

She didn't reply.

"Are we going to see one of those model villages you talked about? Some advance in modern stables?" With Penelope, a man never knew. But her expression never changed. "You're starting to scare me. We're not headed off to Gretna Greene," he teased.

"We're going to Galen's Well," she said at last. "And that is all I plan to tell you."

With no other choice, he spent the rest of the drive just enjoying being with her, savoring the brush of her shoulder against his. There were moments he felt this was a normal carriage ride, and she'd been teasing to make him think otherwise. Perhaps she really was arranging a way to steal some privacy. The very thought sent his cock tightening against the falls of his breeches. He'd spent far too many nights picturing her, her pale thighs open to him, her sweet arousal matching his own. He'd taken to keeping a French Letter in the pocket of his coat just in case. The carnal bent of his imagination made him shift to loosen the tightness of his breeches. But as they'd neared the town, she straightened up, putting a sliver of distance between them, that felt like something far greater.

Suddenly, she reached over, touching his arm. "Stop the carriage. I need to stretch my legs."

The town was just visible on the horizon as he reined in, allowing her to alight. He couldn't help notice the edginess in her as she moved about the verge of the road. It gave Simon a twinge of foreboding. There were no model houses, no secluded interludes. Whatever awaited them, it was clear that Penelope was bothered by it.

"Out with it, Pen," he said, his eyes narrowing. "What is this all about?"

Her breast rose and fell in a quick breath, and she wound

one of her bonnet strings around a slender, gloved finger, so tight he was astonished the ribbon didn't snap. "I came here last week and spoke to someone you might remember from childhood. Dr. Clay."

He frowned, more bewildered as to her purpose than ever. "I remember him. Hard to forget a man who picked gravel out of my elbows and stitched up my leg. How did he end up in Galen's Well?"

"There is an infirmary there, and... an asylum for the insane."

Simon forced a smile, the knot of unease tightening in his gut as he stood beside her. "I'm quite certain my brother and Inchwick would say I belonged there after what I've done with the village, but what has Dr. Clay and such a place to do with me?"

"He came to work there because of your mother."

"What the devil?" Simon staggered back a step, feeling as if she'd jammed a knife into his chest.

Penelope rushed on. "Lady Ravenscroft was locked away there for five years after she left Everdene Hall."

Simon clamped an arm over his stomach, feeling as if he was about to retch. "You're telling me that my mother went mad?"

"Someone *accusing* you of madness, and actually *being* mad are far different."

If that was meant to help, it did not. Simon's heart pounded, racing so hard he struggled to breathe. He'd heard of those hellish places. If she wasn't insane when she entered, how could she remain so after so long? He looked at Penelope with some trepidation. "How did you... discover this connection?"

"I made some inquiries."

"Why...?"

She bit at her lower lip before answering. "I sensed how the loss of your mother haunted you. And the tale of her leaving made no sense. You know how I am when I find anything illogical. It niggles in my brain until I have to untangle it, find answers I can accept."

Simon stalked to the carriage, bracing his forearms against the seat, staring at the polished wood, not trusting himself to speak. Was this some sort of nightmare? It felt as if it couldn't be happening. He shuddered, remembering the holiday his father had forced him and Lucien to go to Bedlam to see the poor devils imprisoned there. It was supposed to be an entertaining outing for the ton, though how, Simon couldn't imagine. He'd never forget the inmates shackled, their chains rattling, the shrieks, their crumpled bodies huddled in corners.

Penelope laid her hand on his shoulder, her voice gentle. "I know that you gave your brother your word that you would not delve further into the past and what happened with your mother. But—I had to know."

A flood of emotions swept through him. Anger, fear, trepidation. It horrified him to think that someone else had seen his mother in such a condition, her dignity lost like those bedraggled souls in Bedlam. "Why? Why couldn't you leave memories of her intact. I would rather think she was dead, than—"

"She's well, Simon." Penelope nodded toward the town. "She lives in a cottage near the infirmary grounds and helps the women there."

Simon didn't know how to feel. Part angry, part eager. She'd re-opened a deep wound he'd kept hidden, insisted had scarred over, even though he knew the poison still trickled through his veins. Penelope had released it in a flood.

She reached up, touching the side of his face, those forest-green eyes locked with his. "It's time you hear the tale from her own lips."

# CHAPTER 29

*S*imon's hands clenched so hard on the reins of the carriage that the leather bit into his palms, despite the gloves he wore. The matched team pranced uneasily in the traces as his tension crackled down the thin strips of leather. Simon didn't put any undue pressure on the bits in the horse's tender mouths, but he didn't need to. They sensed the emotions roiling through him.

A strange mingling of anger that Penelope had duped him, anticipation, and—God curse it—fear of what he'd find.

He'd imagined this meeting a hundred times in his boyhood, when he lay curled on a hard cot at school, his body aching from nasty pinches and cuffs from older boys or the latest caning from his teachers. He'd bitten his own hand to keep from crying, thinking that if he could just reach his mother, find her, everything would be right again in his world. He would be safe. God knew, he still needed to see her, even all these years later.

But nothing felt *safe* now. The foundation of his whole world was shaking.

*It's your choice whether you want to meet her,* Penelope had repeated as the carriage rattled forward. But was it? Part of him wanted to wheel the horses around, heeding Lucien's warning he'd only find disaster delving into the past, honoring the promise he'd given to his brother. But it was too late. He had to know the truth. This was his one chance to learn it.

Pen directed him through the town, the neat streets lined with shops, people going about their daily tasks. It was a pleasant enough view, except for the imposing building looming to the east. A tall brick wall surrounded it. Barred windows from a second and third floor peeked over the barrier like vacant eyes.

Simon knew which cottage belonged to his mother even before Pen tugged his sleeve.

An easel was set up facing the arbor, but the painter had deserted her post to rearrange a still life on a stone bench. A wide, flat-brimmed hat shaded her face, the blonde curls that escaped the knot at the nape of her neck only a little faded. She wore a simple gown in her favorite color—the blue of Simon's eyes.

She straightened at the sound of the approaching carriage, and the sight of her face struck Simon like a bolt of lightning.

It was twenty years since he's seen her, but he knew her crooked smile, that soft cheek, the way her brows swept like a bird's wing.

Her face was care-worn, not the with the hard, stony anger of his father, but a quiet sadness where once there had been laughter and joy. A stranger, wearing his mother's once-beloved face

Part of him wanted to whip up the horses, drive past as if he never saw her, but Pen slid her gloved hand across the space between them, to rest on his thigh. Any other time, it would have been a shocking intimacy, sensual. But this time the warm pressure grounded him. He drew rein, set the brake, then leapt down from the carriage. After securing the horses to the hitching post, he circled around to help Penelope from her seat.

His hands felt clammy as he turned to face his mother.

Age had subtly changed Lenora Harcourt's features, lines softly fanning the corners of her eyes, the skin without the vibrant rosy hue in Simon's memory. Her mouth was still soft with a tenderness almost too deep for the harsh-edged world, her profile like the cameos she once wore at her throat.

She started to reach toward his face to touch him, as if she feared he wasn't real. But, at the last moment, she seemed to think he might not welcome such an intimacy, and knotted her hands together, her knuckles turning white. Her lower lip wobbled, but she stood stock-still.

He'd seen her thus before, with wary animals or children, giving them time and space to grow comfortable in her presence, allowing them the freedom to come to her when ready.

"Simon..." She looked up at him. Her eyes glittered with unshed tears.

An ocean of hurt still flowed between them, questions that might never be answered. He nodded in greeting, refusing to do more. "Of course, you already know Miss Waverly, don't you?" he said, unable to keep the bite from his words. "You got to know each other while arranging this little family reunion."

"We came to know each other far earlier than that. After her accident during the Great Storm." His mother smiled. "You've made a long journey. Please come in and I'll order a tea tray."

She led them up the flagstone path and to the blue-painted door. It stood ajar, as if waiting.

Simon's heart hammered as he stepped inside. He was struck by the simple beauty. It suited her far better than the ornate gilt frames and mirrors in Everdene Hall. The furnishings in the earldom's residences were made to impress, like a peacock spreading its tail and screeching its own importance. This room was designed for comfort, a quiet invitation to rest. A settee stood against a wall. A pair of chairs were tucked near a sunny window. Paintings hung in clusters about the room, one large canvas in a place of honor. Simon's chest felt tight as he peered at it. Four children frolicked on the Everdene lawn with a litter of puppies. Cassandra and Jane, Lucien and Simon, a table set nearby with a pink-frosted cake, and a pile of presents. He'd remembered that day distinctly. It had been Cassandra's birthday fete.

The last birthday they were all together.

She noticed his scrutiny. "I did it from memory when I was overcome by darkness. Recreating that day brought me light." She opened a door, and Simon could hear the sounds of someone putting a room to rights.

"Betsy, we have visitors."

Simon's brow furrowed at the name. Surely, it couldn't be…

A woman, stout as a pudding bag, bustled in with a tray, her cheeks rosy, her cap askew. The tray in her hands rattled dangerously at the sight of him, teacups clinking against saucers, tea spilling from the teapot she nearly overset. "Lor' save us! It can't be… Master Simon?"

"Nurse Betsy!"

"The most loyal friend ever born," his mother said.

Simon rushed to take the tray from the older woman and set it on a table as his mother explained. "Dr. Clay was kind enough to make inquiries and make certain Betsy was all right after the turmoil of my leaving. When he found her, she insisted on coming to stay with me."

His former nurse smiled. "Well, someone had to take care o' you, my lady," Betsy said as she hurried toward Simon. He grasped her hands. Hands that had smoothed across his forehead when he'd had a fever, scrubbed his face when he'd had jam on it, tucked him into bed, and chased away bad dreams.

"I knew you'd be a handsome 'un when you grew!" Betsy exclaimed. "Feet so big and those knobbly knees! Ah, and the twinkle in your eyes! Like to stole my heart, even when I was this close to showing you the back of my hand. There never was a boy could charm himself out of trouble like you."

They sat and spoke in stilted tones, pouring tea, selecting slices of lemon cake or sandwiches from a chipped plate. The food tasted like ash in Simon's mouth. After a few minutes, Penelope startled everyone by rising. "Betsy, could you show me about the garden? After the long carriage ride, I could use the air."

How like Pen to know he and his mother couldn't have the conversation needed with anyone else about.

"There is a lovely little bench out back," his mother said, giving her a grateful smile as Betsy ushered her toward the door. As Pen passed Simon, she paused to squeeze his stiff shoulder, her fingers strong and bracing. He met her warm, green gaze. She was so damned beautiful, her face soft with concern for him, and something more that curled around his heart.

The room suddenly felt empty as the two women closed the door behind them, leaving Simon and his mother alone. He wished to hell he could draw out a flask and let whisky sear away some of the emotions churning inside him. But there was no such relief at hand. He could hear the clock on the mantel ticking, the soft rustle as his mother rearranged her skirts, the faint voices of Penelope and his nurse as they wandered about the garden.

His mother glanced out the window, then back at him. "I was stunned when Penelope sought me out," she said quietly at last. "Even after she left, I wasn't sure you'd be willing to see me."

"She didn't tell me where we were going until we were nearly here."

"Ah." A flash of pain crossed her face at the knowledge that he'd not come by his own choice. "So many times, I tried to imagine what you looked like. I knew you'd be tall and handsome, with that mischief in your eyes." She tried to smile, but it soon faltered. "There hasn't been a day I haven't thought of you, missed you, longed to see your face, and hear your voice."

Was he supposed to say that he missed her, too? As a boy, it had been as if someone had torn a limb from his body when he'd lost her. He'd staggered through those first years, as if he were learning all over how to walk, how to breathe... He couldn't admit that. And so, he waited, distrust mixed with something he couldn't define.

At last, she filled the silence thick between them. "I'd heard Barnabas bought you your commission in the cavalry and you'd been posted to India. All I could think of was you and Lucien playing with toy soldiers on Christmas morning and fighting with wooden swords on the lawn." Her face lit up at the memory. "You always wished to have adventures, but that was not the same as real battles." Her tone was soft, searching.

"No. It's not the same." Images flashed, blood, death, devastation. He pushed them back into a box in his head, locked it away. He hadn't come to speak of these wounds with his mother —rather, far older ones. There were so many questions he wanted answers to, but he voiced the only one that mattered.

"What happened the night you disappeared?"

# CHAPTER 30

*W*hat *happened the night you disappeared?* The question reverberated through the room, making it hard to breathe. Simon watched expressions dart across his mother's face until she stared into her teacup as if it held the answers. After long moments, she raised her gaze to his.

"Your father and I had fought for years, but we'd come to live separate lives, spending as little time as possible together. He stunned me by showing up at Everdene, and informed me that he planned a marriage for Cassandra. Do you remember Lord Thornsby?"

He'd felt an instinctive loathing when it came to the older man. With a knife-slash of a mouth, and eyes so deep set they all but disappeared, save for a mean-spirited glint. And those eyes had followed Cassandra in a way that turned Simon's stomach.

"I remember him." When Simon had been stationed on the Gold Coast, he'd heard that Thornsby still ran slave ships, despite the trade being outlawed in England. Thornsby skirted the law by sailing his ships under the Portuguese flag.

"Lord Thornsby and I had clashed before," she continued.

"You recall the mare we found injured and took to Dr. Clay to mend?"

"Yes."

"That was Lord Thornsby's. I came across him beating the poor thing. There were whispers that he had harmed his first wife." She pressed her lips together, taking a shuddering breath. "I learned that your father intended to force Cassandra's marriage to Thornsby, to consolidate his power in the House of Lords. She was not yet fifteen. Your father planned to send her to be raised in the man's household until the wedding. I couldn't allow it. I packed up our things. A friend had a carriage waiting at the end of the lane. Had I not taken both girls, he would have sent Jane in Cassandra's place."

Simon's stomach turned. The anger he felt toward his father formed a hot ball in his chest. He took a deep breath, willing himself to remain calm, listen to his mother's story.

"I'd hoped that your father might tire, leave the girls be. But if I took his sons... you know how he is. He would hunt me to the ends of the earth."

It was true.

Simon felt sick with horror as he imagined the terror his mother and sisters must have felt, the plans made, the surreptitious preparations.

"We were nearly to the door when..." she paused a moment, a pained look flashing across her face. "When someone raised the alarm. I begged the girls to run, hoping that they could reach the carriage, that my friend could still spirit them away. I remember Barnabas striking me... then nothing. I woke in the root cellar, Jane and Cassandra weeping over me." Her voice choked as she brushed back her tears. "The next day, he dragged me to St. Alban's Asylum for the Insane and delivered both girls to that awful man."

The cruel bastard had known all the time... when Simon had searched for his mother, wept for her, grieved her loss. When the Earl had beaten him for speaking her name, he had known she was locked behind iron-barred windows, her heart breaking with fear for her children.

Murderous rage swept over him. He wanted his hands around his father's throat…

He shot to his feet, stalked away, not wanting his mother to see the demons he'd barely leashed. His fists opened and closed as he fought for control. When he could speak, he said, "Cassandra never married him. Father sent her and Jane to Italy to his sisters to raise." He looked to see his mother's reaction, somewhat surprised by the odd smile on her gentle face. "Why do I get the feeling that you knew this?"

"I may have had something to do with that. I traded my wedding ring to a matron at the asylum in exchange for her help. She wrote Thornsby a letter, warning him that the girls' blood was tainted. After all, their mother was a maniac. Thornsby, much like your father, worried about his reputation should such horrifying news get out. He wanted nothing to do with the girls after that. By some small miracle, I think your father was afraid if he attempted another match for the girls, Thornsby might alert their prospective bridegrooms to my status."

Amazing that his mother had triumphed in spite of the lies and iron bars, besting the ruthless Earl, while saving her daughters from such a hideous fate.

The powerful Earl of Ravenscroft had been no match for a mother's love.

There were still so many questions, and he sucked in a deep breath to steady himself, not sure he wanted to hear the answers to some. "How did you ever escape the asylum?"

"At first, I thought I never would. When I arrived at St. Alban's, it was run by an elderly doctor who believed the traditional values—that a husband had a right to commit his wife for any number of infractions, many of which I was guilty. Disobedience, novel reading, emotional excitement. Refusal of the marital act, as well as melancholia and mania. *That* doctor was in charge of the asylum for the first three years, and I had little hope. It was terrifying at first, the despair near unbearable. My daughters delivered to that monster, Thornsby. You, believing I had deserted you. And Lucien..." She swallowed hard. "A mother is supposed to protect her children, but I had failed in every way."

Simon went to her, took her hands. Held them, regretting all the years he believed the worst of her—a wounded child, abandoned, grieving, then hardening a shell of contempt and anger around that pain, never delving deeper. "No. You gave us so much love. I looked for you everywhere, sure you would come back, not believing you would just leave me, not caring."

"That is what your father told you, then."

"He beat me when I kept looking for you, demanding to know where you were. Insisting I would find you."

"My Simon. It breaks my heart to know you suffered that way. I knew you would be most hurt by my disappearance. You were so small. Forever going with me when I went to the village, telling me stories, asking me questions."

That was how Pen had remembered the two of them, the love, the laughter.

"I... I might have been an inmate forever were it not for Dr. Pierce, the young partner Dr. Yardley brought into his practice during my fourth year at St. Alban's. Pierce's wife was a kindly woman who provided recreation for the less affected patients. Drawing lessons, musicales, gardening in little plots on the grounds. Over time, we struck up a friendship and she was troubled by the fact that she saw no signs of melancholia or mania in me. None of the symptoms of one institutionalized for being insane."

"I asked Mrs. Pierce to contact Dr. Clay, that *he* would be able to explain the circumstances under which I'd been committed." Her smile trembled. "He was the friend who had been willing to help me escape with the girls. He'd left Everdene in fear that your father would discover his part in the plan. When Mrs. Pierce contacted him, he moved here, working with the doctor in charge of the asylum. At great risk to himself, Dr. Clay convinced Dr. Pierce to re-examine my case. They presented two medical certificates declaring me sane."

"Did Father know?"

"They notified him, and he came here. He could not incarcerate me again, but he swore that if I ever attempted to contact any of you children, he would disinherit you and the girls, leaving you penniless."

"That was why you let me continue to think you had deserted us?"

"How could I live with myself, knowing you might be turned out into the streets?"

"I would have paid that price willingly to have you back in my life. To know… the true story of what had happened."

"Perhaps you, but I also had Cassandra and Jane to think of."

"I want you to come home with me," Simon insisted. "Bring my sisters home. I'll see you are all safe."

But could he? He could offer physical protection, but his own financial future was in jeopardy. No, he would find a way, damn it, if he had to turn to highway robbery. He would enlist his brother's help. "Between Lucien and me, I know that we can protect you."

"As much as I wish it, I can't. I have my work here. Women who are suffering the same situation, who are not as fortunate as I have been." She smiled, though her eyes were still tinged with sadness. "There is one woman in particular who is a gifted artist. Mrs. Pierce and I have been selling her paintings and saving the money in hopes we can secure her release, and she will be able to set up housekeeping. Besides," she said, her eyes darkening, "your father would never allow it. And it could only make an already untenable situation more difficult for everyone. You cannot know how—"

"I know my father's ruthlessness very well."

"Yes... your father..." Her words faded, and she reached up, taking his hand in hers, a familiar clasp he'd only remembered in dreams. "You mustn't lose your temper and confront your father, my dear, dear love. He is still my husband. He could spirit me away from here and lock me away somewhere no one would ever find me."

"Not if I kill him first," Simon replied, his voice low.

"Don't even think it!" she cried. "The last thing I wish is for you to risk ruining your future over something that cannot be undone. Miss Waverly told me about your work in the village... Lash out at your father and that would all be at an end." He turned away, not willing to make a promise he couldn't keep. But she didn't let go of his hand, her voice pleading. "I've spent years trying to make peace with what is. Now that you are back in my life... can you not see? Having you visit me, being able to hear your voice, see your beloved face?" She drew his hand to her heart. "Now I have my Simon. Now you know how much I love you... it is more than I ever hoped for. Let us be grateful for that gift."

"I am. But I'm angry—"

"I know. Yet, you mustn't let anger over the past destroy what we have now. Anger festered in your father, poisoned him. No wrong from the past is worth jeopardizing the future that you have built for yourself and those in Everdene. I was so very proud of you when I heard. Perhaps one day I can see it."

"I'll show it to you myself, once it is done."

"Perhaps... we can have a picnic there."

Simon thought of the families who gathered at the site, the laughter, their teasing, children running about while their parents and grandparents watched or joined in or squabbled good-naturedly. What would it be to have his own family thus?

His mother, his brother, perhaps even Jane and Cassandra one day… He closed his eyes, his heart aching as he pictured Penelope there as well… children… He nodded. "I'd like that," he said, his voice roughened with emotion.

"I will bring Lucien to see you as well. When I tell him—"

"No!" Her face paled, her fingers tightening around his hand. "Promise me you will not put him in such an impossible position. His fate is too tightly bound to your father."

Something in her face, made him promise. "As you wish."

"If you will write to me and visit… that will be more than I ever imagined possible. So very, very precious."

She let go of his hand, then glanced at the window where Penelope and his old nurse wandered among his mother's flowers. "Do you care for her?"

*I love her*, he wanted to say, but there was still too much distance to bridge between them. In the end, all he could do was nod.

His mother seemed to understand, though her gaze was still on Pen. "I've always known such love was not to be mine, but it is healing to watch it, to hope one day my own children might find something like it." She looked at Simon. "Marriage can be cruel. And a woman's powerlessness over her own fate is perhaps the cruelest of all. But we can change that. You and Penelope are doing so right now. From the moment you accepted those building schemes from her, took her skills and gifts and opinions seriously, and recognized her worth, there was a shift in the world. Don't lose that. Even a mountain will one day crack."

She stood and cupped his face in her hands, looked into his eyes with that love that was so tender, so familiar. "Go now," she said. "Before anyone discovers you've been here. Do not let anyone know that we've found each other. I beg you."

"For now," he said. Yet how long would he be able to keep such a promise?

# CHAPTER 31

*P*enelope sat on a stone bench in the garden, every fiber of her being straining toward the modest cottage and the man inside it, wondering what he was feeling.

Anger, gratitude, pain, or healing… whatever emotions the time with his mother unleashed would make for a long drive back.

She drew a soft green paisley shawl around her shoulders and shivered. Was the temperature dropping, the wind shifting? Or was it just her nervousness now that she realized what price she might pay?

Her actions caused Simon to betray his word of honor to his brother. It was also possible he would not forgive her for keeping the truth from him until it was too late.

No matter how he felt, the risk had been worth it. Over these weeks, she'd seen the wound in him, felt it as intimately as she had the searing pain from the lightning strike so long ago. She cared too much to let that pain go on burning under the surface, a searing edge to the man who'd worked his way into her heart.

Her heart…

Pen's fingers trembled, and she remembered how it felt to thread them through his hair, the way his hand felt on her skin, his mouth coaxing sensations from her body she hadn't even thought possible. How would he feel about her after this day? Would he ever kiss her again? All she knew was that she wanted to uncover all of the secrets of his beautiful body, his quick mind, that hero he concealed beneath a devil-may-care grin.

A gust of wind rustled the shrubbery around the bench, a branch snagging on her skirt. She bent down to untangle it and went still as she noticed the plant's leaves cupped like a child's upturned palm. Nature's trick to catch the rain when it fell.

She had always busied herself with brisk efficiency when storms came, crushing any residual fear from the one that had almost killed her. Whenever there was the hint of a storm brewing, there was still that prickle at the back of her nape, a frisson of alarm she'd dismiss a heartbeat later. But she was unable to do so now.

The wind changed direction, bringing with it the mare's tails scudding across an otherwise blue sky, the first harbinger of a coming storm.

Echoes from the past awakened.

Her memories of that terrible day had been a blur the first year after the accident. But nightmares had turned darkness into agony, every crack of thunder a monster prowling. She'd been determined not to let anyone guess how frightened she was, but she would wake up screaming. Since then, she'd had years of practice in concealing fear, between her father's drunken outbursts and learning that their home was lost and they were left with little to live on.

Yet, today felt different, memory's shadow-claws scratching at the doors.

She fretted with a button on her bodice as a rim of gray appeared on the distant horizon.

When she couldn't dismiss her unease any longer, she

hurried toward the house, nearly running into Simon and his mother as they stepped out the door to find her.

Seeing the concern on her face, Simon asked, "Is something wrong?"

She tried to smile against her growing concern. "I fear it looks like rain."

Simon and his mother stepped out into the garden and gazed in the direction she pointed.

"Perhaps a bit of haze," his mother said. "As much as I hate to have you leave, I'd not want you to get caught in a storm. You'd best start for Everdene, while you can."

Pen's throat ached as Simon stepped forward, enfolding his mother in his arms. The two clung to each other a long moment. His lashes closed. His voice husky. "I will return as soon as I can. Seeing you… it's been…"

"An answer to my dearest prayer." She kissed him on the cheek. "Remember, *this* is what matters, my darling boy. That we've found each other again. Not anger over the past."

Simon's eyes flashed as if her words twisted like shrapnel in an old wound.

"I love you, Simon. I always have. Never doubt it."

"I won't. I love you."

The moment was too poignant, too private to share. Pen moved to climb into the carriage, but Lady Ravenscroft stopped her. "Penelope." The older woman swept toward her. "Thank you," she said, enfolding her in a motherly hug such as Penelope had rarely known.

For just a moment, she let herself melt into that warmth, imagine what it might have been like to have such love to depend on.

Amidst a flurry of final farewells, Simon helped her into the carriage then turned toward Everdene. They drove in silence, Simon's jaw set hard, a muscle in his jaw working. At first, she thought he was wrestling with emotions that had left him vulnerable. But as the miles passed, she could feel the anger building inside him. She had feared he might have conflicting feelings about what she'd done, regardless of his joy at seeing his mother. Or was there something more, some burden he needed to share?

Once, Penelope had dreamed of independence—living for herself alone. But those dreams had had changed. She now felt a need that unnerved her, an emptiness she longed to fill, in her body and in her heart. She'd seen in exquisite detail what magic Simon's hands could create… Hands that could tame a wild stallion from faraway lands, set a rafter in a cottage roof, wield a saber. Sensitive fingers that could draw inexpressible sensations from bare skin. She wanted to discover just how deep their passion could go, the emotions she'd so fiercely controlled given free rein.

She wanted to share whatever storm was raging inside him after their visit to Galen's Well, to make sure that he knew he wasn't alone.

Unable to bear the silence any longer, she said, "Your mother is just as I remembered her. She hasn't changed."

"She isn't the same," he lashed out. "She never will be."

Pen stiffened and glanced at his face. She'd never seen him like this, his eyes so dark, as if peering out from the very reaches of hell. "You are angry," she said.

"After what my father's done? Tearing her away from her children, locking her in an insane asylum? Betrothing my sister to a monster? I've killed men for less."

Pen winced at the hate in his voice, but at least his rage was aimed at the man who caused his pain, shattered his family. "There were times I felt the same way," she ventured. "When my father lost our home…"

"I don't think so," Simon said darkly. "You might have hated him for it, but you would never actually load a pistol, meet him at dawn, and pull the trigger. I would. I've done it before. And

I've never wanted to feel that pistol grip in my hands as much as I do now."

She laid her hand on his leg, the muscles iron hard beneath her palm. As much as she hoped otherwise, clearly he meant every word. "Tell me," she said softly. "If you want to."

"I'm trying my damnedest to do as my mother asked me to. Not let the beast out."

"The beast?"

"Soldiers train to unleash the beast inside them. We have to, or we'd hesitate on the battlefield and be killed ourselves. But you can't just… just lock that part of yourself away and forget about it. Sometimes it comes roaring out."

"Like now."

His jaw ticked as he concentrated on the road, the horses skittish as the weather began to turn. "I keep picturing my sisters' faces, my mother urging them to run—so close to freedom, and my father dragging them back and throwing them into hell. I'm gutted by what happened to them while I was right upstairs in the nursery, sleeping."

His self-recrimination broke her heart. "You were a child. Even if you'd been right beside them, there would have been nothing you could do to stop your father."

She'd wanted to soothe him. Instead, his face contorted.

"Damn it, Pen, I can't talk about this now. I'm trying to comprehend the fact that my mother was so damn close all these years. If I'd looked for her… Maybe I could have gotten her out of that place sooner. Spared us all those lost years."

"You were in the cavalry then, fighting wars."

"I didn't know the war I should be fighting was right here. But I know it now." Simon's face turned grim. "Yes, damn my father to hell. I know it now."

Was this what his brother had feared? This recklessness, this need for vengeance escaping its leash? Would Simon really do something rash?

She shuddered, Simon's face darkening like the storm clouds on the horizon. Fear closed a hand about her throat, roiling clouds racing toward them with alarming speed. Raw emotion churned inside her, echoing the storm raging inside Simon and in her own chest, the memory of that horrific day she'd been injured so fresh that the old scar burned. It wasn't long before the first drops of rain struck, cold against her skin and her muscles tightened against the stinging drops.

Thunder rumbled, and Pen stifled a cry as a bolt of lightning cracked the sky. Panic clamped around her ribs like iron bands.

She heard Simon curse, urging the horses to greater speed. The bays tossed their heads, snorting and shying from bits of branches that skittered across the road in front of them. The poor animals rolled their eyes, laying ears back at the rumble of the storm. Only Simon's expert hand with the horses kept them from bolting as they neared the edge of the estate.

"We might still be able to make it to Laurel Cottage," Simon said. But they'd barely crossed the border, when the heavens opened. A deluge hammered down on them. Jagged streaks of lighting split the sky, the thunder roaring.

Pen cried out, the horses lunging, trying to bolt as the strike sizzled along the ground, but Simon braced his booted feet against the front of the carriage and tightened the reins. "Hold on," he said.

She gripped the braces on the carriage so hard her hands ached.

"My father has a hunting box just over that ridge," Simon said through gritted teeth. "We can wait out the storm there."

Could they? Was there any way to take shelter from the storm she'd unleashed?

A sizzling bolt struck a tree near them, the crack of wood splitting and the searing flame terrifyingly familiar.

She cried out as leaves and bits of branches struck her cheek, the fingers of lightning ripping away the dark curtain time had drawn over that nightmarish day so long ago.

The carriage jerked as Simon reined to a halt before a small, tidy shelter.

He said something... she couldn't understand... couldn't make her hands release the carriage brace.

"Go!" He snapped, circling her wrist with his hand and pulling her fingers free.

She felt as if she was falling, swirling, completely untethered as she climbed down from the carriage and stumbled toward the door.

She could see it all, the branches whipping wildly, the lambs lashed by rain, she could hear their bleating, feel the weight of the bundle she clutched in her arms...

The wind raked back the shawl she'd covered Fanny's doll with...

Pen's blood froze with horror.

She remembered.

Jesus, God. She remembered.

# CHAPTER 32

Simon stabled the horses, rubbing them down with hay, filling the feed box with grain from bags in the tack room before he barred them in their stalls. The animals paced and snorted, but damn if he could calm them. The storm outside mirrored the maelstrom inside his chest. He stalked across the small space, knowing he bloody well couldn't go into the hunting box filled with a rage so hot he feared it might spill over despite his best efforts.

He smashed his hand into the wall, the pain reverberating up his arm, and bringing with it a moment of clarity. The one thing he knew for certain was that he couldn't trust himself near that tyrannical bastard who had sired him. Not until Simon got some measure of control over the murderous fury coursing through his veins. His mother had begged him to let the past go, but he didn't have her capacity for turning to her better angels. The soulless devil inside him wanted to burn his father's whole world to the ground.

But this time, he couldn't let his demons free. He no longer had the luxury. The people who depended on Simon now had no defense against the force that threatened them. His father could take everything from the villagers, turning them all out, just to spite Simon for going against his wishes.

"Get ahold of yourself," he warned, looking down at his hand, seeing a smear of blood. He never wanted Penelope to see this side of him. Simon braced his palms on the wall, his head dropping between his arms. He sucked in a deep breath and blew it out, repeating the actions until his blood cooled. When he'd managed to tamp down his anger, he straightened and swiped the wet hair from his face. He couldn't stay out here, pacing and furious. Not when Pen was inside the cottage, so badly shaken from the storm. At least now, he'd give her no cause to be afraid of him. He checked the horses one last time, then headed out the stable door.

As soon as he stepped into the rain, he frowned, unease trickling down his spine. The windows of the hunting box were still dark. He'd told her to start a fire… that there was wood and tinder. Why hadn't she done so? He moved to the door, opened it and went still. The room was ice cold, not so much as a flicker of flame in the hearth.

Lightning flashed, momentarily illuminating Penelope—his dauntless Pen—huddled in a corner, water dripping from her soaked hair and clothes pooling around her as she clutched her knees to her chest.

She was crying, wrenching, silent sobs that sliced right through him.

He'd never seen her afraid. Not like this. The remnants of his anger faded, not nearly as important as the woman before him.

He crossed the room in three strides, taking her in his arms, her limbs ice cold. "Pen, my love, what's wrong?

She looked up into his face, hell in her eyes. "Simon, I c-can't breathe."

"Are you hurt?"

She shook her head. "My side burns. Like the storm is–is *alive*…"

Oh, God, Simon knew what she was suffering. He had felt it himself when the horrors of past battles broke through his guard.

He held her tight. "It's all right now. You're safe. I've got you." He drew her face to his chest, stroking the tangle of soaked hair that had fallen from its pins and straggled down her back. She was wet, shaking with fear and cold. She clung to him, and he wished he could just keep holding her. But he needed to get her warm, light the dark corners in the cabin and in her mind. "I'm going to start a fire. I need to get you warm," he soothed, as he placed her gently on a chair.

He pried the flint from her stiff fingers, and went to the hearth, striking a spark to char cloth, gently feeding tinder to the tiny blaze until it caught, the wavering tendrils of flame glowing orange and gold. A faint hint of warmth penetrated the chill that seemed to have soaked in to his bones. Once the fire was crackling brightly, he drew Pen to her feet, leading her closer to the growing blaze.

Her lips were blue, her teeth chattering loudly. Once again she wrapped her arms around her body, the shawl drenched, her gown plastered to her skin.

He held her for long moments, trying to warm her until the fire's heat began to penetrate the cold. Only then did he finally let go. "Sit closer to the flames. You're safe now."

He strode to the cupboard, and rummaged through it, finding trousers and shirts, toweling and blankets. Her eyes were huge in her face, and she jumped when thunder boomed just overhead. "Shh, love," he said, returning to her side.

Gently, Simon undressed her, stripping the wet cloth from flesh covered with goosebumps. Her body was beautiful, just as he'd imagined, those lonely nights as he pleasured himself, hungry for the feel of her. But now, she seemed so vulnerable. He only wanted to hold her, assure her that nothing would ever hurt her while he drew breath.

He grabbed toweling, wrapping one about her shoulders, drying her back, her breasts and arms. He knelt before her, gently moving another over her slender legs, the swell of her bottom, the dusky feminine curls. When he was satisfied that she was dry, he drew a man's shirt over her head, the garment far too big for her slender frame. The top was unbuttoned, the deep vee sagging open to reveal the velvety curve of her breasts. He helped her into a pair of trousers that bagged around her waist, and let the cuffs fall over her feet. Next, he wrapped a blanket around her and drew the large chair close to the now-crackling fire. Settling her on the leather upholstery, he rubbed her feet, trying to warm them with his hands.

"Y–you need to get dry, too," she said at last, and he stood, kissing her before he hastened to shed his own garments and dry himself as best he could. After pulling on a pair of breeches, he draped their wet clothes on wooden chairs near the fire. When he turned back toward Pen, she looked so frag-ile, her face contorting just a little with each flash of lightning, each rattling of the wind against the windows. He peered down at her, his heart seeming to crack open, his mother's wistful-ness in his ear. *Such love is not for me, but I hope my children find it...*

It was then he knew that he would spend his life trying to be worthy if Penelope put her trust in him.

He slid onto the settee beside her, drawing the blanket around them both to share his own body heat with her.

He could feel the soft tremors working through her, knew the sensations she was feeling, the way past traumas could flood back, feel more real than this room, this fire, his arms.

After a while, she melted against him and the trembling stilled. A quiet enveloped them as the rain pattered on the roof, the sound now more peaceful than wild. "I won't let the storm in," he whispered against her temple, her curls brushing his lips. "It's all right now."

"No. No, it's not. It can never be… I remember the day of the storm. What happened."

"It was all a long time ago. You're safe, love."

"I'm safe… but Catherine isn't…she was in my arms…I was holding her, wrapped in a shawl… trying to keep her dry. But the wind tore the cloth away from her face."

"I'm sorry you lost Fanny's doll, love."

"She wasn't a doll, Simon." Her voice broke on a sob. "She was a baby. My baby sister… Catherine."

---

HER WORDS WERE A KNIFE TO HIS HEART. FOR A HEARTBEAT HE couldn't breathe, staring into her eyes. Knowing nothing he could say would help. "Oh, love. I'm so sorry."

"I didn't even remember her…" Pen choked out. "I only knew that, when I came home it was as if… if Father brought me to a stranger's house. Nothing… seemed right. Father. Mother. Even Fanny, crying and crying for Catherine. The baby's clothes, her little blankets, even her cradle… were gone. It was as if they'd… *erased* her. Mother had taken to her bed. She was never the same again. And Father… that was when he started to drink."

She bit her knuckle. Her body shook.

"I'm sorry, Pen, so damned sorry that happened to your family. But you were a little girl. You couldn't know what would happen… Your parents were grieving, but they should have taken care of you. You were alive and hurt and needed them. It wasn't your fault."

"Wasn't it? No wonder my mother got so angry when I wouldn't listen. No wonder she… she couldn't love me the way your mother loved you."

Lightning flashed, thunder roaring so loud it rattled the windowpanes. The rage, the anger and sense of betrayal that had gripped Simon faded, leaving only the need to comfort this brave, bright woman, to hold her, make love to her, shield her from all of the pain life had dealt her. To always be shelter when a storm battered her world.

"I love you," he said.

Her gaze lifted to his, haunted eyes the green of a fairy glade. Her sable lashes clung together, glistened with tears. A feeling he'd never known before swept through him, and buried itself in his heart.

"I'd give anything to take your pain away, but I can't. I know it's there. Even so, I swear to God, Pen. I'll never leave you alone in a storm, whether it's on the heath or in your heart."

She was quiet for so long, he thought perhaps she was about to deny him. Then, finally, her voice, soft, hesitant. "I love you. I'm still afraid, but… Simon, you make me want to… you make me *want*."

She arched her neck to bring her mouth to his, kissed him. Her mouth so hungry, so sweet he crushed her to him, kissing her back with a need so primitive, so consuming he couldn't hold any of himself apart. There was so much left undecided. The reckoning with his father, the village, the mystery with Lucien, and yet, in that moment, he held the answer he'd searched for all his life in his arms.

"Make love to me, Simon," she pleaded, as thunder crashed overhead.

He scooped her up, carried her to the bedchamber with its simple coverlets and brass frame. Rain sluiced in sheets down the glass panes, the world beyond a gray, wind-tossed blur. Lightning crackled, but he was there, the flash across the sky not nearly as electric as the force that blazed between them every time he touched her. The over-loose trousers fell past the flare of her hips with the barest nudge from his hands.

By the flickering light from the sky, she grasped the bottom of the shirt and pulled it off, her naked breasts bouncing just a little as her hardened nipples pulled free of the fabric. Cream velvet, crowned with aureoles the color of ripe berries, lush and exquisitely sweet.

"You are so damned beautiful," Simon breathed. He shed his own clothes in a rush, the two of them diving beneath the coverlets, the bed linens cold on bare skin. He covered her body with his, giving her his heat, giving her everything he ever hoped to be.

Pen opened to him, cradling his lean hips between her thighs. His cock swelled and he rubbed it gently against her feminine cleft. The silky curls and slick heat of her as he slid against her sent waves of pleasure to every cell in his body. He shaped her breast with his palm, toying with the nipple until it was a tight bud. She moaned softly, arched her back, bringing her breast closer to his mouth, curled her hand around his nape and pulled him down to suckle her.

Simon toyed with the rosy crest, then drew her into his mouth, gently nipping and then sucking as he moved against her, nudging the tiny pearl at the peak of her sex.

Pen's fingers dug into his back, sliding down over his shoulders, to his buttocks. The tip of his cock touched the opening of her body, and Simon froze. She lifted her own hips, as if to follow him. He braced himself on his elbows, staring down at her passion-flushed face.

"Pen, I don't... the French letter is in my coat... soaked and..."

"I don't care. Not anymore." She reached between them, taking hold of him, guiding him to where he most needed to be. "I want you inside me, Simon. All of you."

The trust in those eyes crushed any shred of control that remained.

She felt him nudge deeper, opening her inch by inch, a stretching sensation as he filled her. It seemed impossible that he would fit, fill this sudden emptiness that yawned inside her. In places she'd never known needed him so badly.

He rocked his hips, thrusting a little deeper, a little deeper. She felt a tearing sensation, a sharp sting and burn. He kissed her with a fierceness that startled her, and he buried himself to the hilt.

He lay still for a moment, then lifted his head and peered down at her, a crease between his brows.

"Are you… all right…?" he asked on a ragged breath.

"Yes." Penelope peered up at him, tracing the planes of his face. Loving him. *Loving him.* "Please… please, Simon, make the storm go away." She arched her hips, wrapping her legs around him, drawing him deeper. Simon groaned and began to move, a rhythm that made her writhe against him, moans rising from her throat. Sensation built, a deep craving, as she reached for something mysterious and new. The storm still raged outside, but that fear couldn't break through the magic shield Simon's body cast around her.

She reveled in the taut muscles of his back, his mouth eager, his hands calloused but tender as he stripped away the last barriers between them, each thrust leaving them naked and new.

The crest built, then broke, and she cried out as unbearable pleasure erased all other thoughts from her mind.

Simon thrust harder, kissing her, filling her. At the last moment, he tried to pull out, but she clutched her legs around him. She felt him stiffen, a rough cry tearing from his throat. He buried himself deep, a warm rush filling her as he spent himself, then finally stilled.

After long moments, he gently slid off of her. She sat up as he went to find a cloth from the shelf behind them. When he returned, she felt his eyes on her back. He stood silent, in the flickering light, then ran his fingertip over the scar that ran from her shoulder blade down to her hip. Penelope closed her eyes, picturing in her mind. She'd managed to see it herself with a hand mirror and her mother's cheval glass. Those rare times her family had caught sight of it, they'd winced, or swiftly turned away. No one had ever regarded it the way Simon did now. With quiet wonder, exquisite tenderness. "It's not like anything I've ever seen," he said softly. "Thin tendrils branching out from the center, like the fronds of a fern. It reminds me of the way your mind works, forever exploring every direction possible. Unexpectedly beautiful, despite the pain it caused you." Tenderly, he kissed the mark the lightning had seared into her skin.

He cleaned gently between her legs, then set the cloth aside and slid back into bed beside her, drawing her into his arms.

They lay together in silence, the afterglow of their lovemaking holding them in its embrace. The fury outside grew fainter, the sound of the rain turning to a light patter.

"I think the worst of it is over," Simon said after a while. "We should head home."

And yet, she was reluctant. Penelope thought of all they'd discovered since the carriage had rolled away from Everdene that morning. The truth about the love they shared. The truth about Simon's mother and what his father had done. The truth about Catherine… Catherine, the baby sister the storm stole away.

Once they stepped out of this unexpected haven, she knew a somber truth in her heart.

The real storm had just begun.

Penelope peered across the storm-scarred landscape as the carriage wound along the muddy lane that cut through the Harcourt estate. Crops had been battered and flattened, tufts of thatch and shingles ripped from roofs. Cottagers moved about, cleaning up the debris, piling up fallen branches, repairing fences the wind had buckled, or searching for livestock that had escaped and scattered.

Always, when she'd seen the destruction after a storm, Pen had felt a faint nausea curdling her stomach. Had some part of her, buried deep, been thinking of her lost sister? It explained so much, as if someone had stripped away a blindfold, and she was seeing clearly for the first time since she was seven, the sense of grief that clutched at her, that seemed to grip her when there was no discernable reason. The panic when the sky grew dark. The punishments her mother had dealt out, so harsh when she was headstrong or defiant. Her father losing himself year by year in drink, trying to deaden his pain, to forget the child he'd lost. Forgive the daughter who'd survived.

Painful as it was, she'd fit the puzzle pieces together at last, and it all made sense. She felt drained, so tired, and yet, she leaned against Simon, drawing an inner steadiness from his presence.

Her clothes had dried, crumpled and a trifle stiff. Despite that small discomfort, she'd nestled close to him, remembering how he had helped her slip into each garment, his clever fingers doing up hooks and laces, his lips pressing fervent kisses to bare skin before he covered it. Part of her wished they could have remained in the brass bed in the hunting box forever, but there were challenges to confront. She couldn't predict what the future might hold. She only knew that she wanted to face it with the man beside her.

Simon stopped the carriage beside a weathered-faced farmer. A dejected-looking collie trailed behind him, its long coat weighed down by mud.

"Did you suffer much damage from the storm?" Simon asked.

The farmer nodded. "'Twas a rum one, sir. Going to take time to clean up the mess."

*Wasn't that what she and Simon faced as well?* Pen thought as they drove on. The facts Simon had learned in Galen's Well had churned through his world fierce as any tempest. Though his fiery anger seemed banked for the time being, it would not take much to stir it back to life. As for her… What could she say to the mother who had erased her baby daughter? To Fanny who had cried for a little sister while her parents told her she wasn't real. How could she forgive herself for taking Catherine out into the storm and then… forgetting her, banishing her from memory. Because no one in her family could bear the pain.

She looked up at Simon, aware that they were both changed utterly from the pair that had left Everdene that morning.

"What happens now?" Pen asked Simon softly.

He shook the reins, and the horses started forward. "I intend to write my sisters. To tell them I'm sorry for letting them slip out of my life without a fight." He stared off into the distance, his eyes shadowed with regret. "As for Lucien, I broke my promise not to delve into our past. As much as I owe him the truth, my mother thinks it best not to tell him."

"I do wonder why. Perhaps as the heir to the earldom, he's bound more to your father than you or your sisters?"

"Perhaps…" Simon mused. "But I can't help feeling that there is something more buried underneath all of this."

"I think so, too." Pen pictured the warning in the Viscount's letter. "After your visit to Bitterne Tower, he wrote to me," she said, carefully. "He asked me not to probe into the matter with your mother, that the past was too painful, best to leave it buried." She stopped there, not wanting to burden him with the Viscount's threat.

"We did bury it. Both of us. That's how we survived." Simon was quiet a long moment. "Have I told you that Lucien was not in the nursery when I awakened the night my mother disappeared?"

"No."

"I woke to the sound of shouting in the corridor. Then the door slammed open and someone shoved Lucien back into the nursery. He fell, hard against the bed. I remember him being… terrified. And then someone locked the door from the outside. All the next day, we couldn't get out of the room."

Pen shuddered, thinking of two young boys, frightened, alone.

"Something happened that Lucien is still not telling me." He glanced toward her, then back to the muddy road. "In the end, demanding the truth point-blank is the only way to find out. I worry, though."

"Why?"

"My mother fears my father might abduct her again, take her someplace hidden, maybe on the Continent, and have her committed again. He still has that power as her husband."

Pen pictured the barred windows of the asylum staring over

the high stone fence, wondering how anyone could be so cruel as to imprison someone sane there. "It's so unjust."

"It's more than my mother's safety," he said, as he turned down the lane toward Laurel Cottage. "Until New Everdene is finished and the villagers are in their new houses, I don't dare say a thing to anyone. I can't risk that my brother or father will put an end to our project, should either of them find out. But the time will come."

Pen squeezed his arm. "I know you'll puzzle out what to do."

Simon looked down at her. The ice blue of his eyes warmed at her confidence in him. Then she saw tenderness, concern deepen, his gaze a caress. "And what of you, love?"

She looked at Laurel Cottage, the home she would one day lose. Everything about it was familiar to Pen, the faded shutters, the roses climbing one wall, the dilapidated stable. Yet, it was changed forever.

Her mother was cast in a new light, plagued by headaches and secret grief, her often harsh, desperate need to quell Pen's willfulness. Would it make things better between them if Pen dragged everything out into the light, or would it only reopen her mother's wounds? And what of Fanny who had grieved their baby sister so terribly years ago? Kitty who had been named for a ghost?

Simon reined the carriage to a halt and peered down at her, waiting for an answer. *And what of you, love?*

"I don't know."

He stroked her cheek. "So, neither of us are certain what tomorrow will bring. The one thing I am certain of is this: I want to spend the rest of my life with you. I know you said you didn't want to marry," he said. "God knows, after seeing what my mother endured, I understand your reasons. But I'm hoping that, in time, you will trust me enough to give me a chance. I'll do everything in my power to deserve you. If you'll let me."

"I already do. Trust you. I'm scared, but..."

"Pen? Oh, Pen!" Fanny's cry startled Pen, and she turned to see her sisters bursting from the house, Kitty's face streaked with tears. The instant Pen leapt down from the carriage, they both flung themselves into Penelope's arms.

"I'm all right." Pen fought to keep her voice steady. "We were caught by the storm. But we're here now and safe."

"I know how you h-hate storms," Kitty said with a hiccupping sob. "You try to pretend you don't care, but I know you do."

Pen's chest squeezed with affection. Kitty had not even been born the day Pen had been struck by lightning. But when Pen's night-terrors came, Kitty was the one who woke her, who crawled into bed with her and held her until the shaking stopped.

Fanny didn't weep, but her eyes were huge, and she was trembling... Pen's heart wrenched as she pictured Fanny as she'd been so long ago. A tiny girl, staring out the window, crying for what she had lost...

Pen felt the weight of Simon's concerned gaze, knew that he'd seen her with all of her defenses stripped away.

Pen gathered them both close. "Captain Harcourt found us shelter and we waited out the storm."

"Nothing will ever harm your sister while I am alive," Simon soothed. "I swear it."

Kitty gave him a watery smile.

"Where is Mama?"

"In bed. She dosed herself with laudanum, like she always does when there is a storm."

Always before, Pen had thought her mother's dependence on the drug when it stormed was because of her accident. But now, she knew... Her heart ached as she and Simon exchanged glances.

"I'm going to get these horses back to their stable, then head over to the new village," he said. "I hope Daw and the men got things covered with canvas and battened down before the rain hit."

Pen frowned. She'd barely slept, she'd been so worried in the days leading up to seeing Simon's mother. Between that, the memories the storm had awakened, and making love to Simon, she hadn't spared a thought to what might be happening at the building site. "I should come, too," she said.

Simon shook his head. "If there is work to be done, it will be heavy lifting. Nothing you could do, anyway. Stay here and rest. Take a hot bath. You'll need one after what you've been through." His smile brought forth memories of their time together, and why her body ached in secret places he had made his own. "I'll let you know what I find," he assured her. He tipped her chin up, kissing her right in front of her sisters, astonishing Pen as much as he did the two of them. His lips moved over hers, claiming her, offering comfort, support, strength.

The girls stared as Pen caressed his jaw, tracing the strong, chiseled planes of his face. His mouth curved in a smile. "I'll see you tomorrow, sweet," he said. She watched him climb into the carriage and drive away.

"Come sit in the parlor, Pen," Fanny said. "Have some tea and we'll have Clara prepare you a bath."

"And you can tell us all about Captain Harcourt," Kitty said, managing a wobbly smile.

"A bath sounds heavenly. But I think I'll take my tea upstairs in Mother's room, while I'm waiting for the water to heat."

Her sisters stared, nearly as shocked as they'd been when Simon kissed her. Pen mounted the stairs, going to her mother's room. She sat on a chair beside the bed, looking at her mother's face, slack, vulnerable. "It's me, Mama," she said softly. "Penelope. I'm home." Her mother's fingers were curled slightly as if reaching for an invisible hand. Pen slipped her fingers into her mother's, filling that empty space.

SIMON REINED CASPIAN OVER THE RISE, TAKING IN THE SIGHT OF New Everdene with that feeling of deep connection that never failed to surprise him. The storm had definitely done some damage in the half-constructed village. Here and there, crates were overturned, canvas had torn free from its anchoring or a tree limb had snapped. But it could have been far worse.

The stream coursing past the edge of the village, churned in a wild torrent, overflowing its banks. But as Pen had pointed out on suggesting the site, the higher ground where the cottages were being built kept the streets and houses from flooding.

Men moved about the muddy site, setting things to rights. Oilcloth had been draped over piles of lumber and lashed over unfinished roofs. A crew was tending a partially finished wall that seemed to list off-kilter.

Simon frowned as he noted Inchwick surveying the scene, arms crossed over his chest, a smug expression on his face. He'd barely set foot on the village site the past weeks, but of course, the thieving bastard would want to revel in every complication and delay.

"How bad is it?" Simon asked one of the men as he dismounted and tied Brutus to the hitching post.

"Hard to tell," the man said. "Thought we'd got everything anchored down tight. But there seem to be problems we didn't expect. A couple of rafters split, some loft floors sagging. Widow's house is the worst. Daw's got a crew in there with him, trying to figure out what's amiss."

Simon frowned and strode toward the structure, noting that the hopeful seedlings the old woman had transplanted had been flattened in the mud.

As he stepped inside the building, he saw a group of men with Daw in the center. The brawny carpenter balanced on a ladder as he strained to examine the ceiling. Tripp crouched beneath it, the boy's face, shadowed, and intent as he fumbled with something in the corner.

"Daw, how goes it?" Simon called to his friend.

"Still trying to puzzle out what the blazes is going wrong here. I've got Mac and Bailey up in the loft. And Cooper and Michael are shoring things up. Makes no sense, but I swear, this support is listing. That architect inspected it just the other day, and it was sturdy." Daw leaned toward two exposed joists, then suddenly straightened as he caught sight of Tripp's homespun jerkin. "Blast it, lad. I told you to stay out of the way here."

The boy flushed, looking guilty as he shoved something back in his pocket. "I want to stay with you." The boy's chin jutted out, a strained defiance in his voice.

Daw gripped the joist, and stretched over to glare at the child. "You can come back in as soon as I know it's sa—"

Simon heard a strange grinding sound, saw Daw's eyes go wide as the structure shifted.

Daw shoved his shoulder against the sagging beam, as if he alone could hold it. "Everybody out!" he bellowed, his panicked gaze on the boy he was too far above to help. "It's going to go—"

Simon grabbed Tripp around his waist, about to haul the child toward the door, when he heard the sickening groan of timber above them. Simon flung himself over Tripp, shielding him with his body as the support collapsed, crashing down. Pain shot through Simon, a roaring sound in his ears. Cudgels seemed to strike his back, his shoulders as he held tight to the boy.

Outside, he heard men shouting, Inchwick ordering them to stay back. But the other workmen were already clambering over the wreckage, trying to get to the people inside.

Simon's arms wrapped around Tripp and he felt the boy's heartbeat racing. Holding tight, he pushed upward against the debris pinning them down. Wood and plaster slid off, bringing up even more dust.

He'd barely gotten them free of the debris, when the lad pulled from his grasp, scrambling toward the broken ladder, where a patch of Daw's shirt showed under the wreckage. Tripp flung away chunks of wood, trying to get to the injured man.

Daw reached out, white dust matted against his blood-soaked arm. "Get Tripp... out..." he rasped.

Head throbbing, Simon picked his way toward Tripp. It hurt to breathe, the pain intensifying as he reached Tripp, then hauled him outside, the lad kicking and screaming the entire way. He thrust Tripp into someone's arms, then he plunged back into the wreckage.

It was hell, like the aftermath of a battle, men wounded, some screaming as they were dug from under rubble. Simon, in battle mode, rapped out orders to the shell-shocked men, telling them what to do, shifting fallen beams, then moving the injured out of harm's way.

At last, they reached Daw. Simon's stomach twisted at the sight of his friend. His leg bent at a gut-churning angle. A gash arced across his forehead, blood trickling from the corner of his mouth, making Simon worry the worst injury was internal, where no one could see.

He lay there, so still, Simon feared he was dead. He pressed his fingertips to the carpenter's throat finding a thready pulse. "Daw? Daw, it's Harcourt."

"Boy... is he..."

"Tripp's fine. He's right outside, howling to get back to you."

"Thank God... he's safe." Daw's eyelids fluttered shut, and Simon saw a tear run down the man's cheek. "Told him to stay out of the house after storm ... always three steps behind me... My wee shadow..."

"How many men were inside?" Simon asked.

"Eight. Didn't seem... so serious. Never would have... brought them in if..."

They'd pulled out five, Daw and two others still inside.

"What the devil happened?" came a familiar voice.

He glanced over his shoulder. Inchwick stood there, pristine in his fresh gray frock coat. Ignoring him, Simon directed his attention to the two men helping him tend to the carpenter. "I'll get Daw out. We've still two more to find."

They nodded and moved off. "They're here," one of them shouted. "Below the cupboard."

Their jubilation at finding the last two workers was tempered by the sudden screech above them, the grinding of wood against wood.

Simon looked up and swore, another ceiling beam listing. He turned his attention back to his friend, trying to assess his injuries. "Can you feel your hands and your feet?"

"Wish I couldn't," he said, his voice low.

As dangerous as it was to move Daw, if he didn't, the man would die.

Bracing himself, Simon scooped the brawny carpenter up into his arms, the man screaming in agony as Simon staggered toward the door. The other men streamed out in his wake, carrying the two they'd been able to free just as another beam crashed down, the deafening sound reverberating throughout the street.

Simon fell to his knees, laying Daw down on the ground, then struggled up, starting toward the ruined building. "Anyone left?"

"Got them out," Garrick said. "But, Jesus, Mary, and Joseph…"

Relieved, he looked around, saw the injured and those tending them, someone calling for a tourniquet, others for bandages.

Simon rapped out commands to the people gathering around. "Wagons. Get all the wagons you can and take these men to Everdene Hall."

"The manor house?" Inchwick blustered. "Are you mad?"

"We have the staff to tend them, beds," Simon snapped. "Tripp! Take one of the horses and fetch the doctor."

"Doctor Holmes isn't here," Inchwick said. "He's gone to London to replenish his supplies."

Simon swore. "Lancaster, head to the manor house and tell the staff to prepare. Hot water, bandages. Tripp, stop at Laurel Cottage on the way. Tell Miss Waverly what's happened. That we're taking the injured to the manor. We'll need anyone able to help nurse until we can find a damn doctor. Ride, lads. Lives depend on it."

With one last agonized glance at Daw, Tripp swung up on a draft horse's broad back, and dug his heels into its side, thundering off. Pray God, they could get help in time.

Simon finished loading the last man into the wagon, then grabbed Brutus's reins. His eyes locked on the cottage that lay in ruins. "How the devil did this happen?" he snarled as he dragged himself up into the saddle.

Inchwick's lip curled in disgust. "Ask your friend Miss Waverly."

# CHAPTER 34

*P*en curled up in the window seat in her bedchamber, her legs tucked beneath her as she watched stray drops from the eaves trickle down the panes. The bath she had taken had been heavenly, the hot, sudsy water soaking the kinks out of her muscles and soothing the slight sting in her nether regions from lovemaking and jouncing on the carriage seat. She'd emerged from the tub and donned her most comfortable dress, the folds of autumn-leaf gold worn soft with age. But she couldn't bring herself to rejoin her family. Not yet. Her sisters were full of questions, her mother still muddled from the laudanum, but awake enough to fuss over Pen's scandalous behavior.

If only she knew just how scandalous.

Pen smiled, remembering the passion she and Simon had shared. How was it possible to feel safe, protected in his arms, yet stronger than she'd ever been before? No one had ever known her the way Simon did, all defenses stripped away. And he had let her see him thus as well.

He'd responded to every touch as she explored his body, letting her past his inner barriers to the vulnerable, daring, courageous man beyond. Yes, there was pain in the past events they'd discovered, but there was so much more healing in what they'd shared. She brushed her hands lightly over her breast, her nipple hardening at the memory of how he'd placed his lips there, and places she'd never dreamed a man would kiss. What other mysteries would they unravel between them? In their bodies, their hearts... and the world beyond, once they completed their village...

She pictured the celebration there would be, once people were able to move into their new village... imagined Margery Garvey, Widow Bevans and the others making the cottages into homes.

What would it be like to make a home with Simon? She'd never imagined doing so with any man. Yet, now...

She closed her eyes, picturing the stables he'd build, foals frolicking in pastures, perhaps even children running about, loved, laughing, with arms like Lady Ravenscroft's, always waiting to scoop them up. She was jarred from those sweet imaginings by the sound of hoofbeats outside.

Her lashes fluttered open, and she frowned as a draft horse thundered toward Laurel Cottage. Her pulse quickened, as she recognized the small, wiry figure clinging to the horse's back like a cocklebur. Tripp!

Pen leapt to her feet and dashed downstairs, flinging the front door open before the boy could knock.

Her heart stopped the minute she saw Tripp's tear-streaked face. Mud spattered him from head to toe, bits of wood and thatch clinging to clothes and hair. She bent down, grasping his shoulders to steady him as sobs wracked his thin body. "Tripp, what is it? What's wrong?"

His eyes went wide with horror. "The roof... fell in..."

Her stomach plunged to her toes. "The roof?" she echoed.

"At the build site. Widow Bevan's cottage."

Pen tried to breathe, her lungs suddenly constricting. Oh, God... "Was anyone hurt?"

"Daw an'... Captain Harcourt. Others, too."

"Where are the men now?" she demanded.

"They're taking them to the manor but Dr. Holmes is gone to London. Miss W-Waverly, you have to help."

"I will." She wheeled and shouted down the corridor. Kitty! Fanny! Clara!" The three girls rushed in, all wide-eyed at the alarm in her voice. "There's been an accident at the construction site," she told them. "I don't know how many men have been hurt."

"Oh, no!" Kitty gasped. "What happened?"

"What on earth?" Her mother's voice sounded from the staircase. Anastasia Waverly stood at the stair rail, a disheveled figure in her brocade dressing gown. Dark circles smudged beneath her eyes, the pupils still near invisible. She gaped at the filthy urchin who was huddled against her wall.

"The doctor is away," Pen continued. "I'm going to Everdene Hall to help care for the injured."

"No!" her mother slurred, swaying slightly as she made her way down the stairs. "You mustn't!"

Pen paid her no mind. "Clara, have Hughes saddle Epona. Fanny, gather any bandages you can find, put them in a basket and send it to Everdene as quick as you can. Mother, where is the medical kit?"

"In her room," Kitty said. "I'll fetch it." She scooped up her skirts and ran.

"Penelope Eloise, I forbid you to go." Her mother grasped her arm. "All those strange men! You'll be ruined!"

Penelope pulled away, her heart wrenching as she thought of Simon, his beautiful, strong body broken. "Would it help if I told you I'm already ruined?"

Her mother gasped.

Penelope ignored her, heading into the library, taking out an ink pot, quill, and foolscap, scribbling a hasty note as Kitty clattered down the stairs, the leather medical bag in hand. Pen grabbed the bag, then thrust the note into her sister's hand. "Kitty, ride Dobby to Farmer Ellis's house. Tell him to take his fastest horse to Galen's Well and give this note to Dr. Clay. He'll either be at his surgery on main street or at St. Alban's Infirmary. He has to come to Everdene Hall and help us. Hurry as fast as ever you can."

Kitty was already running out the door.

"Why can you never listen!" her mother wailed, as Pen started after her sister. The older woman seemed ready to sink to her knees. Fanny caught hold of their mother, pulling her back. "Go, Pen. Hurry."

Pen's pulse raced, as she ran out the door, Tripp following close behind. Hughes was waiting, Epona saddled and bridled, pacing restlessly beside Tripp's winded draft horse. Pen fastened the medical bag to the saddle. The mare tossed her head, side-stepping as Hughes lifted Pen up onto Epona's back.

"Miss! Miss, take me with you," Tripp wailed.

Pen held out her hand, and the boy took it, swung up behind her, clinging to her waist. Pen leaned forward and spurred the mare into a run.

PENELOPE HAD BARELY DRAWN REIN IN FRONT OF THE MANOR house before Tripp leapt off and darted away. By the time she'd unfastened the medical bag and handed Epona's reins to a groom, the boy had disappeared.

She rushed up to Everdene's imposing door and burst in without ringing the bell. The manor house swarmed with confusion, maids and footmen rushing around amidst a cacophony of barked orders, cries of pain, oaths. A maid rushed out of one of the rooms, a basket full of bloody towels clutched against the front of her uniform. She looked as if she was seconds away from throwing up.

"Where is Captain Harcourt?" Pen cried out.

"They've put everyone in the parlor," the maid said, jerking her head toward a door.

Pen bolted past a brace of footmen who were carrying a mattress. Once inside the room, the scene filled her with panic. What had once been an elegant chamber was utter chaos. Gilt-legged furniture had been shoved out of the way to make room for makeshift beds, injured men either tossing and turning on them, or propped on chairs while servants did their best to tend their wounds. Bloody water sloshed against the rims of basins being carried away, while ewers of clean water replaced them, steam curling from the containers.

She scanned the room, heartsick as she recognized the faces of men she had worked with these past months. Bailey, the wheelwright moaned on his cot. Mac sat on a bench, his body curled protectively around his left arm. In the far corner, three men fought to hold someone down as he writhed in agony.

Pen pressed her fist to her mouth, bile rising in her throat. Had she caused this? Made some crucial mistake in her figures? Were her plans flawed?

Inchwick's scornful words echoed in her mind. *She's a woman! She's not qualified...*

"Easy, Daw," a familiar voice sounded through the clamor. "Lie still."

Simon. Relief washed through Pen with a force that made her choke back a sob. Stripped to his shirtsleeves, he bent over a table where the injured carpenter lay. The white cloth over the broad expanse of Simon's shoulder was stained with dried blood—his own or someone else's, but whatever his injuries, he was moving purposefully, speaking clearly.

As she approached, she saw Tripp holding the remains of a boot someone had cut off. Someone had wrapped a bandage around the carpenter's head. The leg of his breeches had been ripped up to the hip, and gaped open, revealing a pale, muscular calf wrenched at an angle that made Pen feel light-headed. She shoved the sensation back. "What can I do?" she asked.

Simon's gaze flashed to hers with gratitude and resolve. "Give him more whisky," he said.

She found the nearest bottle and lifted Daw's head, cradling it while she pressed the opening to his lips. He gulped the amber liquid, the muscles in his throat standing out in cords. Simon's brow furrowed in concentration as he palpitated the break in Daw's leg. The man's face contorted in pain. She'd known Simon had seen injuries on battlefields, but she'd never guessed he would be so skilled at what he was doing now. "We've got to shift the bones back into place," he said with calm resolve.

Pen took hold of Daw's callused hand as Simon moved to the end of the table and closed his fingers around Daw's ankle. "Hold him." Simon slanted a grim look at the men positioned by Daw's shoulders. A drop of perspiration trickled down the side of Simon's face.

Pen squeezed Daw's hand, tight. "Look at me, Daw. Tripp and I are here."

"M-my good lad..." Daw tried to smile at the boy.

Out of the corner of her eye, Pen saw Simon move. Daw's bloodcurdling scream split the air. His hand crushed Pen's so tight it seemed the bones should snap.

"You're hurting him!" Tripp wailed.

Suddenly, Daw's eyes rolled back, his big body going limp.

"Splints!" Simon ordered.

Pen grabbed two lengths of board, and helped Simon arrange them on either side of the injured leg.

"That's right," Simon told her as he bound the splints in place with strips of cloth. "Hold them right there." When he tied the last knot, his shoulders sagged.

"It's over, Tripp," Simon said as Pen gathered the boy in her arms. "See, it's over."

"Is he dead?" Tripp wept, staring at Daw's slack face.

"He's just fainted," Simon soothed. "Why don't you sit here, and watch over him? Tell me when he wakes up."

A swell of feminine voices penetrated the room, and Penelope looked up to see the women from the village streaming in, carrying whatever might help in their capable arms.

"Mrs. Garvey!" The boy cried, flinging himself at her. Margery Garvey laid down a basket of bandages and remedies, then gathered Tripp in one arm, while curving one hand over Daw's cheek. She leaned over her husband, her face set with a strength that awed Pen.

"How bad is it?" she asked Simon.

"Bad," he admitted. "We've done what we could, but we won't know how the leg will heal until a doctor gets here."

She nodded, glanced at her husband, then adjusted his pillow, directing Tripp to help her remove his second boot and covering him with a thick blanket.

Pen looked around the room, seeing all of the other injured men being cared for. All of them save Simon. "Come over here," she said, drawing Simon toward a small, curtained alcove.

"I'm fine."

"The blood on your back says otherwise. You won't do these people any good if a wound turns putrid."

Simon acquiesced. Pen took up her medical kit and he followed her into the alcove. Setting her leather bag on a small table, she unbuttoned Simon's shirt, and peeled it off one arm, then moved around his back to strip away the other sleeve. Her breath hissed between her teeth. Bruises bloomed in a horrifying array over his back, a mass of cuts tangling where debris had crashed down on him. Tentatively, she probed his ribs. He swore.

"Do you think any of these are broken?" she asked.

"Wouldn't matter if they were unless one punctured my lung," he grated. "The surgeon would just wrap them tight in cloth bands."

"Ah, so you are an expert regarding such wounds, are you?"

"A donkey in the pack train took exception to me walking behind it in Bombay."

Pen signaled one of the servants to bring her hot water and fresh bandages, then rummaged for the salves she'd brought from Laurel Cottage to help keep out infection. She worked cut by cut, cleaning each one thoroughly, then calmly took out a curved needle and silk thread to stitch up the deepest slice.

When she'd managed to close up the gash and cover it with salve, she took wide bands of linen and bade Simon hold his arms away from his body. He winced as he did so, his jaw clamping tight against the pain. She wrapped the bands around his torso tightly enough to give the battered area support. With each loop around his body, she thought how close she had come to losing him.

He could have died. Any of these men could have been killed.

She fastened the wrap by tucking the end of the fabric beneath the disc of his flat nipple, her knuckle tickled by the fine dusting of dark hair that spanned his chest. She let her fingers rest there, tears filling her eyes.

"What is it?" Simon asked, pulling her toward him. He gritted his teeth, but didn't stop until she was in his arms.

She laid her face against his naked shoulder, feeling the warm skin, the taut muscle, the throb of his heartbeat against her cheek.

"I could have lost you," she whispered. "You could have been killed. Any one of your men could have died."

"But we didn't."

"What happened to Catherine was my fault... What if... what if this was my fault, too?"

He cupped her head in his hand, stroking her hair.

"Sometimes things just happen," he murmured against her tumbled curls, and she heard an understanding in his voice, an empathy so deep she felt it in her chest. "Things go wrong, whether we mean them to or not. Either way, we find the will to go on."

---

SIMON GLANCED OUT THE WINDOW, WONDERING WHAT TIME IT was. The sky beyond the panes was dark as his mood. Eight men who were too injured to move to the village lay in beds the footmen had carried down from empty servants' quarters. Simon had ordered comfortable chairs be brought from elsewhere in the manor and drawn up beside the beds, so loved ones could keep watch and support each other through this long ordeal. The villagers, regardless of their connection to the injured, had banded together to help each other, bringing baskets of food or helping bathe faces and change bandages.

When Simon was finally satisfied that he'd made everyone in the makeshift infirmary as comfortable as he could, he slipped out, going in search of Pen. She'd been as busy as he was. When the wives and mothers of the men had come to take over tending the wounded, Pen had organized a retiring room for them. She'd thought of everything, Simon realized with tender pride.

The cook filled the sideboard with cold roast beef, slices of ham, soups, pies, and oranges from the orangery. Watered wine and whisky stood beside the platters to fortify nerves, with a supply of tea and chocolate waiting to keep caretakers awake or calm rattled nerves. There were pillows and blankets in stacks where they could snatch a few minutes of rest, pitchers and bowls of warm water to wash, and handkerchiefs for those who needed a good cry.

Simon found Pen in the receiving room alone. She looked exhausted, her beautiful green eyes haunted as she met his gaze.

"How is everyone?" she asked, starting to get to her feet. He gently pushed her back onto the settee and sat beside her, drawing her close.

"A little better. I found a bottle of laudanum left from my father's illness and dosed the worst cases," he told her. "Mac and Bailey are resting comfortably and Daw is asleep."

"Thank God." Pen fretted her lower lip. "I keep hoping a doctor will come walking through that door. With each hour that passes, I'm worried there is some injury we're missing. I sent word to Dr. Clay."

"I sent riders out searching for doctors as well. I don't give a damn whom they find as long as someone gets here soon."

The sound of heels clicking on the marble flooring made them both straighten, expecting to see one of the frazzled caretakers. Instead, Inchwick strode through the door.

"Someone *will* arrive soon, Captain Harcourt," Inchwick said with feigned regret. "I've sent for the Earl and Viscount. I am sure you are most unhappy to have the failure at the village exposed, but I thought it was necessary."

Of course, the smug bastard had done so. This was just the chance he'd been waiting for, devil take him. "I don't give a damn if you announce what happened in town squares," Simon replied. "I just want to find a surgeon who can tend these men properly."

The land agent glanced at Penelope before focusing on Simon. "Such a tragedy! All of these cottages are doubtless death traps."

Pen looked up at him in horror. "No. I don't believe that."

"We'll be wrecking the lot of them before the snow falls."

Inchwick's words were lost in the rattle of iron coach wheels rumbling up to the manor house. Simon rose so fast, a stab of pain shot through his ribs. Through the window he saw lanterns bobbing wildly from hooks on the equipage, the horses winded and lathered.

His father and Lucien? No—there was no coat of arms displayed on the vehicle. "Please, let this be a surgeon," he exclaimed, his heart thundering as he and Pen raced to the front door.

They were halfway down the stairs when a tall figure in a black frock coat climbed down from the coach.

"Dr. Clay!" Pen cried. "Thank God you're here!"

But the man wasn't listening.

Clay turned back to the coach, offering his hand to help another passenger descend.

Simon stared as his mother leapt down in a wave of skirts and ran to him, sweeping him into her arms.

## CHAPTER 35

"Mother!" Stunned, Simon gathered her close despite the ache in his ribs, feeling a tremor going through her. "What are you doing here?"

"Penelope's note to Dr. Clay only said there was an accident at the building site. I was terrified that you'd been hurt," her voice caught. "I've only just found you again," the Countess said with a grateful glance in Pen's direction. "To lose you…"

Simon reeled inwardly at the raw emotion in her voice, the pain, the fear and relief. Love that sank into his very bones. His throat felt tight. "I'm fine… well, a few bruises and cuts, but nothing serious. It's the men inside who need a surgeon's care."

"Take me to them," Dr. Clay said, medical bag in hand.

"Follow me." Penelope waved him up the stairs. "We moved beds into the parlor and turned it into a makeshift infirmary," she explained, as they hurried into Everdene Hall.

"Easier to care for them all that way." Clay nodded in approval.

Simon took his mother's arm, and the two followed the pair into the manor, her step faltering the moment they crossed the threshold.

It didn't occur to him until that moment that this was the first time that Lenora Harcourt, Countess of Ravenscroft, had reentered the home she'd been stolen away from years before. Her grip tightened slightly on Simon's arm as she looked around the marble entry hall. He wondered if she pictured her children on the upper floor, peering through the stair rail during balls they'd once held? Or Christmas mornings?

Or the moment her husband had dragged her to the root cellar and locked her in.

It was this last, he thought. When Simon had seen her in Galen's Well, she'd been so afraid of returning here, worried about what repercussions she might face. Even so, she'd come here for *him*.

"This way," he said gently, breaking into her thoughts.

She nodded, allowing him to lead her into the parlor-turned-infirmary, where Pen and Dr. Clay had already started to make rounds.

The injured were restless, some moaning, tossing and turning, while their caretakers tried to change bandages or sweat-soaked clothes, or coax broth, water, or whisky between their lips.

"Lady Ravenscroft!"

His mother started at the sound of her name. She looked around, seeing an older woman at the side of one of the injured cots staring at them. Widow Bevans, her mob cap askew, her arms filled with a basket of clean bandages.

"Mary, Jesus, and Joseph!" the old woman exclaimed, as she set the basket down, then rushed toward them, suddenly seeming far younger than her sixty years. "It's a miracle, it is! This is our kind lady, come back to us!"

Those villagers who could, gathered around Simon's mother, their voices mingling in confusion and disbelief. But when the widow reached her, Simon felt his throat knot. The old woman curtseyed so low her skirts pooled on the floor. She took Lady Ravenscroft's hands in her gnarled, chapped fingers and rained kisses on them. "We thought ye dead! Where have ye been?"

His mother looked down at her with tenderness and an innate respect that moved Simon deeply. "Never you mind, Minnie. I'm here now."

Yes, she was here, Simon thought with a sudden clenching in his gut. But his father was coming as well. The Earl would be raging like a wounded bull when he came through that door.

Simon's fists clenched. His own rage was a heartbeat away from flaring, one glance at the man who had destroyed his family, and Simon wasn't sure he could keep his beast in check.

He wanted his mother as far away from Everdene as possible during the confrontation to come.

As soon as he could pluck her from the crowd, he drew her aside, his voice low. "Mother, it was so good of you to come, but you can't stay. Father will be arriving any time now. Let me send you back to Galen's Well."

She met his gaze directly. He saw the shadow of fear in those gentle eyes, but also steely resolve. "No. I'm not leaving. These people need help."

It was true. Dr. Clay was already off in a corner, checking on Daw's broken leg while other men waited for his ministrations.

The Countess gave Simon a resolute smile, taking in the scene around her. "We'll need plenty of extra bed linens, and all of the chamber pots you can find," she told him. "Fetch ice from the icehouse and towels to wrap it in so we can take down any swelling. Tell the kitchen staff to start kettles of beef broth, and make tea and toast to settle people's stomachs."

"Penelope already has the cook tending to that," Simon told her. "And she's arranged a retiring room with food and whatever comforts we can offer to those who are watching over the injured."

His mother turned to Pen and nodded in approval. "Well done, my dear," she said. A child's wail sounded across the room, and the Countess crossed purposefully to where the wheelwright's wife was smoothing a cool cloth over his head while her son tugged at her skirt, whining.

The Countess placed a hand on the harried woman's back.

"Why don't you take this little fellow out into the hallway. Let him run about for a bit. I'll tend to your husband."

The woman stared in disbelief. "Oh, I couldn't possibly… you a lady and all…"

"Of course you can. I promise I will keep close watch here."

Something in his mother's sincerity reached through the woman's reticence. "Thank ye, my lady. Billy hates being cooped up. When he gets restless, he finds all manner of trouble."

"Boys do. I remember my own little ones." She cast a tender glance at Simon, and his chest suddenly felt too small. "Billy, do you know what Captain Harcourt did when he was a boy?"

She launched into a mischievous tale that had the lad giggling.

It was as if she'd never stopped being the chatelaine of a huge manor, as if this were still her home. So little had changed in the household, even some of the staff the same, their faces lighting up at the sight of her.

Simon bit the inside of his cheek as he watched her, the love she bestowed so freely, the loyalty she inspired in those who knew her. The mother he'd known so well in the time *before*.

But watching the way she tended the injured reminded him of exactly what was at stake.

He needed to go to the site, examine things, discern what had caused this accident. But damn if he could leave her here alone. Something seemed to reach out from that dark, deep well of his childhood, echoes of the despair he'd felt when he'd realized his mother was gone. He was a man now. Had faced hordes of enemies aiming guns and swinging blades without fear. But this…

He had to convince her to leave Everdene before his father arrived.

# CHAPTER 36

It was astonishing how quickly Dr. Clay and Lady Ravenscroft had brought order to their makeshift infirmary, their quiet confidence and skill quieting the racketing nerves of everyone in the room, from the injured to those who cared for them.

Pen rolled her stiff shoulders, trying to fight back a yawn as she brought a cup of tea to Margery Daw. Her heart squeezed at the sight of Tripp, asleep on a pallet someone had set beside Daw's bed. The little boy curled up like a puppy, still holding Daw's ruined boot. Daw himself was awake. The splints Pen and Simon had used to stabilize the break leaned against the side of the bed, while Daw's jaw clenched as Dr. Clay examined his leg.

"Whoever set this bone is to be commended," the doctor said. "I couldn't have done better myself."

"Will my leg heal?" Daw rasped, his face white with pain. "I have to be able to do hard labor to provide for my family."

"The bones will knit, but there is no way to know if there will be lasting damage." Dr. Clay's voice was level, but the way he avoided Daw's eyes for just an instant, was enough to register doubt.

The carpenter turned away, a tear trickling from the corner of his eye. The cup of tea Penelope held trembled, and she tried to swallow her own tears as Margery reached for her husband's hand. Unwilling to interrupt the moment, she set the cup beside Margery, then stole away to get her own emotions back under control.

When Simon and Lady Ravenscroft found her organizing a table of supplies, Simon looked as miserable as she felt over Daw's prospects.

"I'm sorry there isn't better news about your friend," Lady Ravenscroft said quietly, her anguish mirroring Simon's. "I've seen astonishing recoveries in the past, though. The Garveys mustn't give up hope."

"No," Pen said, trying to quell her own fears. "But I just can't imagine Daw not being able to do carpentry work." Her voice caught, and Lady Ravenscroft slid an arm around her.

"My dear, dear girl. You've done an astonishing job, managing all of these injuries, setting the house in order, but you've run yourself off your feet. It is time to let someone else deal with things. Simon, have one of the maids settle her in a guest room and lend her a fresh nightgown so that she can sleep."

"I will." Simon said. His gaze was guarded in a way it hadn't been earlier.

Pen started to protest. "I can go back to Laurel Cottage…"

"No," Simon began, but his mother cut in.

"My dear, you would fall off of your horse and we'd have to bandage you as well. You needn't shoulder all of this burden any longer. I'm here now." Lady Ravenscroft smiled.

Even if Penelope could have gone home, the prospect of dealing with her mother's anger over her defiance, never mind her sisters' questions, was more than she could endure.

"Thank you," Pen said. "If you need my help—"

"I promise I'll wake you," the Countess assured. "We'll send a servant to let your family know you are staying here, and to bring back a change of clothes. You just rest."

"Come with me," Simon said, offering Pen his arm.

She took it, feeling the tension rippling off of him in waves. When they were free of the crowd, she took a good look at his face, realizing it wasn't just Daw's injury that troubled him. "What is it? I know there is much to worry about, the accident, the injured, but this… I sense there is more."

Simon's biceps hardened beneath the superfine of his coat. "I've begged my mother to leave, but she refuses."

Pen slanted a glance up at him. "Would you run if you were faced with the same situation? Leave people who are injured, who need you? People you feel responsible for?"

The muscles in his jaw ticked. "Of course not."

"Then why do you expect your mother to?"

The question seemed to take him aback. Then he glared at her. "You've heard what my father is capable of."

"When your father snatched her away last time, it was in the dead of night. Here, she's among people who love her, and are loyal to her. You saw how the tenants reacted to seeing her again. And *you're* here to guard her." She released his arm and stepped closer to him, so their bodies pressed together as they walked.

Simon drew a deep breath. He winced as he expanded his ribs, but she could feel him relax just a little. "Yes. And I'll have Lucien to help guard her as well."

*Would he?* Pen wondered, as Simon showed her to a bedchamber in a quiet hall, and summoned a maid to help her change.

She wished that she knew whatever had driven the Viscount to write her his letter of warning. And why Lady Ravenscroft had begged Simon to keep their reunion secret from his brother.

In spite of all she and Simon discovered about the past, there was something more beneath the surface. Something Lucien Harcourt and his mother considered dangerous to Simon. What was it?

She couldn't shake the feeling that they were about to find out.

She barely kept her eyes open as Ruby helped her wash then dropped a simple cotton nightgown over her head. By the time the maid had unpinned her hair and brushed it, Pen's head was nodding with exhaustion.

"In you go, miss." Pen slid under the covers. Ruby was still talking when Pen fell asleep.

SHE HAD NO IDEA WHAT TIME IT WAS WHEN SHE HEARD THE DOOR creak, then opened her eyes to see a figure in the open doorway. "Simon...?"

"Go to sleep, love. I just wanted to check on you." He started to pull the door closed.

"Stay..."

He froze. She heard a quick intake of breath, before he stepped into the room, closed the door, then turned the key in the lock.

Certain she was dreaming, she glimpsed his shadowy form beside the bed, heard the thud of his boots, the swish of his coat being discarded. The mattress moved as his weight pressed down upon it, and suddenly, she felt his warm, hard body against her back. He molded himself to her curves and planes, her bottom cradled against his groin, his thighs curved under hers. He drew her hair away from her throat and pressed his lips to the slope where her shoulder and neck met. His breath tickled her there, and he looped a heavy arm around her body, one hand closing over her breast.

She sighed, snuggling more tightly against him, taking

comfort in the feel of him, the rhythm of his heartbeat against her, the soft stirring of his breath on the fine hairs against her neck. She covered his hand with hers and slept.

---

LIGHT WAS STREAMING IN THE WINDOW WHEN THERE WAS A discreet knock at the door. "Captain?"

Pen started awake, suddenly aware that last night had not been a dream. The mattress shifted, a sudden coolness against her back where Simon had been. He was already yanking on his coat as quickly as his bruised ribs would allow.

"What is it?" he called to whomever stood outside in the hall.

"A coach coming up the drive, sir."

"Thank you." He looked at Pen as he pulled on his boots. "Damn, I didn't mean to stay so long…"

"Who–who is that?"

"I told Flynn I was going to check on you. To let me know if anyone needed me. To summon me at the first sight of my father. He must have guessed I stayed in your room."

As shocked as she was that Simon trusted anyone with the knowledge that he was coming to her bedchamber, it was nothing compared to the Earl's impending arrival.

Simon stooped and kissed Pen hard on the lips. His face flushed. His eyes blazed fire. There was no mistaking that wild, fearsome anger that had nearly consumed him on their drive back from Galen's Well.

# CHAPTER 37

*Hold the line!* The thought came unbidden, memories of battlefields past, as Simon stood in the entry hall before the parlor's closed doors, watching the man who had destroyed his family limp toward him, with Lucien a step behind. The injuries the Earl had suffered months earlier had left his skin the color of clay. But his eyes were hot coals of rage.

"What the devil have you done with my village!" the Earl bellowed, sending maids skittering down the hallway. "I had the coachman drive past Blagden Valley and there is not so much as a stick of lumber! I never should have acceded to your wishes, Lucien," the Earl blustered. "Simon has made a mess of things as always!"

His brother gave a pained shrug. "I explained that we moved the site," Lucien said.

The Earl took a step forward, then jabbed his gold-tipped walking stick at Simon. "I ask you to accomplish *one* thing for the good of the Harcourt name. And what happens? I receive word that you've made a disaster of it. Explain yourself!"

Before Simon had a chance to respond, a maid bustled out of the parlor with a basket full of soiled bandages, and behind her, two tenants' wives peeked out, obviously dismayed by the racket.

The Earl's eyes widened as he took it all in. "What the devil are all these people doing in my house?"

"This was the easiest place to care for a large number of injuries," Simon explained with grim control.

"*Get them out!*" The Earl roared. "They'll make the whole place stink of blood and filth—"

"Quiet, if you please!" a feminine voice broke through his tirade.

The Earl's head jerked, his eyes bulging as he stared at the woman gliding toward them from the makeshift infirmary.

Lucien's breath caught, and the color drained from his face. "Mother...?"

It had been nearly two decades since Lady Ravenscroft had ruled over this manor with her velvet-soft hand. The apron she wore over her gown was spotted with blood and rumpled, tendrils of hair escaping from her pins, but as she approached, she looked every inch the lady of the manor. Her shoulders squared as she faced the man who had imprisoned her in an asylum. "If you must complain, Barnabas, do it in another room."

For an instant, Simon's father looked as if he was having apoplexies, his face red, veins standing out in his neck. "Lenora! How dare you set foot—"

She cut him off smoothly, though her hands trembled as she clasped them at her waist. "I heard there had been an accident at Everdene. I feared Simon had been hurt."

"You *knew* Simon was at Everdene?" The Earl's eyes narrowed in accusation. "How long have you been in contact? Lucien, were you part of this conspiracy to deceive me?"

"No." His voice came out in a rasp.

The Earl strode toward the Countess, his cane gripped as though he might use it against her. "I *warned* you never to contact my sons. I swear, I'll make certain this time—"

"Stop!" Simon ordered, stepping between his parents, just as Penelope came down the stairs. He felt the sweat beading upon his brow as he fought for balance, a knife's edge away from losing control. He wanted to grab the old man by the throat, shove him up against the wall. Demand answers. Make his father pay.

But they were not alone, he realized as Pen strode toward them, immediately assessing the situation and positioning herself next to his mother, somewhat blocking the view of the tenants and servants in the room behind them, all watching with wide eyes.

Much as he'd love to tell the whole goddamn world what a monster his father was, he couldn't expose his mother's suffering for people to gossip over. She deserved to keep her dignity.

He turned his attention back to his father. And though he kept his voice low, he made sure his tone left no doubt as to the real meaning behind his words. "*You* will *not* hurt her again."

"You *dare* threaten me?"

Inchwick chose that very moment to make himself known. "My lords!" he said, sweeping into the foyer. "You have arrived at last." The man bowed and offered a solicitous smile to the Earl who still glared at Simon. Receiving no response from that quarter, he turned his attention toward Lucien. "After not receiving word, I feared you had encountered some mishap on the way."

"The deuced roads are still muddy after the storm. We had to stay at an inn halfway here."

"Shall we go to the village at once?" Inchwick asked. "I

confess, I've been distressed by the goings-on there, and fear you will find it shocking."

The Viscount, looking infinitely relieved at the interruption, nodded. "Let us go assess the damage." His gaze rested for a moment on their mother and Penelope. "We can deal with private matters later."

*Private matters?* Simon stared at his brother, incredulous. Was that how Lucien regarded their mother suddenly appearing after so many years? "Jesus, Luce—"

"The estate is our first concern," Lucien insisted, not hiding his eagerness to get Simon and his father out of the house. "Come, Father."

Simon glanced back at Pen, who had linked her arm through his mother's, the pair of them proud, strong, yet so vulnerable it unnerved him.

Perhaps it was better this way. The three Harcourt men could settle things at the building site. Away from his mother and Penelope—and the injured villagers.

But damned if he was going to be cooped up with his father in a coach. He'd be far too tempted to kill him. "I'll meet you there," Simon said, and headed for the stable.

---

Simon, arriving first, tied Caspian to the hitching post, then surveyed his surroundings as he waited for the other men to descend from the coach. He had spent years fighting in foreign lands, walked onto countless battlefields after the killing was done. Places that had once bustled with life, now reduced to wasteland, only soulless shells left behind.

That was what New Everdene felt like now.

Such a contrast to how it had been but a few days before. The jovial calls of the workmen, their coarse jokes, the laughter of children who played on the outskirts of the construction as their parents labored to build their new homes. He crossed to the ruins of Widow Bevans' cottage, the tiny garden she had started nothing but trampled mud. A knot tightened in his chest, but he turned to face the three men striding toward him.

His father scowled beneath the brim of his top hat. "These are not the buildings I approved. Inchwick, how could you allow this?"

"I had no choice, Lord Ravenscroft. When I questioned the changes, Captain Harcourt produced a letter from the Viscount saying he was to be in complete control."

"Is this true?" their father demanded, watching Lucien walking around the ruined cottage.

He didn't reply, his attention focused on the damage he could see. When he'd examined it, he approached the Garvey cottage next door.

"I wouldn't go inside, my lord," Inchwick warned. "All of the cottages are likely structurally unsound."

"Who is responsible?" demanded Lucien. "I swear, I'll take him to court for damages."

Inchwick' eyes gleamed. "They were designed by a woman."

"A *woman?*" Lucien and their father echoed.

"You might have noticed her at Everdene Hall when you arrived," he replied. "The dark-haired lady who was standing next to the Countess. She is a governess who dabbles a bit in architecture." He cleared his throat, his glance flicking toward Simon, as he added, "Apparently, Captain Harcourt felt that qualified her to design an entire village."

Lucien wheeled on Simon. "Have you completely lost your senses? I agreed you could move the site, not throw the cottage plans into the rubbish and let one of your women play at building houses!"

"Her late father was an architect," Simon replied, his icy gaze on Inchwick, before turning toward his brother.

"And that makes her an expert?"

"No. But she arranged for her former employer, an accomplished architect from London, to examine the design. He inspected the buildings not two weeks ago and judged them sound," Simon defended. "Richard Tremayne's credentials are flawless."

"She worked for him?" Lucien asked.

"As his *governess*," Inchwick said, his voice laced with contempt.

"Good God," Lucien said bitterly. "You let a *governess* take charge?"

Blood pounded in Simon's temples. "That governess is far more qualified to oversee the plans than the thief in your employ. She showed me that hideous place he wanted to build on, proved to me that it was ill conceived."

"Do you even hear how ridiculous you sound, Simon?"

"She *compelled* me to do better. And she found our mother, Lucien. Can't you see—"

"Damn it," Lucien snapped, his face suffusing with red. "She had no right to meddle!"

"Had she not, I would never have discovered that Inchwick has been embezzling from the estate. We have proof."

Inchwick gave a self-deprecating smile. "You needn't bother calling me out. I was honest about my faults during our coach ride. I informed you father and brother that I have taken a bit more than my due—"

"A *bit*?" Simon scoffed. "You lied and stole—"

"Enough," his father said, with a savage wave of his hand. "How is that different from what *you* have done? You blackmailed my employee in order to deceive your own father!"

Before Simon had a chance to reply, Inchwick interrupted. "You mustn't blame Captain Harcourt, my lord. To put it delicately, he has been infatuated with Miss Waverly from the first."

"Waverly?" the Earl sputtered. "Waverly's *daughter* is the one who caused this?"

"Yes, my lord. May I be so bold as to suggest a way to avoid such complications again? You own Laurel Cottage. It was a mere courtesy to allow his widow and her daughters to remain there. But since the elder Miss Waverly has such a penchant for trouble, perhaps you might terminate the lease."

"You rotten, scheming bastard!" Simon stalked toward Inchwick. The man scrambled backwards, falling into the mud. Simon turned to his brother. "Listen to me, Luce—I know this looks bad—"

Lucien gave a harsh laugh. "That's an understatement."

Lucien had always seemed so fiercely controlled, as if the slightest bend would make him break. But now, as Simon looked at the man standing next to their father, he realized there was something unnerving, seething beneath the surface. How long had he been this way? And how was it that Simon had failed to notice until now?

They had always been close, Lucien willing to listen to Simon's side of things, and he tried to appeal to the brother he'd known, not this stranger standing before him. "Moving the village here was sound," he insisted. "I'd stake my life on it. Half the county was flooded when we drove from Galen's Well, but here the streets are clear. I was right there beside Tremayne when he inspected these buildings. Something is not right about this cave-in."

"Are you sure this Tremayne wasn't also ensnared by Miss Waverly's charms?" Lucien demanded. "More intent on pleasing her than doing his job?"

"If you doubt me, you can have Tremayne examine every inch before we proceed."

"Such idiocy," the Earl scoffed. "Even for you, Simon. All you had to do was monitor things from a distance, stay out of Inchwick's way."

"Inchwick knew damned well Blagden Valley wasn't a fit place to build."

"It was out of my sight and that was good enough for me."

"He was cheating you!"

"And what do you think *you* have done?" The Earl swept his hand as if New Everdene was something foul to be thrust off of his plate. "You've thrown my coin away on these ridiculous houses, making me look like a fool to my fellow Tories. I've spent years making speeches in Parliament decrying the unreasonable demands of the masses. Crushing uprisings and making sure that the laws are severe when punishing any rabble who would defy God's own order."

"One more thing you and Inchwick have in common," Simon said. "Using God as your excuse for exploiting those less fortunate than you. Like your wife."

The Earl raised his cane, as if to strike. Simon's hand flashed out, clasping the ebony length and halting it midair. Their gazes locked. Finally, Simon let go of the cane.

His father shook with rage. "She didn't appreciate all I did for her, any more than you do! My wealth put a fine roof over your head. Provided you with the best of everything, the finest homes, the finest schools, admittance to London's most exclusive clubs. Now you object to the very hand that feeds you? Tell me, what are you worth on your own? Have *you* the funds to finish this—this village of yours? Well, *do you?*"

Simon's jaw clenched and hateful triumph suffused his father's face.

"I'll not invest another shilling," the Earl said. "Inchwick, put an end to any new construction my son cannot pay for."

Simon looked in dismay at the wooden stakes that mapped out where a dozen more houses were to be built.

Inchwick lips curled up in distaste. "And what of the buildings already here?" he asked the Earl.

"I intend to recoup every shilling beyond what I originally agreed to pay. Finish those still standing and raise the rent. Evict anyone who cannot pay."

Simon thought of Tripp and his grieving mother, so desperate she'd sold a beloved child, trying to help her other children survive. The image nearly choked him and he leveled an imploring gaze at his father. "Don't do this to exact some kind of sick revenge on me. Where will the other people go?"

"Let them drown themselves in the Thames for all I care."

Simon turned to his brother. "Lucien, you can't let this happen. These people depend on us. We can't let him keep destroying lives. He hid our mother from us all of these years. When you know all she suffered you'll be as horrified as I."

Lucien looked sickened, but not shocked. His expression confused Simon, and yet, Lucien was their father's heir. Who better to know what the Earl was capable of?

The Earl braced both hands on his cane. "That was quite an impassioned plea on your mother's behalf," he sneered.

"You mean the innocent woman you locked in an insane asylum for daring to disagree with you?"

His father's chest swelled, his face purpling. "She was *my wife*! It was my duty to make her submit!"

Simon squared his shoulders, resolve coursing through him. "You won't hurt her anymore. Lucien and I will stop you."

"Lucien?" His father's mocking laugh made Simon's skin crawl. "Oh, yes, you always had such blind faith in Lucien, ever since the day your mother disappeared. Clung to him when you begged to know where she was, what had happened to her. When you *cried* for her."

Lucien grabbed the Earl's arm, shook it. "Father, that's enough!"

But the Earl's gaze only lit with unholy glee. "Lucien was *there*! In the hallway when your mother tried to run away. Otherwise, I never would have caught her." The Earl's face twisted in satisfaction as he said, "Who do you think raised the alarm?"

Simon staggered back, the blow of his father's words hitting him harder than cannon blast. He reeled, trying to shove the words away, the events from that horrible night falling into place. As the shock and agony settled in his gut, he looked at Lucien. "Is it true?"

The answer was written across his brother's stricken face.

# CHAPTER 38

The moment the four men had left Everdene Hall, Pen wanted to follow. Lady Ravenscroft, however, kept a much cooler head by reminding her they had the injured to tend to.

She was right, of course. The tenants and servants who had worked together, cried together, fought pain and fever and fear, were a stark reminder that other lives were at stake.

While Dr. Clay and the Countess tended the more serious patients, Penelope took charge of changing bandages and distributing medicine to those less injured. When she was finally able to catch the Countess alone half an hour later, she noted the woman's troubled frown. "Is something wrong?" Pen asked.

Lady Ravenscroft's gaze swept the room. "I am afraid my husband's appalling display of temper has caused unrest. The families want to take their loved ones home. Nor can I blame them."

"Is it safe to move the men in spite of their injuries?"

"Dr. Clay believes they will heal better away from the Earl's poisonous anger. No one knows that better than I do."

Penelope would never forget the courage and dignity the Countess had shown, and could only imagine the jolt she had suffered, being subjected once again to her husband's vitriol. "How are you faring after seeing the Earl again?" she asked.

"Strangely enough, it was something of a relief. For years I had nightmares… I would round a corner and Barnabas was there, looming over me like some ogre from legend." She gave an odd half-smile, more to herself than to Penelope. "He's actually a lot smaller than I remembered. Nothing but a bitter, sick old man. Now that Simon knows the truth, he has no weapon to use against me. And…" Her voice softened with a deep, wistful ache. "I have seen Lucien."

Pen pictured that emotion-charged moment, the hard-edged Viscount's face going white at the sight of his mother. "Why is it that you didn't want the Viscount to know Simon had found you?"

"Things between Lucien and me became… complicated. But his love for Simon never wavered." The Countess, her expression bittersweet, reached over and took Penelope's hand, a tender touch that made Pen's own heart ache with yearning. "You should have seen them as boys, my dear. From the moment I laid Simon in the cradle, Lucien was so protective of him. And Simon, he made my solemn Lucien smile. I knew they would take care of each other when I could not. My one comfort in the times I most despaired."

She looked down at the Countess's delicate fingers, holding her own. They had once been those of a noblewoman, soft and pampered, required only to lift the weight of an embroidery needle or select delicate gowns. In the years since she had left Everdene, they had become callused and capable in service of women at St. Alban's.

Pen hesitated to cause her more pain, and yet, so many secrets had entangled this family. She knew the only way to be free of them was to speak the truth. "When I began making inquiries in an attempt to find you, the Viscount wrote me a threatening letter, commanding me to stop."

A dart of pain shone for an instant in the Countess's eyes, but she did not look surprised. "Lucien and I each have our reasons for keeping such distance, reasons that I cannot share. I can only tell you this. My husband was cruel to my daughters, to Simon. To me." She blinked back tears. "But what he did to Lucien was cruelest of all."

Before Penelope had a chance to ask what that might be, the Countess looked her in the eye, her smile perfunctory, indicating that—for now at least—she was done answering any questions. "Come along. We have much to do if we are to help our charges back to their homes, preferably before my husband makes his return."

Within minutes, the exodus from Everdene Hall began, Lady Ravenscroft taking charge to make sure all went smoothly. One of the Harcourt coaches had been brought out from the coach house, and fitted with pillows and coverlets, and whatever else could assure an invalid's comfort. The steadiest team available waited in the traces, as Dr. Clay and the Countess prepared to accompany home the first group of men and their families.

As the equipage rumbled away, Pen peered in the direction of New Everdene.

There was still no sign of the four men who had left hours ago. She'd been uneasy when she'd watched Simon ride off, suspecting that Inchwick would do everything in his power to show the buildings in the worst possible light. It wouldn't be hard to undermine what they'd accomplished, especially since they still had no idea what had caused such destruction.

As for Simon's brother, she thought, returning into the house, perhaps the pair had shared a bond as children just as the Countess claimed, but that was years ago. She saw no signs of that now. If anything, the Viscount was desperate to hide something, something so dangerous that the he was willing to threaten Penelope to keep it buried.

Several times the coach returned then left again, until at last, Daw and his family were the only ones who remained. As two burly footmen settled the carpenter in the coach, Tripp climbed up onto the seat beside him. Margery Daw stepped in after them, then looked down at Pen. "I suppose you will be glad to get home as well, Miss Waverly."

"I suppose I will," she replied with a smile, though truth be told, she wasn't quite sure how she felt, since returning home meant she'd be away from Simon. She thought of the stolen moments they had shared when he'd slipped into her bed the night before, the feel of being held in his arms as she slept, waking to the sound of his breathing and his hand cupping her breast.

As difficult as this time had been, those moments had made her long to spend every night in his arms, his face the first one she saw in the morning, and the last at night.

Oh, there had been the danger of being discovered, but she hadn't cared. Being with Simon felt so right. Now, she would go back to Laurel Cottage, to her mother's familiar complaints, her sisters forever looking to Pen for answers. To the questions about Catherine she might never ask, might never have answered.

Lost in her reverie, it was a moment before she realized the coach was readying to depart. She stepped back, waving at the occupants as the vehicle lurched forward, then on down the drive.

Her glance strayed out to the pasture where Epona was grazing beside three of Simon's golden mares, their bellies rounded with foals to come. Worried about Simon, she asked one of the grooms to have her horse saddled, so she could ride out to New Everdene herself. About ten minutes later, she started out to the stables, then stopped short on seeing the

Earl's coach in the distance. She scanned the horizon, but saw no golden horse and rider, wondering what was keeping Simon.

Hurrying back to the house, she was waiting when the three other men came through the door. The Earl muttered some unintelligible order to Inchwick, who seemed pleased with whatever was said, because he flashed Pen a smirk, then hastened off on some errand. The Earl cast a surly glance in her direction, then headed up the stairs, his brass-tipped cane punctuating each step.

Only the Viscount remained. He stood, staring into the now-empty parlor, before turning toward Penelope, a flash of emotion crossing his face, something she couldn't quite decipher. "Why did you have to meddle? I warned you not to."

"Where is Simon?" she asked.

"I don't know... He rode off somewhere, and..." His voice faded, his eyes turning dark, haunted.

She felt a sudden, cold sinking sensation in her chest. "Is he all right?"

It was almost as if he no longer saw her, his gaze turning distant. Finally, Lucien shook his head. "No..."

Her limbs turned leaden. "What happened? Tell me!"

Whether he heard her or not, she didn't know. He turned and followed his father up the stairs.

# CHAPTER 39

orn between following Lucien to demand answers, or trying to find Simon herself, Penelope chose the latter. What had happened that the Viscount had looked so despairing? And why, oh why, hadn't Simon returned? After the trauma of the roof collapse and her own sense of responsibility for it, caring for the injuries and enduring the Earl's rage, she wanted—no, *needed*—to wrap her arms around Simon, feel his heartbeat, his mouth on hers, and know that no matter what had caused the torment in Viscount Everdene's face, Simon was safe. That she and this man she loved could, together, resolve whatever threatened him.

She ran to the stables, seeing Epona still saddled and tethered just inside. She burst into the door, surprised—and relieved—to find Simon leading a freshly brushed Caspian into his stall.

He closed the stall door, then looked over at her, his face haggard, his hair tousled.

"What happened?" she asked.

"My father." His eyes darkened with suppressed anger. "He

not only ordered a halt to all new construction, he intends to raise the rents to a ruinous amount. Evict those who can't pay."

"No…"

"That is, unless I can make up the difference in cost between the cottages he approved and the ones I built."

Guilt swept through her. If she'd left well enough alone, the people might be housed in cramped cottages in Blagden Valley, but at least they would have had a roof over their heads. Pen bit her lip and groped for something to say. "What about Lucien? Your mother told me how close you and he once were. Is it possible together—"

"No." The swift denial cut through the air like a blade. "We are on different sides of this battle. It's—" His voice cracked as he stared at Caspian in his stall. "It's over, Pen."

"We'll think of some way forward, Simon."

"There is none," he said, tearing his gaze from the stall to look at her. "None, but to go to Tattersall's, and sell Caspian and the mares."

Pen reeled, trying to imagine Simon without his horses. While she loved her Epona dearly, Simon's bond with Caspian was different. They had survived the battlefield together. The horse had been his strength after losing his friend Jamie, his reason to fight, his future. "Surely there must be another way," she said.

His fists clenched at his side. "Would that there was. My father all but laughed in my face, saying I had nothing of any value to sell. But I do. I invested every shilling I had in Caspian and the mares. After that, there's nothing left for me here. Once they're sold, I will rejoin my regiment."

"Rejoin your regiment…?" Her heart started hammering at the hollowness of his words. "And what of me?"

He shook his head, not meeting her gaze. "I'm sorry, Pen. I can't take you with me."

His words hit her like a blow to her gut.

She thought of everything that had happened between them. Could he just walk away after what they had together? No. She refused to believe that he could even entertain the idea. He was hurt. Lashing out. "Leave, then. But don't be surprised when I follow you. I refuse to go back to the half-life I knew before I loved you."

Simon pressed his fingertips against his eyelids. "Damn it, you have no idea the danger you'd be in!"

"I don't care as long as I'm with you."

He let his hand fall to his side, his expression steely. "I won't have you stranded in some foreign land, unprotected if I'm killed."

"It's my life, my risk to take." She took a steadying breath, searching his face, hoping to find some way to reason with him. "We are *not* letting that bitter old man wrench more away from you."

"Wrench more? There's nothing left for him to take. Not after what he told me..." Anguish flashed in a searing path across Simon's face. "Do you know why my mother didn't want me to tell Lucien that I'd found her? Why Lucien discouraged me from trying to find out what had happened to her?"

"Why?"

"Because Lucien *knew*." The words tore from Simon like twisted shards. "From the night she disappeared, he and my father lied to me. *Lucien* was the one who raised the alarm."

*That* was the reason the Viscount had wanted Pen to leave the past alone? In a burst of clarity, she could see what Simon could not. She wanted to hate Lucien Harcourt for hurting Simon this way. And yet... she thought of the Countess's words. How her sons had loved each other, how Lucien had always protected Simon. Suddenly she pictured them as she'd known them so many years ago. Boys... like Tripp. Small, vulnerable... motherless. Victims of their father's rages.

She didn't want to feel empathy for the Viscount who had threatened her, but it was possible to feel for the boy he had been. "He was just a child."

"Far older than I was!" he said. "Old enough to know better. She was our mother, for God's sake."

Knowing he was blinded by his own devastation, she groped desperately for some way to ease his torment. "I can only imagine how painful this has been for you. But your brother had to be frightened and confused... Helpless, even..."

"How can you take his side?"

"I'm not."

Simon glared at her, clearly betrayed by her words as well. "And all the years after? He kept lying. My God, he was the only person I truly trusted until Jamie and you. He *sided* with my father. Made my mother's life a living hell."

"Simon, please..." She tried to draw breath, but it felt as if her heart was in tatters. "Don't let the Earl shatter your relationship with your brother now without a fight. Think of your mother. She told me how close you and Lucien were, how you helped each other survive her loss, the loss of your sisters, your father's cruelties."

"You don't understand," he said through gritted teeth.

As much as she wanted to reach out to him, they seemed suddenly oceans apart. He needed time now. Space to deal with this new betrayal, sort through all he'd learned. So did she. "I should go..." she said.

He nodded, his hands tightening as if to keep himself from touching her. "That would be best."

The words pierced her heart. Was he truly going to end things between them?

He might, but she was not. She went to him, kissed his cheek, then walked to the door, where Epona was tethered. She paused and looked back at this man who had taught her to love, made her believe in herself as no one had before.

He'd turned his back to her, his shoulders stiff with pain. She paused a long moment, willing him to look back at her one last time. He never did.

# CHAPTER 40

There was nothing more to do or say. Heart heavy, Pen mounted Epona, and was trotting down the drive when she saw Inchwick step from his cottage, heading to the manor. Her first instinct was to avoid him.

He'd been embezzling from the estate for years. He'd twisted matters around, from evicting Tripp's family, to stoking the Earl's wrath over the village, pleased in knowing he would turn so many out of their homes.

The thought he was gloating over his triumph angered her, the words welling up inside her, words she damned well had to say. She urged Epona to a light canter, then reined her in before the land agent could pass. "Mr. Inchwick. I have something to say to you."

"Ah, Miss Waverly. Perfect timing. I was actually in search of you as well. There is a private matter of some importance the Earl has asked me to address. Might I suggest we talk in my office?"

She regarded him warily. "I find I'm short of time and temper."

"Then we shall settle things here. Did you really think that you and Captain Harcourt could best me?" His smile made her skin crawl. "It seems our little *contretemps* is at an end. Since the day you took my ledgers, prying through my personal finances, I've resolved to make you regret it."

"The only thing I regret is not convincing Captain Harcourt to have you arrested the moment he discovered your years of theft."

"Well, it was an opportunity missed. I confess, I was not certain how the Earl would react to my private enterprises. However, I have been able secure his clemency after your debacle in the new village. Even the most stable wall will fall if one knows where to weaken it."

Shock swept through her. When she finally found her tongue, her voice came out in a sputter. "*You...?* You did this?"

"I have no idea what you are talking about. Just try to convince any sane man that the roof falling wasn't the result of some ridiculous *female* playing at a man's work."

Epona must have felt her unease. The mare sidestepped nervously. Penelope tightened her grip on the reins. "How could you...? I will see that you—"

Inchwick actually laughed. "Anyone who hears you accusing me, a respected land agent of long standing, will dismiss you as one more woman given to hysteria—not unlike the Earl's wife. The queen herself would condemn you!"

Epona snorted, growing more restless as Pen looked down at him, trying to keep her temper in check. "I'll find a way to prove what you've done."

"*You* will not have the chance, thanks to my employer. You made a fool of the Earl of Ravenscroft, deceiving him about the village, unearthing what happened with his wife. You exposed him as a liar to the Viscount, possibly the only person in Christendom that he gives a damn about besides himself." He jumped back as Epona stomped dangerously close. "Know this, Miss Waverly," he said, turning a wary eye at the horse, then focusing on her. "The Earl intends to use every weapon at his disposal to destroy you, and it has been my great pleasure to put the perfect means at his disposal."

A chill ran down her spine.

His eyes gleamed with an intensity that she found disconcerting. "I would advise you to begin searching for a new place of residence. Your tenure at Laurel Cottage is at an end."

She wanted to scream at him, strike him, tell him he couldn't do this terrible thing. But she wasn't about to give him that satisfaction. Instead, she urged Epona forward.

"What?" he asked, as she started to trot past. "No pretty plea begging me not to evict you? No protests? Or are you planning to run crying to your lover?" He made a scoffing noise. "He cannot even save himself, let alone you. You have no lease. It was a mere a courtesy to allow you to remain this long. His lordship expects you to quit the property at the end of the month."

She wouldn't let him see her cry. Dear God, how was she going to tell mother, Fanny and Kitty? She wheeled her mare about so that she faced him once more. "You and the Earl are despicable."

"And in complete control of the situation, as God intended." He was about to turn away, then stopped, looking up at her. "Oh, and one last caveat for you to consider. Do not count on securing a governess position any time in the future. The tale of what happened here will spread like wildfire. I intend to see to it. You will forever be labeled as the woman whose delusions of grandeur brought an entire town to ruins."

"How dare you…"

"Your time at Everdene is done. You've brought everyone you care about to ruin—Captain Harcourt, your mother, your sisters. They'll suffer the consequences of your unwomanly ambitions." He smirked. "Tell me, Miss Waverly… Was it worth it?"

Her throat constricted, and she tasted bile. Taking a deep breath, willing herself to calm, she trotted forward so that she was directly beside Inchwick. She looked down at him, giving what she hoped was her most chilling smile. "Don't think you are rid of me quite yet, Mr. Inchwick. I'm going to find a way to prove what you have done. If it's the last thing I do."

# CHAPTER 41

As much as Pen longed to go to Simon, face this challenge the way they had so many others, she couldn't add to his burden, not tonight. She needed time to think. Her head was aching almost as much as her heart. The moment she returned home, she fetched a piece of foolscap, pen and ink from the desk, then wrote: *Meet me at New Everdene in the morning. P*

Entrusting it to Hughes to be delivered, she counted the hours until the next morning. She could only hope that Simon would come.

Once Hughes had ridden away, Penelope could no longer quell the jolt of terror that struck through her at the thought that in a month, her family would leave this place forever. Kitty and Fanny would be set adrift, and her mother would lose her home… God knew, Anastasia Waverly had tried Penelope's patience, and there were times frustration and resentment had driven her to the edge of madness. But the thought of her mother accepting charity in some distant relative's home filled Pen with regret.

By the time she gathered the courage to go downstairs, and

face her mother and sisters, Clara was lighting the first candles to drive back the gathering shadows. Kitty and Fanny rushed to greet her from the kitchen. A smear of flour marked Fanny's cheek, and Kitty's apron was askew, reminding Pen of when they were little girls, giggling, begging her to stitch a torn doll, or build towers out of books, or tell them tales as they sat in front of the fire.

Pen stiffened, knowing that she was about to shatter their worlds as surely as if she'd hurled one of Zeus's lightning bolts.

"Is something wrong?" Fanny asked.

"You look tired to death!" Kitty said, giving Pen a hug. "Come in and sit down and let us fuss over you!"

Their solicitude was almost more than she could bear in the face of the news she had to impart.

Her mother walked in just then, eyeing her oldest daughter, a somewhat eager glint in her eye. "You didn't come home last night," she said in a tone that suggested she was expecting her statement to be followed by some word of Pen's engagement. "Will there be an announcement to follow?"

"Sadly, yes. But not what you think." She explained in as few words as possible about what had transpired, then took a deep breath. "I'm afraid the situation made the Earl very angry. There were… unexpected consequences that will affect all of us." Penelope hesitated, steeling herself for what would follow. "The Earl has given notice that we are to vacate Laurel Cottage by month's end."

Her mother paled.

"Wh-what?" Fanny choked out.

Kitty gasped, her eyes saucer-wide as she looked at her mother, then back to Penelope. "Surely, he wouldn't?"

"He can and he will unless I find some way to stop this. He owns the property."

"Oh, Penelope." Her mother sank into a chair, her eyes shimmering with tears. "How many times did I beg you not to meddle in things that weren't your concern? Now your head-strong ways have cost us our home."

Penelope wanted to say was it was their father's gambling that caused them to lose their home. But in her heart, she knew the blame did not lie fully with him. He had merely drowned his grief in the only way he knew how, with devastating conse-quences, just as her mother had cloaked her grief in headaches and retreating into an imaginary world where indulging in luxuries they could not afford would disguise her pain.

Penelope could not have prevented the consequences from that long-ago storm, things beyond her control, but had her certainty that she was right, her need to push through any obstacle resulted in all of this? If she'd left things alone, Simon would not be disinherited, her mother and sisters suddenly evicted, and the villagers? The men who were injured, the fami-lies with nowhere to go...

She turned toward her mother, wishing she could change the past, but she couldn't. Her voice caught as she tried to speak. In the end, all that came out was, "I am sorry. I'm sorry for this. I'm sorry... about the storm... what I lost in it..." Her mother's eyes brimmed with tears.

"The storm?" Kitty asked, confused. "When you were with Captain Harcourt? Have you spoken to him about this?"

"Yes!" Fanny said. "Surely, Captain Harcourt will intercede with his father. It's clear the gentleman adores you."

Perhaps he had at one time, Penelope thought, recalling that wild, sweet passion she had shared with him. Would it have been easier to reconcile herself to the future if she hadn't known what it felt like to love, to fight, to have someone believe in her in a way beyond what was dictated by being a woman? Who saw all of her—the strengths, the weaknesses, the ridicu-lous, and the wise, and loved it all.

She shook her head. "Such an appeal would be fruitless. Captain Harcourt is estranged from his father, so we can count on no help from that quarter. And to make matters worse, he is planning to return to his regiment."

Fanny reached over, clasping her mother's hand, the poor woman looking ready to faint.

Kitty tipped her chin up, saying, "I know you think us flighty, caring only about hair ribbons and balls, and eating ices with our friends. But we know the only reason we're able to do so is because you have shouldered responsibility for the whole family." She looked at Fanny, who nodded in encouragement. "We've been talking since you left for Everdene Hall. Seeing how you dealt with the accident, what you've done at New Everdene. You always told us we should reach for more. Now that we've seen you do so, we know you're right."

"It's just as Kitty says," Fanny insisted. "We will take some of the load off of your shoulders. We're going to make you proud of us, prove that your faith in us was justified."

"I never doubted it." Tears pricked the backs of Pen's eyelids. "I love you both so much."

Their mother broke into a sob, then quickly rose from the table, fleeing from the room.

As much as Pen wanted to follow, she knew that her presence was the last thing her mother needed right now.

Tomorrow, she would square her shoulders and go back to New Everdene. She would not let Inchwick and the Earl win. She would find a way to prove what Inchwick had done, save her sisters and mother. The villagers.

And Simon's dream of a pasture full of golden horses.

---

SIMON TRUDGED UP THE DARK STAIRCASE TO HIS BROTHER'S chamber, feeling the echoing emptiness in the house. Pen was gone, the manor emptied of the tenants he'd worked with these past months. The servants, perhaps too scared to make themselves known after all that had transpired, hadn't even bothered to light the sconces in that wing of the house, and so it was dark when Simon knocked on Lucien's door. He had done so, many times over the years. Sometimes to share brandy, to talk about a horse or a pretty girl who had caught his eye. But more often than not, to drive back memories of the family they'd lost, a secret part of him needing to be certain that his brother, this one anchor in his life, had not vanished as well.

Now, all sense of solid ground was gone.

"Come in." Lucien sounded wearier than Simon could ever recall.

He opened the door. His brother sat at a writing desk that was scattered with ledgers and papers, notes scribbled in a frenetic hand. A nearly empty bottle of wine stood beside the branch of candles that cast the desk's contents in wavering light.

Lucien looked up, Simon catching a glimpse of anguish on his brother's face as he stood, folding his arms across his chest. He faced Simon. Their gazes crossed like swords.

"I assume," Lucien said, "you have things to get off of your chest?" He nodded at the mess of papers on his desk. "First, know that I'm calling in a group of architects and builders from my other estates to look over construction at the site. If there is a flaw in Miss Waverly's design, they will fix it."

"There isn't."

"We will soon find out. I still think it was a damned reckless thing to do, having her draw up these plans, but…" The years of their bond seemed to catch hold of him, and he took a deep breath. "I can also see that you've accomplished more than I would have thought possible at the site in a very short time. Unfortunately, it is also over budget. You know how Father is. He insists we stop construction."

"That's what I've come to discuss with you. I intend to pay the difference so that work can continue. Every shilling."

"How?"

"By selling Caspian and the mares I bred him to. They're in foal, and I should get enough to make a large dent in the debt." When his brother made no immediate objection, he continued. "But I need your help. Once I pay back the funds, will you guarantee that they go to finishing New Everdene? That the tenants won't be evicted because of my actions?"

"You would do that for these people?"

Simon met his brother's gaze with a steely one of his own. "Yes."

"Exactly how am I supposed to force our father to do anything? You know how he is."

"Find a way. He liked having a son in uniform, a cavalry officer he could brag about in the House of Lords. I'll rejoin my regiment as soon as the sale is made, fight for his goddamned empire. Payment in blood should satisfy even him." Simon saw his brother flinch, didn't want to see the sudden pain in Lucien's eyes. He wheeled and walked out the door.

# CHAPTER 42

The following morning, after a restless night with little sleep, Penelope saddled and bridled Epona, setting out for New Everdene. She'd not seen it since the disaster at Widow Bevans' cottage, and the sight of the blighted building as she rode toward it made her shudder. She tore her gaze from the ruins, searching the seemingly empty street, dismayed not to see Simon.

It wasn't until she passed the wreckage, that she caught the sight of Brutus tethered to low branch of a nearby tree, Simon waiting beside him.

He helped her dismount, his hands strong and familiar around her waist as he held her for just a moment longer than necessary, then lowered her to the ground.

"You read my note, then?" She didn't wait for him to answer, plunging on with, "I know who caused the cave-in. Inchwick."

"What proof do you have? Without it, we've got nothing."

"I don't have proof. Still, he all but gloated over it when he told me my family is to be evicted at the end of the month. Apparently, at the direction of your father for my part in all this."

Simon's eyes burned with anger as she told him what Inch-wick had said.

That he'd make certain she'd never work again as a governess, ruin her reputation, and any chance of resuming construction beyond the cottages already erected.

"I know he's behind this," she insisted. "Even if I could find the proof, he says no one will believe me. But if it came from you…? Maybe we can find something if we look."

She started toward what was left of the cottage, but he caught her hand, stopping her. "Be careful," Simon warned. "We don't dare move anything until we're sure it won't upset the balance of whatever's left and cause further damage."

She nodded, letting him enter first, then followed.

Dust motes floated through the air around them, sunlight pouring in through the now-open roof, onto the fallen beam that lay across the floor, crushing everything beneath it. The sight of the damage was a stark reminder of the shock and fear the men must have felt in that frozen instant just before every-thing came crashing down.

Simon pointed near the center, the dark stain beneath the splintered ladder rungs. "Daw was there. They'd laid tarps over the place where a chimney was to be built. He was inspecting the roof for damage from the storm. I heard Mac and Bailey in the loft… then a cracking sound. Everything happened so fast."

"There's so much damage. How do we prove anything?"

"That's just it. Inchwick was using inferior materials. Maybe we missed a rotted place or a crack that couldn't withstand the weight of the rainfall."

Penelope frowned. "Doesn't it strike you as odd that the beam, inferior or not, would break at that location?"

"From what I can see, it's where most of the weight would have been centered—" He stopped, moving closer, examining the break. "Come look at this."

She joined him, leaning so close she could feel the brush of his sleeve.

He ran his finger along the exposed wood. "It's a clean cut. Marks from the teeth of a saw."

Penelope's breath caught. She had modeled her plans on one from her father's architecture books. There was not meant to be any cut there at all. Which did not, however, rule out possible human error. "Could have it been cut by mistake? Someone hoping it wouldn't be noticed?"

Simon eyed the break more closely. "No. Mr. Tremayne inspected every beam. There is no way he would have missed it. This cut would have to have been made after the beam was put in place. But if Inchwick is responsible, he couldn't have done this alone. I doubt he had the knowledge. Whoever made this cut knew exactly how to weaken the support." Simon rose, then looking around with new purpose. "Sooner or later, it was meant to fall. The force of the wind and the weight of the water took care of the rest."

They heard a sudden rustle from what was to be the bedroom, then a stifled cough.

Pen froze. Had one of the conspirators returned to see his handiwork?

Simon held his finger to his lips. With the agility and stealth of a tiger, he picked his way to the other room.

A few moments later, she heard a scuffle, then Simon's surprised voice, saying, "Tripp?"

Penelope made her way carefully to the room where the boy cowered against the wall, his eyes huge.

"What the devil are you doing in here?" Simon asked. "Can't you see it's dangerous?"

"Come to put something back 'fore he found out about it," the boy said.

"Before who found what?" Simon asked.

Tripp swallowed hard. "That man who was here, th' other

night. I didn't mean nothing by it, I swear! But sometimes I can't sleep, thinking of my mam and sisters, and—and so I took to walking through here, thinking about what it'd be like, if we was here altogether. But I never meant for anyone to get hurt! You have to believe me!"

Simon's shoulders stiffened at the boy's words, his voice low, on edge. "What do you mean you never intended for anyone to get hurt...?"

Tripp shrank back at the urgency in Simon's voice, his eyes darting around as though searching for a quick escape.

Penelope, seeing the fear in his face, reached out, taking his hand in hers. "You needn't be afraid. You know we only mean to help...?"

He searched her gaze, gave a timid nod.

"What happened?" she asked gently.

"Bunch of 'em came out here. Inchwick with Okum an' some o' those other folk that kicked up a fuss at the meeting when Captain Harcourt tol' 'em about wreckin' the village."

Pen fought to keep her voice level, trying not to scare the child. "You saw them here that night before the storm?"

Once again that timid nod. "They caught me, they did. Inchwick said he and the men was checking to make sure the roof was sturdy. I wanted to tell you, 'cept he told me if I squealed on 'im he'd see to it Daw was throwed into the poorhouse, an' his wife set out like me ma." He brushed the tears from his face, forging on. "Then Okum grabbed me an' said he was going to finish what the chimney sweep started. Stuff me up a chimney an' set a fire. Scared me so bad I near pissed myself. Kicked an' clawed, I did. 'E dropped me an' I ran."

Simon's gaze hardened, his fists clenching at his side.

Penelope kept her attention on Tripp. "You were very brave. But why do you think those who were hurt had anything to do with you?"

"Because of this." He dug in his pocket and pulled out what

looked to be a bronze disk, a leather cord strung through a hole in its center. "I know they'll come looking for it."

"What is it?" Simon asked taking it from him.

"Okum's China coin. Wore it 'round his neck, he did. Always braggin' how he took it off a sailor in a tavern brawl. I must'a grabbed onto the cord and snapped it when I was fightin' him. Didn't know it was in my hand 'til I was all the way home."

"I don't understand," Penelope said, eyeing the coin Simon held, before turning back to Tripp. "Why would you think that made you responsible for the workers getting hurt?"

"Because—" His voice choked as he looked away, tears starting anew, the fear evident as he fought to take a breath. "'Twas my fault Daw got hurt. I was tryin' to put the coin back, when he caught me that day. If he hadn't been hanging onto that beam, leanin' way over to scold me it wouldn't have come down —I knew I shouldn't 'ave been there."

Pen drew him into her arms. "It's not your fault. I promise."

"It is," he said, his sobs shaking his thin body, his hot tears soaking into her shoulder. "Daw warned me not to come in when they were working, lest anyone get hurt. And now..."

"Oh, Tripp." She patted his back, letting him cry, her gaze meeting Simon's. "That beam didn't fall because of you. Those men you saw here—Okum and the rest—they're the ones responsible."

"Miss Waverly is right," Simon said, as the boy's sobs eased. "Daw doesn't blame you. None of us do. But there is something you can do to help us. Help Daw."

Tripp wiped his face with the back of his arm, a look of hope appearing in his swollen, red eyes as he focused on Simon.

"Can you tell the magistrate what you've told us?"

He bit his thumbnail, and Simon knew Tripp was picturing the dark chimney and fire in Okum's threat. But after a moment, Tripp gave a resolute nod. "Mrs. Garvey says I have to tell the truth."

"There's a good lad. We'll be right there with you. Miss Waverly and I."

"What if Inchwick turns the Garveys out like he did me mam?"

Simon stood, looking at the wreckage around them. "We're going to make certain he never has the power to do such a thing again."

# CHAPTER 43

S imon stood across the table from his brother as Lucien turned the Chinese coin over in the palm of his hand. "You're sure about this?" Lucien asked.

"Very. Had we been a moment later, Tripp would have put the coin back in the corner for Okum Landry to find and we'd never have known."

"But Okum? I can't believe he'd have anything to do with this. My God. He's been the cooper here for years."

"It's possible he was corrupted by Inchwick long ago. But it's not just him. From what Tripp says, Okum had several of his mates with him. I remember the group, hanging out at the tavern, looking for trouble. Maybe the news about the village was just more than they could take. Probably wouldn't have taken much for Okum and Inchwick to convince them they were doing the right thing by vandalizing our work."

"But Okum…?" Lucien stared at the coin as though trying to imagine how the villager they'd known for much of their lives could possibly be responsible for such an act.

"If you have the magistrate bring the lot in and question

them, they'll turn on each other like rats in a sack…" He waited, knowing it was his brother's decision.

"I expect they will." Lucien tossed the coin onto his desk, a look of distaste crossing his features. "No doubt, they'll all be too happy to take down Inchwick in the process."

Simon merely nodded, not wanting to ruin this tenuous connection to his brother.

"So, Miss Waverly found the answer to this mystery as well," Lucien continued after a moment.

"She is nothing if not tenacious."

Lucien looked down at his signet ring and twisted it on his finger. The family crest gleamed. "God knows, I didn't want you digging into the past, Simon." He let out a ragged sigh. "For what it's worth, I'm glad she told me to go to hell and found our mother. Alive."

There was so much Simon wanted to confess in that moment. How, at first, he didn't know how the hell he felt about Penelope prying into something so painful, something he'd long buried. He'd been so damned angry. At the same time, he wanted to know why his mother had left them. He would never have heard her side of the story had it not been for Pen. But all he said was, "I'm glad she did, too."

Lucien closed his eyes. Simon wondered what he was picturing. Their mother the night she was running away? Their father's derision and echoed threats the moment he first saw her after so many years, standing before him.

Simon drew a deep breath, looking at this brother who had once been his hero. The brother he'd loved above anyone else. Until Penelope. It occurred to him in that moment, he had to know. "Why…?" he finally asked. "Why did you lie to me?"

"How could I tell you the truth," Lucien said, his voice thick with emotion. "After what I did? I watched you, saw your grief, your anger, your pain. Knowing there was so much more to the story than what had happened the night Mother tried to run away. Our parents were miserable…"

Lucien was quiet for so long that Simon wasn't sure he intended to continue.

But then, after a moment, a look of resolve crossed his face. "I'm sure you realize Father married her for her dowry, expected her to be a glittering political hostess, and aid in his campaigns in Parliament. Mother failed so miserably at it that he exiled her to the country. When he did visit Everdene, he would call me into his study. He said the rest of you were nothing but a drain on the earldom, while I was like him in every way—strong, ruthless when necessary, honoring the earldom and bloodline instead of consorting with lowly peasants."

He still turned the ring on his finger, his gaze distant, remembering the past. "I should have been disgusted by his words. Part of me was. Yet, there was that small place inside me that felt… proud that he thought me his equal. It became almost like opium to me, and I craved that approval to the point that I would do things that now make me cringe. As much as I wanted his regard, I also feared his anger. I had seen how far he would go to crush anyone who defied him."

He took a deep drink of his wine, as if to burn away the memory.

"You were never afraid," Lucien told him. "You never backed down, no matter how he raged or rained blows upon you." He saluted Simon with the half-empty goblet. "God, I wanted to shake you until you fell in line. Wanted to bellow at you not to make things so difficult. Yet, frustrated as I got, I admired you underneath. I was ashamed of my own cowardice."

Simon stared at him, transfixed, remembering. Lucien, placing cool cloths over the welts on Simon's back, left by his father's razor strop, or bruises from blows from the Earl's fists.

The empathy in his brother's face. Why had he never recognized the faint shadow of shame?

"During that last visit," Lucien continued, almost as if he was no longer aware of Simon's presence, "Father must have suspected Mother was getting desperate. He called me into his study and confided to me that Mother was... not in her right mind. It was to remain a secret between us two men. It was up to me to keep watch, he said, to report anything unusual. He was depending on me."

Just as Simon had always depended on Lucien. Pen's words echoed in his head. "You were just a boy..." The words came out unbidden.

Lucien seemed not to hear. He looked down at his goblet, his expression haunted. "It was frightening. I sensed something was wrong with her that night when she tucked us in bed. There was something... brittle, and she cried. I heard a noise and went downstairs, and I saw Mother, Jane, and Cassandra creeping out with their valises. If you had seen her that night..." He finally looked at Simon, and there was no mistaking the pain in his eyes. "She fought him like a madwoman, terrified. Cassandra and Jane... they were screaming... And then she was gone. Father told me if you knew what had happened you might go mad, too. What was I to do? When you cried, and kept searching for her, I lied and kept secrets all that time in an effort to protect you. And to protect myself. I fed your anger, let you believe she had left us, because *I* was afraid if you knew the truth, that I was the one who had sounded the alarm, I'd lose you, too."

His brother's raw anguish twisted Simon's gut, ate away at the anger he had harbored for so many years, the anger he'd directed at Lucien after finding *he* was the one who'd betrayed their mother. "You should have told me..."

"How? As I grew older, I thought... *if Simon had seen Mother and Jane and Cassandra running away, what would* he *have done?* Pieces of the story didn't make sense. I began to question. But I was too afraid."

A part of Simon wanted to hold onto the anger. Blame his brother for the lost years with their mother, his sisters. But as he watched the emotions chase across Lucien's face, he wanted to comfort him. Comfort the brother who had shouldered so much of the burden, been his champion when their father had directed his temper Simon's way. "How could you not be afraid?" Simon asked, after imagining what he would have done in his brother's place.

"You wouldn't have immediately called for Father," Lucien said. "You would have found out what was happening. Would have asked them... before you betrayed them. When I finally gathered the courage to confront Father, pressed him for the truth..." He shuddered at the memory. "Do you know what he told me...? That it didn't matter anymore. She had died in that hideous asylum, like the one he took us to as boys." He choked back a sob. "What was I to do? *I* killed her. It was my fault she'd died."

His words hit Simon as though he'd been punched in the gut, lost all air in his lungs. He knew without a doubt their father had let Lucien believe exactly that. It was his way of controlling Lucien, ensuring that he would never tell Simon what had happened.

Lucien drained his glass, then immediately refilled it. "But you, Simon, you were the only one out of all of us who wasn't afraid of him. Even as a boy, you wouldn't buckle under his bullying, no matter what he threatened, and you haven't bent to his will here." He gave a cynical laugh. "You realize he meant for you to fail?"

"It occurred to me."

"When I saw what you'd accomplished at New Everdene,

how you took his cruel act, and transformed it into something to improve the lives of every tenant… You found the truth about our mother, opened my eyes to how Father manipulated me to bend to his will. Father said that I would lose you if you knew the truth. Now I have. Maybe I deserve to." He looked up at Simon, unabashed by the tears in his eyes. "I'm sorry. I'm so damned sorry."

He looked so alone.

Simon wasn't sure what to say or do. Too many years of repressed emotions welled up, coming out at once. He picked up the coin Okum had lost, twisting the leather thong that dangled from his fingers, wanting—no, *needing*—to change the topic, put them both on even ground. "Then with your permission, I will inform the magistrate."

He turned to leave, nearly to the door, when Lucien slammed his goblet to the table, wine sloshing over the sides as he stood.

"Don't go," Lucien called out.

"I don't think we should wait to notify the magistrate. If Inchwick and his minions suspect we know what they've done—"

"Don't rejoin your regiment."

Simon stopped in his tracks, surprised by his brother's words.

Lucien crossed the room toward him, saying, "I don't know if we can mend what is broken between us, but there is no chance at all if you're a continent away. Let me invest in this stable of yours." He held out his hand toward Simon. "Let me help. Even if I don't think there is any way to make our father accept our vision of the village, I would like to try."

As much as Simon wanted to accept his brother's offer, he knew there was no way either of them could win against their father. The man wielded too much power. And they had their mother to think of. Even so, he was grateful for the effort. He grasped his brother's hand, about to decline the offer, when it suddenly hit him as to what they needed to do. "What if there is a way?"

Something akin to hope gleamed in his brother's eyes. "I'd like to hear it."

# CHAPTER 44

Simon took grim pleasure in the expression on the Earl's face as he entered the Sky Chamber, the room where it had all begun. Where his wife had sought refuge from his cruelty, where he'd sounded a death knell over the village, where he'd struck his unholy bargain with Simon, entangling another son in a depraved scheme to destroy lives.

The old man had done his best to drag them all into hell, Simon thought. Cassandra and Jane. Lucien and him. But the ruthless Earl of Ravenscroft was about to enter a hell of his own making.

The Earl's hard gaze swept the room, his eyes clouding with suspicion as he viewed the other occupants. Lucien leaned against one wall, his arms crossed over his chest. Their mother, pale but resolved, had sought out the blue brocade chair in which she'd loved to gather her children and spin stories or play games, or merely stare out at the village she'd loved.

And Penelope. Simon's chest squeezed. Penelope, who sat beside his mother, lending quiet support. Who'd risked everything for the people of Everdene, and for him. Who had broken open the midnight-hued hell his father had built, unearthed the lies, and drawn out the poison, exposing the wrong done to Simon's family, leading them into the light—shaken, still dazed and uncertain, but new. He'd insisted that she witness this, despite Lucien's objections. She'd done more than any other person to see the Earl's crimes against his family and tenants be laid bare, to thwart the old man's heinous plans.

If only Cassandra and Jane could be here to witness this as well, it would be perfect, Simon thought. But he'd bring them back to the family. He would.

The plan Simon had devised had seemed like a solid one when he had conceived it. But… Now that his father was here, he wasn't sure. God knew, he'd seen officers who'd been willing to burn the world down just to save face.

He felt that honing of instinct he'd experienced before battle, every cell of his body alert, ready to spring into action, his senses sharpened to translate every nuance in the enemy he faced.

He'd never waged a battle with higher stakes than this.

"What the devil is this about?" the Earl demanded as he made his way into the room, his cane tapping on the floor. His nostrils flared, lips curled as he surveyed people gathered there. "What is the meaning of this? If we're meant to conduct business, why aren't we in the study?"

"We wished to inform you that construction on New Everdene will go forward as planned," Simon told him.

"The devil it will!"

"If it does not, I will see to it that you will have a difficult time passing any sort of legislation in Parliament when session opens."

"A mere cavalry officer having influence in Parliament?" the Earl scoffed. "As if you have that kind of power! Do you think you can threaten me?"

"It's not a threat." Simon retrieved a sheaf of papers from the desk and held them out to his father.

"What is this?" the Earl demanded, refusing to take them.

"A sample of what will be distributed outside Parliament if you refuse to finish the village. You know the populace loves nothing more than the scandal sheets. I will personally see that it falls into the hands of every member of the House of Lords and the Commons, telling them what you've done.

He read aloud the list of the Earl of Ravenscroft's crimes. "Your wife's unjust incarceration, as testified to by two respected doctors. The fact that you were swindled by Mr. Inchwick for years will show your incompetence, and your cowardice in not prosecuting him will give rise to everyone wondering what dirty secret the thief must have on you to blackmail you so. The damning words of an earl who was willing to wipe away his estate's village just so he could have a more picturesque view. Add to that the fact that you're refusing to finance the last of the cottages. I think there are ruinous debts out there somewhere that you are keeping secret as well, don't you, Lucien?" Simon cast a smug glance at his brother.

"I am sure of it," Lucien said.

"I have no ruinous debts!" the Earl sputtered.

"Our accusation doesn't have to be true, as long as other people believe it. You proved that with your slander against our mother. People will seize on the scandal as the perfect explanation for your actions. Why else would you stop work in the midst of construction in this village of yours?"

"You know damned well why!"

"You've made plenty of enemies over the years," Lucien said. "They'll be all too happy to believe the worst of you and spread the scandals all over England. You worry about uprisings against landlords? This should cause a spark to set off an inferno, with you at the very center."

The Earl's face turned purple.

"You should know it was Inchwick who gave us this idea," Simon told him. "He planned to shred Penelope's reputation out of pure spite. At least ours will result in a positive outcome for families you were willing to render homeless."

"You cannot prove that!"

"Who would doubt your own sons if we were the ones who let these rumors slip out? A sorrowful word when Lucien is at White's. Or I'm in some gaming hell or at the races."

The Earl stood, fairly shaking with rage. "I believe you capable of any outrage to your name, Simon. But Lucien? Never! He would be tarred with the same brush! Lucien would never drag the Harcourt titles through the muck!"

Lucien's eyes narrowed as he spoke. "You are the one who has done that, Father, whether the rest of the world knows it or not. You made me your accomplice when I was a boy." Lucien looked at his mother, his voice thick with regret. "I intend to do whatever I must to make things right."

"Lucien, you were a child," their mother said gently. "Afraid of a father who was violent. I never blamed you."

"That is just like you, spewing sentimental pap," the Earl cried, pointing an accusing finger at the Countess. "You were abandoning your children, defying your lord and master!"

Simon cut him off. "She was trying to save her daughter from suffering as she had suffered. With a vicious husband who would make her life hell. And she did," Simon said in awe. "Even from the depths of the asylum you imprisoned her in, she found a way to save Cassandra and Jane from your schemes."

How had she found the courage, the will and resourcefulness to do what she had done? Love. The kind of fierce love Penelope had shown when she fought for the people of Everdene, when she sheltered Tripp, when she refused to let Simon believe lies about the mother who loved him.

"When we get finished with you, you won't be invited to a single *ton* event, won't be able to pass any legislation, no one in the House of Lords will speak with you, lest the taint of your crimes spill over on them. A few reminders of what happened in

France during the revolution should be enough to have these accusations taken seriously."

Simon's gaze clashed with his father's, unyielding. "So, Father, what say you? Do I take these to the printers? I'm quite sure there are many who would fight for the privilege of bringing you down."

"Lucien, you can't allow this!"

"Yes, Father. I can," Lucien said with grim satisfaction. "You were willing to evict four women from their home because one of them had the courage to do what was right and didn't meekly accept your command. I wouldn't just allow you to be drowned in scandal, I'd take pleasure in it, the way you doubtless did when you and Inchwick imagined that you had Miss Waverly at your mercy."

The Earl's jowls quivered with indignation. He clutched a hand to his chest, the gray in his face even more alarming.

"Barnabas, it is over," the Countess said. "All of the lies you constructed, the walls you built, the damage done. And for what? In the end, you've lost everything worth having."

"Lucien, you know what it means to be a nobleman," the Earl pleaded, "that you must be ruthless. It has been this way for centuries... We hold on with an iron rein or there is chaos. Ruin. Tip the balance, and where will it end? You know what happened in France when the lower orders seized control."

"You're right in one way," Lucien answered. "I don't know how it will end. But I'm willing to look at the future in a new way, help it take shape, thanks to what Simon and Miss Waverly began in Havelock Meadow."

Penelope stood, crossed to Lucien. "I know what it is to have regrets, to wish you could undo mistakes you made as a child. I think you've paid enough. That is why I believe you and Simon are wrong in this pact you've made."

"Wrong?"

"The Earl should pay for the new village. All of it."

The Earl blustered. "How dare you interfere—"

Pen leveled him a glare, her voice calm, yet cutting, sharp as knives. "You owe it to families like Tripp Raffy's. Daw Garvey's. Widow Bevans', after leaving them victim to Inchwick's greed and petty cruelty. You owe it to Simon and your daughters and to the Viscount. You owe it to my mother and sisters, to your wife, and to me for the needless suffering you've caused. If you'd had one tenth the courage and honor your sons and wife have shown, this would never have happened. But it did. You caused all of it."

Simon had never admired or loved her more.

"You're a disgrace to your sex," his father raged. "Nothing but an uppity woman who doesn't know her place."

Penelope's neck arched with pride. "You're wrong in that as well. I do know my place. I've claimed it at New Everdene. In time other women will as well."

"The walls fell down!" the Earl sputtered. "Your absurd attempt at a man's work is a failure."

"No. We found proof that Inchwick, Okum Landry, and their cohorts sabotaged my work. They're with the magistrate now."

He seemed to shrink into the chair. His eyes went to Lucien one last time, an appeal.

"You cannot allow them to do this! To your father? I thought we understood each other, all of these years. That the Harcourt legacy would be safe in your hands."

"It will be." Simon nodded to his brother, certain it was so. "We are done bending to your tyranny," Simon told him. "Do what you wish with the earldom. Run it into the ground before the eyes of the *ton* and let your allies in Parliament see who you really are. Lucien has his estates, the viscountcy. He will inherit the earldom. We've proven we can rebuild Everdene from the ground up. We can do the same with the entailed estates. Even you can't live forever."

Lucien straightened his cuff. "My brother and I are going to breed the finest horses England has ever seen. When I have questions regarding my estates, Simon will be the one I turn to. If New Everdene is the success I believe it will be, I will have him oversee similar projects on my other estates."

"He'll bankrupt you and run your estates into the ground. And for what? For these tenants who are no more than plough animals who scrape along."

"I'll give them the best life I'm able, while keeping the estate on firm financial ground. It will take time to make what I aspire to a reality, but I'm ready to start now. What about you, Father? Do your cohorts in the House of Lords, and the ballad sellers on the street start circulating scandal sheets about the Earl of Ravenscroft?"

The Earl ground his teeth in frustration.

"You wish to keep the Harcourt legacy intact?" Simon asked. "Deed control of the estates to Lucien. Retire to Bitterne Tower and remain there for whatever time you have left. Considering the way you behaved toward your injured tenants, you might become a target for those you've tried to crush. Retribution you well deserve."

His father's breath was rasping now. Sweat beaded on his brow. He looked at Lucien, and for a moment, there was something pathetic, something sick and weak and clinging in his expression. As if he were drowning. Simon knew damned well that if his father could, he would happily drag every one of his children down.

"We've already had some other papers drawn up. Giving me control of the estates, of the girls' dowries, of Mother's, as well." Lucien gestured to the delicate escritoire his mother had used. A bottle of ink, sealing wax, and freshly sharpened quill stood at the ready. He handed his father the pen.

The Earl read the carefully crafted document. Glared. For a

moment, the whole enterprise teetered as if above a chasm, and Simon expected the Earl to fling down the quill and stalk off.

"Sign it," Lucien commanded. "Or you will truly get the loathing you deserve. Your precious title will be one of infamy, one people spit on or make bawdy songs about. One wreathed in shame."

Simon would never forget the moment of his father's surrender. The Earl scrawled his name across the bottom of the document in a sprawling signature he'd used on countless bills to hold that iron gauntlet of superiority over families like Tripp Raffy's

Barnabas, Earl of Ravenscroft, the signature read. Simon softened the sealing wax over the flame of a candle, then dripped the blood-hued liquid beside the signature. Five drips. One for each of the children wounded so terribly. One for the wife betrayed. He watched his father remove his signet ring, then press it into the pool of wax. It was done.

The Countess stood, went to her sons, laid a hand on each of them. Simon tried to smile, as she looked into Lucien's eyes. "Oh, my Lucien… I'm so, so sorry I couldn't protect you. Never once in all these years did this change. I love you."

The Viscount's voice broke. "I'm sorry. I'm so sorry. Forgive me, Mama."

She gathered him into her arms. Her big son, the perfect, unflappable viscount. Simon saw his brother's broad shoulders shake as he buried his face in his mother's shoulder.

Simon felt a featherlight brush of a hand on his back, then heard a soft click. He turned, and saw Penelope's skirts vanish through the door.

# CHAPTER 45

Quiet wreathed Laurel Cottage as Penelope walked into the house. Running her fingertips over the crooked door latch, one of the beloved roses she'd plucked tucked behind her ear. She'd left in a hurry when Simon's summons had come. *I believe we've found a way to resolve things with my father. Please come to Everdene Hall.*

Now, as she walked in, she went to her mother's room, needing absolution.

"Mother?" Her mother sat in a chair by the window, sorting ribbons from light to dark, then muddling them up and beginning again. She looked so vulnerable, small, and broken, so different from the Countess. And yet…

"Penelope. It's you."

"Yes."

Pen went to her. Not wanting to tower over her, she sank to the floor at her feet. Her mother tucked a tendril of hair back behind Penelope's ear.

Pen took a deep breath. "Mother, I know what happened the day I was struck by lightning. When Captain Harcourt and I were caught in the storm the other day, I remembered."

Something wary darted into her mother's eyes. "These ribbons are such a mess. I really must—"

Pen took the ribbons from her mother's lap and threaded her fingers through her mother's own. "Please, Mama. Please let me say it. I'm so sorry I didn't listen to you… I'm so, so sorry I took Catherine with me that day."

"Catherine…" Stark awareness and grief flashed across her mother's face. The pale column of her throat worked. Pen waited for her mother to speak.

"I kept waiting for you to remember… expecting you to. You carried her everywhere. Loved her so much. *We* loved her so much." She paused, chafing her thumb over Pen's hand. "I should have gone with you that day to see the lambs, or stayed awake and minded you. You were forever into mischief. I should have known you would try to go. When I woke up and realized you and the baby were gone…"

Her grip on Pen's hand tightened.

"We almost lost you, as well. The doctor said how–how *fragile* you were. That a shock could set you back. When you never mentioned her, your father thought it best that there were no reminders. He didn't want you to live with the guilt."

Her mother stood, went to her jewelry box, opened the bottom drawer. She drew out a brooch she sometimes wore. She placed it in Pen's hand, and Pen stared down at it. A curl of baby-fine hair pressed with a spray of forget-me-nots.

"I always thought this was Kitty's curl… but it was Catherine's, wasn't it?"

"Your father had it made for me, before he changed."

Pen felt tears push at the backs of her eyes.

"It was so hard, pretending she never was. He said that naming the new baby Kitty would help me forget, too. But it didn't. You had blocked Catherine from your memory, and Fanny would never question… But I kept her locked in my head, in my heart. I know I've not always been fair to you.

When you kept being headstrong, I was so afraid I'd lose you, too."

Pen thought about the fears that had tormented her mother, how desperate she must have been when she misbehaved. She'd not change herself, and yet, she regretted the pain and worry she'd caused her. If only she'd known what had truly happened during the storm, she would have understood. Perhaps she and her mother could have comforted each other, healed…

"Where is Catherine now?" Pen asked.

"In a churchyard near Aunt Phaedra's, where we were visiting when the storm struck."

Pen looked into her mother's eyes, perhaps seeing her for the first time. "Will you take me there someday?"

Her mother touched her cheek. "When the forget-me-nots bloom. We'll plant some there."

---

Two weeks had passed before Simon rode up to Laurel Cottage. She'd known that he would come.

She melted into his arms, breathing in the scent of horses and wind, spices and shaving soap that was Simon's own.

"God, I've missed you," he said, taking her mouth in a kiss that made her knees go weak. "I would have been here sooner, but there's been so damn much to do. I had to take Father back to Bitterne Tower and see to it he dispatched a letter to the Prime Minister and certain members of the House of Lords. They are either rejoicing or mourning the fact that he'll not return when the new session opens."

"And your mother?"

"She and Mrs. Pierce, the other doctor's wife, had arranged for their patient's paintings to be displayed in a gallery, and she wanted to attend—as herself this time. The appearance of the long-absent Countess of Ravenscroft should bring quite a crowd. Mother, Lucien, and I have all written to Cassandra and Jane, telling them what happened and asking them to return to England, at least for a visit. I hope that they will. Their lives have been in Italy for so long. I keep trying to picture them as they are now, but I can only see girls with golden curls plaiting ribbons in their ponies' manes. Even if we're reunited, we'll be strangers."

"You'll come to know each other again. Is there any news on the village?"

"Tripp did catch Inchwick, Okum, and some other malcontents in the act of sabotage, though the lad didn't know it. Inchwick swears he only wanted to make the cottage seem structurally unsound. He didn't intend to bring the structure down on anyone's head. The storm made the damage far worse than intended."

"People were hurt. Could have been killed. It was only by the grace of God that no one was. And we still don't know if Daw will fully recover."

"I know."

"The architects Lucien hired will submit their reports Thursday next. But Inchwick is frightened enough that he's willing to point out any other place they tampered with things. We'll make repairs and families should still be able to move before winter hits."

"I'm glad."

"I spoke to Lucien," Simon said. "Really listened and I thought about what you said.

You were right. I thought of how it was for him as a boy, everything that was expected of him. That he had to live up to being an earl one day.

"We were children when my mother was torn away from us. My father manipulated us, lied. He told Lucien my mother died in the madhouse. It was easy to convince him. Lucien was a frightened boy when he saw my mother that night and she was half-mad with desperation, trying to protect my sisters. What could describing what he'd seen do but hurt me? He owned that he made mistakes, but he was trying to protect me; then, once he was older, began to question what he'd seen. He was afraid that I would hate him if I learned the truth. The guilt he carried for sounding the alarm has been horrible all these years."

She grasped his hand, carried it to her lips, thinking of the shadow of guilt she would always carry as well.

"Our father won't divide us again," Simon said. "We plan to rebuild the Harcourt estates from the bottom up. Starting with a stud farm. I'll be keeping my promise to Jamie. We're going to make my vision a reality."

"That's wonderful!"

"Lucien has asked me to be in charge of managing the building projects for the estates. But we're going to need expert advice on construction, on the latest advancements."

"I'm sure that you can hire an accomplished architect."

"We intend to. You."

"What? But I'm not fully trained. After what happened—"

"You can bring Tremayne in to consult if you feel the need, but that is up to you. I've fought in a dozen battles, but I've never met anyone braver than you. You make me want to be the man who stands beside you. Who gets to watch as you reach for whatever it is you want. There's no goal too difficult. You want to change things. They need to be changed. I'll support you in any way I can. When I returned to England after the massacre, I didn't believe in anything anymore. I'd seen officers destroy men I loved and fought beside. I'd seen what it meant to try to 'make the world England.' And my family—you know the ugliness there. In the end, even Lucien…" He stopped and she could see the pain at secrets kept. "It will take time to fully trust him again. But there is one thing I do believe in. With every fiber of my being. I believe in *you*."

Her heart thundered against her chest.

"I've heard it said that anyone who survives being struck by lightning is touched with some kind of greatness. Singled out by fate. I believe that is true. You were touched by fire, and I want to see you drive back the darkness that tried to consume my mother and my sisters, that would throw our daughters into the shadows. Marry me. Let's forge our marriage into something different, something new. We'll start with this," he said, drawing a document from the pocket of his coat. "The deed to Laurel Cottage, in your name. I've had the barrister draw it up so that legally, no one can touch it, not even your husband."

She stared down at the document, her heart welling with love. "Yes. I'll marry you, Simon. I never imagined I could feel this way," Pen said. "That loving you would make me feel..."

"What, love?"

"Free."

He drew back, looked at her with heartbreaking tenderness. "Free?"

"I'm not afraid anymore."

"Of storms?"

"No. Of this–this part of myself I always tried to deny. Wanting to be... loved. You showed me I can be true to myself, have my independence, *and* your love. I don't have to sacrifice one for the other."

"I'd never ask you to be less than who you are, Pen."

"I know."

He drew her into his arms, kissing her with all of the love they'd both denied themselves for so long, looking into a future that was far more of an adventure than they had imagined.

"What happens now?" Pen asked softly.

Simon smiled down into her eyes. "We create lightning of our own."

# EPILOGUE

## ONE YEAR LATER

The forget-me-nots were blooming. Clumps of delicate blue flowers here and there, where Penelope had quietly planted the seeds. He'd found them for her after she'd shown him her mother's brooch, and they'd scattered them together, reminders of storms they'd survived, of what they'd lost and what they'd won. And the sweet aches they knew remained in each other.

A year had passed since the tempest that had torn through the county, collapsing the roof of Widow Bevans' cottage, stranding Simon and Penelope in the hunting box, revealing secrets that had held them prisoner for too long.

Some wounds were still healing. Daw's limp was a testimony to that. But the carpenter was growing stronger every day. The lad Daw had taken in and nurtured had been tireless during his recovery, and Daw insisted that it was due to the crutch Tripp carved him that he was walking so well. Daw had set that crutch aside three months ago, but it stood in a place of honor in the chimney corner of the Garveys' new cottage—something Daw would keep forever.

That slow recovery had been a lesson to Simon. It would

take time and patience to knit the broken pieces of his family together, but Penelope had taught him to build a strong foundation, and in time, he hoped the Harcourts and Waverlys could create a haven where they'd all feel safe again.

It was easier now that Inchwick and his cronies were imprisoned, though the Earl still clung to life in his gilded prison. It was as if Lord Ravenscroft had dug his nails into the curtain of time, afraid to face St. Peter and punishment for his crimes.

Lucien worried Simon most of all. His brother had flung himself into cleansing the Harcourt holdings of the old earl's poisonous stewardship, burying himself in ledgers, correspondence, and meetings with land agents, trying to get some handle on work that was long overdue. As to an heir, he'd vowed never to wed. Simon's sons would one day inherit the titles due the Harcourt name. It grieved Simon that his brother was determined to hold himself apart, alone, as he had been for so long. Simon could only hope that when Cassandra and Jane returned, and he asked their forgiveness, he'd change his mind. They'd exchanged letters with their sisters, tentative efforts to get to know each other, somewhat stilted and unsatisfactory. But with one of their elderly aunts ill, they'd postponed visiting until this fall.

Whatever was to come in the future, today was beautiful and bright. Simon looked across the field to where the new mews were nearly finished, a marvel that he and Penelope had designed. For the time being he and Pen made their home in Everdene Hall, the Sky Chamber once again filled with laughter, warmth, and love, and visits from Pen's sisters and friends, as well as the Countess, who'd been welcomed back again. In time, he'd have Penelope design a house of their own. But for now, it was only right to drive back the shadows and bring life back to the home he'd so loved.

As for his dream, his vow to his friend Jamie, one look at the pastures proved it was coming true. The green fields were bursting with new life, foals playing chase games, kicking up their heels and racing each other, while Caspian, their proud sire, looked on. Simon had added four more mares to their stock, and already, horse-mad Englishmen were eager to buy golden horses from Everdene.

The village itself bustled with activity, the houses filled with families. Simon's heart swelled with pride whenever he surveyed what he and Pen had created, what they'd all built together, something new and wholesome and hopeful where his father had intended to leave only rubble.

It would take years to untangle all of the difficulties, but Jane and Cassandra would be in England this fall, the new crop of foals was thriving, and his wife, his Penelope, was glowing. Weaving joy where there had once been only loss.

Simon had never believed he could know such happiness. Such a feeling of wholeness.

Penelope had been so right about healing, releasing poison… Building things instead of tearing them down.

But then, she still never had any trouble telling him when he was doing things wrong. He smiled, remembering her, with her daisy crown and smudged dress, the summer of treehouse magic.

By next year, perhaps they would have a babe of their own. Being a father made him nervous as hell, after what he'd grown up with. But she'd taught him how to build on wholesome ground, and he'd learn to trust himself.

He went to claim his wife, and she stood, brushing dirt from her hands, showing him that smile he loved, that clever, dauntless, teasing smile that heated his blood even more than it had in the hunting box, in the storm that had broken something open in both of them, torn down their defenses, shattered secrets, and let them be completely vulnerable with each other.

The storm that had brought his mother back to Everdene, and unburdened Lucien of his tormented secrets.

Perhaps storms were necessary…

"Simon, I think another groom has come to see your horses," Pen said, gesturing to the paddock where a man leaned on the fence, looking out at where Caspian stood, king of all he surveyed.

"I'll tell him what I tell them all. He'll damn well have to wait. The foals are not for sale… until we have pastures full of our own."

She laughed softly, and reached up on tiptoe, her lips on his cheek. "Hoarding all that treasure for yourself, are you?"

"Yes. Especially my most precious treasure of all." He peered down at her, the wife he'd never dreamed of having, the life he'd only begun to believe was really his. He kissed her full on the mouth, not giving a damn who saw them as they strolled toward the newcomer together, arm in arm.

The man's back was to them. His coat sagged despite his broad shoulders, the fabric faded and as misshapen as his floppy hat. But his body was taut as a drawn bowstring.

From his vantage point across the meadow, Caspian raised his head, liquid dark eyes fixed on the interloper. The stallion's ears pricked forward, and he tossed his mane, whickering as he cantered toward him. As he neared the man, the stallion stretched out his elegant neck.

"Be careful," Penelope called warning. "He's wary of strangers."

"I'm no stranger."

Simon's feet rooted to the spot at the sound of a familiar Scottish burr as the man turned and pulled off the battered hat. Coppery hair flashed in the light.

He could barely feel Pen's hand on his arm, heard her voice as if from an ocean away.

"Simon, what is it? What's wrong?" she asked anxiously.

"Jamie," Simon choked out in disbelief. "Jesus God. It's Jamie. Alive."

# ABOUT THE AUTHOR

When Kimberly Cates was in third grade she informed her teacher that she didn't need to learn multiplication tables. She was going to be a writer when she grew up. Kimberly filled countless spiral notebooks with stories until, at age twenty-five, she received a birthday gift that changed her life: an electric type-writer. Kimberly wrote her first historical romance, sold it to Berkley Jove, and embarked on a thirty-year career as an author.

*Kimberly Cates*

Called "a master of the genre" by Romantic Times, her thirty-three bestselling, award-winning novels are noted for their endearing characters, emotional impact and their ability to transport the reader to the mists and magic of the British Isles.

Kimberly has also penned historical romances as Kimberleigh Caitlin and contemporary romances under the pseudonyms Kimberly Cates and Kim Cates.

9 781648 393754